The Evil Within

By S. M. Hardy

DARK DEVON MYSTERIES
The Evil Within
Evil Never Dies

The Evil Within

S. M. HARDY

Allison & Busby Limited
11 Wardour Mews
London W1F 8AN
allisonandbusby.com

First published in Great Britain by Allison & Busby in 2020.
This paperback edition published by Allison & Busby in 2020.

A CIP catalogue record for this book is available
from the British Library.

10 9 8 7 6 5 4 3 2 1

ISBN 978-0-7490-2560-1

Typeset in 11/16 pt Sabon LT Pro by
Allison & Busby Ltd

The paper used for this Allison & Busby publication
has been produced from trees that have been legally sourced
from well-managed and credibly certified forests.

Printed and bound by
CPI Group (UK) Ltd, Croydon, CR0 4YY

To David
and our evening in a Brighton hotel bar
talking ghost stories
Thanks for the inspiration
This one is for you

CHAPTER ONE

I squinted at the alarm clock trying to focus on the fluorescent numerals. One-thirty; I'd been in bed forty-five minutes and asleep for about thirty. Two hours less than last night and three less than the night before. At this rate I was going to die of exhaustion.

I wasn't sure whether it was the same goddamn awful dream; I could never remember much about it other than I wake up in a cold sweat, my sheets wrapped around me like a shroud. It was getting that I didn't want to go to bed.

Dragging myself into a sitting position I slumped back against the headboard and waited for my pounding heart to calm before swinging my legs over the side of the bed and staggering to my feet. I needed to sleep, but I didn't want to dream, though how I was going to manage that I wasn't sure. The strongest thing in my medicine cabinet was paracetamol, or possibly Night Nurse. When I looked, I had neither.

I padded into the lounge and over to what I laughingly called the bar. The bottle of Smirnoff had a dribble at the bottom, the gin had about two measures, but if I drank it, I would be sick to my stomach; gin and I didn't get along. The bottle of Grouse was fumes only. I should have known I'd be dry. My least-best friend had come to squat two weeks ago and had only left the day before yesterday. Waking him with my yelling two nights in a row had seen him off. I couldn't say I wasn't relieved. His constant 'Jim, it's been two years, mate, you're a young, good-looking fella, you need to get back out there, you need to get back on the pony' had me wanting to shout in his face: 'Shut the fuck up – what would you know? Have you ever fucked up your life so badly that you'd lost everything that meant anything to you?'

Of course he hadn't. He was a shallow, know-it-all, know-nothing prick and I was glad to be rid of him. Sad to say he reminded me too much of me. Me before I met Kat; me before I knew what it was like to care deeply about someone other than myself. Shame I didn't realise how much I cared until she was gone.

The empties went in the bin, which left me with a bottle of Baileys, two years out of date – I didn't need to look at the label – and a quarter-bottle of Amontillado sherry, probably just as old.

I sat down on the settee cradling the Baileys in my hands. If she'd been here she would explain the bad dreams away. She'd have made me feel better. I sighed and dropped the bottle down on the floor beside me. She wasn't here and never would be, so no point getting 'all my yesterdays'. She was gone, I was here, and I was maybe beginning to face the consequences of my actions – ambitions – life. Hot fuck and buggeration. I didn't deserve this.

Feeling sorry for myself was definitely the pits and way down lower than I needed to go. Kat would have been ashamed of me; I was ashamed of me. I wiped my hand across my face, stood up and dragged my sorry self back to the bedroom.

If I dreamt the dream I would try and take control. Isn't that what the mind doctors told you? That's what she used to say. Take control. Yeah right, just like she did, then my eyes filled up and I whispered, 'Sorry, babe. I didn't mean it. You know I didn't mean it – right?' I prayed she knew, and I guessed she did. Didn't the inhabitants of the hereafter know everything? I hoped so. I hoped she knew.

And then, for the first time in nearly two years I began to cry, and I felt weak and I felt worthless and I wanted to go to sleep and never wake. I wanted to be with Kat.

I flung myself down on the bed, our bed, and thankfully I did sleep and there were no more dreams, at least none that I remembered.

I woke to the alarm. Just as well, I had a meeting. I'd had my best work suit dry-cleaned but forgotten about ironing a shirt. After a frantic throwing out of clothing from within my wardrobe I found a shirt that was clean, relatively unrumpled, but white. I hated white; it reminded me of funerals and I'd had enough of those.

I searched some more, but white it would have to be. The suit at least wasn't black but a charcoal grey. Not a lot different, but to me a relief. I didn't want to be seen as a grieving widower. Not that I was. We hadn't made it to that one final step. Two weeks and one day it would have been different.

I looked in the mirror, took a deep breath, blinked back tears and tried to block all the bad thoughts out of my head. I at least looked the part: smooth, slick, a clean-cut, up-and-coming young exec. Today I had to act like one and be sharp and focused. This was what I was paid exorbitant amounts of money for. Two years ago, I'd have said I was worth every penny.

The meeting went on longer than it should have, but not as long as the clients would have hoped. How you could call businessmen whose legs you were about to cut out from beneath them clients I wasn't sure. After the meeting I guess they were ex-clients.

In this case the clients were a small family business. On the surface financially sound, but someone, somewhere within the organisation had decided not sound enough. After months of wrangling and solicitors' letters this was D-Day. The clients and their representatives walked into the room hoping there was a modicum of a chance of their survival. The suits sitting on the other side of the table, of which I was one, had already written them off. The meeting was perfunctory and for the first time it left me with a sour taste in my mouth. I couldn't do this any more.

'That went well,' Clement said as we left the room.

I glanced back over my shoulder at the clients' shell-shocked faces. 'You think?'

He frowned at me. 'Well, we all knew it was a waste of time.'

'They didn't.'

His frown deepened. 'Don't let Sir Peter hear you say that.'

I raised an eyebrow at him. 'Maybe I should.'

'What the fuck?'

'Did you not read their file? Didn't you go through the figures?'

'The account was terminal,' he said, clearly exasperated that we were still talking about it when as far as he was concerned there was no more to be said.

'Only because of our punitive interest rates, yet they'd never missed a payment and in fifteen months the loan would have been paid off. With the loan repaid, on their current turnover, the overdraft would probably have been gone as well within five years.'

'Five years is a long time – too long.'

'When they came to us for help the loan was meant to be a lifeline, now they owe us a great deal less than they did at the outset and even so we've gone and pulled the plug on them.' I shook my head in disgust. 'I've had it, Clem. What we did in there was brutal. Immoral. Even criminal.'

'What we did was our job.'

'Makes it right, does it?'

'The salary makes it right,' he said and by God he meant it. From his expression he couldn't see anything even mildly wrong with what we'd just done.

I looked back down the corridor; the clients were being shown out, shoulders slumped, faces slack, spirits broken. The father, the man who'd started the business over thirty years ago, looked frail, almost as though he'd aged ten years since the beginning of our meeting. When they entered the lift they shuffled around to face me. I had to turn away; I couldn't bear to see the look of betrayal in their eyes.

Sir Peter was pleased. The fact he gestured for us both to sit down was the tell. He dropped the phone-book-thick file on his desk and buzzed his secretary.

'Coffee?' he asked us, although didn't wait for a reply. 'Pot of coffee and three cups,' he said as he sunk down behind his desk.

A seat *and* coffee? I was surprised and when I glanced at Clem a self-satisfied smile was creeping onto his face. Was he expecting promotion? A pay rise? Sir Pete was hardly going to call us both in together for either of those things. Christ, if you were found to have even discussed your pay scale with anyone else within the company you were out on your ear.

The coffee appeared, brought in by a tall, slim, tight-arsed secretary, with a plastic smile. She served us and was dismissed with a nod from the great man and something clicked inside my head and it was as though a veil had been lifted from in front of my eyes. This wasn't what I wanted to do. This wasn't where I wanted to be.

Sir Pete started to speak, at least his lips were moving, though I didn't hear a word he said. All I wanted was to get out of that room, and out of this life. I reached for my coffee, slopping some into the saucer. If I tried to drink it now I was going to drip it everywhere and the suit was fresh on today. Fresh on . . . I put the cup and saucer back on the desk and got to my feet.

'James?' Sir Pete said with a frown as I interrupted his speech.

'I'm leaving,' I heard myself say as I walked out of his office.

As I reached the lift Clem came up behind me and grabbed hold of my sleeve. 'Jim, are you OK? Jim?'

'I'm leaving,' I repeated as I stepped into the lift.

He stood there glancing about him as though he wasn't sure what he should do, then, with a sigh, joined me.

'You just walked out on the boss while he was in mid flow.'

'So did you.'

'He sent me after you, you jerk. What are you playing at?'

'I'm leaving.'

'So you fucking said.'

13

'No, Clem, I'm leaving. Resigning, handing in my notice.'

'No fucking way.'

'Yes fucking way,' I said and I started to grin. 'Yes fucking way.'

Sir Pete couldn't believe I was throwing away a successful career and was convinced I'd had some sort of breakdown. Maybe I had. The bank's shrinks certainly thought so. Worried about lawsuits citing work-related stress, I was signed off on long-term sick leave and, if worse came to worst, would be let go after an appropriate period of time with a handshake good enough to deter any claim of unfair or constructive dismissal. Sir Pete's biggest mistake; he should have accepted my resignation.

For the first week there were no more dreams and I'd more or less convinced myself they *were* down to stress. On night eight of my sabbatical they started again. And boy they were full-blown gorefests.

These I remembered. Nightmares so bloody and vicious and full of rage that after the fourth day I was wondering whether I hadn't just had a breakdown but was going full-on insane and heading for a long-term stay in the funny farm.

After a particularly harrowing night when I'd woken screaming Kat's name and for a moment could almost feel her cold, dead body lying within my arms, I went to see my doctor. Fortunately for me she was a no-nonsense, matronly figure who didn't believe in most of today's PC psychobabble.

'Mr Hawkes, all you need is a good, long rest,' she had said, her voice laced with sympathy. 'You've had three major events in your life within as many years. You lost your mother and father, then your long-term partner within a very short period. Having a highly pressurised job hasn't helped. Now that's behind you, I suggest you get away somewhere new. Somewhere you can relax.'

And that was it. No pills, no potions, just a prescription of rest, rest and more rest. So that afternoon I started scanning the classifieds for a country retreat somewhere. And this is when I found Slyford St James.

CHAPTER TWO

The drive down was better than I'd expected, but then the school holidays had finished about a week earlier and now it was mainly the granny brigade who were migrating south-west for the autumn in their camper vans, caravans and overloaded estates. All I had was the car, two suitcases, one for clothes and one for bedding, towels and other essentials and a holdall containing shoes, walking boots and a pair of trainers. And my laptop; I wasn't completely giving up on the outside world. I'd debated upon getting a pair of wellies and decided against it. If need be, I'd buy some while I was away.

I'd rented a cottage on the outskirts of the Devonshire village of Slyford St James. The owners were overseas and not returning anytime soon so I'd paid upfront for one month with the option of maybe one or two more if the isolation didn't drive me even madder than I was already.

The letting agent said it was tucked away down a private lane, with no close neighbours and was probably a ten-minute walk from the village centre, which boasted a pub, the obligatory church and a small village shop. A travelling library visited every other Thursday and a fishmonger every Friday. There was a bus twice a day, once to pick you up and once to take you back. When I asked how that worked I was told the route was a continuous loop. My joke that 'it was a bit like the M25' fell on stony ground.

According to my satnav, Slyford St James didn't exist and the road atlas wasn't much better. It did show up on Google Maps, but only just. It must have been a dark and dreary day when they took the satellite photograph as the village looked more like a grey smudge on the landscape and I could only just make out a church spire through the murk. There was no street view, but at least I knew how to get there.

As I drove into the village it started to drizzle, making the grey stone cottages appear even greyer, and by the time I'd driven out the other side, big fat raindrops were splattering against the windscreen.

'Great,' I muttered. My jacket was in the boot along with my golfing brolly.

Just outside Slyford St James there was a road sign directing me to the next village and, as promised, there was a turning off to the left into a narrow lane, which hopefully led to my temporary home.

Thick, overgrown hedges pressed in on the car, in

danger of scratching the paintwork, and scrubby sprigs of vegetation had sprung up along the centre of what was not much more than a rock and dirt track. It made me wonder just how long the cottage *had* been vacant.

The property was at the end of the lane on the right. I pulled up outside and peered through the rain-splattered window, getting my first glimpse of what was to be my new home. A white-painted gate opened onto a narrow, paved path, leading to what I supposed would be a picture postcard cottage on a dry and sunny day. This afternoon it looked plain bleak. With a sigh I decided to bite the bullet. I didn't think the rain was about to let up anytime soon and I couldn't stay in the car indefinitely so, keys in hand and at the ready, I flung open the car door, pushed open the gate and made a run for it.

By the time I reached the front door my shirt was plastered to my back. I struggled to put the key in the lock as I swiped my sodden fringe back out of my eyes. Then the key turned, the door swung open and I overbalanced, almost ending up in a heap in the entrance hall.

I pushed the door closed, shutting the pounding rain outside, and stood there, dripping water onto the carpet. I took a step back onto the doormat. Great, I was inside and soaking wet with all my clothes, towels and sheets outside in the car, so unless I braved the rain I was doomed to shivering to death. And my God was it cold. It was like I'd walked into a fridge.

With a despondent sigh I opened the door and stared out at the persisting rain. If anything, the downpour had got worse. Black clouds raced across a dark slate sky and it could have been the onset of dusk instead of three-thirty on an autumn afternoon.

Muttering obscenities to myself I threw back the door and ran down the path and out through the gate. On the press of a button the boot sprang open and began to rise. I grabbed my laptop bag and slung it over my shoulder, hefted out the case containing my clothes and scooped up my coat, shoving it under my arm. The rest of my stuff could wait until later. I slammed the boot shut, locked the car and ran back to the cottage, the rain pummelling down on me every step of the way.

Back inside I dumped my stuff in a pile and pulled off my shoes, dropping them on the mat.

'God, it's bloody cold,' I muttered as I fought to open my case with numb fingers. The combination padlock slipped beneath my fingertips, and in the gloom I was finding it hard to see. I glanced around to find the light switch. As I suspected, it was just inside the front door. Unfortunately, the light bulb was of the 'I'll save the planet while you die of old age' variety and it took its own fine time in brightening enough so I could see.

I twisted the line of numbers into position and – nothing. 'What the fuck?' I scrubbed at my eyes and peered down at the little black numerals. One – four – zero – six; my birthdate. I flicked each wheel up one and then back down. Still the padlock remained firmly locked. 'This is ridiculous,' I muttered to myself as I spun the numbered wheels around and started again. One – four – zero – six.

Still no joy. I'd locked the padlock less than . . . Out of habit I glanced at my wrist, too late remembering I no longer wore a watch. I swore under my breath. It could have only been four hours ago. I'd even checked the bloody thing several times before putting it on the case.

I rocked back on my haunches and glared at the lump of dysfunctional metal. 'Fucking marvellous.' I was tempted to stand up and give the case a hefty kick, but a broken bottle of aftershave soaking my clothes would just about finish the 'perfect' start to my self-inflicted banishment from the City.

I stood and padded along the corridor to a doorway, which I hoped would lead me into the kitchen. Maybe, if I was lucky, there would be something languishing in one of the cupboards I could use to break the bloody padlock open.

It *was* the kitchen and, if anything, it was even colder than the hall. I was beginning to think my first impression that the place had been empty for some time was more than likely correct. The floral aroma of cleaning fluid scenting the air only just covered the underlying mustiness of abandonment.

First off, I lit the oven and the hob hoping it would take the frigid edge off a bit. I'd thought the estate agent was going to turn on the central heating. She'd said someone would pop in to get it all ready for my arrival, read the gas and electricity meters and give it a clean. Obviously making it comfortable for the incoming tenant wasn't part of the deal.

I pulled open the drawer closest to the oven; knives, forks and the usual. The next drawer down was lined with cooking utensils all laid out a uniform distance apart; who on earth did that? Either the owner or the cleaner suffered from some sort of compulsive behavioural disorder. I slammed the drawer shut and the clink of the implements colliding together made my lips twitch into a morose smile.

The rest of the drawers and cupboards were either empty or contained pots and pans or cleaning cloths, brushes and sprays. Nothing that would prise open a defective combination lock. There was only one thing for it: a trip into the village to buy a hacksaw – if there was a local store that sold such a thing.

I slouched my way back into the hall and scowled at the object of my misery. 'One last chance or it's the hacksaw and bin for you.' I dropped back down to have one final go. 'One – four – zero – six. Fuck.'

I took off my shirt – there was no point getting the lining of my coat any wetter than I had to – slipped on my coat and turned to the door just as someone knocked three times, making me jump, and my stomach gave a flip.

Bang, bang, bang. A second volley of knocks echoed throughout the passageway. I took a long, deep breath, kicked my rain-soaked shoes out of the way and pulled open the door.

The man almost filled the doorway. His clay-coloured, long, waxed coat giving him the appearance of a highwayman. The hood flopped over his brow almost touching his bushy, grey eyebrows; the bottom of his face obscured by a salt-and-pepper beard that disappeared beneath his coat's collar. He took a step towards me and I stumbled backwards away from him. If he noticed, he didn't say. He stuck out a hand, then, looking down at the water dripping off his fingertips, thought better of it.

'Mr Hawkes?' he said, ducking his head and stepping across the threshold, although I hadn't invited him to come inside.

'Yes.'

He smiled, showing off-white, tombstone teeth. 'I'm Jed Cummings. It's me you call if you need anything fixed. I turn my hand to most things, so if I can help I will.' He rummaged in his pocket and handed me a card. Plain white with his name and number printed on one side. I turned it in my fingers, but the other side was blank.

'Thanks,' I said, 'I will.'

He looked me in the eyes and his head skewed to one side. 'Are you all right?' he asked.

'Yes, I'm . . .' I let out a shuddery sigh and wiped my face with my hand.

He glanced down at the screwed-up shirt on the floor. 'I'll go and get the heating going,' he said, and before I could refuse his help, he'd pushed past me and opened up the cupboard under the stairs. 'It's on,' he said, 'but the silly buggers probably forgot to crank up the thermostat.' He pushed the door shut and sauntered into one of the other rooms. 'Yes, I thought so. The dial is just inside the door. Not very modern, I'm afraid, but it works. You'll probably find you can turn it right down again once you've got rid of the chill.'

'Thanks,' I said, 'you've saved me searching around.'

'Anything else I can help you with?'

'No,' I hesitated, glancing down at my case. 'I don't suppose you have a hacksaw?'

He raised an eyebrow. 'Not on me, but I can bring one by later on. What's the problem?'

I gestured to my suitcase. 'The bloody padlock won't open.'

He squatted down and took a look at it. 'You sure you've got the combination right?'

'My birthdate.'

'One – four – zero – six?'

I nodded.

He reached out and then hesitated; his fingers hovering about an inch away from the lock. He glanced up at my face and gave me a strange look before resting his fingers upon the combination wheels.

'Your birthday, you say?'

'The fourteenth of June.'

'Not the sixteenth of April?'

My mouth went dry and I had to swallow twice before I could reply. 'No,' I said.

His fingers twisted each of the four barrels and the lock sprang open. 'One – six – zero – four,' he said as he got up from his crouch.

'It can't be, I checked it. I checked it several times,' and

23

my legs began to shake and if he hadn't grabbed hold of my arm I would have fallen.

'Come on,' he said, leading me through into the sitting room and lowering me down onto the settee.

I flopped forward, head in hands. What was happening to me? I'd checked the combination at least twice, maybe even three times. Could I really have set it to the wrong date? Was my subconscious trying to tell me something?

'Here,' Jed said, handing me a tumbler with two fingers of something amber-coloured in the bottom. He looked at the hip flask in his other hand, then with a shrug took a slug himself.

I tipped back a mouthful and swallowed. A burning trail starting on my tongue hit the back of my throat and gradually warmed my chest, then my stomach.

'Better?'

I gave him a nod. 'Sorry, you must think I'm an idiot.'

'I know a troubled soul when I see one.' I stared up at him. 'Do you want me to get the rest of your stuff out of the car?'

'No, it's OK.'

'Hmm,' he said, tucking the hip flask inside his coat pocket and holding out his hand. 'It won't take me a moment.'

I pulled the keys from my pocket and dropped them onto his palm. 'Thanks.'

His fingers closed around the keys and he disappeared into the hall. I heard the front door open and less than a minute later the sound of the car boot slamming shut.

He didn't come straight back and when I heard the thud of feet on the stairs I realised he'd taken my things upstairs to the bedroom; by the time he strolled back in I'd finished the drink.

'I'll be off now,' he said, 'but if you need anything more give me a ring.'

'Thanks.'

He peered at me beneath bushy eyebrows. 'And if you find yourself lonesome you can find me most evenings in the Sly between eight and nine.'

'The Sly?'

'The Sly Fox; the village pub.'

I smiled up at him. 'I guess I owe you a drink.'

'Be seeing you,' he said and left, leaving me staring into an empty glass and trying to remember when everything had started to get so weird.

CHAPTER THREE

I gave the pub a miss and spent the evening unpacking my stuff and making myself at home. I ate baked beans out of the saucepan with a wedge of bread I'd brought with me. I'd have to check out the local supermarket in the morning. I washed the beans down with a can of lager and made a mental note to buy some more when I found the store.

Batteries replenished I flopped down on the sofa in the lounge and channel-hopped, looking for something to catch my imagination. The choice was between two soaps, an American sitcom and a documentary on World War II. The comedy was the best out of a bad bunch. I wanted to lighten my mood not deepen my depression.

Halfway through the programme I found my thoughts drifting to a small, shiny combination padlock. How could I have set it to Kat's birthday? I know it was a reversal of numbers, but even so, I'd checked it. I couldn't understand how it had happened.

This brought something else to mind. How did Jed know? He didn't try several different combinations. He twiddled the wheels straight to one – six – zero – four. How could he have known that? I hefted myself up off the couch and went out into the hallway. The padlock lay where he had left it glinting at me.

For some reason I shivered. It wasn't because I was cold, I'd actually had to turn the heating down once the unlived-in chill had been chased away. Even so, goosebumps speckled my arms and icy cold fingertips ran down my spine.

I reached out to pick up the padlock and hesitated. The engraved black numbers all in a line were clear enough and the hoop remained open. I took a deep breath and picked it up, the metal cool against my fingers. I pushed in the hoop and spun the numbers. Tried to pull it open and couldn't. I twisted them back to the combination of numbers that made up my late lover's birthday. It sprung open.

'That's it. You are finally ready for the funny farm,' I said, then pushed the hoop back into the hole, spun the numbers again and dropped it back on the hallstand. It was time for bed.

I woke to a warm and misty day. Smoky tendrils of grey floated against the kitchen window and when I opened the front door and stepped outside my clothes felt limp against my warm and fast-dampening skin.

The mist followed me into the car and even with the air conditioner going full pelt I had trouble clearing the inside of the windscreen. In the end I had to resort to wiping it with the back of my hand, leaving glistening droplets smeared across the glass.

According to the Internet, the nearest supermarket was on an out-of-town estate about ten miles away. The murky weather made me wonder if I should leave it until another day and perhaps risk the village shop, but I had a larder and fridge to fill plus drinks to buy and that was enough to deter me; I wasn't yet ready to become the topic of village gossip.

I eased out of the lane, not knowing how busy the main road in and out of the village would be at this time of the morning. It was a little after nine, so I suspected there could be mothers returning from the school run. Even so, I didn't see one other car as I drove through the village and out the other side other than those blanketed in smog parked at the edge of the road.

I drove out of the village, along a narrow lane onto the main road and into sunshine with not a cloud of mist to be seen.

'Well, at least I can see where I'm going,' I muttered to myself as I looked out for signposts directing me onto the road towards Torquay.

The retail park was like most I'd been to before, with stores for practically everything I would ever need, though I wasn't planning to stay in Slyford St James that long. Hopefully my laptop wouldn't need to be replaced within the next month or two, nor my wardrobe of clothes, though I pondered on buying a new padlock for my case; one that used a key.

When I turned into the lane leading back to the village the first thing I noticed was that it was still misty, not as bad as when I left, but the road ahead and fields on either side were covered with a thin veil of grey.

This time when I drove through the main street I did see a couple of residents going about their daily business. A man with a blue and white striped, button-straining shirt was outside the local pub chalking up a sign with the day's menu. He looked up as I passed by and followed me with an empty stare.

A stick insect of a woman with long, greying hair and wearing a cheesecloth shirt and mid-calf, floral skirt she'd probably bought in the seventies was coming out of the village shop, a jute bag over one arm and a loaf tucked under the other. She too looked up and I returned her hesitant smile. Further along the street a ginger and white cat sat washing himself on the pavement. His paw paused mid swipe as I drove past and I could see his green eyes following me through my rear-view mirror. Slyford St James obviously didn't get many visitors.

The postman had called while I was out. I'd arranged for my mail to be redirected while I was away, but there was only one plain, white envelope, which felt like it contained a card. It was addressed to me at the cottage and, as I'd told very few people where I was going, I couldn't imagine who it could be from. Intrigued, I slit it open before going back outside to unload the car.

It was a card from the estate agent wishing me 'good luck in my new home'. A nice thought, I supposed. There was also one of Jed's cards inside with a note saying I should call him if I needed a handyman. At least now I knew I hadn't been visited by the neighbourhood nosey parker or axe murderer.

I packed everything away and sat down in the kitchen with a coffee and a local paper I had picked up. It contained mainly news about what was going on in the surrounding area, which was to be expected, though I did find a mention of the neighbouring village, whose pub had apparently only recently had a change of ownership and was offering discounts on meals during its first week of opening.

I folded it and slapped it down on the table with a sigh. I chugged back the last mouthful of my coffee and got up to wash the mug.

Now the mist had cleared a bit I could see more of the garden, through the kitchen window. It was larger than I'd imagined, about a hundred feet long, and it splayed out as it stretched away from the cottage, making the far end probably three times the width of the building. The grass looked as though it was regularly mowed, and I hoped this was something Jed dealt with. Gardening wasn't one of my favourite pastimes.

Beyond the garden there was a patch of woodland and it crossed my mind that this would be the ideal place to have a dog, a thought I immediately discarded. When

I went home I wouldn't have time for a dog. Then I remembered how much Kat had wanted one.

'It'll keep me company,' she'd said, but I'd said no, selfish as usual; thinking how it would mean no more holidays abroad, no impromptu weekends away. Not thinking about all the evenings and nights she spent alone when I was working or was too pissed to come home or . . . There was no need to go there and even though she never knew, I still felt it was part of the reason for what happened happening. Stupid, really, though now I really wished I'd let her have a dog.

I let the water run, impressed how quickly the water came through hot. By the time I'd rinsed the mug it was almost too hot. I left the mug to drain on the side of the sink and as I glanced up saw a glimpse of movement at the end of the garden. I squinted at the trees on the other side of the fence, but there was nothing there.

'Bird?' I muttered to myself. 'Yeah, must have been a bird.'

Then there was a thud upstairs like someone had dropped a substantial book. 'What the f—?' I said, frowning at the ceiling before striding out of the kitchen, along the hall, then taking the stairs two at a time.

I swung into the doorway to my bedroom and glanced around. Nothing on the floor, nothing where it shouldn't be. The bathroom was the same. I stopped outside the closed door to the spare bedroom. I'd given it a cursory look around last night, but apart from a double bed, a wardrobe, chest of drawers and a chair it was empty.

Still, where else could the thump have come from?

I reached out to turn the doorknob, my fingers barely grazing the polished brass as the door swung open. I swallowed, but it did nothing to clear the tightness in my throat. I was sure I'd closed the door last night.

'Faulty catch,' I said out loud, then wished I hadn't; what if there was an intruder hiding in there? In retrospect, I should have picked up something to defend myself. Then thought, how stupid was that? Like I was going to stab or poleaxe an intruder. If I found someone hiding in there I'd scream like a tiny tot and run for it. I stepped into the doorway. The room was empty. I stretched out and pushed the door right back against the wall to be sure no one was hiding behind it and let out a deep breath.

Did I dare look underneath the bed? If I didn't, would I sleep tonight? Keeping a safe distance away I got down on my knees and peered beneath the bed, letting out a sigh of relief when there wasn't some psychopath staring right back out at me.

One more place: the wardrobe. I stood in front of it, building up the nerve to pull it open. On three, I told myself. I stood to one side. *One, two, three*. I grabbed the door handle and jerked it open. The wardrobe juddered and swayed in an alarming fashion then fell still. I peered around the door. Another empty space another sigh of relief, then another thud from right above my head and I practically jumped out of my skin.

With a racing heart I looked upwards. The attic; I hadn't thought about the attic. I couldn't even remember whether I'd noticed a hatch. I padded into the hall, pulling the bedroom door shut behind me, and this time rattling the doorknob and pushing against it to make sure the lock had actually taken.

The trapdoor was about a metre from the end of the passage. There was a small brass ring screwed into the edge, but I didn't have anything to use to hook it down. Even if I had, did I really want to pop my head through the hole into pitch-dark to see what was up there?

I stood in the hallway listening and was rewarded with silence. There must be a logical explanation. Could it be the pipes clunking? It was a very old cottage, though judging by the heat of the hot water in the kitchen and the shower I didn't think it could be serviced by the original plumbing.

I waited for a minute and then another. Still not a sound and I was pretty sure if someone or something living was up there, they would have made a noise of some description; a creaking joist, a footstep on boards, a cough or a rasp of material against wood. I waited a bit longer and there was nothing but complete silence.

I briefly thought about calling Jed and asking him to stop by to take a look and almost immediately thought better of it. I would look a right idiot and I could imagine it being all around the village that the 'townie' had only been in residence five minutes and was already imagining things.

I went back downstairs and thought about methods of locking the hatch shut. A bolt would do it, except I didn't have any tools. Another brass ring screwed into the ceiling and secured with a padlock might work. I could probably manage to screw a ring in by hand, though if someone was up there and wanted to get out they would simply smash their way through.

Hell, what was I thinking? Did I really believe there was someone hiding in the attic? Why would they, for Christ's sake? I took a deep breath; I needed to get a grip. There was no one in the attic and if there was anything up there at all it was probably a squirrel or a bird and it had knocked something over in its panic to get out.

Then why no scrabbling of claws or flapping of wings? a little voice inside my head said. I pushed the thought away. I was a grown man, not some little kid scared of the bogeyman.

I sat back down at the kitchen table and, although I tried to tell myself differently, as I flicked through the local newspaper I was waiting for another thud from above me.

For the rest of the day I wandered around like a lost soul waiting for something to happen and when nothing did was curiously disappointed. I wasn't really hungry, so I skipped lunch and when it came to dinner time I had cheese on toast with pickle. I did consider washing it down with a can of lager, but decided to wait and perhaps wander into the village and try out the pub. I was going to have to show my face at some time or other so it might as well be somewhere that I had at least half a chance

34

of seeing someone I knew. Jed said he usually got there about eight. I would arrive at ten past.

As it happened, by the time I had washed up, showered and changed it was nearer twenty past and it would probably take me about ten minutes to walk into the village's centre.

Now that it was getting dark the mist had finally disappeared and it was a fine, balmy autumn evening.

Once out of the lane and walking on a proper pavement my footsteps seemed inordinately loud as I strode along. The post office, which doubled as the village shop, was in darkness. I had thought it might stay open late, being the only shop for miles, though when I checked the times on the door, I saw it closed every day at six o'clock except for Sundays, when it didn't open at all.

As villages go it was sparse. Usually there is an obligatory antique shop and sometimes a store selling crafts and knick-knacks just in case a tourist happened by. Slyford St James didn't even have a phone box, and when I passed the church it looked sadly neglected, the grass between the old, toppled tombstones long and uncut.

The ginger and white cat was sitting on the doorstep of the pub watching my approach, and as I pushed the door open he got to his feet, turned and slipped inside, slinking past my legs.

The man behind the bar was the same rotund gentleman I'd seen earlier marking up his chalkboard. He gave me a nod as he finished polishing a pint jug with a red and white striped tea towel.

'What can I get for you?' he said with a West Country burr.

'A pint of Jail, please.'

The cat hopped onto the stool next to me and stood there, his front paws leaning on the bar. He gave a yowl and began to paddle the polished wood with his paws.

'You'll have to wait,' the publican said to the cat as he pumped my pint.

'Your cat?'

He gave a snort. 'He sort of adopted me and the wife when his owner died,' he said. 'He comes in every evening as regular as clockwork. Stays until chucking out time and leaves with the last customer.'

'Where does he sleep?' I asked.

'Buggered if I know,' he said handing me my pint then tapping the price into the till. 'Do you want a tab?' I looked at him. 'Most of my regulars do and pay at the end of the evening, unless they're too many sheets to the wind, then they pay me in the morning.'

'Well,' I said, 'if you're sure.'

'No skin off my nose unless you do a runner, and as you're renting the Morgan place for the month, I can't imagine you'd be doing that,' he said. 'I'm George, by the way.'

'Jim,' I said, shaking the offered hand.

The cat yowled again and reached out a paw to pat George's outstretched fingers. 'All right, all right,' he said, turning to the shelves of liquor and grabbing a bottle containing a thick, yellow liquid. 'Advocaat,' he told me, pouring some into a wine goblet.

The cat started to purr and hopped onto the bar to sit in front of the glass. It then dipped the tip of its paw into the liquid and with delicate flicks of the tongue licked off every drop before repeating the process.

'Well, I'll be damned.'

George leant on the bar watching the cat as he slowly but surely devoured the glass's contents. 'I was making a snowball for one of the youngsters a few Christmases ago and slopped a bit. Old Ginge was there like a shot. Now, as you can see, he expects it.'

The front door opened, and while George saw to his next customer, I glanced around the place to see if I could spy Jed. I didn't have far to look; he was in the corner nursing a pint of ale, with what was probably a whisky chaser waiting by his elbow. He gestured with his head for me to join him.

'So how's it going?' he asked as I sank down on the seat opposite his.

'OK,' I said.

He raised an eyebrow. 'You don't sound too sure.'

'Oh,' I said, embarrassed that he could see right through me so easily, 'it's nothing.'

'What's wrong?'

I hesitated. How exactly was I going to put this so I didn't sound like an absolute arse? 'I think that maybe something has got stuck up in the attic,' I told him, trying to sound nonchalant. 'There was a loud bang and I thought it was from upstairs, and when I went to check I heard it again. I'm pretty sure it came from the loft.'

He stared at me for a long time. I took a swig of my drink and tried not to fidget like some naughty kid. 'I'll come and take a look on my way home.'

'Are you sure? I don't want to put you to any trouble.'

'Will you get a wink of sleep if I don't?' he asked, knocking back half his pint.

'Hmm?'

'I thought not.'

'I'm probably being stupid.'

Jed shrugged. 'If there is something up there you don't want it causing any damage or scratching about all night.'

'No, I suppose not.'

'I'll—' He broke off and frowned over my shoulder, then gave a sigh and took another swig of his drink.

I glanced behind me. Two young girls who couldn't have been much more than teenagers were standing a few yards away. They were both dressed in Goth black with so many piercings I wasn't sure how they kept their heads from slumping over onto their skinny chests. One was scowling around the room as though daring anyone to speak to her, while the other chewed on her lip gazing at Jed with black-lined, doe eyes.

When I looked back at Jed, he had finished the ale and started on the chaser. He threw it back in one, then glowered into the glass before slamming it down on the table.

'Can I get you another?' I asked.

'Thanks,' he said, but his mind was clearly elsewhere and it wasn't a happy place.

As I walked to the bar the girl who'd been watching Jed slipped past me, and when I glanced over my shoulder, he jerked his head towards the chair I'd just vacated and she slumped down.

George was already pouring the drinks when I reached the bar. 'You ready for another?' he asked.

I nodded and leant back against the bar to watch Jed and the girl. I couldn't see her face, but I could tell she was talking as Jed was shaking his head. The other girl was watching them too, arms folded across her chest and lips curled downwards in a sulky pout.

George put my pint next to Jed's ale and chaser and when I went to pick them up said, 'I'd give them a moment, if I was you.'

'Who is she?' I asked.

'Julie Finch; comes from the next village,' he said, then ducked his head when the girl's friend cast a glare his way.

'Come on outside,' I heard Jed say, and when I looked, he was on his feet and walking towards the door. 'I'll be back in a minute,' he said to me as he passed. The girl, Julie, was trotting along behind him. Her friend gave an overloud, affected sigh, and followed them both outside.

George shrugged and made a fuss of the cat who'd finished his advocaat and was purring away happily and it did cross my mind that Old Ginge was perhaps a little drunk. There were a few questions I would have liked to ask George, but didn't feel I could – after all, it was none of my business. It didn't stop me wondering; Jed was old enough to be the girl's father, though if he was, she must have inherited her looks from her mother.

I carried the drinks over to the table and sat down. By the time Jed returned I'd finished my first pint and was halfway through the second. He dropped down onto his seat with a grunt and threw back half his jar of ale without drawing breath. He rubbed the froth from his lips with the back of his hand and slouched down further into his chair.

I sipped at my pint, not saying a word until the silence between us began to get a mite uncomfortable. 'So,' I asked, 'have you lived here all your life?'

He gave a nod and drained the rest of his pint. He was clearly not in the mood for talking and I was beginning to wish I'd stayed at home.

'Look, you really don't have to come back to the cottage tonight. I'm sure it can wait.'

He raised an eyebrow.

'It is probably only a bird or a squirrel.'

'And what if it isn't?'

I frowned at him. 'What else could it be?' Now he had said what I'd been thinking, I must admit it did sound ridiculous; what else *could* it be?

'You know.' I shook my head and he stared at me long and hard. 'You really don't?' he said, his expression puzzled.

'No, I really don't.'

He blew out air through puckered lips and reached for his whisky. He knocked it straight back and lumbered to his feet. 'Come on,' he said.

I drained the last of my beer and followed him to the bar. 'I'll pay for his,' I said to George.

'Got any whisky back at yours?' Jed asked.

'Yes.'

'Good, I think you're probably gonna need it.' He gave George a nod of farewell and made for the door while I collected my change.

'Don't let him play with your head,' George whispered under his breath as he dropped a pile of coins into my palm. I frowned at him, but he had moved along the bar to serve another customer.

Jed was waiting for me outside on the pavement in front of the pub. The two girls were standing with a lad maybe a few years older than them. He had his arm around Julie's shoulders in a protective hug and was scowling at Jed. If Jed noticed he didn't show it as he dropped into step beside me.

'Oy yow,' the boy shouted. I glanced back over my shoulder, but Jed kept on walking. 'Yow, ald-timer, I'm talking to yow.'

Jed hunched his shoulders and muttered something under his breath. There was the thud of feet on pavement and Jed was spun around as the lad grabbed his arm.

Jed stared at the lad and then at the hand on his arm. The boy flushed pink but didn't let go.

'What's going on?' I asked.

'Yow mate is filling her head with shite, that's what,' the lad said, his face twisted into a sneer. 'Superstitious ald twaddle.'

'Leave him be,' Julie said as she and her friend joined us. 'I asked him, he didn't want to.'

'Want to what?' I asked.

The lad glared at me and back to Jed. 'Keep out of my way, ald-timer, and if yow know what's good for yow, stay out of her way too.'

Jed shrugged his arm out of the boy's grip and turned his back on him. 'Fucking arsehole,' the lad said.

'Takes one to know one,' Jed muttered to himself, but loudly enough that the kid could hear.

I gave the kid a look. 'Don't even think about it,' I said. The kid's lips curled into a sullen scowl, but he left it and I followed Jed along the road. As I fell into step beside him it occurred to me that the evening wasn't getting any better.

When we arrived back at the cottage I let us in, and Jed headed straight upstairs and into the bathroom. When he reappeared he had a pole with a hook on the end in one hand and a torch in the other. In a matter of seconds he had opened the trapdoor and pulled down an aluminium loft ladder.

He handed me the pole and after turning on the torch clambered up the steps. His shoulders disappeared inside the hatch and he stood there a few minutes, I assume shining the torch about.

'Nothing much up here but empty space,' he said as he climbed down.

'I heard something.'

'I didn't say you didn't,' he said and then disappeared

back in the bathroom. He didn't close the door, so I peered inside to see where he hid the torch and pole. He looked over his shoulder and gestured inside a cupboard at the far end. 'If you need it again it's in here, but I wouldn't be going up there if I were you.'

'Why ever not?'

He just looked at me, then gestured that I should go back downstairs. 'I'll be having a glass of that whisky,' he said.

He sat himself down at the kitchen table while I went to get the whisky and two tumblers from the cupboard in the living room.

'What was all that about at the pub?' I asked as I poured us both three fingers of the Scotch.

He leant back in the chair and stretched out his legs. 'I'm not sure you'd want to know.'

'The kid said something about "superstitious old nonsense".'

Jed took a sip of his drink and grimaced as the alcohol hit the back of his throat. 'Nice drop of whisky.'

I nodded. 'My boss used to give us each a bottle every Christmas and I acquired a taste for it.'

He picked up the bottle and studied the label. 'You didn't get this down the village shop,' he said with a laugh.

'Do you think whatever was up in the attic has gone?'

He peered at me over his glass. 'I doubt it, but I'd advise you to ignore it.'

'Ignore what?'

'Ever have a near-death experience?' he asked, the sudden change of subject making me blink.

'No, have you?'

He gave a laugh. 'Plenty of times, lad, but they had nothing to do with the way I am. I was born this way. Maybe you were too; I just wondered, that's all.'

'Jed, what the hell are you talking about?'

'You know why this cottage is empty?'

I frowned at him. 'The owners are overseas.'

'That's true. Mr and Mrs Morgan moved to New York to be close to her parents. It's doubtful they'll be coming back, and if you decide to stay, I suspect you'll get this place real cheap.'

'I'm here for a month; two at most.'

'Don't be so sure,' he said.

'The estate agent didn't say anything about them moving away long-term.'

'She wouldn't.'

I shivered, the saying about someone walking over your grave springing to mind, making me shiver again. I took a sip of my drink. 'You're talking as though there's some big mystery.'

'No mystery about it. Do you know why Charles and Yvonne Morgan moved to New York?'

Now I was more than a little puzzled and frustrated by Jed and his cryptic comments and questions. 'You said to be near to her parents.'

He looked at me over the rim of his glass. 'But why?'

I shook my head. 'How the hell should I know?'

He took another sip of his drink. 'They had a daughter, Krystal, six years old, cute kid. A few years back she thought she'd go searching up in the loft for her Christmas presents, at least that's what they thought she was doing. Anyway, she fell. Broke her neck.' He gave a shrug. 'Neither of them was ever the same and as soon as they could they moved out.'

'That's terrible,' I said.

His eyes met mine. 'She's who you heard.'

I stared at him for a moment. 'That's not funny.'

'Don't I know it. I've been seeing and hearing this kind of thing all my life.'

'What kind of thing?' I was getting angry now. The last thing I wanted was some drunk old man winding me up with tales of ghoulies and ghosties. Maybe this was what George meant about him messing with my head.

'The girl, Julie,' he said as though he hadn't heard me, 'her dad worked on the oil rigs. Died a few months ago in a freak accident.'

I frowned at him; he was making no sense at all and I began to wonder whether he'd been in the pub a lot longer than half an hour by the time I'd arrived.

'She's having trouble coping so she comes to me.'

'Why?' I asked, and a whole load of nasty scenarios started to roll through my head. Was Jed the local drug dealer – or worse?

'For messages.'

Now I was completely flummoxed. 'Messages?'

He stared into the bottom of his glass, swirling the liquid around and around before lifting it to his lips and chugging it back in one.

'Aye, lad, messages from her dear departed father.'

Then the penny finally dropped. 'Are you telling me you're some kind of psychic?'

He looked at me, his eyes staring into mine. 'You say it as though you don't believe it and yet you and I share the same curse.'

'I don't know what you're talking about,' I said, and I could feel my expression turning mean.

He sucked air in through his teeth and was about to say something, then thought better of it and got to his feet. 'I'll see you tomorrow.'

'You will?'

'I'm paid to cut the lawn and tidy the garden once a week. I usually do it every Thursday, so unless you'd prefer I did it another day I'll be along tomorrow.'

'Right,' I said.

'I'll show myself out,' and with that he was gone. I waited until I heard the front door slam before reaching for the whisky bottle.

CHAPTER FOUR

I didn't sleep well, but at least I didn't dream. The clock said seven twenty-five when I finally swung my legs out of bed and shuffled to the bathroom. I had a faint ache in the centre of my forehead, which I put down to the whisky, and when I looked in the bathroom-cabinet mirror my red-rimmed eyes confirmed my diagnosis.

I washed and, although tempted not to just for once, shaved and by the time I'd dressed I was feeling a whole lot better. Shaving had been a good idea; my reflection was less wild and haggard. My hair was already getting long and I really should have had it cut before I left the city; the last thing I wanted was to end up looking like Jed. And that took the smile from my lips. What *had* that all been about yesterday?

Deciding to forgo bacon and eggs, I instead toasted some bread while I sipped on a mug of coffee and stared out through the kitchen window at the garden. The grass didn't look like it warranted a cutting, but I supposed Jed's regular ministrations kept it that way. Better a quick mow once a week than having the major job of hacking through six inches of grass.

I munched on my toast at the kitchen sink, still staring out through the window. It was another murky old morning, but there was a brightness coming down through the mist that made me think the sun would burn it away by midday.

Dropping my plate into the sink I turned on the tap and, as I reached for the washing-up liquid, caught a glimpse of movement out in the garden. I peered across the lawn, but there was nothing except for the swirling mist.

Seeing and hearing ghosts where there were none; maybe this break away from it all wasn't what I really needed. Ghosts? No, what I really didn't need or want was Jed filling my head with his old nonsense.

I scrubbed at my plate with more force than was probably necessary. When he arrived I would be polite but keep my distance. Sadly, it meant I would have to restrict my visits to the pub until he got the message, though if he got there at eight there was nothing to stop me popping in for a pre-dinner drink. I couldn't isolate myself; that would do me no good at all.

Throwing the scrubbing brush down on the side of the sink, I placed the plate on the drainer and glanced out the window – just in time to see a small, red-cardiganed figure disappear through the mist and into the trees bordering the end of the garden.

'What the hell?'

Not bothering to dry my hands I hurried to the back door, threw the bolts and ran out into the garden.

'Hey you!' I called. My voice sounded hollow, like the mist was devouring it.

There was no reply. Why would there be? The kid was trespassing and she knew it. I was pretty sure it was a she. I thought I'd glimpsed a grey-pleated skirt and long, possibly fair hair tied in braids.

I jogged across the lawn, too late remembering I was wearing my favourite pair of nubuck deck shoes I'd bought in Jamaica and was getting them soaking wet for my trouble. Still I carried on until I reached the low wooden fence surrounding the garden. For a moment I was nonplussed as to how she had got out, then saw the small latched gate to my right. I pulled it open and hurried through and was immediately within the patch of woodland bordering the property.

After the first few feet the mist petered out, the leafy canopies above me forming an impenetrable barrier. It was disconcertingly quiet, like I was the only living creature inside this wooded sanctum. There was no rustling of foliage from above or the sound of birdsong, just the crunching of years of leaf litter beneath my feet and the steady beat of my heart, which sounded overloud in the near silence.

I opened my mouth to call out again but changed

my mind. It would be like shouting in a church. Then I wondered why I'd thought of that.

'This is ridiculous,' I muttered to myself and stopped. She could be anywhere. In amongst all the trees and shrubbery she could be hiding only a few feet away and I'd probably not see her.

I glanced around me, breathing in the mixed aromas of living vegetation and the loamy musk of decaying wood and leaves. This would be a good place to have a dog. I could almost see Kat dressed in waxed jacket and jeans striding ahead of me, Jack Russell by her side. This was another thing we would have argued over – the breed of dog, though I think she'd have settled for anything if I'd said yes. I was more for keeping a big dog if I were to have one at all. Kat had said it was a man thing: big dog, big dick. She was probably right. I'd been full of pride and ego. How she'd put up with me I'd never know.

'I've grown up, Kat – the last two years have made me,' I said, then realised I'd spoken out loud.

I closed my eyes and took a deep breath. I heard a giggle. My eyes snapped open. I'd heard a giggle, a child's giggle.

I took a few more steps and I heard it again, coming from in front of me and to the right. I started towards the sound. Then more childish laughter, but this time it sounded further ahead and to the left. How was she moving so silently? My progress was being proclaimed by the crackle of my feet upon the wrinkled, dead leaves.

She giggled. She was having a lovely time. She obviously wasn't scared of the stupid townie trying to find her.

Why was I trying to find her? And if I did, what was I going to say to her? I almost stopped there and then, but something made me carry on. I wanted to see this little girl. I heard her laughing. Or was she sniggering – sniggering at the stupid, stupid man who thought he could catch her?

I'd show her. I'd show her who was the stupid one. I started to run. I would find her and I'd show her. Little brat.

Then I was out in the open, crossing mown grass, and up ahead through the swirls of mist was a grey, crumbling stone wall. I stopped for a moment, suddenly disorientated. The anger, no, rage I'd been feeling drained away. Why had I been so angry? The thoughts that had been flowing through my mind were . . . terrible – shocking, even – and more than a little reminiscent of the awful dreams I'd been having. I ran a hand across my face. I was losing it. I was truly losing it.

I turned back towards the trees. I was going straight to the cottage and phoning my doctor. The girl giggled again and I almost ignored her, but a little spark of the anger returned and I spun around and strode towards the wall and, as I got closer, I could see a shadow of a building loom up through the murk. It was the church. I was at the back of the church and over the wall I could see the first of the many headstones and tombs that filled its grounds.

I hadn't realised how vast an area the cemetery covered, but then I'd only seen it from the road out front.

I followed the wall around for a few yards and came to a place where the grey stone had collapsed into an avalanche of rock and dust that was only a foot or so tall.

I clambered over and then wondered why. Why would I want to wander around a graveyard on a misty, murky morning? Almost immediately the thought was gone as I heard the child once more, but this time she was singing.

Now I lay me down to sleep.

Ice-cold fingers traced my spine and I felt the first inkling of fear. Her voice had a haunting, eerie quality to it. A little girl's voice singing a child's lullaby in a graveyard shrouded in mist probably had something to do with it, I told myself, but it did nothing to dispel the cold fist clutching at my heart. Even so, I carried on walking and I'm pretty sure it wasn't me making my feet move; if I was in control of my actions, I'd be returning the way I'd come – at speed. Yet I didn't stop. I carried on walking into the mist that in places was so thick it could have been low-lying cloud.

My shirt was sticking to me and my hair plastered my forehead. The long grass between the tombstones soaked my jeans almost up to my knees and when I got back to the cottage I would have to change. *If you ever do get back*, a voice that sounded very much like Jed's whispered in my head.

I was tempted to turn and run. I didn't want to be here. I was cold, I was wet, I was . . . angry. I was so bloody angry and I had no idea why. A little kid had been running about in my garden – big fucking deal.

I scraped my wet hair back from my brow and forced myself to stop. I was going to return to the cottage right now. I began to turn, and as I did, to my right I saw a flicker of red amongst all the grey. Just a glimpse before it was lost again in the spiralling mist.

Despite my earlier conviction that I should immediately get away from this place I started towards where I thought I'd seen her. I had to weave between gravestones; some crooked, some fallen, some rough and crumbling, some probably only erected in the past ten years or so. Had I the time or inclination, this would be as good a place as any to learn something of the village's history.

Another flash of red through the smog; it appeared closer now. I hurried on. I wanted this over with and yet I had a feeling of déjà vu. Like maybe I'd been in this place before, like maybe I'd dreamt this.

Now I lay me— A few more words of song that abruptly stopped, so close I could only be steps away. I felt a breeze against my cheek and the mist twirled and twisted as though being blown away as the sun at last found its way through, bringing some light to this place of darkness.

Directly ahead of me was a grave; newer than the rest, more cared for than the rest. Flowers only a day or so old lay on the freshly trimmed grass cover; an oasis of colour amongst the gloom.

The headstone was of white marble with gold-painted lettering engraved into the surface in a font similar to Times New Roman. I began to read and, for a moment the world swung out of kilter and I felt like I was falling.

Here sleeps Katherine Moran born 16th April 1989.

Kat? I ran my hand across my face. It couldn't be – it couldn't . . . My eyes swum and then focused.

Here sleeps Krystal Morgan born 14th June 2009. I drew in a ragged breath. The Morgans' dead child shared my birthday.

'Tragic, very tragic,' a voice said from beside me. I jerked around. 'I'm sorry, did I startle you?'

'No! Yes. Sorry, I was miles away.'

'Peter Davies,' the bespectacled and rosy-faced reverend said, sticking out his hand.

I hastily wiped mine on my jeans before taking hold of his. 'Jim Hawkes.'

'My, my, you're freezing cold,' he said, his bright smile fading a tad. 'Why don't you come in and have a cup of tea?'

'I wouldn't want to impose.'

'Ah, come on, Jim – may I call you Jim? Do an old man a favour; I don't get to meet people from the big, bad city all that often and it'd be nice to get to hear what's happening in the outside world from someone who's seen it first-hand for a change.' And with that he shepherded me through the grass and onto a stone path and guided me towards the rectory, chatting all the way.

The rectory wasn't in much better fettle than the church. Even through the gradually clearing mist I could see the paint around the windows and door frame was chipped and peeling. The reverend pushed the door open and gestured for me to enter.

The hallway was dark and gloomy and smelt musty,

bringing to mind the yellowing pages of long-forgotten books. A staircase led up to the top floor of the house; a narrow, worn carpet of indistinct colour and pattern covered its centre, flanked by dark-brown varnished wood.

He ushered me along the corridor past a coat stand harbouring a long, waxed jacket and an even longer once-black coat that looked as though it had seen better days. Beside it was a cylindrical, brass container holding two umbrellas: one funereal black, the other a kaleidoscope of red, green and blue and probably more at home on a golf course. The brass hadn't seen a duster for many a year and was fast turning green with neglect.

He showed me into a sitting room that clearly doubled as his office. By the window was an oak desk cluttered with papers, files and books with a large, black leather-bound Bible balanced on the top as if to weigh down the melee of paperwork that was likely to explode off the desk if left to its own devices.

'Sit down, sit down. Make yourself comfortable and I'll get you that cup of tea,' he said.

'Please don't trouble yourself.'

'No trouble, dear boy. No trouble at all. I could do with a cuppa myself,' he said as he bustled out of the room, leaving me to perch on the edge of the large leather sofa flanking the fireplace.

I could smell damp soot and it occurred to me that a fire hadn't burned in the grate for some time. I supposed as we were coming to the end of summer he hadn't needed a fire thus far, though the grey ash and the remains of blackened logs said otherwise. I was beginning to suspect the good reverend lived alone, without even a housekeeper to maintain order. It certainly looked that way.

I glanced around the room. An old upright gramophone player stood in the corner with lid open. I levered myself off the couch to take a peek, and sure enough an old 78 rested on the turntable, a film of dust coating the once-glossy, black disc.

I slumped back down on the couch and sank into the leather where the springs had given up the ghost. I felt a bit sorry for the poor old boy. No wonder he craved company: I doubted he had much of a congregation – the village was tiny.

The door swung open and he backed in clutching a tray. He'd taken the trouble to get out his best porcelain; a white and floral teapot with matching cups, saucers, sugar bowl and milk jug rattled about as he searched for a clear spot amongst the clutter on his desk.

'Here, let me,' I said, scrambling to my feet and moving a couple of files out of the way.

He muttered his thanks and busied himself pouring the tea. 'Milk? Sugar?'

'Just milk, thanks.'

He handed me a cup and saucer and then settled down behind his desk. 'So, how are you finding it here in Slyford?'

'It's certainly different,' I said.

'A quieter pace of life to what you're used to, I'm sure.'

'Hmm,' I said.

'You're staying at the Morgans',' he said. 'A real shame about them. It was at their daughter's grave where I found you.'

'I heard there'd been an accident.'

The reverend put his cup and saucer down on the desk and leant back in his chair. 'That's what they say.'

I gave him a puzzled look. 'You say it like you don't believe it.'

He picked up a lump of sugar with a pair of tarnished tongs and dropped it into his cup. I raised my own cup up to my lips and almost gagged. The milk was off. I looked his way as he dropped another lump of sugar into his tea and began to stir. While he was otherwise occupied, I hastily put my cup and saucer down on the floor beside me.

'I'm not sure what to believe,' he said, and I watched in morbid fascination as he took a sip of his own tea.' He gave me a sunny smile. 'Ah, that's better.'

I inwardly shuddered. No wonder he laced it with sugar. 'You make it sound as though there's some mystery over how she died.'

'The poor child was found at the top of the stairs with a broken neck. They said she fell from the loft while looking for Christmas presents.'

'That's what I heard.'

'It was September.'

I frowned at him. 'September?'

'She'd only been back at school a week and yet there she was at home on a school day, allegedly on her own.'

'Allegedly? What are you getting at?'

'When you get back to the cottage, take a look at where the loft hatch is in relation to the stairs.'

I remembered charging up the stairs to search for the cause of the loud thump the previous day and afterwards looking up at the loft hatch. It was about a metre from the end of the hall; at least two metres from the top of the stairs.

'But there must have been an investigation?'

The reverend sipped at his tea, peering at me over the rim of the cup. 'You're not in the city now, you know,' was all he said.

As soon as was polite I made my excuses and left. He saw me to the door, and I could feel his eyes watching me as I followed the path from the rectory back into the churchyard. This time I walked to the front of the church and took the main street back to the cottage. I had seen enough gravestones for one day.

CHAPTER FIVE

I was greeted at the cottage gate by the sound of the mower coming from the back garden. I let myself in through the front to avoid disturbing Jed, in truth wanting to avoid him. He had left me disconcerted the previous evening. I was now doubly so after my conversation with the Reverend Davies, though any anger I'd had for Jed and his bullshit had temporarily subsided.

I changed my wet jeans and ruefully wondered whether my deck shoes would ever be the same again after their soaking. I then made myself a coffee and sat down at the kitchen table, considering whether I *should* make that appointment with my doctor. It would mean going all the way back to the city, and what for? She'd only repeat what she'd told me before. I was stressed and needed to relax. Unfortunately, thus far I was finding Slyford St James far from relaxing.

There was a rap on the back door and Jed poked his head inside. 'I've done the lawn. Is there anything else you want doing?'

'No,' I said. 'No thanks.'

'Then I'll be off,' he said, his voice gruff, and I suddenly felt mean.

'Would you like a coffee before you go?'

His craggy face creased into a smile. 'I wouldn't say no.'

He came in and sat down at the table while I boiled the kettle and shook out some biscuits from the packet onto a plate.

'The mist's clearing,' I said, glancing out the window.

'It's gonna be a nice day,' he said. 'I think we might be heading for an Indian summer.'

I handed him a mug and offered him the biscuits, then we chatted for a bit. 'Who does the wood at the bottom of the garden belong to?' I asked.

'The Morgans,' he said. 'That's why they bought this place: they fancied having a bit of woodland for their kids to play in.'

'Kids? I thought there was only the daughter.'

'I'm guessing they wanted more.'

'So the woodland comes with the cottage.'

'Thinking about making an offer?'

'What? On this place?' I grimaced. 'I don't think so.'

'It's early days yet. After a few weeks you might find you don't want to leave.'

'Hmm, we'll see.'

'Any more bumps in the night?'

'No,' I said with a little too much venom and had to force my face not to settle into a frown.

'Good,' he said, chugging back his coffee and getting to his feet. 'I'll be off, then.'

'Be seeing you.'

'Aye, lad, you will,' he said and was gone. No sooner had he shut the door I wished he hadn't left so soon.

I was going to have to find something to do with myself. It was all very well going away to chill out, but empty time on my hands wasn't going to help me any. Instead of forgetting my misfortunes I'd be dwelling on them.

Perhaps I should find myself a hobby – but what? It was Thursday, so the travelling library would be coming to the village today – or was that every other Thursday? I couldn't remember. I wasn't much of a reader, anyway. What else could I do? Art? No – not one artistic bone in my body. Photography? Wasn't that a kind of art? I mulled on it for a bit. One thing was for sure, I'd have to find something, otherwise I'd go crazy. Crazy with boredom.

I spent the rest of the morning on my laptop googling all sorts of hobbies and almost immediately discarding them. By lunchtime the idea of owning a dog was beginning to seem like a good one. Except you couldn't own a dog for just a month. A dog is for life, not just for extended holidays.

Then the fourteen per cent warning flashed up telling me my laptop's battery was about to expire. I logged off and dutifully plugged it in to charge and did the same with my mobile after checking for missed calls. At one time if I didn't look at my phone for even an hour there would be one or two messages waiting for me. Now there was nothing. As far as my London friends and ex-work colleagues were concerned I could have died.

I thought about having some lunch and decided against it. I wasn't hungry and eating for eating's sake was not a habit I wanted to get in to. I wandered listlessly from room to room, opening drawers and cupboard doors. I'm not sure what I was looking for or what I hoped to find.

The Morgans had left a few bits and pieces behind, as though they might someday return, but mainly impersonal, practical stuff. There were a few books on a bookshelf in the lounge. I suspected they were more for decoration and maybe even put there by the estate agent to make the place appear more homely.

In the cupboard under the stairs beside the boiler there was a vacuum cleaner, a set of steps, a couple of umbrellas and an old biscuit tin containing nails, screws and other paraphernalia together with a variety of tools. A red leather lead hung from a hook at the back. I leant in and lifted up the thin strip and traced a finger down its length. The surface was still shiny but crazed with cracks. It was well used but not old. So the Morgans had kept a dog. I wondered where it was now; they surely couldn't have taken it to New York.

I let the leather slip from my fingers to swing back and forth until it stilled to dangle there surplus to requirements and a sad reminder of a family torn apart. I shut the door with a sigh. I was getting maudlin.

I stopped at the bottom of the stairs and glanced up into the hallway, remembering what the reverend had said, and it occurred to me he was right: if the child – Krystal? Yes, Krystal – had fallen from the attic she'd never have been found at the top of the stairs. I was about to turn away but before I knew it, I was climbing the staircase. Not only was I maudlin, I was also getting morbid.

When I reached the top I stopped and stared down at the carpet. This must have been where they found her. This very spot. I shivered, hugging myself. I wasn't surprised the estate agent hadn't mentioned why the Morgans had gone away. I'm not sure I'd have rented the place had I known. My eyes were drawn to the loft hatch. The Reverend Davies was right: it didn't make any sense whatsoever, unless she somehow managed to crawl to the top of the stairs. Would she have been able to do that?

I shivered again. Poor little girl; poor parents.

I went and stood beneath the trapdoor, peering up at the square of wood. How on earth did she get up there in the first place? Jed had reached it with a pole. OK, it was a cottage and the ceiling wasn't that high, but could a six-year-old girl reach the brass ring and pull the hatch down?

My curiosity got the better of me. I went into the bathroom and fetched the pole, and as an afterthought picked up the torch. The pole was actually an odd length. It was only about two feet long and when I examined it I could see why. The end had been cut off. Had Mr Morgan, worried about his over-inquisitive daughter, cut the pole down?

I had no idea how tall a six-year-old would be, but it would have been a bit of a stretch for a child of that age to reach the catch, I'd imagine. I lifted the pole and caught the ring with the hook and pulled – nothing.

I thought for a second, then pushed upwards before pulling again. The hatch dropped down on creaking hinges. Maybe she could have opened the hatch. The aluminium steps were another thing altogether. They were laying back inside the loft space and a good five or six inches higher than the hatch.

I snagged the bottom rung with the hook. It took me several attempts to gain purchase and when I did I had to pull hard to get the ladder to tilt downwards. I was pretty sure a six-year-old child wouldn't have been strong enough to do it.

So what did happen that day?

I was about to push the ladder back up then thought, what the hell? Now I'd opened it I might as well take a look and see if there was anything of interest lurking in the space beneath the roof. I remembered when my father had cleared out my grandparents' attic after they'd died it had been like an Aladdin's cave. Sorting out other people's rubbish might not be much of an occupation, but it'd give me something to do.

Balanced halfway up the ladder, with my head and shoulders poked through the hatch, I swung the torch around the loft space. The inside of the roof had been lined, fairly recently, by the look of it, and the rafters had been boarded so it was actually a good storage space, but apart from a roll of what looked like an old carpet the attic was near empty.

I swung the torch around one more time. There was a water tank in the corner and some pipes clad in grey foam running along just under the eaves, but nothing else except specks of dust and fluff floating like tiny phantoms in the swathe of torchlight. I turned around on the steps to look behind me, swinging the torch in an arc across what was the largest expanse of space, and something moved.

For an instant, caught in the roving beam was a white, startled face. I turned right around, jerking the torch back. My feet slipped on the metal rungs and I dropped the torch as I scrabbled to grab hold of something to stop my falling.

I bashed my chin on the edge of the hatch snapping my head backwards, saw stars and next thing I knew I was sitting on the landing.

I took a couple of deep breaths and looked up at the empty hole in the ceiling above me. I think I half-expected to see a face peering down at me, but no, just a square of dark.

I lifted both arms – they at least were working – and then tried to stand. I creaked a bit and my calves and back complained. I think I must have whacked them on the aluminium ladder on the way down, but otherwise I appeared to be uninjured. I gingerly touched my chin with the tips of my fingers and they came away a sticky pink. I hadn't so much cut my chin but scraped it and it felt bruised.

The torch lay abandoned a few feet away and surprisingly enough was still working. I picked it up and looked back towards the hatch. I'd seen someone; I was sure I had.

I took another couple of breaths and started back up the ladder. This time when I reached the top I turned completely around and wedged my backside in between the rungs.

I slowly moved the torch back and forth. Nothing. Carefully, I moved myself around and searched the water tank end of the loft space. Still nothing, other than the roll of carpet, pipes and tank. No white, startled face. Nothing.

I wasn't sure whether to be relieved or not. At best I'd imagined it, at worst I was seeing things. *And hearing things*, a little voice reminded me.

I clambered down the ladder, pushed it into the loft and shut the hatch. I was overwrought, that was all. My conversation with Jed the day before and then the reverend this morning had rattled me, and my morbid curiosity had got me seeing shadows where there were none.

I put the torch and pole away and went in search of some antiseptic to bathe my battered chin.

It actually felt worse than it looked. If anyone noticed it at all they would think it was a shaving rash. My calves were in a similar state, pink and grazed. I'd got off lightly and the image of a small, red-cardiganed girl lying at the top of the stairs sprang into my mind unbidden.

Despite telling myself it wasn't a good idea, at ten past eight I was walking through the village towards The Sly Fox. I needed company and, although I could probably do without Jed's at the moment, he was the only person I knew in the village other than the reverend, who was another one I could do without seeing for a while. So, Jed's companionship it would have to be, that is if he was there and not holding seances or whatever damn thing it was that he did.

When I walked in, Old Ginge was sitting on the bar licking advocaat from his paw. He looked up with huge eyes and, upon seeing me, went back to licking off the last of the yellow, sticky liquid.

'Pint of Jail?' George asked.

'Thanks,' I said, glancing around the bar.

Jed was sitting at the same table as before. He raised his pint to me when he saw me looking.

'Another pint of whatever Jed's drinking,' I said to George.

'I'll start a tab,' he said by way of reply.

I carried the drinks over to the table and sank down opposite my new best friend – or should that be *only* friend.

He downed the rest of his pint and murmured his thanks for its replacement. Then he frowned, studying my face.

'You all right?' he asked.

'Why shouldn't I be?'

He stared at me for a few long seconds more and I slumped back in the chair, staring back and hoping the sudden burst of hostility I was feeling didn't show on my face. For a moment I did wonder where all this anger was coming from.

Eventually he looked away and picked up the pint I'd bought him. 'I've got someone coming to see me in a bit and, if it's going to offend your sensibilities, I suggest you leave when she arrives.'

'That girl – Julie?'

'Nah. I doubt I'll be seeing her again now her big brother's got involved. Probably just as well, I had nothing more to give her. This is a believer.'

'Won't she mind? Me being here, I mean?'

He chuckled. 'No. *She* won't mind at all. *You,* on the other hand, might.'

'How do you mean?' I asked, frowning at him.

'You know the saying "it takes one to know one"? Well she'll know what you are, no mistake, and won't be afraid to say so.'

'I don't—'

'Here she is,' he said, getting to his feet.

I glanced over my shoulder, not at all knowing what to expect. I supposed maybe some elderly hippy if she was into clairvoyance, tarot cards and the like. Perhaps the woman I'd seen outside the village store. The lady walking across the bar towards us wasn't any of those things. She was older, but that was about it. And by older I don't mean old. She was one of those women who have an elegant, timeless quality about them. She could have been fifty or sixty, or maybe even a decade older. Fine lines wrinkled the corners of her eyes and lips when she smiled, and I suspected she smiled a lot. Her blonde hair curled down over the collar of her cream silk shirt and, although it was cut short at the back and sides, the top was long and more Helen Mirren than Dame Judy.

'Jed,' she said, kissing him on both cheeks.

'Can I get you a drink?'

'V and T, please.'

'I'll bring it over,' George said, giving her a smile that suggested she was one of his more than welcome customers.

Jed led her over to the table and I got to my feet. 'Emma, this is Jim. He's renting the Morgans' old place.'

She gave him a quizzical look and then reached out her hand for me to shake. Her cool fingers closed around mine and she smiled, her eyes glittering. 'Nice to meet you, Jim.'

'And you, Emma.'

She gave my fingers a squeeze before letting them go and sinking gracefully down onto the bench seat beneath the window.

'How are you?' Emma asked Jed, and there was an inflection to her voice that made me think it was more than a rhetorical question.

'Good,' he said. 'Better.'

Her forehead crinkled with concern. 'Which is it? Better or good?'

'Good,' he said.

She studied his face and I was sure she was about to

say more, but George arrived with her drink, and by the time they'd exchanged a few words and he'd gone, the moment had passed.

'How are you finding village life?' she asked me.

'I've only been here a few days so it's a bit early to tell.'

'Hmm.' It was my turn to fall under her thoughtful scrutiny. 'Do you like the cottage?'

'It's a fair size, bigger than I was expecting, actually, and in a lovely location.'

'You'd not seen it before you rented it?'

'Only in photos, but I'm only staying for a month or so.'

'We'll see,' Jed said.

'Two months tops,' I told him.

'That's what I said when I first came to Slyford,' Emma said, 'and that was more years ago than I care to remember.'

'Emma lives at The Grange,' Jed said.

'I'm not sure . . .'

'It's the big house just outside the far end of the village. You probably haven't been out that way yet,' Jed said.

'We're practically neighbours,' Emma said with a laugh.

'So you knew the Morgans?'

'Yes,' she said, her smile softening. 'Lovely couple, and Krystal was a poppet. Such a shame.'

'What happened to their dog?' I asked and the look that passed between them wasn't lost on me. 'I found a lead hanging up in the cupboard under the stairs.'

'Benji,' Jed said.

'An adorable little Jack Russell,' Emma added.

'What happened to him?'

Emma gave a sigh. 'No one knows,' she said. 'He went missing the day Krystal died.'

Jed took a long draught of his pint. 'I looked for him everywhere, but it was like he'd vanished into thin air.'

'That's a bit strange, isn't it?' I asked.

'The local plod thought he might have got scared when she died and ran away.'

'Idiots,' Emma said, 'bloody idiots.'

'What do you think?' I asked.

Jed and Emma exchanged another look. 'Something happened that day, something more than anyone let on. Even Charles and Yvonne were in denial.'

'They were in shock, Emms,' Jed said, reaching across the table and patting her arm.

'Yes, they must have been,' she said, picking up her glass and cradling it between her hands. 'It was all so terrible.' She gave me a tight smile. 'Let's talk about something else before we all start crying into our beer.' She took a sip of her drink. 'So, Jim, what do you do for a living?'

'Not a lot at the moment, as it happens,' I said.

'Really?'

'I was a banker up in the City, but I decided I needed a career change.'

Emma gave me a sympathetic look. 'You lost someone,' and it wasn't a question.

'My girlfriend. Fiancée, actually.'

'It was an accident, you know.'

'What?'

'She didn't mean to . . . I'm sorry,' she said, seeing my expression, 'I shouldn't have said anything.'

'Jim here doesn't believe.'

Emma frowned at Jed. 'But he's—'

'He still doesn't believe.'

She turned her frown on me. 'How can you not believe?'

'Believe what?' I asked, knowing full well but beginning to get a little irritated – in fact, a lot irritated.

'He's another one in denial,' Jed muttered.

She waved a hand at him, telling him to shut up. 'Jim, what you have is a gift – you should embrace it.'

'I have no gift,' I said, leaning back further into the chair and crossing my arms.

'He's been hearing things at the cottage,' Jed said.

'A thump from up in the loft is all.' *What about the face?* a little voice in my head reminded me. *What about the child in the graveyard?* Where did that come from? It was some kid trespassing, that was all.

I swallowed some beer. This was crazy. They were crazy. It'd do me no good at all meeting up with people like them. I started to get to my feet. I needed to leave. I needed to leave Slyford and get back to London. Coming here had all been a big mistake. I needed to go.

'Sit down,' Jed said. 'Sit down and listen.'

'I've got to go,' I said, pushing back my chair and pulling my wallet out of my back pocket.

'Jim.'

'No,' I said and hurried over to the bar, taking a couple of notes out and flinging them on the bar.

'Hey, don't you want your change?' I heard George call as I practically ran from the bar. When I was out on the street I began to run. And I ran and ran and didn't stop until I reached the cottage.

CHAPTER SIX

As soon as I walked in through the front door I knew I was going to throw up. I pounded up the stairs and made it to the bathroom – just.

Afterwards I felt like I'd lost all strength in my limbs and the short stagger across the hall to the bedroom could have been a marathon. When I got there, I didn't undress but flopped down face first onto the bed, mind and body exhausted, and almost immediately fell asleep. I didn't wake until morning.

When I came to, it took me a few moments to work out why I was lying on top of the covers, fully dressed. I was sure I hadn't had that much to drink. Then I remembered and I could feel my face heat up with embarrassment. What must Emma think? Not to mention Jed and George. Oh God, George must think I'm a right prick the way I ran out of there with no word of thanks or farewell.

I showered, shaved and dressed while wondering whether there was anywhere in the village I could buy some flowers to take around to Emma's to at least try and make amends for my rudeness. Jed I wasn't too bothered about, but George . . . I'd have to pop in the pub later and make some excuse like a dicky belly, which as it turned out wasn't so far from the truth. I'd certainly puked my guts up.

I made myself some toast and leant back against the kitchen sink as I munched my way through a couple of slices, washed down with a mug of tea.

As I dropped the plate into the sink there was a scratching sound at the back door.

'What the . . . ?' I wiped my hands on the dishcloth and took a step towards the door. There it was again, a scrabbling noise like a dog pawing the bottom of the door. The memory of the red dog's lead hanging at the back of the cupboard skittered through my head.

Nah – not possible, the dog had gone missing two years ago.

Another rapid scrabbling of claws against wood. I strode across the kitchen and wrenched the door open.

Nothing.

And yet I'd heard scratching. I stepped out into the garden and looked around.

Nothing.

I pulled the door to and crouched down to examine the woodwork. It had been repainted but beneath the gloss I could see the scars. Yes, once a dog had pawed the door begging to be let in, but not recently. Not a few minutes ago. I went back into the kitchen. Sir Peter's Christmas gift of twenty-year malt was sitting on the worktop next to the microwave and beside it was a glass. It hadn't been there earlier. I was sure it hadn't. I kept the whisky in a cabinet in the lounge. Along with six whisky glasses, one of which was now in the kitchen.

I picked the bottle and the glass up and carried them back to where they belonged, but God help me as I opened the cabinet for a brief moment it crossed my mind that I could do with a drink and would one little snifter hurt? Yes, it would. I'd been to that dark place before, albeit briefly, and I didn't want to go there again. I shoved the bottle to the back of the cabinet. Shut the door and turned the key in the lock.

I went straight through to the front door, snagged my jacket off the banisters where I'd dropped it the night before as I'd charged up the stairs to be sick, picked up my keys from the hallstand and left, deadlocking the door behind me.

When I turned towards the gate it was to find Emma standing there waiting, and it crossed my mind that she was doing just that – waiting.

'That's lucky,' she said. 'I almost missed you.'

I gave her what I hoped was an apologetic smile. 'Actually, I was coming to see you. To apologise.'

'What for?'

'Last night. Running off like that. It was rude.'

She flapped a hand at me. 'No offence taken. It's I who should apologise. I was taking you somewhere you didn't want to go. Sometimes I get carried away with it all.'

'Do you want to come in for a coffee or something?'

She looked past me towards the house and a strange expression fleetingly clouded her face. 'Not now, not today.'

I frowned at her.

'I know,' she said, forcing herself to smile. 'Let's go for a walk.' She hooked an arm through mine and started guiding me down the lane. 'I can show you all the sights.'

'Not a very long walk, then,' I remarked.

She laughed and patted me on the arm. 'We'll walk *very* slowly.'

She chattered away, telling me who lived in each property we passed and a little about each of the residents.

'How did you get to know Jed?' I asked when there was a lull in the conversation, just as we came to the church.

'Jed was an old friend of Reggie's and it just so happened he looked after the garden for the people who owned The Grange before we moved in. It seemed sensible for him to carry on doing it for us.'

'You're married?'

'Widowed.'

'Oh, I'm sorry.'

'A long time ago,' she said, patting my arm again. 'It wasn't long after Reggie died that Jed and I found we had something in common.'

'Being psychic?'

She gave me a sideways look. 'I know you're not a believer so let's just agree to disagree.'

'Had Jed told you about me before we met?' I asked.

'Only that there was a new resident at the Morgans'.'

'Nothing else?'

'When I'd last spoken to him he hadn't met you. He was on his way to introduce himself.'

We walked in silence for a few yards. 'Is it always so misty in the morning?' I asked. 'I haven't woken up to a clear day since I've been here.'

'It's the time of year. When it's wet but warm the mist comes off the fields. It usually burns away by mid morning.'

'It makes the churchyard look like something out of a horror movie.'

She glanced towards the church. 'It does look a bit creepy,' she said with a smile. 'It'd help if they had someone go in and keep the place tidy, but it's gradually going to rack and ruin.'

'I'm surprised the reverend doesn't have Jed go in and do a bit.'

She gave a sniff. 'Jed used to keep it tidy, but he and the vicar before last had a falling-out and he's not been in there since.'

'I'd have thought Reverend Davies would've made peace with him rather than let the place get into a state.'

Emma abruptly stopped and looked across at me. 'Reverend Davies?'

'I met him yesterday. He seemed like a nice chap.'

'You met Peter Davies yesterday?'

'I was—' I suddenly wished I hadn't said anything as I'd now have to explain why I was wandering around the graveyard first thing in the morning. 'I decided to investigate the strip of woodland at the bottom of the garden,' I said, thinking quickly of a way to not make it sound like I was losing my mind, 'and when I came out the other side I saw the church. He found me looking at some of the old gravestones.' She studied my face for so long I could feel my cheeks beginning to flush red. 'I know it seems a bit odd, wandering around . . .'

'Did he speak to you?'

I frowned at her. 'Of course he spoke to me. He introduced himself and invited me in for a cup of tea. I felt a bit sorry for him, actually. If the grounds are a mess you should see inside the rectory.'

'You went inside the rectory?'

'He made me tea.'

She squeezed my arm and we began to walk again. 'What did you talk about?'

I was beginning to feel a little uneasy. It was almost as though I'd been caught out doing something I shouldn't. 'This and that.' Then I remembered something I thought she might be interested in. 'He was of the same opinion as you and Jed that there was something not right about Krystal Morgan's death.'

'He said that?'

'He said her body was found at the top of the stairs, which didn't fit with her having fallen from the loft. Also, that it was unlikely that she was searching for Christmas presents as it was months before.'

She stopped again, head bowed, shoulders slumped, and then with a sigh she drew herself up straight and looked me in the eyes. 'I think you'd better come back to The Grange.'

'Why?'

'Because Jed's there working on my garden and I think the three of us need to have a talk.'

She turned back the way we'd come and I reluctantly went with her. I wasn't at all sure I felt like having to deal with Jed this morning.

Maybe it was my imagination, but I could have sworn Emma speeded up a tad as we passed the church and didn't really slow down until we passed the end of the lane to the cottage. The Grange was about a hundred yards further on.

Huge double gates marked the entrance to a long tarmac drive flanked by manicured lawns, which swooped around to a house the size of a small mansion. She led me past the side of the house and out back to more lawns and what could have been a walled garden.

Jed was sitting on steps leading to a stone-paved patio area fiddling with some sort of mechanical device. He glanced up as he heard us approaching.

'Tea?' Emma asked Jed.

'Please.'

'Jim?'

'Coffee if you have some.'

'Coffee it is. Sit down and make yourself comfortable,' she said, gesturing towards a white wrought-iron table and four chairs on the patio as she passed Jed on the steps.

'She found you, then,' Jed said with a nod of hello and he went back to threading some nylon cord onto a strimmer.

'I was on my way to try and find her.' He glanced up. 'To apologise.'

'She was worried about you.'

'Why?'

He climbed to his feet and gestured that I follow him. 'It's the sort of person she is.'

He led me across the patio to the table and chairs and we both sat. 'You look after all of this on your own?' I asked, looking around what could have been acres of lawn.

'Mostly.'

'It must take some doing.'

'She's got one of those sit-on mower things, so it doesn't take me long. I only come over once a week, twice if she's having guests.'

'It's a lovely garden.'

'The house isn't bad either,' Jed said and then jumped up and hurried to meet Emma, taking the tray from her. 'Here, let me help you with that.'

Jed dumped the tray on the table and they both sat as Emma handed out the cups and saucers. Once she'd finished acting the hostess she leant back in her chair, her expression serious.

'I think you need to tell Jim about Peter Davies,' she said.

Jed gave her a strange look, then glanced my way. 'The Reverend Peter Davies?'

'The very same.'

'Why, may I ask?'

'Jim needs to hear it from you.'

Jed ran a hand through his shaggy hair and blew out through pursed lips. 'There's not much to tell really. Peter Davies took over as reverend from Donald Pugh, a sanctimonious ass of a man.'

'Emma said you had a falling-out.'

He gave a snort. 'Bloody man.'

'He accused Jed of being a charlatan and con artist,' Emma said, and she wasn't smiling.

I very sensibly kept quiet.

'Anyway, he and Slyford St James parted company when he started having health problems about four years ago and that's when Peter Davies came to the village.'

Jed took a sip of his tea and began to stroke his beard, his eyes focused somewhere over my right shoulder.

'After my dealings with the Reverend Pugh I kept my distance for a while, but then he came to me asking if I could do a few jobs at the vicarage for him. Pugh had left it in a bit of a state.'

I heard the cry of a peacock in the distance and when I glanced out across the lawn, I could see the mist had almost totally cleared and feel the warmth of the sun upon my face. Freshly cut grass scented the air as a soft breeze ruffled my hair. It was a beautiful spot and I could think of nothing more typically English than drinking tea and coffee on this terrace on a sunny autumn morning.

'Peter was a nice bloke; too nice, really.' Jed took another swig of tea. 'There'd been some sort of trouble at his last parish, that's what the rumourmongers said, and he had a bit of a problem with the . . .' Jed lifted his hand and made a motion like he was knocking back a snifter.

Despite the warmth of the sun I shivered. 'You're talking about him in the past tense.'

Jed frowned at me, then at Emma.

'Jim told me that he met Peter Davies yesterday morning and had tea with him at the rectory.'

Jed's eyes jerked to hers and then to me. 'You spoke to Peter Davies?'

'I met him in the graveyard, and he invited me in for a cup of tea,' I said, crossing my arms and leaning back in the chair.

'My, oh my,' he said, rubbing his chin. 'I knew you had the sight, but this . . . this is something else altogether.'

I stared at him as the realisation of what he was saying began to dawn on me. 'No,' I said, shaking my head. 'No, it's impossible. We shook hands. He made me tea. We talked for twenty minutes or more.'

Jed slowly shook his head. 'Peter Davies died eighteen months ago,' he said. 'I should know – I found his body.'

CHAPTER SEVEN

I jumped to my feet, sending my chair clattering back onto the paving stones. 'He can't be! I spoke to him.'

Emma stood up and took hold of my arm, as Jed righted my chair, and guided me back down onto it.

'Someone must have been winding me up,' I said, grasping at anything that might make sense of it all. 'Pretending that they were him.'

'Why would anyone do that?' Emma asked.

'People do not have conversations with dead people.'

'Seems you have,' Jed said, helping himself to more tea. 'What were you doing in the graveyard, anyway?'

I ran a hand across my face; this was crazy. 'I was chasing after a kid that'd been playing in my garden.'

They exchanged another look.

'Don't start,' I told them, 'it was just some kid.'

'Boy or girl?' Jed asked.

I hesitated. 'A girl, I think.'

'What did she look like?' Emma asked.

'I only caught a glimpse of her.'

'Then what did this glimpse you saw look like?'

'Red cardigan, grey skirt, braided fair hair.'

'Sounds a bit more of a look than a glimpse,' Jed said with a wry smile.

'She led me to—' Then I stopped. This was all getting too weird.

You're staying at the Morgans', the apparently long-dead Reverend Peter Davies had said. *It was at their daughter's grave where I found you.*

'What was it you were about to say?' Emma asked.

'Nothing. Nothing really, just that I followed her through the woodland and when I reached the church I decided to take a look around.'

Neither of them appeared convinced, but they didn't say as much. I guess they thought I'd already heard enough.

'More coffee?' Emma asked me.

'No. No, thanks.'

'Have you seen or heard anything more since yesterday?' Jed said.

I shook my head, telling myself if I didn't say the word 'no' I wouldn't exactly be lying. It was a trick I used on Kat, though in the end she knew when I was keeping things from her. It was a game we both had been playing in the lead-up to her death. Stupid, stupid games. We were both at fault.

I got to my feet. 'I'd better be off.'

'I'm having a few people around tonight for drinks,' Emma said. 'Would you care to join us? You'll get to meet some of the locals.'

'Thanks, that'd be good.'

'Here at eight-thirty,' she said, getting to her feet. 'I'll see you out.'

I said goodbye to Jed, and Emma saw me around to the front of the house and down the drive. When we got to the front gates she kissed me on both cheeks.

'We'll see you later.'

'I wouldn't miss it,' I said, lying through my teeth and with a wave started back down the lane towards home.

My head was spinning. The man I'd spoken to in the rectory was flesh and blood like me. I replayed our meeting and conversation over in my head. He had shaken my hand. He'd said mine was cold and that's why he'd invited me in for tea; tea with rancid milk, which he had drunk, appearing not to notice.

Then I remembered the state of the place. The musty smell and chill in the hallway and office, the unlived-in feeling, the sense of neglect.

No. No, it couldn't be. When I reached the end of my lane I carried on walking. I was going to the church. I was going to the rectory.

I strode along, a man with a purpose, until I came to the beginning of the church's low stone wall. I faltered, slowed and stopped. If I proved Emma and Jed right, if the man to whom I believed I'd been speaking was a dead man, then I must truly be going mad. Dead was dead.

What about the child? What about the dog? What about the face in the attic?

I put my hand on the wall to steady myself. Mad; I was going insane. I took a deep breath and another. He'd been so real.

I pulled myself up straight and set off again towards the rectory. I'd prove it to myself one way or another. Either I was cracking up big time or someone was trying to make a fool of me. Maybe it was some kind of joke the villagers played on newcomers. That's it, a way of scaring the 'grockles' away. Wasn't that the derogatory term they used for newcomers and visitors to the West Country?

The gate to the rectory hung open, although I remembered closing it. The lawns to either side of the path were overgrown and the flower beds were already being overrun with brambles.

I remembered the paintwork on the windows and front door as being faded and peeling, but I hadn't noticed that one of the windowpanes was cracked and the net curtain inside was hanging in grimy, yellowing tatters. Did they say he had been dead eighteen months? It could have been eighteen years from the state of the place.

No – he'd been here. I'd seen him. I'd shaken his hand and walked with him from the cemetery. We'd spoken for ten or fifteen minutes, maybe more.

I walked along the path and to the door. I raised my hand, fist clenched to rap upon the paintwork. The door swung open, leaving me staring into the dingy passageway and slightly breathless.

'Hello?' I called. My voice sounded forced and hollow. I made myself take a step inside. Paper crackled beneath my feet. I looked down. How had I not noticed before? Several curled and yellowed flyers and a few envelopes lay on the doormat. 'Hello?'

I took another couple of steps and the door shut behind me with a solid click, making me glance back in panic. No one was there. I was all alone. I took a shuddery breath.

Dust and several dead flies coated the hallstand where a phone book lay open, a pen resting between the pages. I carried on walking past the staircase until I reached the office-cum-sitting room. The door was ajar. I pushed it open, afraid of what I might find.

The desk had been cleared. All that remained was a blotter and a desk tidy containing an assortment of pens, pencils, a stapler and paperclips. The large, black leather-bound Bible I'd seen before lay at the corner of the desk. Otherwise the room was the same. Logs burnt to ash and charcoal in the fire grate, and an open old-fashioned record player in the corner.

I glanced down at the floor next to the sagging leather couch where I'd sat. No abandoned cup and saucer to confirm my visit, but then he would have picked it up and taken it away, I told myself, though I was increasingly beginning to believe that maybe, just maybe, Jed and Emma were telling me the truth.

I wandered out into the hallway and towards the back of the house. The large kitchen was all that I'd expect there to be in an old rectory: old-fashioned but functional.

A once-white butler sink, green-stained from a now-dry dripping tap, solid dark wood cupboards and worktops, a large oak table and chairs in the centre.

An old gas cooker sat against the outside wall between more cupboards and next to the sink was a fairly modern washing machine, which together with a stand-up fridge-freezer in one corner looked incongruous alongside the pre-war decor.

Yellow gingham curtains hung at either side of the one grimy window overlooking the garden and another wilderness of overgrown grass and brambles, the product of at least two summers of neglect.

I ran a finger over the kitchen table; it came away thick with dust. An overwhelming sense of despair flowed over me. How could I go on like this? How could I stand this loneliness? And for a moment a very deep darkness scuttled around the edge of my consciousness and was gone, then I wondered what the hell I was thinking.

What was I thinking? It was like the sudden senseless anger I'd felt the day before; an uncalled-for and unwarranted emotion that had risen up inside me from nowhere. I hurried out of the kitchen and started towards the front door, but as I reached out to open it, I felt a sudden chill on the back of my neck like cold fingers caressing the soft down at the top of my spine.

I hesitated, my hand dropping to my side. A feeling of dread tightened my chest and my stomach gave a little flip. I didn't want to turn around, but I knew I must. I had to. Although I knew without doubt I was about to see something

I didn't want to see, I knew I had no choice. I turned.

'Oh, dear God,' I whispered and swung around to frantically grapple with the door to try and get out.

For a few panicked moments I thought I was trapped. Somehow the latch had clicked down, dead-bolting the door, and it took me a few interminably long seconds to release it. Then I was outside, door slammed shut behind me, bent double with hands on knees, hyperventilating.

'Oh God, oh God, oh God.'

Gradually my heart stopped its hammering and my breathing slowed to something near normal and I managed to stand upright. I slowly made my way to the gate but had to stop for a moment, not quite sure whether my legs were about to give way beneath me.

I glanced back at the rectory, at the peeling paintwork and dirt-streaked windows, and quickly looked away again. I guessed I was scared I might see Peter Davies pull back the rotting net curtains to give me a farewell wave. Though maybe not now I'd seen what had become of him.

I assumed he must have tied the rope to the banister rail at the top of the stairs as he wasn't hanging neatly in the middle of the staircase like in the films but sideways on, the toes of his scuffed black leather shoes peeking through the downward posts.

I'd only seen one side of his face and that was bad enough. Dark purple, mottled flesh had swollen to practically engulf the rope around his neck. His wire-framed glasses had slipped off one ear and hung there lopsided across his face.

His lips had pulled back into a rigor grin, the tip of his bloated, purple tongue peeping out between yellowing teeth.

And Jed had found him like this. Poor bugger.

By the time I'd reached the cottage my legs were working normally again.

I fumbled around in my pocket searching for my keys and couldn't find them. I was sure I remembered snagging them off the hallstand as I left. I rammed my hands back in my pockets. No keys. My day was getting better and better.

I leant my shoulder against the front door; it was as though all my strength had drained away leaving me limp and bone-achingly tired.

I forced myself to stand upright. If I had truly either lost or left the keys behind I was going to have to walk back to Emma's to ask Jed to lend me his set. That's if he had one. If not, it would probably be a trip to the estate agents in town, and without having my car keys, which were left safely inside the house, that wouldn't be much fun.

In one last forlorn attempt to find my keys I patted down my jacket pockets, starting at the top, even though I knew they definitely wouldn't be there, and worked my way down, postponing the inevitable for as long as possible.

Nothing there, nothing there, nothing there or there. Then something hard and lumpy at the bottom of the right-hand side of my jacket. I stuffed my hand back inside. Nothing!

I wasn't about to give up without one last-ditch attempt. I pulled out a crumpled but clean tissue and ran my fingers along the bottom of the pocket and there, right in the back corner, the stitching had given away. The hole felt tiny, too small for a set of two keys to push through, but somehow they had. Grasping the bottom edge of my jacket, slowly but surely I eased the keys along the lining to the hole until my fingers touched cool metal and wriggled them through, a few extra stitches giving in the process. What the heck – it would need mending anyway.

I was almost there but something had caught in the stitching. I could feel both keys between my fingers, they were through. Maybe the ring they were attached to had caught. I turned it around and around hoping to free it without doing any more damage to the lining, but I was beginning to lose patience. I gave the keys a tug and felt more stitches give, but even so the damn things still wouldn't come free. I pushed my finger through the hole. There was something else there, something cylindrical. What the hell was that?

'For Christ's sake,' I muttered and gave another more violent tug, and with the sound of ripping material I yanked the keys out of my pocket.

I lifted them up to the lock and stopped. There should be two keys; two keys on a plain ring. Nothing else, only two keys. There were two keys. I recognised them both. One was plain and gold-coloured; it opened the back door. The other was one of those cutesy, patterned keys you could get cut these days. This one was of a red, white and blue Union Jack design. There was also something else, something I had never seen before, a two-inch-long tube. It wasn't caught up on the keys or the ring – it was attached.

The keys jangled together as I lifted them up with shaking fingers to take a better look at the mysterious interloper. It was a whistle; a silver dog whistle.

I laid one hand against the door to hold myself upright. I couldn't have not noticed. The estate agent had sent me the keys by post in a Jiffy bag. Two keys, that was all. I tugged on the whistle. It was attached to the ring by a triangular link. Even after a tug the ends of the link stayed firmly closed together. I put the Union Jack key in the lock, secretly hoping it wouldn't open the door. That these were another set of keys. Someone else's set of keys. The key turned, I pushed against the door and it swung open.

'OK, OK, there's an explanation for this. A simple explanation,' I told myself as I walked into the hallway. 'This is a spare set. That's it.'

I went straight to the hallstand. No second set, my set, lying on top. I pulled open the narrow drawer at the front – it was empty. I dropped down on my knees to search the floor. No other set of keys.

This was madness. It was madness and it was me who was going mad. I strode into the kitchen and dropped the keys on the table. I needed a drink. I flicked on the kettle, turned to reach for the coffee and stopped. On the work surface below the cupboard where I kept the jar of coffee was my bottle of malt and next to it a single whisky glass.

I stared at it. I had put it away. I remembered putting it away, putting *them* away, the bottle and the glass. I had put them away in the cabinet in the living room and locked the door.

I closed my eyes and opened them again. The bottle and glass were still there. I rubbed the back of my hand across my lips. Oh God, I could do with a drink. I could hear the kettle starting to boil, see the steam streaming out of the spout. My eyes were drawn back to the bottle and glass.

Slowly and deliberately I reached up above them, opened the cupboard and took down the coffee jar. I needed coffee. Just coffee. I took the mug and spoon I had used earlier from the drainer and gave them a cursory wipe before spooning coffee into the mug and filling it with water.

My eyes were drawn back to the whisky. Just a small drop in my coffee instead of milk would be OK. I'd had a bad morning. It would be for medicinal purposes. My nerves were shot; whose wouldn't have been after seeing what I had seen?

The image of Jed, his hand raised, tilting it back and forth when he spoke of the reverend's *little* problem sprang into my mind. I made myself open the fridge, take out a carton of milk and slop a large slug into my mug.

I slumped down at the kitchen table, my back to the bottle and glass. Out of sight, out of mind. Not a hope. The coffee didn't taste right. I gave it a sniff. It didn't smell right either. I slammed the mug down onto the table, got up and yanked open the fridge door with a force that rattled the contents. I snatched at the milk carton, unscrewed the lid and took a sniff. It didn't smell off. Putting the lid back on, I peered at the use-by date. By my reckoning it was good for at least another three days. I shoved the milk back in the fridge and slammed the door.

'It must be the water,' I muttered to myself. The water company were always messing about with it, filling it with chlorine or fluorine or some other damn chemical that none of us needed or wanted. Hadn't there been some village in the West Country who had almost been poisoned by an overdose of something the water company had put in their supply? Fucking nanny state.

I stomped the two paces it took to get back to the table and as I pulled out the chair I glanced back over my shoulder and caught a glimpse of the whisky bottle and glass. I licked my lips. It was almost noon; not as though it was ten o'clock in the morning. If I'd been on holiday, lying on a beach somewhere in Spain or the south of France, I wouldn't think twice about having a beer or rum and Coke. And I was on holiday, after all.

Fuck it, I was a grown man. I could have a drink if I wanted one. I deserved a drink, didn't I? Why should I care what anyone bloody well thought? Was there anyone left who I cared enough about that I worried what they thought? They'd all left me or forgotten me. She'd left me. She'd bloody well left me.

'Yeah, fuck her,' I said, reaching for the bottle, when my mobile began to ring from somewhere within the cottage.

I stopped, stock-still, my fingers hovering a hair's breadth from the whisky. The phone continued to ring, a familiar jaunty little ditty made famous by Barry White. My eyes began to bubble up and my hand dropped to my side as I looked around the kitchen. Where was my mobile? Where was my fucking mobile? I had to take the call. No one else who rang me had that ringtone. It could only be one person, but she couldn't possibly ever ring me again.

The phone carried on ringing as I ran out into the hallway, then stopped to listen. It sounded like it was coming from the living room. The door was open, but when I went inside I could hear that the phone wasn't in there. And still it rang.

I ran back into the hall. When was the last time I'd seen it? In the bedroom? In the bedroom on the bedside table? I pounded up the stairs, the sound of the ringtone getting louder with each step. I ran along the corridor and swung into the bedroom. The phone lying on my pillow filled my vision. I strode across the room, picked it up and the ringing stopped.

'No,' I murmured, 'please, no.'

I tapped in my code. No missed calls. No unlistened-to messages. I keyed in 1471. I recognised the number as the estate agents, who I'd spoken to a day or so ago. I sank down onto the bed. What was happening to me? I'd heard the phone ring. It had rung. It had been Kat's ringtone. 'My first, my last, my—' A small dark patch appeared on the leg of my jeans and then another. I swiped a hand across my face and it came away wet.

'Oh, Kat,' I said and flopped back on the bed and closed my eyes. 'Oh, Kat.'

* * *

The light was beginning to fade, and my eyelids felt sore and gritty, my face tight. For a moment I was disorientated, then I realised I was still clutching the phone in my hand. I checked the time and dropped it onto the bedside table with a sigh. She hadn't phoned me; she couldn't phone me. It had been a malfunction of some kind, or wishful thinking.

Then I remembered I had somewhere to be. Emma's get-together and I really, really did not feel like mingling at the moment. I wondered if I didn't turn up, would she think it incredibly rude? Then an awful thought occurred to me – what if she'd arranged it especially so I'd get to meet a few locals? She hadn't said as much, but judging by the sort of lady she was I wouldn't be at all surprised if she'd made a few hasty phone calls.

If there was any possibility that this was the case, I'd have to go. Funny, I'd always been the gregarious one while Kat was happier to stay at home. I literally had to coax her to come out sometimes. She had particularly hated work dos, though I couldn't blame her. Even so I think she would have liked Emma and she certainly would have girded her loins for this event. In fact, she'd have fitted right in here. This is something we should have done together. It would have been right for us.

Money had been my god. Pity it had taken me so long to realise it was a false one.

I guessed Emma's gathering wouldn't be a formal kind of event, so after downing a quick sandwich I dressed in slate-grey chinos, teal shirt and grey jacket. I didn't bother with a tie.

As I opened the front door it occurred to me that I should take something with me as a thank you gift or at least a contribution. I hurried back into the kitchen and opened the fridge, hoping for inspiration or at least a bottle of wine. Then I remembered. I hadn't bought any white. Why would I? It was Kat who drank the stuff; apart from the occasional lunchtime glass, I almost always drank red.

I pushed the fridge door shut with a sigh, my earlier misery bubbling up inside me again. Feeling sorry for myself was not good, not good at all and achieved nothing. I stalked into the living room to get a bottle of red. I knew I had a couple of those.

I turned the key in the lock of the drinks cabinet and pulled it open, reaching for a bottle of red. My fingers closed around the bottle's neck and I paused. Six gleaming whisky glasses nestled together in two perfect rows and beside them, right at the back, was the malt; where it should have been, where I was sure I'd left it before it turned up in the kitchen.

I slowly drew out the wine. This was ridiculous. I practically ran back into the kitchen. The work top where the whisky and glass had been was empty. It would be, they were back in the cabinet.

This was crazy. They'd been there – or had they? Common sense told me they couldn't have been. I'd just seen them in exactly the place they should have been – where I'd put them.

Maybe I had dreamt it? That was it. I was agitated

when I'd arrived back home. Maybe I'd gone straight upstairs and fallen asleep and dreamt it. That would explain the phone call from beyond the grave. That would explain my mobile lying on my pillow. That would explain the whisky.

Wine bottle clenched in my right hand I went straight to the front door, checked my pocket for my keys. My keys. I glanced at the hallstand. They weren't there. They wouldn't be, I'd dropped them on the kitchen table. So I couldn't have gone straight upstairs. I'd gone into the kitchen. I'd gone into the kitchen to make myself a coffee while I'd tried to make sense of how suddenly a dog whistle had appeared on my set of keys. Maybe that was a dream as well.

The keys were where I'd left them. The keys and a silver cylindrical tube. I picked them up and shoved them into my pocket.

I'd go to the party, but tomorrow I was leaving and going back to London.

CHAPTER EIGHT

There were a couple of cars parked in Emma's drive, and the sound of voices and laughter spilt out through the open front door along with a swathe of light from the hallway.

Inside, the house was as impressive as it looked from the drive. A large entrance hall surrounded a massive staircase with rooms going off to its left and right. Small tables, supporting large Japanese vases overflowing with fragrant flowers, flanked each doorway and my feet actually sank into the richly coloured carpet covering the floor as I crossed to the room where all the activity appeared to be going on.

As I entered I was greeted by a young woman who offered me a flute of champagne or glass of orange juice from a silver tray and I began to regret bringing the wine. Before I could find somewhere to discreetly leave it, Emma appeared from within a group of her guests and after kissing me on both cheeks, linked her arm through mine.

'Um, this is for you,' I said, holding up the bottle.

'Oh, you are a darling. Merlot, how did you know it's a favourite of mine?' she said, giving me another kiss on the cheek.

She glanced around and another young woman appeared at her side to take the bottle. I'd guessed Emma was probably fairly well heeled, but I was beginning to get the impression that she was a lot wealthier than I'd previously imagined.

She led me over to a couple of middle-aged women who were animatedly chatting to Jed, his social-gathering smile fixed. 'The two ladies are the Garvin sisters,' she murmured to me. 'They live at the other end of the village.'

She gave my arm a squeeze as the two women looked towards us expectantly as we approached. 'Miriam, Darcy, I'd like to introduce you to my new neighbour, Jim.'

Miriam, a motherly looking woman of about fifty, stuck out her hand and gave mine a firm shake. 'Good to meet you, Jim.'

Darcy was equally enthusiastic, although as opposite in appearance to her sister as she could possibly be. Where Miriam was pink-faced and with soft, chubby curves covered in a voluminous floral dress, Darcy was stick-thin and all angles, dressed in a silver-grey trouser suit that did nothing for her complexion, leaving her pale-faced and drawn.

'You're renting the old Morgan place, I hear,' Darcy said.

'Yes,' I replied, taking a sip of my champagne and wishing it was something a little stronger.

'How are you finding it?' she asked.

'It's a nice cottage.'

'Do you think you'll stay?' Miriam asked.

'No,' I said and wondered whether I should break the news now that I intended to leave for London first thing the next morning.

'He says not, but he will,' Jed said.

'What makes you say that?' Darcy asked him.

Jed gave me a strange look. 'He has things to do.'

'Like what?' Darcy asked.

'Like meet all his wonderful neighbours,' Emma interrupted and drew me away before Jed could reply.

'Sorry,' she said as she led me over to another group of people. 'Jed isn't always the most discreet of people.'

'What did he mean – things to do?'

She stopped and drew me around to face her. 'He thinks you've found your way to Slyford for a reason.'

I inwardly sighed. 'And what would that be?'

She cocked her head to one side as she studied my expression. 'I don't know,' and a small frown creased the centre of her forehead, 'but I suspect we might find out over the next few weeks, maybe even months.'

'Look, Emma.' I really did need to tell her there wasn't going to be any weeks or months – not even days, if I had my way – but we were interrupted by one of the maids.

'There's a phone call for you, Mrs Mortimer. Mrs Sims asking for a word.'

'Excuse me a moment, Jim. I'll be straight back,' Emma said, giving my arm a pat and then she was gone.

Another maid appeared to take my glass and hand me a refreshed champagne flute. I sipped my drink and took a surreptitious look around. There were too many people, mainly a lot older than me: ladies in floral posh frocks and men in navy jackets and old school ties. I caught a glimpse of Jed, red-faced and laughing. He'd moved on to another couple, who were obviously more to his liking, but his eyes were on me. I didn't want to risk him bowling over and taking me somewhere I didn't need to go, so I strolled towards the door and out into the entrance hall, taking another swallow of my drink and hoping to appear nonchalant and at ease.

In the hallway I had a quick glance around. Emma was nowhere to be seen, and before I'd even a chance to consider what on earth I was doing I turned left and hurried past the staircase. Seeing the door to the next room ajar, I pushed it open and stepped inside, closing it behind me.

This was a smaller room and was kitted out like an office-cum-library. There were certainly a lot of books lining the walls. A large fireplace dominated the room, taking up more than two-thirds of one wall. There was no fire burning in the wrought-iron grate, although there were logs and kindling piled to one side in readiness for the fast-approaching winter months.

On either side of the fire were the obligatory leather, high-backed, winged armchairs and the opportunity to sit down in one to hide from Jed and the other guests was too great for me to resist.

I padded across the room and it was only as I sank down into one of the chairs that I realised that its twin was occupied.

'You trying to escape from all the frivolity as well?' a voice asked.

'I'm sorry,' I said, starting to stand, 'I didn't mean to intrude.'

He raised a hand, gesturing that I sit. 'I don't mind a bit of company, but some of Emma's friends I find a little wearing,' he said, giving me a pleasant smile. 'Now, as I've never seen you at one of these things before, I'm guessing you must be our new neighbour recently arrived from London.'

'Jim, Jim Hawkes,' I said, half-getting up and leaning forward to stick out a hand.

We shook and we both sank back into our respective chairs. He retrieved a crystal glass from the small table beside him, cradling it in long-fingered hands as he studied me and I studied him right back. Soft lamplight glinted on the golden contents of the glass catching my eye and for the second time in not so many minutes I wished that my glass contained something a lot stronger than champagne. I pushed the notion from my mind. I wasn't here to get smashed, then wondered where that thought had come from.

'So, Jim, how are you finding Slyford?' Then he laughed. 'I suspect you're getting fed up with people asking the question.'

'Just a bit,' I told him with a wry smile.

'It was exactly the same when I first moved here, and from experience I can tell you it won't change until someone else new comes into the village, then I'm afraid you'll find yourself asking them the self-same question.'

He put the glass back on the table and plucked at the blanket covering his bony knees, pulling it up to his waist. How had I not noticed the blanket when he had half-stood to shake my hand?

'You're better off hiding in here with me,' he said, drawing my eyes back to his face.

When I'd first sat down I'd have said that he was in his forties, but looking at him now I realised I must have been mistaken, he appeared considerably older, then it could be because he was ill and I wondered how I'd missed this as well. Looking at him again it was plainly obvious.

He had high cheekbones and in his youth would have been handsome, now they just accentuated how sunken his eyes and cheeks had become, though his eyes were bright and from the lines around his eyes I could see he was a man who laughed a lot. He was laughing now. A cheerful sort who wouldn't let anything that life threw at him get him down and suddenly, as ill as he appeared, I wished I could be like him.

He glanced down at the watch that hung about his painfully thin wrist. 'Hmm, you've probably got another hour or so before things next door start to get serious.'

'Serious?'

'Emma and Jed,' he said with a sigh. 'Not their faults, really. The Garvin sisters will start begging for a seance and Jed will've had too much to drink to remember it isn't really a good idea. Emma will feign reluctance, but that's all it'll be. No, it's better you stay in here with me.'

'They're going to have a seance?'

'More than likely.'

'Maybe I should leave.'

He picked up his glass and raised it shakily to his lips, the veins tracing the backs of his hands looking a dark purple in the lamplight.

'Maybe it'd be for the better if you did – somehow I think not. I think you're meant to be here and now. Maybe then it can all be done and dusted. Maybe then a few of this village's ghosts can be laid to rest.'

My mouth felt very dry. 'Ghosts?' I asked, and it came out more as a raspy croak.

His smile was very gentle. 'I know you want to leave Slyford, but give it time, a few more days, a week, a month, but give it time. This village needs you. Emms and Jed need you.'

'I don't understand.'

'You—'

'Jim?' a voice called.

'You'd better go,' he said.

'Oh, Jim, there you are,' Emma said, and I glanced around the wing of the chair to see her crossing the room towards me with Jed in her wake. 'I thought we'd lost you.'

'I'm sorry,' I said, hastily getting to my feet, 'I just needed a moment of quiet and I got talking to . . .' Then I realised he'd never told me his name. I glanced down at the other armchair and the world about me gave a little lurch. The seat was empty. I forced myself to carry on even though my head was reeling. 'I just needed a moment,' I finished lamely.

If either of them noticed I was talking rubbish they didn't show it. Emma linked an arm through mine. 'Come on. I have some more people to introduce you to.'

As she led me from the room I glanced over my shoulder at the back of the empty chair and it occurred to me that maybe Sir Peter had been right. Maybe I *was* in the middle of a breakdown.

I didn't have time to brood. The next hour or so passed in a confusion of names, faces and inane small talk, when all I wanted to do was escape back to the cottage. No, not to the cottage. I didn't really care if I never saw the place again. What I really wanted was to escape back to London and if I could say 'Beam me up, Scotty' and suddenly appear back in the familiar surroundings of my own home, I would.

At about eleven-thirty people began to leave and to my relief there had been no mention of a seance. That the Garvin sisters appeared to be ensconced for the night did give me cause for concern and, when they gravitated towards Jed as the elderly couple he was talking with said their farewells, I decided it was time for me to leave.

Emma was in the front hall saying goodbye to her guests and I dutifully joined the queue wishing they'd get a move on. Why it was some people when they decided to leave just couldn't get on and do it I'd never know. It was always the same. They'd say their goodbyes and then stand on the doorstep yattering on and on for half an hour or more.

When it finally got to my turn Emma gave me a bright smile. 'Leaving so soon?'

'Emma, it's been great. Thanks for inviting me.'

'You're not going?' a voice boomed from behind me, making me jump.

I glanced over my shoulder as Jed crossed the hall to join us. Behind him the Garvin sisters hovered. Miriam's expression was possibly one of disappointment; Darcy's was more like tight-lipped disapproval.

'Why not join us for one last nightcap?' Emma suggested.

'That's very kind, Emma, but it's been a long day,' I said.

'Ah, come on, Jim. Have one last snifter with us for the road,' Jed said, slapping me on the back.

I wanted to refuse. I wanted to leave. All the same I found myself being drawn across the hallway into what I imagined was Emma's sitting room.

Four lamp stands were positioned around the room, the light passing through their amber glass shades bathing the gold and cream striped walls in a cosy, warm glow. Several floral-covered couches and armchairs were arranged around a central coffee table and to my relief it crossed my mind that never had I seen a room less conducive to the calling upon of spirits.

Jed fetched glasses, moving around with a familiarity that made me wonder at the relationship between him and our hostess. Emma poured two fingers of Scotch into each of the glasses and handed them around. Then, when we were all seated, she dropped down into a chair herself with a happy sigh.

'Cheers,' she said, lifting her glass.

'Cheers,' we all echoed.

It was good stuff. Sir Peter would have loved it.

I rolled the first mouthful around on my tongue, savouring the slightly peaty flavour, and when I swallowed the golden liquid left a trail of warmth down my throat and into my chest that had me closing my eyes and feeling grateful I'd stayed.

'This is lovely,' I murmured.

'Reggie's favourite,' Emma said. 'I was never much of a whisky drinker before he introduced me to this blend.'

We all relaxed back into our seats, sipping our drinks in a companionable silence and I couldn't help thinking it was the perfect end to the day and perhaps my stay in the village. It wasn't the right time to mention it, though. I thought maybe in the morning I'd pop round to see Emma with a bunch of flowers to give her the news. If I was all packed up and ready to go, she could hardly talk me out of it.

'Have you seen any more of the Finch girl?' Darcy asked Jed.

I inwardly winced. Maybe I should have left.

He looked up from his glass. 'The last time I saw her

was a few days ago. Her brother warned me off.'

'Warned you off?' Emma said. 'It was she who needed warning off.'

'He didn't see it that way.' He took a swig of his drink. 'Anyway, I'd already told the lass I didn't have anything else for her. If the dead don't want to talk, I can't make them.'

'And her father didn't?' Miriam asked.

'He'd said all he had to say and moved on, and that's the way it should be.'

'Had any other messages?' Miriam asked, her eyes bright, and Darcy shifted forward on the couch, elbows on knees, hands clenched together as if in prayer.

I shivered. There was something in their expressions that I found unsettling, repugnant even. A fervour, a zealous excitement. I now understood what my companion in the study meant. This was the moment they'd been waiting for all evening. Getting Jed to perform for them. I didn't want to see this. I didn't need to see this.

I went to stand, but my legs didn't want to work and my head swam. Had I drunk more than I thought? I'd only had three glasses of champagne, four tops, and I still had a finger of whisky left in my glass.

I looked up. Fortunately, all eyes were on Jed and no one had noticed my momentary incapacity. His cheeks were flushed and his lips wet. He'd certainly had more than three or four flutes of champagne.

'I'm sorry, ladies,' he said. 'I've nothing for you tonight.'

I relaxed back into my seat. Thank the Lord for that.

Jed's parlour games I did not need. I took another sip of my drink closed my eyes and everything went blank.

Blank – no, not blank. It was like I was blind, deaf and dumb. It was like I'd been submerged into a sea of black. I couldn't breathe; I was drowning in darkness. I began to panic. I was sitting in Emma's lounge with four other people who had no idea I was dying in front of them. I tried to speak; I tried to scream, but no words came.

Then, almost as though I had imagined the whole thing, the veil was lifted. I gasped in air. I could breathe, hear and see.

'Oh my God, oh my God,' I heard a woman's voice saying over and over again.

'Jim. Jim, can you hear me?' That was Emma.

I looked up. Emma was crouched in front of me, her eyes wide, her face pale despite the sunny glow of the lights. Jed was doing something to my hand. When I looked down he was wrapping a towel around my palm, but even as the material wound around my hand it rapidly turned scarlet.

'Should I call an ambulance?' Jed asked.

Emma ignored him. 'Jim, are you all right?'

I looked back at my hand and the bloody towel. 'What happened?' I suddenly felt very cold. Had I had some sort of fit? Had I had another episode of craziness?

'Don't you remember?' Emma asked, biting her lip, then she and Jed shared a look.

Jed had lost the ruddy glow to his cheeks, and I wasn't sure whether it was the sight of my blood but he appeared to have sobered up pretty damn quickly.

Over his shoulder I could see Miriam and Darcy huddled together on the settee. They'd lost their eager expressions; Miriam was staring at me in cold-eyed shock – no, her expression was more like horrified, and Darcy's complexion looked bloodless. Bloody hell – what had I done?

Jed stood. 'I'll see you out,' he said to them.

'You didn't tell us,' Darcy said.

'I didn't know,' Jed said, glancing my way as he ushered the two women out of the room.

I instinctively flipped a wave of farewell. Darcy's expression was troubled, but Miriam . . . I caught a glimpse of something else. She was looking directly at me, her eyes narrowed. There was something there that made me shiver and then, within an instant, it was gone and she gave me a weak smile. Good God, I was seeing menace where there was none. She was a middle-aged woman, for heaven's sake.

Emma unwound the towel from around my hand and started to dab at my palm with the least bloody patch of material she could find. When I looked I could see an inch-long, jagged gash across its centre. She peered down at the wound, still dabbing at it as the flow of blood began to slow.

'You'll live,' she said, giving me a tight smile, 'and I don't think there's any glass in it.'

'Glass?'

She gestured over her shoulder at what remained

112

of one of her whisky glasses. Now a pile of broken, blood-smeared pieces.

'I'm sorry – did I do that?' Though I couldn't see how I had; the glass was of thick, good-quality crystal. 'What happened? Did I have some sort of seizure?' I babbled, my fear fast turning back to panic.

'No, not a seizure. Don't worry. It's nothing to worry about.' Jed appeared next to her and handed her a packet and a roll of bandage. She muttered her thanks and, dropping the bloody towel on the coffee table next to the shards of crystal, began to dress my hand.

'Well, I've got a feeling we won't be seeing the Garvin girls for some time to come,' Jed said and started to chuckle.

Emma shot him an angry look. 'I'm glad you're amused.'

'It is kind of funny.'

'You think?'

'What happened?' I asked, my fear turning to irritation as they appeared to be talking around me.

'Make yourself useful and pour Jim a drink,' Emma said.

'You want one?'

'I think I could do with one.' She pinned the bandage into place. 'There. All done,' she said and got up to sit in the chair next to mine.

Jed handed us both a glass then went and recharged his own. 'You don't remember what happened?' he asked, dropping down on the sofa recently vacated by the Garvins.

'Just everything suddenly went black and I felt like I was drowning.'

Emma rested her glass upon her knee and tapped the side of it with the nail of her forefinger. 'You've never had this happen before?'

'No,' I said, shaking my head.

'I don't know how to break this to you,' Emma said.

'Am I having a breakdown?'

That brought a smile to her face, the first real one since I'd come round.

'No, dear boy, you're not,' she said, 'but I'm afraid you're going to have to start facing a few home truths and, judging by your previous reaction, I don't think you're going to like hearing them.'

'What?'

'You just passed us a message from beyond the grave.'

CHAPTER NINE

Had my legs not felt like jelly and my hand throbbed like shit I would probably have got to my feet and left. I think I almost would have preferred it if they had told me I'd had a seizure or was going mad, though perhaps it was a kind of madness. I'd always thought psychics were conmen preying on the vulncrable and anyone who actually believed in that kind of hogwash was either desperate, deluded or stark raving bonkers. Now they were asking *me* to believe in the very same thing.

'I know you don't want to accept it, but if all you've seen and heard over the past few days hasn't convinced you that you can communicate with the dead, I don't know what will,' Emma said.

'It's never happened before,' I said, leaning back in the chair and crossing my arms.

'Before you came to Slyford, you mean,' Jed said with a grunt.

'Are you sure?' Emma asked. 'Having a connection to the dead doesn't just snap on like flicking a switch.'

'Quite sure, thank you, and if it's all the same to you I'd rather it didn't happen again.'

'You can't just switch it off, either,' Jed commented.

We sat there in an uneasy silence for a while, and in the end I had to ask the question despite myself, even if only to break the difficult atmosphere between us.

'You said I gave you a message from beyond the grave – what did you mean? What did I say?'

'So now you want to know?' Jed grumbled.

Emma gave him another of her looks and Jed suddenly found the bottom of his glass very interesting.

'I warn you, it was harrowing.'

Jed leant forward in his chair and picked up a small oblong object from the coffee table. 'Emma usually records any messages I have to give. She wasn't expecting anything tonight so she missed the first few seconds.' He pressed a button on the side and a reedy, young voice filled the room.

'. . . hide. He found me. Had to run. Make him stop. Make him go away.'

'Oh my God,' a woman said, I think it was probably Darcy, and someone told her to shush.

'He's coming. He's coming.'

Then there was ragged breathing over the whir of the machine.

'Do you think that's it?' A faint whisper.

'I don't think so; look at him,' Emma's voice and then several gasps.

'Oh, dear Lord,' Darcy again, I think.

Then a man's voice. Loud, angry and sounding like he was out of breath. 'Where are you? Little brat. Think I'm stupid, do you? When I find you, I'll show you who's stupid. I'll show you.'

I shivered, getting a really bad feeling. I recognised the words or at least the sentiment.

'When I find you, I'm going to make you sorry. I'm going to make you very sorry indeed. Little bitch.' More heavy breathing.

'You have to make him stop,' another voice, but this one I recognised. Peter Davies. 'He's going to hurt more children. You have to find him and make him stop.'

Another gasp. 'Oh my God, oh my God,' the woman's voice I'd heard when I came to my senses, then another low, barely distinguishable voice snapping at her to, I think, shut up.

'Jim, Jim, can you hear me?' That was Emma, and a loud click then silence.

I took a swig of my drink. 'Are you telling me that I said all those things?'

'You didn't just say them, Jim, you physically changed. I've never seen anything like it before. Your face changed, not a lot, but enough that if I hadn't recognised the voice I'd have seen something of Peter Davies in you,' Emma said.

117

'What about the other man?'

She grimaced. 'Him, I didn't recognise.' She glanced at Jed and he shook his head.

I sat staring into my glass while Jed poured us all another slug of whisky. If he was trying to take the edge off how we were feeling I think he was deluding himself. I doubted I'd ever feel the same again.

'Who do you think the man was?' Emma asked no one in particular.

'No idea,' Jed answered.

'Do you think he's dead?'

'He must be, people don't get psychic messages from the living.'

'If he were, why would the reverend tell us we had to stop him?'

I sat listening to them, trying to make sense of what to me was nonsensical. The first voice, the little girl, was that Krystal Morgan? Had the second voice been that of the man who'd killed her? Then it dawned on me. I was beginning to believe in all this. I was beginning to believe someone had killed Krystal Morgan and for whatever reason someone somewhere was trying to make me discover who and why.

I got up and walked to the window. The curtains hadn't been closed and I could see myself and the room behind me reflected upon the glass. I took a sip of whisky, still staring at the reflection. Emma was leaning forward in her chair, deep in conversation with Jed. I don't think they'd even noticed I'd left my seat. The room really did appear to glow in the lamplight; all that was needed was a roaring fire in the grate and it'd look like a magical Christmas scene.

I felt small, cold fingers slip into mine. I let out a shuddery breath, not looking down but instead at the reflection of the little girl standing next to me. She smiled up at me as I watched our reflections. I didn't dare look to my side: I was afraid if I did, she might disappear. I was afraid if I did, I might just see a small figure standing beside me.

I saw Emma look our way, but then her attention returned to Jed. She clearly hadn't seen my ghostly friend. The child rested her head against my arm, gave my fingers a squeeze and slowly faded away until all that was left was the memory of her soft, cold hand in mine and her heartbreaking smile.

I was about to turn away when there was a movement outside. I leant forward, my nose almost touching the glass and a face loomed up at me out of the dark. I staggered back a step and straight into Jed.

'Are you all right?' he asked.

'Did you see that? I thought I saw something.' My pounding heart began to slow, and I moved forward to once more peer outside. There was nothing but darkness. It was Jed's reflection, that was all. It must have been. A little voice inside my head told me different, but I refused to listen. It was an illusion, a trick of the light. Then I remembered the cold fingers wrapped in mine.

I walked back to the couch and sat down.

* * *

We talked all night. Emma made coffee and toast and we carried on talking. At least they did. I said very little. I didn't tell them about the reflection of the child, nor did I tell them about the face looming at me out of the darkness. I'd more or less convinced myself it was indeed Jed's reflection as he came up behind me. More or less, but not completely. For one thing I was pretty sure the face didn't have a beard. Could it have been Jed's reflection combined with mine?

It was a question I would never be able to answer. Still, I was more than glad that by the time I left to walk home the sun was coming up and it was light outside, although as ever a pall of mist floated off the fields and gardens flanking the lane.

When I arrived at the cottage I went straight up the stairs to bed, stopping only briefly to use the bathroom and clean the patina of whisky and coffee off my teeth. I closed the curtains, undressed and crawled under my duvet. As weary as my body was, my mind was still buzzing.

The whole of the previous evening felt surreal. Jed was the one who spoke to the dead, not me.

Eventually sleep found me, and boy did I sleep. At one point I woke long enough to look at my clock, which read three o'clock and in a dozy haze I read it as three in the morning. It didn't register it was light outside and before I did my head had fallen back on my pillow and my eyes had closed as exhaustion took me again.

The next time I woke I was interrupted from my sleep by an irritating sound that wouldn't go away. I pulled the duvet up over my head, but still it went on and on until my mind began to clear and with a start I sat up.

My bedside clock read eleven-twenty and it took a few moments for me to realise it was dark and therefore eleven-twenty at night. Still the noise went on and on and eventually the sleep-induced fug began to slip from my brain and I began to listen. It was scratching. A rapid scrabbling of claws against wood. I swung my legs over the side of the bed and listened some more. The scratching was coming from the hallway. Something was scratching at my bedroom door. I pulled on my jeans and padded across the room barefoot to stand in front of the door.

Claws continued to attack the wood in an urgent clatter and the red lead hanging in the cupboard under the stairs came to mind. I reached for the light switch, the clatter of claws became frantic and another of my senses kicked in. What was that smell?

My hand dropped to my side and the realisation of what I had almost done made my chest tighten. I could smell gas.

The scratching stopped. I threw open the door, but there was nothing there, nothing except the thick reek of gas filling the hallway. I ran down the stairs and flung open the front door and then swung along the corridor to the kitchen.

I stubbed my toe as I blundered past the table and chairs in the dark, but I barely felt it; I had too many other things to worry about. The oven door was open, and the gas was on full, as were all four burners. I switched them off and opened the back door – the unlocked back door – and stepped outside into the sweet night air.

After filling my lungs I went back inside, walking through every room trying to open windows but gave up as they were all screwed shut. When I reached the lounge the door was closed when I always left it ajar. My hand touched the doorknob and from the kitchen I heard a dog yap.

'What the fuck?' I ran back to the kitchen. There was nothing there, but then I heard a dog bark, this time from out in the garden. I hurried outside – still there was nothing.

My head was beginning to ache. Whether it was an after effect of the whisky from the night before, my deep sleep or the gas, I wasn't sure, nor did I really care. If I'd flicked that light switch, if the scratching at that precise moment hadn't become more insistent, making me pause, I didn't like to think what might have happened with all the gas in the house. These days the inhalation of the gas itself didn't kill you, it was well-meaning neighbours ringing on your doorbell or switching on lights and the associated sparks of electricity that did.

I stood barefooted on the grass considering my own mortality, the ghostly scratching and why someone had turned on the gas and who that someone could be, all the time hoping the dog would bark again and a real live terrier would bound into the garden.

When I went back inside the kitchen the stink of gas had almost gone. I wiped the grime off my feet and pounded back upstairs to find some shoes and open my bedroom window to clear the last remnants of the odour.

Back downstairs the hallway was clear so I closed the front door and flipped the latch, not that it appeared to make much difference. Someone had obviously come and gone as they pleased. On my way back to the kitchen I hesitated by the living-room door.

I had been about to go in when the dog had interrupted me again with its barking. Why had it done that? I rested my hand on the doorknob. This time there was no ghostly yapping or scrabble of claws. *Maybe because the danger had passed.* The thought scared me. Had an assailant been hiding in the room? Had he slipped outside while I was back in the kitchen or out in the garden? The door was still shut – would he or she have bothered to take the time to close it behind them? With some trepidation I turned the handle and let the door swing open.

The ache in the centre of my forehead began to throb. The door to the liquor cabinet was open and just inside it next to the whisky glasses was a large candle flickering away. I wasn't sure there would have been enough gas in the hallway for the flame to have caused an explosion had I opened the door earlier, but if I hadn't woken when I had and gas had begun to seep into that room, who knows what would have happened. There was one thing of which I was pretty much certain. Someone had either tried to kill me or was giving me a serious message. I was clearly no longer welcome in Slyford St James.

CHAPTER TEN

It occurred to me as I slumped down at the kitchen table that I shouldn't have still been in the village. Last night I'd intended to leave. Was it really only last night? It felt like a million years ago. Fate had, however, conspired against me. Fate? No, not fate, something altogether different.

I got up to put on the kettle and stared out into the garden, not that I could see much in the dark. Then I remembered the night before and the face outside the window, and quickly moved across the kitchen to lock and bolt the back door. It didn't help. I still didn't feel safe.

What on earth was happening to me?

I made myself a mug of coffee, despite the urge for something stronger, and plonked myself down at the kitchen table. I'd heard the evidence and I'd seen . . . What had I seen?

I thought I'd seen the reflection of the ghostly image of a child standing by my side. I'd felt her touch. Was it Krystal? Was it the same child I'd followed through the woods to the churchyard? I pushed back my chair and began to pace. I couldn't have done. It was madness. I was having a breakdown. Everything pointed to it.

What about the dog barking?

My imagination, that was all. I'd never heard a dog before I saw the lead in the cupboard.

It woke you from your sleep.

I dreamt it.

It woke you from your sleep.

I slumped back down on the chair. It *had* woken me, or at least something had.

It woke you before too much gas seeped into the bedroom, then distracted you when you were about to make a life-threatening mistake. It saved your life.

It did seem that way.

All right – let's forget about ghostly apparitions and messages from beyond for a moment and concentrate on what happened tonight.

One thing was for sure the dead couldn't hurt me – or could they? I sat up straight in the chair. Shit! Things had physically moved when no one else could have possibly been in the cottage. Peter Davies had made me tea, for God's sake, so maybe they could. I closed my eyes and breathed in deep, trying to calm my agitation. Consider the facts, I told myself. Someone, whether living or dead, had damn well tried to harm me – but who and why?

I'd start with the living. I didn't know anyone in the village other than Jed, Emma, George at the pub and the people Emma had introduced me to last night, and although I knew I could sometimes piss people off, last night I hadn't spoken to anyone for long enough. Except . . .

Who was the man in the study? And where had he suddenly disappeared to? He would have had to have stood up and passed between Emma and me within not much more than a split second. Dear Lord, I was definitely losing it. It was no good. This place was not good – not for me, anyway.

Tomorrow I'd pack up my bags and leave. Or should I say today – it was past midnight.

He said the village needed you.

Did it matter what a figment of my imagination had said?

He said Jed and Emma needed you. He said you were here in the village for a reason.

Maybe he did – someone else had other ideas on the subject, otherwise why the gas? Why the lighted candle?

Don't you want to find out why?

No, not really.

My inner voice fell silent.

Not if it was going to get me killed.

More silence.

Fuck it – I was talking to myself and expecting answers – how mad was that?

Someone tried to kill you – that wasn't a figment of your imagination.

Wasn't it? Did I have a shred of evidence? Maybe I'd turned on the gas. Maybe subconsciously I was trying to kill myself.

Now, you are talking crazy – you know that isn't true.

I jumped to my feet and hurried through to the living room. The candle was where I'd found it. I'd blown it out, but from the wax that had pooled around it I would have said it had been burning for some while, though probably no more than an hour, possibly less. How long would it have taken the cottage to fill with gas? No time at all, I supposed, not with the oven and all four hobs turned on full.

I had been fast asleep. Could I have walked in my sleep?

That is crazy.

And actually, it was. I'd have had to have come downstairs, blown out the pilot light, turned on the gas. Then I'd have to have gone into the living room, found a candle from somewhere, and I certainly couldn't remember ever seeing that thick, stubby lump of wax before, and light it. And for that I would have needed matches.

I glanced around the room. No matches. I went back to the kitchen. Still no matches, only one of those gas lighter thingies that lights the gas with a spark. I patted my pockets, empty except for a few coins and a five-pound note.

I couldn't have lit the candle; I didn't have anything to light it with. I slumped down onto a chair, my legs weak. Were the dead capable of such a thing? I glanced towards the cooker. Could the dead . . . ? I didn't complete the thought. I didn't need to. Maybe the dead could harm the living. I hoped not, or at least that I'd never find out. I wasn't sure if I felt better or worse as the realisation slowly dawned on me that, yes, someone really had tried to kill me. A person; a real, honest-to-God living person. On the floor right in front of the cooker was a dead match, a dead match and a footprint. I crouched down to take a better look. It was faint, but it was undeniably a print of the sole of a boot or maybe even a wellington, and I was pretty sure it wasn't one of mine. I raced upstairs to my bedroom. I checked my walking boots, trainers, my shoes. There was nothing even close to the print in the kitchen.

I sank down onto the bed feeling like the breath had been knocked out of me. Someone had really and truly tried to kill me and that someone was certainly not a ghost.

Who would do such a thing? Why would anyone do such a thing? Jed possibly had keys to the cottage, but I couldn't think of a single reason why he would want to kill me unless he was the crazy one. Maybe he didn't like having competition. Maybe that was how he saw me. He could see the dead and now so could I.

That's even crazier.

Is it? I mulled on it for a bit. Actually, it was. If anything, Jed had tried to encourage me to accept my . . . gift? Curse? What the fuck was I thinking? Real life people didn't talk to or see the dead.

You did last night. You did a couple of days ago. You recognised Peter Davies's voice on the tape. They recognised his voice on the tape. Face it, why don't you?

Something weird was happening to me, whether it was madness or not was debatable.

You'd prefer you were going insane than believe you could possibly be seeing the dead?

Not prefer – it was just the more plausible option.

Right!

Then something else occurred to me. The second voice on the tape; he'd been practically ranting with rage. The same rage, the same words that had flowed through my head when I'd been chasing after the child through the wood. I'd been full of inexplicable anger and some of the terrible thoughts that had flickered through my head, there but not fully forming, were more than a little disturbing. They were downright sickening and not the thoughts of a normal, rational man. They were not my thoughts. No, never. Never, never, never.

But if I was going mad . . .

Don't start that again. Look at the evidence.

What evidence? There was no fucking evidence.

There's the tape. There're four witnesses to something out of the ordinary happening last night. There's the footprint.

'I need to talk to Emma and Jed,' I said out loud.

You need to tell them everything.

Everything?

Silence.

I suppose I did. But where to start? It was something I would think on; after all, I had all night. Unless my would-be murderer tried again.

We'll keep you safe. And this time it was like a whisper caressing the inside of my skull. The tension inside me drained away and with it any energy I had and, despite having slept away the day, I flopped back on the bed and was asleep before my eyes had barely closed.

I must have woken at least once during the night, although I couldn't remember it, as when I finally opened my eyes to the first inkling of dawn seeping beneath the curtains I was under the duvet.

The need to pee had me reluctantly leaving the cosy comfort of my bed and by the time I'd done the necessary all that had happened over the previous two nights came flooding back, bringing with it a tsunami of emotions, most of which were unrecognisable even to me. Fear and panic were the biggies. I actually got as far as dragging my suitcase from the wardrobe before I managed to get a grip.

I sank down on the bed. Was running back to London going to solve anything? There were just as many ghosts there to haunt me. Maybe not the kind that went bump in the night or scratched at door frames; probably a far worse kind – memories.

She'd been dead for over two years and yet I still saw her everywhere. In the house, on the street. A couple of times I'd even embarrassed myself by accosting total strangers, women who, when they'd turned to face me with startled and slightly alarmed expressions, I'd realised looked nothing like her. Nothing like her at all, and I wondered how I could have even thought they might have been her.

No, I couldn't go back. I'd thought I could; I'd thought I must, but I couldn't keep running away every time the going got tough. Something was happening in Slyford and, like it or not, I'd become embroiled in it. There was also the small matter of someone wanting to see me dead – or at least gone. Had they waited a day they'd have got their wish, I'd have left. Then all at once it became clear to me and I could feel my lips curling into a grim smile.

I was going to stay. I was going to stay and solve the mystery, if there really was one. I was buggered if I was going to let someone scare me away without at least finding out why.

Mind made up, I shoved my suitcase back into the bottom of the wardrobe before I had a chance to change my mind, got washed and changed and hurried downstairs.

The garden outside the kitchen window was shrouded in mist, but the sun was already beginning to break through, making it a whole lot brighter and less like something out of a horror movie. I could even see the trees looming up on the boundary.

I wondered if it was too early to go and call on Emma. I didn't actually know where Jed lived, although

I did have his card somewhere with his number on it; two cards, the estate agent had sent me his card as well. Where had I put them?

There was a pinboard on the kitchen wall with various bits of information tacked to it. Maybe I had put it there. Mug in one hand and slice of toast in the other I strolled over to take a look, munching away as I did so.

It was as I thought. I'd tucked one of the cards down in the corner edge of the board. I stuffed the last piece of toast in my mouth, licked butter from my thumb and forefinger and reached for the card. As I pulled it out from under the strip of wood, I dislodged another card which fluttered to the floor. I bent to retrieve it and there was a loud knock on the door, which had me jerking upright and slopping my coffee over my fingers.

'Shit!'

There was another knock and, dropping Jed's card on the table and transferring my coffee to my other hand, I crossed the kitchen to answer the door, rubbing my wet fingers off against my jeans.

'Hang on a mo,' I called, putting down my mug to fumble with the bolts. I'd forgotten I'd locked the place up like Fort Knox the evening before.

Key turned and bolts drawn, I pulled the door open. Jed was standing with his back to me, only turning as he heard the creak of the door. He was carrying a white carrier bag tucked under his right arm, which he transferred to his left hand upon seeing me.

'Still here, then?'

'Still here,' I said.

'Wasn't sure you would be.'

'I nearly wasn't,' I told him, gesturing that he come in, 'but not by my own devices. Coffee?'

He nodded his thanks, and I put on the kettle while he settled himself down at the kitchen table, putting the carrier bag down on the floor beside his chair. I leant back against the sink while I waited for the kettle to boil. He'd picked up his card and was turning it over between his fingers, staring at it, forehead lined. He was nervous, pent-up – angry or anxious, I wasn't too sure.

'I was going to call you this morning,' I forced myself to say; his nervousness was catching, 'I think we need to talk. You, me and Emma.'

He tapped the corner of the card on the table and then carefully laid it down as though he was giving himself time to think. When he looked up, a worried frown creased his brow and, now I had the opportunity to look at him properly, I could see that although I'd slept for almost twenty-four hours, he had the appearance of not having slept for probably even longer.

'Something's happened,' he said, studying my face.

'Are you asking me or telling me?'

He continued to stare at me until I began to feel uncomfortable. It was a relief when the kettle stopped boiling and I had an excuse to busy myself with making him a coffee and refreshing my own mug. When I sat down opposite him he was still watching me.

'What's going on?' I asked.

'You tell me.'

'I think perhaps I should wait until we're with Emma.'

'Someone broke into her house last night.'

'What?' The smell of gas and the image of the flickering candle instantly coming to mind. 'Is she all right?'

'A bit frightened, is all.' He cupped the mug within his huge hands as though trying to warm himself. 'She heard a noise downstairs and called me.'

'You live nearby?'

'Just past the Sly. I was there within five minutes.' His face was solemn. 'Probably the longest of my life.'

I'd thought so. If there was nothing going on between the two of them, it wasn't down to Jed. He was well smitten. 'Did you catch anyone?'

He gave a slow shake of his head. 'As soon as they saw my lights as I pulled into the drive they were probably on their toes.'

'She could have been mistaken. It's a large, old house. Sometimes they creak and moan.'

'I reckon she knows the sounds of her own house. Anyway, he left a calling card.'

I again thought of the candle. Perhaps they'd left her a matching one. Then I realised he was studying my expression so hard it was as though he was trying to see right inside my soul.

'OK, Jed, what's going on?' I repeated.

He stared at me for a moment longer, then leant down and picked up the carrier bag and placed it in the centre of the table. 'I found this lying on the floor just outside her bedroom. It must have got dropped in his hurry to get away. The carpet up there is so damn thick it didn't break.'

'What is it?' I asked, but I had the feeling I wasn't really going to like the answer.

He gestured with his head at the bag. 'Open it.'

'What is it?' I repeated, not moving.

'I said open it,' and I saw the first faint flicker of anger in his eyes.

I lifted my hand and pushed the edge of the bag down with my forefinger. In it was a bottle. I looked across at Jed and frowned. His expression was grim enough that I didn't ask any more questions. I took the bottle by the neck and pulled it out of the bag. It was an almost empty bottle of Scotch.

'Recognise it?'

I did. I had a bottle of it in the liquor cabinet – or did I? I looked at Jed and he stared right back at me. Then I got it; he thought it'd been me. The stupid bastard thought it'd been me who had broken into Emma's.

'No,' I said.

'What do you mean "no"?' he said. 'You and I sat at this very table supping the stuff together no more than a few nights ago.'

'I didn't mean that,' I said. 'I meant it wasn't me at Emma's, if that's what you're thinking.' I got to my feet. 'Come with me.'

I led the way into the living room and to the cabinet. 'I slept most of yesterday and didn't wake up until almost half past eleven,' I told him. 'The cottage was full of gas and when I finally came in here, I found that,' I pointed at the candle, 'and it was alight.'

He crossed the room and stooped down to look in the cabinet. 'And no whisky?'

'I hadn't noticed, but knowing what I know now, probably not.'

'Emma never thought it was you.'

'But you did,' I said, and I know I sounded a little bitter.

He sighed and stroked his beard. 'I didn't know what to think. I thought not. I didn't want to believe it had been you but . . .' He gave me an apologetic smile. 'I hoped not,' he repeated somewhat lamely.

I gave a small, unamused laugh. 'If it's any consolation, for a few moments I did wonder whether it could have been you who had broken in here. Whoever it was must have had a key.' He frowned at me, his hand going back to his beard. 'I couldn't find how they had broken into Emma's either.'

'You think they had a key?'

'I'm beginning to wonder.'

'But how? I mean, who would have a key to the cottage and Emma's?'

'Other than me, you mean?'

I flopped down onto the couch, my mind working overtime, and then began to smile, but it was nothing to do with me feeling at all happy. 'He's one clever bastard.'

Jed sank onto the armchair opposite me. 'What do you mean?'

'An almost depleted bottle of Scotch left at Emma's; an unusual brand you'd identify as mine. Me possibly blown up so unable to defend myself and, if all else failed, just to confuse the matter, you had keys to both our homes. If one or both of us had died last night I doubt the police would have looked at anyone else.'

'You think whoever was at Emma's was after killing her?' Jed asked, his expression bleak.

'Someone sure as hell tried to kill me and planted evidence I'd been to Emma's for a reason.'

'But why?'

I didn't know either, but more than ever I was determined to try and find out.

CHAPTER ELEVEN

Jed persuaded me to go back with him to Emma's. He hoped between the three of us we might come up with a motive for someone wanting to see me, and possibly Emma, dead. I had an idea he was hoping he could convince one or both of us to report what had happened to the police. I didn't think this was a good idea. All it would achieve would be to put all three of us on their radar, and if anything else happened they would have already made up their minds it was down to 'one of the three weirdos'.

If asked, my last employer swearing I'd left after having a breakdown wouldn't exactly help matters. That I was beginning to think Sir Peter was probably right wasn't going to do me any favours either.

Jed waited out front while I locked up, double-checking the back door and every window. After slamming shut the front door, I got out my keys to deadbolt it and the silver tube hanging from the key ring had me pause for thought.

'What's the matter?' he asked.

I held up the keys so he could see. 'Recognise these?'

He took a step towards me, squinting at the three pieces of metal hanging from my fingers and his hand went to his beard. 'Where did you get those? They're not the ones the Morgans gave the estate agents.'

'I'm pretty sure it's not the same set of keys they sent me,' I told him, then explained about having thought I'd lost my keys and finding them in the lining of my jacket.

'They were Krystal's keys,' Jed said. 'She had the whistle to call for Benji, but the damn dog would never come to it. I don't think it actually worked.' A half-smile played on his lips. 'She kept saying "It's meant to be silent to humans, silly".'

We started off down the path together and as we stepped out into the lane, Jed said, 'Strange how they should turn up just like that.'

I gave a non-committal grunt in reply. It wasn't the only strange thing that had happened, but I wasn't at all sure how much I should admit to. I might think I was going mad, but I didn't want other people thinking it too.

Emma looked pale and tired, but her smile when she saw me was genuine enough that I knew she didn't believe it was me who had paid her a clandestine visit. Sadly, her smile disappeared to be replaced by shocked concern when Jed told her in his gruff, direct way what had happened at the cottage.

She led us out back into the conservatory, a bright and airy sanctum, where a young woman was already placing a tray on a low wicker table. Emma gestured towards the matching armchairs while she settled on the couch. I sank into the brightly coloured cushions thinking I could happily spend hours sitting in this room, staring out into the garden or engrossed in a good book.

'We won't be disturbed here,' she confided as soon as the woman had gone. 'The girls are setting up for the Sly Committee Autumn Luncheon.'

'That today, is it?' Jed said with an ill-disguised sneer.

'Don't be such an old grouch.'

'Bunch of stuffed shirts and blue rinses.'

'Not one of the ladies has a blue rinse.'

'You know what I mean.'

She sighed as she handed out the coffee cups. 'They have good hearts, but yes, I do.'

'Hmm, you think too kindly of people.'

'You're an old cynic.'

I listened to their bantering for a few minutes, but I really wasn't paying much attention. Slyford's Village Committee sounded as dull as dishwater. Then Emma said something that made my ears prick up.

'It's such a shame, Charles and Yvonne Morgan made all the difference. It was just what the committee needed – some fresh, young blood to buck up our ideas.'

'The Morgans were on the committee?'

She looked at me over her coffee cup as she took a sip.

'Hmm. They'd only been members for a month or

two when . . .' Her expression became pained. 'Well, the least said about that the better.'

'They certainly livened things up a bit,' Jed said, 'but not everyone thought they were a good addition.'

'You always get some deadwood in committees, who don't see any change for the better.'

'They certainly put the Garvin sisters' noses out of joint.'

'Really?' I asked.

'You don't want to hear about all that nonsense,' Emma said with a wave of the hand.

'I'm not so sure,' I said, looking her straight in the eyes. 'Someone tried to kill or at least scare me off last night and the same goes for you. I think I want to know about every single person in this village and the Garvins would probably be as good a place to start as any.'

Jed gave a snort. 'Two silly old biddies who have nothing better to do than gossip and jibe about folk.'

'Jed!'

'Well, it's true and you know it. They never had a good word to say about the Morgans once they were elected onto the committee.'

'Why's that?' I asked.

'Charles Morgan was all for having events the whole village would enjoy. Pub quizzes, village fetes, fun runs – that sort of thing,' Emma explained.

'They don't sound particularly radical ideas,' I said.

'The Garvin sisters have a very high opinion of themselves,' Jed said with a snort. '"Public Houses are *so* not for us",' he said in a falsetto voice and wrinkled his nose like he was smelling something nasty as he lifted his coffee cup to his lips with his little finger stuck out in a curl.

'You're being a bit harsh,' Emma said, but she was trying hard not to laugh. He raised a bushy eyebrow at her, and her lips gave a little twitch. 'All right, all right. Yes, they are a bit snooty.'

'Emma, they're dreadful.'

'Then why did you invite them to stay late the other night?' I asked.

Jed gave a snort of disgust. 'Emma didn't so much as invite them as they invited themselves,' he said, leaning back in his chair. 'It's the same every time Emms has "a bit of a do". They hang around at the end hoping I'll give them a performance. The other night I was fed up with it all and was going to disappoint them, but then you suddenly went off into one and scared the crap out of them.'

Emma frowned into her coffee cup.

'What?' he asked.

'Don't you think it a bit strange?'

'How do you mean?'

'They always get so excited about anything they consider "supernatural",' she said making quotation mark signs with her fingers, 'so why the fit of the vapours over Jim's efforts? I'd have thought they'd be over the moon.'

Jed's eyebrows screwed together in a furry caterpillar line that had me stifling a slightly hysterical giggle, the sort one gets at the most inappropriate of moments like funerals or deadly serious board meetings. I took a deep breath and tried to draw my expression into one that suited the mood.

'You're right,' Jed said. 'It makes no sense at all.' He slumped back in the chair and I could almost see the cogs whirring around in his head.

Emma tapped a fingernail against the side of her cup, staring into mid-air. 'Reggie's keys,' she suddenly said.

'Pardon?' Jed said, straightening up in his seat.

'Reggie's keys,' Emma repeated. 'After he died, I couldn't find them. I never did.'

Jed sucked in breath. 'But that was,' he breathed out through pursed lips, 'nigh on fifteen years ago.'

'I know, but that's the only set of keys that aren't accounted for. I'm pretty sure of it.'

'How about Tilly or Rachael?' Jed asked.

'They both have a key to the back door,' she admitted.

'Have you asked if they still have them?'

Emma gave an exasperated tut. 'Of course not. They come in at least twice a week, sometimes more. How would they get in if not with a key?'

'Could one of them have misplaced their key and asked the other to get a replacement cut?' I asked.

Emma frowned at me. 'No,' she said with a small shake of the head, 'no, they would have mentioned it. I'm sure they would.'

'It wouldn't hurt to ask,' Jed said.

'It might,' she said. 'They'd be most upset if they thought someone had broken in using one of their keys or even worse if they got it into their heads that I was accusing them of being complicit. No, I can't ask them.'

'It could explain how whoever it was gained entry.'

I realised my hand was in my pocket my fingers curling around the set of keys to the cottage. A dead child's keys. *Little brat, I'll teach you. I'll show you.*

I pulled them out of my pocket and held them up. 'You say these were Krystal's keys.'

Jed licked his lips and nodded.

'Did they go missing when she died?'

'I don't know,' Jed said. 'I don't think so.'

'But you don't know for certain?'

His shoulders slumped. 'No, no I don't.'

'Where did you find them?' Emma asked.

I stared at them lying on the palm of my hand and then dropped them back into my pocket. 'In the lining of my jacket. I never did find the set I'd been sent by the estate agent. They disappeared and these turned up in their place.' I slumped back in my chair. 'I know this will sound crazy, but what if somehow they were swapped? What if Krystal somehow swapped them?'

Jed raised an eyebrow and he and Emma exchanged a look that wasn't lost on me.

'Jim, Krystal's dead, and dead children can't swap keys or play tricks. They're not physical; they're spirits,' Emma said, her voice gentle like she was comforting a small, upset child.

'I don't suppose spirits make you cups of tea either,' I said with a resigned sigh.

'You're talking about Peter Davies?' Jed said.

I looked up at him. 'Yep. He made me a cup of tea.' I took a deep breath – *here goes nothing*. 'What about moving things about the house? Can spirits do that?'

They exchanged another of their looks.

'I've heard all the usual stories, but I've never seen it happen,' Jed admitted.

'Neither have I,' Emma agreed.

'Tell us,' Jed said.

So I did. I told them everything. Well, when I say everything, I mean from when I arrived at Slyford St James. I didn't tell them about Kat, although I think they had an idea about her. I didn't tell them about falling apart for a while after she died, and I didn't tell them that I'd been given a golden handshake from my job on medical grounds. If I had, I know what they'd have thought; I knew what I'd think. Nutter. A complete headcase. But wasn't that what I'd been thinking?

Another thing I didn't mention was the man I'd been speaking to at the party. I don't know why, really. I just didn't feel comfortable speaking about him.

Even so, by the time I'd finished they were both looking at me a little strangely. I think it was when I told them about the face looming at me out of the darkness the night of Emma's party that finally did it. Even as the words tumbled from my mouth I realised how mad I sounded. As it happened Jed surprised me.

'I knew you had the sight from the first moment I met you,' he said, 'but if it hadn't been for the other night, and seeing you and hearing you do and say what you did, I'd think you'd lost the plot.'

'Playing the devil's advocate here,' Emma said, 'the instances with the bottle and the glass could have been . . .' she hesitated and her cheeks flushed, 'they could have been down to you being tired.'

'Tired and emotional, you mean,' I said with a bitter laugh.

She leant over and laid a hand on my arm. 'You lost someone not so long ago and you've still not moved on. It's understandable.'

'How *did* you know that?' I asked.

She gave a little laugh. 'I'm nowhere as gifted as Jed, but I can feel things about people, see things sometimes. A sadness radiates off you and when I touched your hand the first time we met in the pub I could feel your grief and underlying confusion.'

'You said it was an accident – what did you mean?' I asked. It was a question that had been on the tip of my tongue ever since we'd met that first time, but until now I'd been too scared to ask.

Emma gave me a sympathetic smile. 'It was a whisper in my head. *Tell Jim it was an accident.* I can't say more than that.'

'A whisper in your head?'

'I'm not like Jed – when he gets messages, most of the time he knows who they're from and who they're for. I just get whispers.'

'So, this whisper, was it' – I let out a shuddery breath – 'was it Kat?'

Emma patted my arm. 'I don't know, but I suppose it could have been.'

'I wish I could see her again.'

'I've never heard from Reggie and nor has Jed.' And the man I'd spoken to the night of the party came into mind, but I pushed the thought away.

'Sometimes, when it's someone you're close to, it just doesn't happen,' Jed said, 'and Reggie and I . . . Well, we were close, I couldn't have had a better friend,' and he looked away and I'm sure I saw a glint of tears. I was slightly taken aback; Jed didn't strike me as an overly sentimental type.

'I never had anything like this happen to me before I arrived at Slyford,' I told them after a brief silence, 'then practically from the first moment I stepped into the cottage everything got very strange.'

'Like the combination to your padlock.'

'Yes.' This was something else I'd been wanting to know. 'How did you know the combination? You just picked it up and immediately knew.'

'Fourteen zero six, sixteen zero four; a reversal of numbers, an easy mistake to make and a logical explanation,' Jed said.

'As simple as that?'

He made a non-committal grunt.

'Jed?'

'Emma isn't the only one who hears whispers sometimes. And she's wrong, I don't always know who's talking to me.'

Emma looked surprised. 'I didn't know; you never said.'

He smiled at her and once again it skittered through my head that if there was nothing going on between the two of them it wasn't down to Jed.

'It's not something I've given much thought,' he said. 'I've always heard voices; they just don't always announce themselves.'

'Have you ever seen things?' I asked. 'People, I mean – dead people.'

'Not like you. I've seen glimpses sometimes. Shades of figures but nothing I could mistake for the living.'

Emma leant forward to pass around a plate of biscuits. I took one more for something to do with my hands and give me time to think rather than wanting a sugar rush. Even to Jed and Emma I was an oddity and the spectre of madness had returned to loiter at the back of my mind.

'I'm wondering whether I should go to see someone,' I admitted and took a bite out of my biscuit.

Both Emma and Jed looked genuinely surprised. 'Like who?' Jed asked.

I swallowed and washed it down with a mouthful of coffee. 'A doctor, maybe a shrink.'

'Ah,' Jed said, leaning back in his chair.

'Do you really think that would help?' Emma asked.

'Only if he wants to find himself on Prozac or Valium, or even worse, locked up in the funny farm.'

'So you think I'm crazy?'

'That's what a quack would think. They deal with

science and logic. Do you really think they'd believe you see the dead?'

'I'm not sure I believe I see the dead so why should they?' I said, feeling downright miserable.

'Look,' Jed said, fixing me with a stare, 'I know you're having a hard time taking this in. Hell, I've lived with it all my life and still sometimes it can surprise me, but you're not going mad. At least if you are, the seeing of dead people isn't part of it. What happened to you the other night was extraordinary; it was nothing like I've ever experienced before.'

'I've never seen anything like it either,' Emma said.

'But why is it all happening to me now?'

'I have no answer to that.'

We sat in silence for a while and once again I could hear the faint call of a peacock from across the garden, and I wished I could stay here for ever where it was safe and calm and I didn't see things I really didn't want to see.

'Maybe . . .' Emma said and hesitated. Jed and I both looked up. She was running her finger around the rim of her cup, a small frown creasing her brow. 'Maybe it's happening for a reason. Perhaps you're seeing and hearing these things because there's a need to put them right.'

'What do you mean, Emms?'

'If Jim has only just started having these' – she frowned down into her cup – 'episodes, it could be that he's tuned into whatever happened at the cottage. Perhaps Krystal is crying out to him for some kind of closure or maybe even justice.'

'You think it might stop if I discover what really happened that day?' I asked.

'I don't know,' she said, 'but I really am beginning to believe you're seeing and hearing these things for a reason.'

I sank back in my seat. Hearing Emma say what I'd already considered was making me feel a whole lot better and that my decision to stay was the right one. Besides, if it hadn't been for the scrabbling of claws at my bedroom door I might no longer be here. I owed it to Krystal's little dog to at least try and find out what happened to her. *Even if it's likely to get you killed?*

I thought on it. Yes – even then.

CHAPTER TWELVE

When I left Emma's I couldn't face going straight back to the cottage; instead on impulse I carried on down the lane to see where it led. A walk would do me good and hopefully clear my head, even if it couldn't help me answer the questions whirling around inside it. It would take more than a walk to do that.

A wonky, weather-worn, wooden signpost at the lane's end pointed the way down a path to 'Fisherman's Cove and Saints' Bay'. Below it was a more modern sign – 'Care! Dangerous When Wet'. Well, it wasn't wet today. The path was little more than a track, only just wide enough for two to walk next to each other. Over the summer the surrounding undergrowth had begun to encroach from either side, sometimes meaning I had to shrug my way past long grass and shrubbery or swat aside low-hanging branches from the occasional self-sown sapling.

It was rocky underfoot, the soil worn away to a dusty cover littered with sharp-edged, loose stones. The track curled and twisted ahead with nothing else to see other than wave after wave of vegetation and the blue of the sky above. Now and then a seagull would cry out as it soared towards the sun and swooped down again, wings outstretched soaking up the warming rays.

A line of sweat trickled down my brow and I shrugged off my jacket and threw it over my shoulder. It was turning into a beautiful day.

I didn't appear to be getting anywhere near the coast and I was beginning to wonder whether it was worth going any further, when the path began to slope downwards and I caught a whiff of salty air encouraging me to carry on.

The track began to zigzag back and forth, then the vegetation appeared to drop away and there outstretched into infinity was the ocean. I stood still for a moment taking in the view along the cliff, the sharp scent of the sea and the warmth of the sun upon my face to the soundtrack of waves crashing against the rocks below. This was why I had come to Slyford St James. This was the feeling I'd been hoping to find.

I started off again; to one side of me gorse and shrubs, to the other a rocky landscape with some intermittent patches of brambles, heather and grass gradually dropping away to the sea. Once or twice the path curled a few yards towards the cliff's edge, but nowhere close enough for the health and safety brigade to have a fit of the vapours.

Ahead of me the path dropped into a dip and out of sight for a few yards before coming up again the other side. I carried on walking and at the bottom of the dip I found what I was looking for, another track going downwards towards the bay below.

The first few yards had my calves working overtime as I shuffled down the steep incline, loose bits of rock skittering from beneath my feet, then, to my relief, I came to the first of many steps carved into the earth and rock. They were steep but wide. On some I had to take two paces before I could step down to the next. It was going to be a hard slog down to the bay.

Even harder coming back up.

I ignored the warning voice in my head. I'd take it nice and slow. I had all the time in the world and nowhere to be and nowhere to go.

From the steps I couldn't see the bay beneath me, and it was only after about five minutes that I began to wonder whether it actually did lead to Fisherman's Cove. It could just take me to a lower path. What the hell? It had to go somewhere.

The scent of the sea filled my nose and mouth and when I licked my lips they tasted of salt. Then the vegetation fell away until to one side of me there was only sheer rock and to the other a handrail of tubular metal hammered into the cliff, then nothing except thin air. I stopped to peer over the edge. Below me was a beach of sorts. Mainly rocky fissures filled with pools of seawater and strands of weed floating like tendrils of mermaids' hair.

The kid in me, enthused by thoughts of investigating the rock pools searching for crabs and other sea life, had me bounding down the steps, my feet barely touching the ground. In my head I heard a childish giggle and the yap of a small dog. Krystal used to come here.

The flight of steps ended in a sea of pebbles as I took that last pace down onto the beach. The tide was out, and I could see strips of sand between the swathes of solid rock at the shoreline.

The shingle crunched beneath my feet as I made my way across to the first slab of dark-grey stone and it felt so much better than the shifting pebbles as I climbed up to take a look. It was as I thought: dips and crevasses filled by the retreating tide made fine homes for all sorts of interesting sea life. Blood-coloured anemones clung to the sides of the pools while small fishes darted between clumps of seaweed. A hermit crab scuttled away to hide from my shadow and a mollusc of some description slowly made its way down the rock to find deeper waters.

Krystal would have loved this. I could almost hear her excited cries as she hopped from pool to pool searching for one more creature. The thought brought me up sharp. What had happened to her? Why had her young life been cut short so cruelly?

Any joy I had felt as I descended down onto the beach was replaced with one of melancholy. As if to reflect my mood a cloud passed across the sun, darkening the landscape, and a gull cried out, a plaintive sound against the swishing of pebbles as they were tumbled back and forth by the tide.

I shivered. Without the warmth of the sun upon my back and the exertion of walking the cliff path I was suddenly cold. I pulled on my jacket and carried on across the rock until I could jump down onto the sand at the water's edge.

The tide was on the turn and in the brief time I'd been on the beach it had already started to climb its way back up the shore.

I stared out across the bay. It was a sheltered spot and so small that despite its name I doubted very much that fishermen ever came here, other than maybe to shelter from a storm, though it was more likely any vessel would end up smashed against the rocks than be able to wait in safety.

On impulse I stooped and picked up a palm-sized, fairly flat stone and skimmed it out across the water. It was a good throw, bouncing across the surface three times before it disappeared beneath the waves. I had another go and another and soon realised I should have stopped while I was ahead.

How long ago was it that I'd last tried skimming stones? Then I remembered and I let the stone clutched in my hand slip from my fingers.

Kat and I had been away for a weekend break in the Channel Islands and we'd found a bay very similar to this one. The day had been dull and overcast, and with not much better to do we had decided to take a walk along the cliff paths that circled the island to investigate the long-deserted gun emplacements built to protect the islands during wartime.

We'd laughed a lot. I remembered that much. When was it we'd stopped doing that? When was it we'd begun to take life all too seriously? Sadly, I remembered that too.

I gave myself a mental shake, pinching the bridge of my nose and closing my eyes for a moment. I was getting maudlin and no good would come of it.

It was time to go home – if I could call it that. I doubted I could ever think of the cottage as my home, too many bad things had happened there.

I took one last look out across the bay. Dark clouds were rolling in and what had started off as a warm and sunny day was beginning to look decidedly stormy. The sea had turned grey, mimicking the sky, and the waves were building themselves up into a white froth as they beat against the cliffs surrounding the cove.

I'd better get back otherwise I was in for a soaking.

I shivered again, but this time it had nothing to do with the chill in the air. I could feel eyes upon me, unfriendly eyes. Someone was watching me and that someone meant me harm, I was sure of it.

I spun around to look towards the cliff top and high to the right of me I saw a movement. Had he kept still I might not have seen him. He was there for only a split second, but it was enough. A large, hulking figure in grey, and I was pretty much sure, even from this distance, he was the man I'd seen through the window at Emma's.

He was on the cliff path coming from the opposite

direction to Slyford, but I had to climb the steep steps and get onto the path before he reached the intersection. I ran. The shingle beneath my feet had me slipping and almost falling, slowing me down until I at last reached solid rock. Even then, in my panic, several times I nearly fell before I reached the steps.

I pounded upwards, chest aching, calves screaming. There were so many steps and they were so damn steep. Halfway I stopped to catch my breath, clinging onto the railing as I stared at the cliff top above me, my eyes searching for movement. If he was there, I couldn't see him. But he was there, I knew he was. He was coming for me and I knew if he found me here, found me alone in this remote and secluded place, I would never be going home again.

The logical part of my brain said, *No, things like this don't happen in real life – you're being paranoid*, but another insistent little voice was whispering for me to *Hurry, hurry, otherwise you'll never make it.*

I forced myself upwards. I'd known it would be a hard slog, but when I'd bounded down the steps I hadn't considered that when I made the return journey I'd be running for my life.

When I reached the top of the steps the path above me was empty, but I still had the sharp incline to go. I scrambled up practically on my hands and knees. If he caught me here, all it would take was one hefty shove and I'd be joining Krystal in the hereafter.

At the top of the slope I glanced from right to left. There was still no sign of him. Had he passed this point?

Had he got ahead of me and was hiding somewhere in the undergrowth waiting for me? I didn't think so. If it'd been me, I'd have waited at the top of the steps to catch my prey when they were vulnerable and out of breath, when they wouldn't have much fight left in them.

I started along the path, hurrying as fast as my tortured calves would allow. When I returned to the city I was going to start running again, I was going to get fit. Too late for now, though.

I kept glancing back over my shoulder, half-expecting to see a bulky figure barrelling along the path behind me, but if he was there he was lost from view in the twists and turns of the path amongst the gorse and bracken.

I stopped for a moment, leaning forward to rest my hands on my knees and ease the stitch fast forming in my side. I was beginning to think I was mistaken, that my paranoia had created a grey, hulking figure up above me on the cliff. Surely he'd have made it to the top of the steps before I had?

I stood upright, held my breath and listened.

Long grass rustled in the fast-cooling breeze coming in from the sea. An insect buzzed past my head. A bird twittered then broke cover to fly out of the vegetation to the right of me. Otherwise nothing, nothing except . . . the thump of boots. For a big man he must have been practically dancing along the path, but I could hear him now and it was almost as though he somehow knew I'd heard him for his feet began to pound upon the path as he picked up speed and began to really run.

But could I outrun him? I had to try. It was now a race for life. Panic spurred me on. Aches and pains ignored if not forgotten, I ran as I'd never run before, careering along the narrow path, swerving around corners as it turned back on itself, blood pounding in my ears – or was it the sound of his boots upon rock?

He was getting closer, I was sure of it. I wasn't going to make it. He was going to get me, and I was going to die on a deserted cliff top and disappear, probably never to be seen again, like Benji. Whatever had happened to Krystal's little dog? And I wondered why at a time like this I should even care.

Then ahead of me I saw a flash of red and grey. Krystal? I thought I'd been running as fast as I could, but seeing her had me forcing myself to go that little bit faster than even I thought I could.

The path curved inland, and as I reached a bend I saw another flash of red. I almost called out to her but stopped myself just in time; that really would give my position away. From memory the path would soon stop its zigzag ascent and although it wasn't exactly straight, he would probably get a glimpse of me, which would give him a pretty good incentive to speed up and catch me.

I swung around one final corner and ahead of me I saw white-sock-covered legs scrambling into the undergrowth. I ran to the spot and despite having no time to waste crouched down. There was a long narrow tunnel within the gorse and shrubbery, and I was just in time to see a white fluffy tail disappear into the dark ahead of me.

Behind me on the path I could hear him coming. *He's going to catch us, Benji, he's gonna catch us!* I dropped down onto my knees and crawled inside. It was narrow, dark and smelt of fresh earth and greenery. I scrambled forward on my elbows and knees, brambles and twigs tearing at my jacket and hair, all the time praying that a pair of hairy hands wouldn't suddenly clutch hold of my ankles and drag me back. After about two and a half yards I came out of the tunnel and found myself entering what I can only describe as a den. Someone, probably a good few years ago, had crawled into this space carrying planks of wood, nails and other bits and pieces, and constructed a small cabin out of scraps of whatever he could find. Bits of packing cases formed the walls and the roof was made of what looked like it could have been the front of an old shed, including a small window giving me at least some light through the grimy glass.

It was only about four feet tall and about five feet square, but I guessed to a couple of kids it would have been as great as any castle. I crawled into the far corner and sat cross-legged facing the entrance.

He won't find us here, Benji. He'll never find us here.

'Oh, Krystal,' I whispered, 'what happened to you?'

If I'd been expecting a reply, I was to be disappointed. I pulled up my legs and rested my arms on my knees and my head on my arms. I was in for a long wait. My pursuer wouldn't be giving up so easily. But how long would be long enough? If he was really that tenacious, he could wait all day.

No, he would think I'd made it to the end of the path and into the lane and was on my way back to the cottage. Would he carry on to see if I was there? He'd gotten in before – what was to stop him getting in now and, finding the cottage empty, just sitting there waiting for me to get back? Is that what he did to Krystal? Did he lose her when she and Benji scuttled into this hidey-hole, but instead of giving up went on to her home to wait for her?

Bastard. Fucking bastard.

She deserved it, little bitch.

Whoa – where was that coming from?

Stuck up little townie bitch. Butter wouldn't melt, little brat.

And he said a whole load of other stuff that had me clamping my hands over my ears in an effort to block it out, but it was a forlorn hope. It was like when I was running after Krystal through the woods, the same vitriolic monologue ran through my head. The same rage, the same cruelty.

What did it mean?

Jed and Emma said I communicated with the dead – could I somehow also hear the thoughts of the living? No, that was one step too fucking far. I was going bonkers; I must be even to consider it.

Then whose voice is it you're hearing?

'I don't know,' I whispered and covered my face with my hands. 'I really don't know.'

* * *

161

I'm not sure how long I sat there for. It must have been hours. I'd stopped wearing a watch not long after I'd given up the job; I'd read somewhere that an important part of de-stressing your life was to make time your friend instead of your enemy, and the best way to do that was to make sure you couldn't constantly check the time.

Another bit of advice was to ditch the mobile phone so you weren't at others' beck and call twenty-four seven and only to check your email once or at most twice a day. Hence my phone was sitting on the kitchen table instead of in my back pocket when I could really do with it for calling for help.

Eventually, when my backside was so numb I couldn't feel it and I was pretty sure it must be getting dark outside or was seriously overcast as the limited light in my hideout was beginning to fade, I got on my hands and knees and crawled out into the tunnel.

I cautiously stuck my head out of the hole to look along the path. It was empty, but then why wouldn't it be? My pursuer would have either gone home or could even be waiting for me back at the cottage. If he was still loitering on the path I was done for. I could hardly stand up straight, let alone make my cramped legs run.

It hadn't rained, that was something, but the heavens were dark and gloomy, and I still reckoned we could be in for a storm. As if to prove me right I felt the first spots of rain on my face as I stepped off the path and out into the lane.

I was in two minds as to what I should do. Return to the cottage and risk being confronted by a madman or return to Emma's and chance looking like an idiot. If I'd had my mobile, I could have phoned Jed, and I decided from now on wherever I went my mobile went too. I was probably going to feel less stressed with it than without it.

When I reached Emma's gate I hesitated out on the lane and a horrible thought occurred to me. It wasn't only me the man had been after – he'd also paid Emma a visit. Shit! I'd been holed up for hours, during which time he could have vented his frustration on her.

I hurried through the gate and up the drive, and with my stomach doing cartwheels and my heart somewhere up near my mouth, I rang the doorbell. I waited a minute then rang again. Maybe she was out.

Maybe she can't answer.

I looked back to the gate, paranoid that the unknown man would be there watching me. I rang the bell again.

'Come on, come on.'

Then I saw movement through the bevelled door panes as a shadowy figure approached the door. I took a step back. What if I'd interrupted him in his grisly work? What if he'd known I'd come here instead of going straight to the cottage alone?

A chain rattled and there was a rasp of a bolt being drawn before the door opened a crack.

'Jim,' Emma said, 'hang on a minute,' and she pushed the door closed to remove the chain. 'Come in. I didn't expect to see you again so soon.'

'I hope I'm not interrupting.'

'Not at all. Come through,' she said, leading me

163

into the living room. 'Can I get you a tea or coffee?'

'No thanks. I was wondering if I could phone Jed from here?'

'Problem?' she asked, her smile being replaced with a concerned frown.

'Possibly,' I said and told her everything that had happened since I'd left her earlier that morning.

She listened in silence until I'd spilt the whole sad story out, though halfway through she did get up to pour us both a drink and by God I needed one. When I took it I don't think I was the only one who noticed my hand was shaking.

'Do you still think it's a bad idea going to the police?' she said when I'd finished.

'And tell them what? Say what?'

'Well, we both had visits the other night.'

'And the only evidence of either visit is a near-empty bottle of my whisky. Christ, Emma, even Jed thought it might have been me.'

She made a dismissive gesture with her hand. 'Well, I didn't, and Jed didn't really, not in his heart; he was just being protective, as is his way.'

'What would the police do, anyway? Nothing, most probably, other than take a few notes.'

'At least it would be on record.'

'Yeah, great, so when one of us is murdered in our beds they'd "have a record" that we'd been worried for our lives.'

Emma grimaced as she looked down into a drink and

I felt mean. She didn't need me to make her feel more scared than she already was. The chain on the door and the cautious way she had peered around it proved that she was already nervous.

'I'm sorry,' I said, dragging my hand through my hair and dislodging a bit of bracken. I picked it off the arm of the chair, then wasn't sure what to do with it.

Emma began to giggle. 'Did you really crawl through the bushes?'

I placed the piece of vegetation on the edge of the coffee table. 'Yes,' I told her, 'I followed Krystal and Benji.'

'I don't understand what this all means.'

'Nor do I. And I could hear *him*, Emma. I could hear what he was thinking inside my head.' Then something dawned on me. 'No, not what he was thinking, what he had *thought*. What he'd been thinking when he had chased Krystal.'

'Like a memory?'

A cold draught tickled the back of my neck and I shuddered, suddenly cold. 'Oh my God,' I murmured to myself. 'Oh my God.'

'Jim, what is it? What have you thought of?'

'What if he wasn't chasing me at all? What if he's still chasing Krystal?'

CHAPTER THIRTEEN

Emma called Jed while I was using the bathroom, and ten minutes later we were sitting in the kitchen while Emma rustled up something for us to eat and I told Jed everything that had happened. Like Emma he listened in silence, only speaking when Emma asked whether we'd like cheese and ham in our omelettes.

'And you think it was the same man you saw at the window?'

I nodded. 'Though I didn't really get a good look at him. It's just a feeling.'

'Hmm. And you could hear him speaking?' Jed said, his expression dubious. 'Are you sure you weren't just remembering what he'd said before.'

'Like I'm imagining things?'

'I didn't say that.'

'It would help if we knew who this man was,'

Emma said over her shoulder as she pottered around over the stove.

'Well, he certainly doesn't come from Slyford,' Jed said. 'We'd know him if he did and from your description he doesn't sound like anyone from the village.'

'Jim said he saw him up on the point. It could be he was coming along the path from Chalfont.'

'Chalfont?' I asked.

'Chalfont St Mary, it's the next village up the coast.'

'It's where all the local children go to school,' Emma said as she placed a steaming plate in front of me and then Jed.

'Did Krystal?' I asked.

Emma and Jed shared one of their looks as she sat down at the table with her own plate. 'Yes,' Emma answered. 'They all do until they go off to seniors.'

'So this could be how he knew Krystal. He saw her on her way to and from school.'

Jed uttered a curse, then immediately apologised to Emma for the profanity. By her expression and the dismissive flap of her hand I think he only said what we were all thinking, including Emma.

'But why would he target me? And why would he target Emma? I never knew he even existed until—'

'Until you heard his voice in your head,' Jed said.

'Maybe he somehow knows you've connected with him. Maybe he felt you too?' Emma said.

'Ah, come on, Emms – now we are flying into the realms of fantasy,' Jed said. 'Jim may be a truly talented psychic, but no one can read the thoughts of the living, let alone it go both ways.'

'Thought transference,' Emma said.

'Not possible.'

'Some people say the same thing about communicating with the dead.'

'That's different,' Jed said through a mouthful of egg.

'Well,' she said, 'somehow Jim's heard the thoughts of this unknown man and somehow the man knows it, otherwise why the attempt on his life? Why follow him today?'

'I still don't understand why he would have come here that night?' I said. 'What had you to do with anything?'

She tapped her forefinger against her lips. 'I think you were right before. He wanted to make us distrust you if he didn't manage to blow you to high heaven. Alienate you from us.'

'All he's doing is drawing attention to himself,' I said.

'He's certainly done that.'

'I missed an opportunity today,' Emma said.

Jed and I both looked at her quizzically. 'Why's that?' Jed asked.

'At the committee luncheon – I should have asked if anyone knew anyone who fits the description of our mystery man.'

'We haven't much of a description. A big hulking man could be anyone; even me,' Jed said with a grunt. 'Anyway, they would have asked why, and would you really be comfortable telling them?'

'You have a point,' Emma said with a sigh.

'Besides, if he does come from Chalfont, I don't think anyone has much to do with the place other than the Garvin sisters, and you don't want to give them any more excuses to keep turning up here unannounced.'

'That's another good point.' She paused a puzzled frown creasing her brow. 'Actually, they were acting a bit weird today, not that they stayed long, and that was strange in itself. I usually can't get rid of them.'

'Weird? They're always acting weird.'

'Then weirder than usual.'

'How do you mean?'

'Oh, Miriam was all giggly and asking about Jim and did I see him often. Had we known Jim before he came to Slyford? Did he give seances? That sort of thing. As for Darcy, she was . . . I don't know, a bit off somehow. She wasn't saying much and kept giving Miriam these odd sideways looks. Miriam was oblivious. You've got a real fan there, Jim.'

'That's all Jim needs, those two turning up on his doorstep.'

'I thought I scared the hell out of them the other night.'

'Well, they didn't seem at all scared this afternoon. Anyway, I told them Jim was a very private person and no, he didn't hold seances.'

'Doubt that'll stop them. I've never met such a pair of nosey parkers.'

'Miriam's right smitten.'

'Good God, Emma, the woman's old enough to be Jim's mother.'

Emma grimaced. 'I suppose you're right. I think Miriam is in her fifties and Darcy is probably a year or so younger.'

'Really?' I said. 'I would have thought Darcy was the older of the pair.'

'Are you sure you've got that right, Emms?' Jed asked. 'I always thought Darcy was the older sister.'

'No, I'm positive. I remember Miriam making some comment about when they were children and how she always looked after the baby. Darcy got really grumpy about it, actually.'

'Bit of a control freak that one,' Jed said.

When we finished our meal I didn't want to outstay my welcome, but I was a little unsure how to ask Jed to come back to the cottage with me without looking like an idiot. Fortunately, when I stood to leave, Emma voiced her concerns.

'Are you sure you'll be all right? I mean, what if he's still hanging around somewhere waiting for you?'

'I'll walk with him,' Jed said, getting to his feet.

Emma crossed her arms and leant back in her chair to look up at him. 'And what do you think you're going to do if he is waiting for Jim, you old fool?'

Jed grinned. 'I might be getting on a bit, but I've always been good in a scrap.'

Emma rolled her eyes. 'Men!'

She saw us to the door and gave us both a peck on the cheek goodnight. 'Make sure you lock and bolt your doors,' she said to me.

'You too,' I told her.

'I've been setting the alarm since the other night. Maybe you should consider getting one fitted.'

'I won't be staying that long,' I said, but couldn't help thinking it might be a good idea. I'd at least be able to sleep at night.

The rain had stopped but the moon was cloaked by clouds and there was a heaviness in the air foretelling there was more to come. The lane was dark and filled with shadows and I was more than a little grateful for Jed's bulky presence striding along beside me.

When we reached the cottage, Jed followed me through the gate and stood waiting for me to unlock the front door.

'Mind if I come in?'

'Not at all,' I said, 'I'd be grateful for the company.'

I stepped inside, surreptitiously sniffing the air for gas before clicking on the hall light and leading the way into the living room.

'Want a drink?' I asked.

'Have you got any?'

'Not any of the good stuff, I'm afraid.'

'Let's check the rest of the house first, shall we?' All pretence of why he had actually come inside being swept away.

I gave him a wry smile. 'That obvious, huh?'

'Emma would have my guts for garters if I didn't take a look around and something happened to you,' he said, following me out into the hall and to the kitchen.

He stopped halfway along the hallway and opened the cupboard under the stairs to peer inside.

'Just being careful,' he said when he saw me looking.

The kitchen was how I'd left it, even down to the footprint and spent matchstick, so we trooped upstairs to check out the bedrooms. Once again Jed checked the cupboards and wardrobes and even pulled back the shower curtain around the bath.

When we went back out into the hallway his eyes went straight up to the trapdoor in the ceiling.

I frowned at him. 'You don't think . . . ?'

'One can't be too careful,' he said and went back into the bathroom to get the pole to pull down the ladder.

As I watched him I could hear my heart thudding in my ears. *Think you can hide from me, little bitch.*

As he put his foot on the first step of the ladder I reached out and touched his arm. 'I'll go.'

He shook his head. 'Probably best you don't,' and carried on climbing. He stood at the top, swinging the torch back and looking around him, then slowly climbed back down. 'I think I'll be having that whisky now.'

While he was putting the pole and torch away, I went and sorted out the drinks as my heart gradually slowed to normal and the herd of wildebeest in my stomach stopped rampaging about the place.

Jed came in from the hall and slumped down on a

kitchen chair, gratefully reaching to take the glass I offered him.

'I've been thinking,' he said as I sat down opposite him.

'Sounds serious,' I said with a forced smile.

'Maybe we should take a trip to Chalfont and have a look around.'

'What, and hope we just happen to bump into this mystery man?'

'It's a small place.'

'It must be bigger than Slyford if it's got a school.'

He stared into his glass as he swirled the contents around. 'It's a bit bigger. They have a small supermarket, a bank and a wine bar as well as a general store, a shoe shop and a couple of pubs.'

'Blimey, almost a town,' I said.

'I use the general store over there when I need something and can't be arsed to go to the trading estate. It's more expensive, but I use less petrol so it's swings and roundabouts,' he said, ignoring my facetious comment.

'If we both go there and he sees us together, it'll draw you into this mess as well.'

'Too late to worry about that, I think,' Jed said. 'If he knew enough about you to involve Emma, he sure as hell must know about me.'

I chugged back the last of my Scotch and studied his face for a moment. I already knew Jed could be a good friend, but the expression on his face told me he could no doubt also be a bad enemy. Whoever this mystery man was, he shouldn't have involved Emma.

'One for the road?' I asked, unscrewing the bottle.

Jed glanced at his watch. 'Why not?' he said, putting his glass in the middle of the table.

I poured him a stiff one and another for myself.

'Tomorrow morning I'll take you over to Chalfont,' Jed said.

'I'm still not sure—'

Jed raised his hand to stop me. 'You need your locks changed; we can get new ones while we're there. It wouldn't hurt to get one of them gas alarms if they've got one.'

He had a point. 'OK,' I told him, 'if it's not too much trouble.'

'No trouble at all, lad,' he said, and his mean expression had returned.

After Jed had gone, I locked and bolted the front and back doors and went round checking all the windows, even though I'd already done so before I'd left the house in the morning. I supposed if someone was determined to get in they would break a window, but at least there was a chance I would hear them.

As I drew the curtains in the living room I noticed the first spots of rain beginning to splatter against the window and hoped Jed would reach home before it began to pour as I was pretty sure it would. There was a still heaviness to the air and a closeness that usually precedes a storm and, sure enough, as I climbed the stairs to bed I heard the first rumblings in the distance.

By the time I'd finished in the bathroom I could hear

the steady patter of rain on the roof and against the windowpane and as I entered the bedroom there was a flash that lit up the sky. I pulled the curtains shut. I usually enjoyed a good storm, but I wasn't in the mood; tonight, the crashing of thunder and the bright flashes lighting up the room brought with them a tight feeling of anxiety in my chest.

I undressed down to my T-shirt and underpants but stopped as I was about to pull the shirt over my head. I usually slept naked; tonight was going to be an exception. The thought of being alone and naked in the cottage set my pulse racing and the fear I'd felt earlier in the day returned to haunt me.

I sat on the bed, turned on the bedside light and glanced around the room, feeling edgy and vulnerable. There was another flash of lightning and I counted one, two, three, four, then came the crash of thunder. It was getting closer and my nerves were already jangling. On impulse I jumped from the bed and picked up the chair by the window and carried it over to the door propping it under the handle. I knew I was being paranoid, but I couldn't ignore the fear bubbling inside my chest.

Another flash of lightning lit the window. One, two, three, crash. I climbed into bed, reached out to turn off the light and hesitated, fingers outstretched. What was I – a child now too scared to sleep in the dark?

I groped for the switch, went to click it, then stopped and sunk back on the bed. Damn it. Damn this mysterious man who had me acting like a small, terrified kid. I curled up and wrapped the duvet around me, tucking my head down and covering my eyes. Damn him.

Outside the rain thrashed down, the lightning flashed and the thunder roared. I pulled the duvet over my head, but it made no difference. The storm's cacophony wasn't about to be silenced. Then there was a flash of lightning that beneath my covers appeared as though it had cut right through the room, followed by an almighty bang that I swear shook the cottage right down to its foundations.

'Bloody hell.' I stuck my head out from under the duvet, then pulling it around me got up and padded across to the window to look outside.

I wasn't sure what I expected to see. Maybe flames and smoke from a tree that had been struck or God forbid someone's house in the village. The garden was in pitch-black darkness and the rain was falling so heavily I doubted I would be able to see much had it been daylight.

Then there was another zigzag flash across the sky illuminating the garden and the trees beyond. Over the pounding rain I somehow heard a dog yap twice and when I looked down, standing in the middle of the lawn was a small figure in red and grey holding a little dog in her arms. As the light faded away she lifted a hand and waved. I pressed my nose against the window, straining my eyes to see through the darkness and thrashing rain that had enveloped her, but it was no good.

I waited and waited and then there was another flash, but she was gone. One, two, three, four, five – the storm had passed over. I padded back to bed, curled up, and with the image of Krystal smiling and waving at me fell into a deep sleep.

True to his word Jed was knocking at the back door just after nine. 'Wanted to miss the school run,' he explained.

I'd been expecting Jed to drive some beaten-up old van, so it was a bit of a surprise when we walked around the front to find an old but pristine maroon Jaguar parked in front of my car.

'Nice wheels,' I commented as I dropped down onto the dark-red leather passenger seat.

'Bit of a beast when it comes to petrol, but she's my one luxury,' he said, his cheeks taking on a ruddy glow.

'Had her long?'

'Since new,' he told me and that made me glance back his way. This model of Jag was an expensive car in its day, which made me think Jed couldn't have been the village handyman for all of his life. It occurred to me I didn't actually know very much about him at all.

The inside of the car had a comforting smell of old leather with a slight tang of citrus, which I suspected was furniture polish; the walnut veneer dashboard certainly gleamed in the sunlight pouring through the window.

As far as I could remember this was the first morning I'd left the house to a clear day without a layer of mist surrounding me. The storm had at least been of some benefit, although pools of water had been left on the tarmac and pavements to steam in the sunshine.

As Jed drove us out of the village we passed a car coming the other way. The narrow road forcing both cars to slow as they passed. I recognised Darcy Garvin hunched over the steering wheel, peering at us with narrowed eyes and pinched lips. Her sister Miriam's mouth opened into an 'O' and then she forced it into a smile and waggled her fingers at us. Jed muttered something derogatory under his breath, and when I glanced his way the mean look was back.

'You really don't like those two, do you?' I said.

He grunted. 'I don't like the way they try and insinuate themselves into everyone's lives. You're lucky you scared the crap out of them, otherwise they'd be camped on your doorstep.'

I leant back in the seat and crossed my arms. I really didn't need reminding about the night of Emma's get-together. The Garvin girls weren't the only ones who'd been scared.

'Mind you, from what Emms said they seemed to have got over it by the committee meeting, so you may have that pleasure yet to come.'

'Oh joy,' I said to a snort of laughter from Jed.

Chalfont St Mary wasn't very far away at all, only about fifteen minutes or so by car. 'If you're fit it's a good walk along the cliff,' Jed told me. 'Though you have to watch the weather, it can get a bit slippy.' He absently rubbed at his beard. 'Come to think of it, someone took a tumble along there a few years back.'

'Hmm.' It was doubtful I would ever walk that way again, not alone at least. Even thinking about it made my heart rate speed up and my chest tighten.

I breathed in deeply and then out again trying to quell the anxiety bubbling up inside me. Hyperventilating in Jed's car would be too humiliating for words. It had been bad enough when I'd woken this morning to find myself still in my underwear with the bedside lamp burning and a chair wedged under the bedroom doorknob. I hadn't needed to look into the bathroom mirror to know that my cheeks had flushed scarlet.

Despite what Jed had said, Chalfont had more of the feel of a town about it, and compared to Slyford was large and sprawling. It actually had a high street with proper shops. It even had a chemist.

Jed parked up in a small pay and display car park around the back of the high street for the princely sum of twenty pence for an hour. 'Two will be more than enough,' he muttered.

'So what do we do now?' I asked as he fed two ten-pence pieces and a twenty into the machine.

'Buggered if I know,' he said, snatching the ticket from the slot, 'but I suppose we could start with getting you some new locks and that gas alarm.'

I waited while he placed the ticket on the dashboard and then fell in step beside him. At the far end of the car park there was a narrow alleyway, which took us out about halfway down the high street.

'How about I give you the grand tour and we walk up one side and back down the other? It should take all of fifteen minutes.'

'Sounds good.'

We passed a hairdressers. 'Emma comes here now and then,' Jed told me, and I wondered how he knew that and whether he brought her. Then it occurred to me that whatever he might say, the locals of Slyford came here more often than he might think.

There was also a fishing supplies shop, the window cramped with rods and reels and even a few brightly coloured fishing nets and buckets for the kids.

The hardware store was a few shops along and, surprisingly, considering the number of varied modern appliances stacked on its shelves, had one of those old-fashioned tinkling contraptions announcing your arrival. The window and front few shelves were stacked with ice cream and bread makers, food processors and microwaves, and plenty of other modern technology, some I didn't recognise. I even saw a few flash drives and USB cables hanging on a rack.

Jed made his way to the back of the store where it was like we could have stepped through a time warp. A long counter stretched the width of the store and behind it, rising up from floor to ceiling, were row upon row of small cubbyholes filled with wooden drawers, each labelled with a yellowing, handwritten card within a small brass frame.

A young man glanced up from the register and smiled upon seeing Jed. 'Dad,' he called over his shoulder.

'Morning to you, Tim. How's yer pa today?'

Tim grimaced, though it was with a smile. 'Moaning

about the government, moaning about taxes – you name it. I'm gonna stop him from reading the paper before home time, it only puts him in a bad mood for the rest of the day.'

'What's life if you can't have something to moan about?' an old boy said, coming out from a door at the back. 'Morning, Jed, what can I do you for?'

Despite his son's comments, his father had the face of a man who was happy with life. Merry blue eyes sparkled from below sandy, bushy eyebrows and his rosy apple cheeks had me thinking of him as a diminutive, though beardless, Father Christmas, or maybe one of his helpers. The store was certainly a Santa's grotto of goods.

'Morning, Sam,' Jed said, sticking out a meaty hand.

The two men shook, and Tim sauntered off to serve another customer, leaving his father to it.

'This here is Jim Hawkes,' Jed said, 'our newest arrival to Slyford. Jim, this is my old mate Sam.'

'Nice to meet you, Jim.'

'And you, Sam,' I said, and we shook.

'What can I do for you this fine morning?' Sam asked.

'New locks with deadbolts for front and back doors. One of them gas alarm gadgets if you have one and a couple of internal lockable door fittings.'

Sam gave Jed an odd look but didn't say anything other than to say he had all 'them thar' things in stock, before ambling away to find them for us.

'Two internal door fittings?' I asked out of the side of my mouth.

'One for your bedroom, one for Emma's.'

'Oh,' I said.

'You can never be too safe – not now anyhows.'

I didn't disagree. I was happy to have all the protection I could get and it made me feel not so stupid about the chair under the doorknob.

'Here,' Sam said, putting a couple of packets on the counter. 'What sort of internal door fittings? Brass, chrome or bronze effect? Key or integral lock?'

'Both brass and with keys,' Jed replied. Sam gave a nod and trotted off again. 'Oh, and could you let us have two matching bolts?'

Sam hesitated mid step, but once again kept his thoughts to himself. He probably thought I was some really nervous townie who was scared shitless by every hoot of an owl or cry of an over amorous fox. The man in me felt embarrassed, the scared kid of the night before didn't care.

Sam returned with everything Jed had asked for, including the gas alarm, and put them on the counter. 'Anything else?'

'That's it for the moment,' Jed said, and I reached for my wallet. 'One of them bolts and door fittings is down to me.'

I shook my head. 'I'm more than happy to pay,' I told him and counted out several twenty-pound notes as Sam rang the purchases up on a cash register that I could swear was the same as the one in *Open All Hours*; it certainly appeared to be out of the same batch.

Jed leant over the counter and Sam, seeing he wanted to talk, moved closer. 'Young Jim's had a bit of trouble with intruders and so's Emma.'

Sam's eyebrows bunched together. 'Really?'

'Hmm.'

Sam looked up at me. 'Sorry to hear that.'

'One of those things, I guess. The cottage is a bit isolated compared with the rest of the village.'

'Where are you at?'

'The Morgans',' Jed said before I could answer.

The two men exchanged another of those looks. 'Well,' Sam said to me, 'I hope these do the trick.'

'I'm sure they will,' I told him as I handed over the money, though I was equally sure they probably wouldn't if the mysterious man was really that keen to do for me. Still, they would make me feel a little bit more secure.

Sam bundled up our purchases, wrapping them in brown paper then popping them in a stiff, brown-paper carrier bag.

'Tim wants them to do their small bit for saving the planet,' Jed confided to me as we left the store. 'It costs them a damn sight more for paper bags than plastic, but it's made their little business popular with the local fishermen and conservationists.'

We carried on up the high street and it soon became apparent Jed was a well-known face as several people we passed acknowledged him with a nod or a 'good morning'.

'They just know me by sight,' he said when I commented on it.

On the way back down the other side of the street Jed suggested we stop for a coffee. We'd paid for two hours and we'd spent less than a third of that, so I thought *why not*?

Again, it was immediately apparent Jed was a known face. The woman behind the counter gave him a bright smile and hurried over with menus as he wedged himself into a corner seat by the window.

'Morning, Jed, where's Emma today?'

'Back at The Grange. Lil, this here is Jim Hawkes, her new neighbour. I thought I'd show him around some of the local high life.'

Lil patted him on the shoulder and laughed. 'You are a one.' She took a small notepad and a stub of a pencil from her pink overall pocket. 'The usual?'

'Just a coffee for me,' he said, 'and one of them chocolate cake things.'

'One coffee and a chocolate muffin.' She gave me a smile. 'And how about you, Jim?'

'The same, please.'

She scribbled it down, taking back the unread menus and returned behind the counter to bustle about with white china cups, saucers and a stainless steel coffee machine that had so many knobs and dials that you probably needed a degree to work it.

'What are we really doing here?' I asked.

'You needed some home security.'

'But here?'

'You also needed to get away from Slyford for a while.'

'You know, if he does come from Chalfont the chances of us seeing him on the street are practically non-existent,' I said.

'Tell me – what else were you planning to do this morning?'

He had a point. Before I had a chance to answer, the coffee and two fairly substantial chocolate muffins arrived with milk, sugar and the usual customer–proprietor associated chatter before she left us to get on with our mid-morning snack.

Jed took a sip of his coffee and then began to peel back the corrugated paper cup from around the base of his cake.

'I'd never have tried these if it weren't for Emms,' Jed said, breaking a piece off and popping it into his mouth.

'You come to Chalfont with Emma often?'

He swallowed the piece of muffin and took another sip of coffee. 'Not very. I sometimes bring her over when she's getting her hair done, if I need a haircut or something from Sam's.'

'Emma drives?'

'Have to, living in Slyford. If you relied on the bus, you'd never leave the place.'

'I did sort of get that impression from the estate agent.'

'Oh, it's not so bad. We're a bit isolated during the winter, but we rarely get snow down this part of the country so it's not often we can't get in and out of the village, though last year was a bit of a challenge.'

I took a bite out of my muffin and, as the rich cake melted on my tongue, I instantly got why Jed was so smitten.

'Good, eh?' he said with a grin.

'God, it was worth coming just for this.'

'I've tried 'em elsewhere but none are as good as the ones you get here.'

I took a sip of coffee to wash it down. Why chocolate and coffee were such a fantastic mix I'd never know, but they definitely were.

We sat in companionable silence, savouring the muffins and coffee until with a sigh I'd eaten the last crumb.

'That was . . . great,' I said, and Jed chuckled.

'I sometimes tell Emms I've got to come over when she needs her hair done just so I can sit in here,' he said.

'I think I might have to start joining you,' I said with a laugh.

'Can I get you gents anything else?' Lil asked as she cleared our plates.

'As tempting as it is, I'd better not,' I said.

Lil dropped the bill on the table, and I took out my wallet.

'I'll get these,' Jed said.

'I wouldn't hear of it,' I told him, 'you paid for the parking and petrol.'

Jed didn't seem in any hurry to leave. He leant back in his chair and stared out onto the street. I saw him frown and looked out to follow his gaze. Julie Finch and her friend were walking along the pavement on the other side of the road. His expression became pained and then it was almost as though he was pushing any negative thoughts he might have been having away as he gave a little shake of his head, pulled himself up straight in his seat and forced a small smile onto his face.

'Do you think you'll hear from her again?' I asked.

He gave me a sideways look. 'Nah,' he replied, 'I made it clear I'd nothing else for her. The dead don't usually hang around for long without good reason.'

'Krystal and Peter Davies are.'

His eyes met mine. 'I said "without good reason".'

It was my turn to look out upon the street. 'Why me? Why not you? You knew them.'

'That's probably why,' he said. 'You haven't any emotional connection.' He got to his feet. 'Come on, let's go for a walk.'

I followed him out onto the street, and we carried on up towards the other end of the village and then down a small cul-de-sac. I could hear the children before I saw them.

'This is where Krystal used to go to school,' Jed said as we stopped outside the gates.

Children in grey and red uniforms were running, jumping and skipping around in the playground. All little tykes of no more than six or seven.

A whistle blew and a tall woman in a navy suit began ushering them inside. Some ran towards the school doors, others were more reluctant, dragging their feet, as my mother would have said. I knew the feeling – I'd hated school.

Gradually the kids disappeared inside, leaving silence where only a few minutes before there had been excited shouting and laughter. I shivered as a feeling of melancholy swept over me and inexplicably tears pricked my eyes. I lifted my hand, pretending to pinch my nose, surreptitiously wiping away the tears. I glanced at Jed, he was staring straight ahead into the schoolyard.

'Did he stand here? Did he stand right here in this spot watching her?' he said. His face took on a ruddy look and I could see the pulse throbbing in his temple.

'We're assuming a lot,' I told him. 'We could be wrong. Her death could have been an accident.'

'Do you believe that?' he asked, still staring straight ahead. 'Do you really believe that after all you've seen, after all that's happened?'

The vitriolic words of the unknown man poured into my head like scalding water, making me flinch. I didn't feel his anger, but I didn't need to, the words were enough.

I sucked in breath and when I glanced at Jed he was watching me. 'I guess not,' he said.

'But even you said it was impossible to pick up on the thoughts of the living.'

'Maybe I was wrong. Maybe such strong messages of violence hang around with the victims of it. I don't know,' he said, stroking his beard. 'I'd never have believed someone could physically change the way you did the other night.'

188

We slowly trudged up the road away from the school and back onto the high street, both wrapped in our own thoughts. I wasn't too sure about what Jed was thinking but mine were all over the place. I was a finance man. I believed in hard facts and figures. While Kat had watched scary supernatural films from between her fingers or behind a cushion, I just sat and laughed at the absurdity of it all.

Laughing now? a little voice inside my head that sounded remarkably like Kat asked.

I guess I wasn't.

I made an effort to look in the shop windows we passed, but I wasn't really interested. I had too much other stuff going on. There were two charity shops: one for the aged, another for children suffering abroad. The quality of the items on display was surprisingly good – no old tat here in Chalfont. There was a pet shop that appeared to cater mainly for tropical fish and reptile lovers, and next door to it was a florist with an assortment of tubs containing sweet-smelling bunches of flowers outside on the pavement. Then, when we crossed the road and started on our way back towards the car park, we came across a toyshop.

The window had already been decorated up for Halloween, with orange and black paper, cotton wool spiderwebs and various witches and demon masks and costumes. I stopped for a moment to admire the display; it was surprisingly good. They had even dressed dolls as ghouls, ghosts and witches, and someone had taken a felt tip to Barbie's Ken, giving him a widow's peak and adding a black silk cape to make him vampiric in appearance.

I glanced along the street. Jed was only a few feet further on. He had been stopped by a short, rotund gentleman and they were chattering away like long-lost friends. My attention returned to the grisly display. Huge black rubber spiders with ruby eyes and long white fangs were scattered amongst the other toys, some menacing recumbent Barbies. Diamond-backed snakes meandered between trolls with multicoloured hair and boxes of Meccano.

At the back of the display someone must have spent hours building a huge gothic castle from grey and black Lego – it even had turrets from which hung brightly coloured triangular flags.

Jed was still chatting so I took a step closer to the window to peer at the posters forming the backdrop. Medieval, pale-skinned princesses petting green and gold scaled dragons, fairies dressed in black and purple riding dragonflies, a full-length photo of Maleficent in all her furious glory – someone had spent a great deal of time and thought when designing this display. Krystal would have loved it.

The thought brought a lump to my throat. This was ridiculous. I went to stuff my hand in my pocket to try and find a tissue, but instead small, cool fingers wrapped themselves around mine. I focused out of the display and to my reflection. Her image wasn't as solid as at Emma's, but Krystal was there, one hand in mine, her other arm wrapped around the little dog pressed up against her chest.

'Jim,' I heard Jed say and my head jerked around. 'You ready?'

I gave a mute nod and looked back to the window, but she was gone, and for all the people in the street and Jed by my side, I felt terribly alone.

CHAPTER FOURTEEN

On the way back Jed drove us around a bit, his excuse being that he was showing me the local should-see places; really, I was pretty much sure it was more about killing time until we could stop off at the pub for some lunch. I wasn't really in the mood, but since Jed was going to be fortifying the cottage against would-be attack I could hardly complain. As it happened, once I had a pint and a plate of pie and chips inside me I felt all the better for it.

The post had been delivered while we'd been out. A plastic envelope with my redirected mail was waiting on the doormat. I dropped it on the hall table along with my door keys – I couldn't imagine any of it would be important – and went and put the kettle on while Jed set out his tools and began taking out the front door locking mechanism.

'Will the owners mind?' I asked.

'I'll tell the estate agent I recommended you changed them after having an intruder. The Morgans left me in charge of maintenance, so they won't worry.'

I supposed he knew what he was doing. I left him to it and took my bag of post into the kitchen. It was mostly bills, all paid monthly by direct debit, so nothing to be done. I left a thick white envelope emblazoned with my late employer's logo until last as I couldn't imagine it was good news.

As it happened, I was wrong. My boss having stated on several occasions to anyone who cared to listen that I had, in his opinion, had a breakdown had worked in my favour. The company doctors had agreed and to avoid possibly getting involved in a lengthy lawsuit with me claiming for damages for all manner of things, they had finally worked out a figure for my golden handshake that made even me blink.

If I had a mind to, I could probably buy the Morgans' cottage straight out with money to spare. I spread the letter out on the table and read it again, and I couldn't help chuckling to myself. Sir Peter must have dictated it through clenched teeth.

On the downside, I would never again get employment in the finance industry and I guessed it might be difficult to get any sort of high-profile job at all after being tarnished with having suffered from a mental disorder of sorts, as unfair and wrong as that might be.

It wasn't something I was going to spend too much

time worrying on for the moment. If need be, I could sell the house in London and the proceeds from that along with my payout would keep me going until I'd worked out what I was going to do with myself. I folded the letter and tucked it back in the envelope, then set about making some coffee.

Jed had already taken out the door lock, leaving pale wood and a hole, which I eyed with some trepidation. If he didn't know what he was doing, the door wouldn't even click shut, let alone lock. He didn't appear worried as he finished drawing a line onto the wood and absently stuck the pencil stub behind his ear.

I handed him a mug. 'Is it a long job?'

'Nah, I'll be done before you know it.' He took a slurp of his coffee. 'Where do you want the gas detector?'

'In the kitchen, I suppose.'

He gave a distracted nod, still eyeing the hole in the door. 'I'll get that sorted, then the lock on your bedroom door.'

'Thanks. What about Emma's?'

'I'll pop around there on the way home.' His eyebrows bunched together, his expression darkening.

'Do you think he'll try again?' I asked, seeing the grim look at the mention of Emma.

'He'd better not, cos if I get my hands on him . . .' He gave a snort. 'Whoever this fella is, he really shouldn't have drawn Emms into all this.'

He was right and I couldn't see why he had. Other than to try and cause a rift between us, it was hardly worth the additional risk of discovery when, if his plan had worked, I'd have been blown to smithereens. Another mystery – my life was full of them at the moment.

I left Jed to it as I doubted he wanted me peering over his shoulder.

By half past three he was done. We celebrated with a pot of tea and a biscuit, and then he was gone – off to Emma's.

And once again I was alone.

I'd never before been worried by my own company and, sometimes, when I'd been living with Kat, I'd been grateful for the times when she was off somewhere and I could spend some time by myself. Now I was beginning to loathe every lonely moment.

Or was it more that I was scared?

It was a sobering thought, probably because it was true. I was scared of being alone. Scared of what I might hear, scared of what I might see, scared of what I might do. Frightened that I may succumb to the fresh bottle of whisky I'd put in the drinks cabinet in the living room, or that on returning to the kitchen it would have spirited its way onto the worktop, a shiny crystal glass by its side ready and waiting.

I found myself pacing from room to room, and with each step my anxiety levels rose up another notch. I made myself stop and take a deep breath. At this rate I was going to drive myself to an early grave without the help of anyone else.

I went back into the kitchen to dry up and put away the mugs, and the mundane simplicity of it all began to calm me. As I absently picked up the teaspoon and began polishing it, I glanced out of the window at the trees at the bottom of the garden. Apart from my manic chase through to the church I hadn't given the small wood much thought.

My mind began to drift back to that morning, and I wondered why Krystal had wanted me to chase her? I dropped the spoon in the drawer and gazed down the garden, looking but not seeing. She *had* wanted me to follow her. Every time I'd been about to give up she had let me catch a glimpse of her or hear her singing. But why?

Was it so I would meet Reverend Davies?

I dropped the tea towel over the back of the chair.

Or was it so I would feel her killer's rage?

I mulled on it. I doubted she could control either of those things. I was missing something, I was sure of it. I opened the back door and stepped outside. But why else would she have wanted me to follow her to the church? Or was I reading too much into it?

I pinched the bridge of my nose and closed my eyes for a moment. All I was doing was giving myself a headache. Did I really believe a dead child was trying to pass me a message from beyond the grave? Peter Davies had spoken to me – why couldn't she?

Because in your heart you knew she was dead?

Good point. I turned to go back inside. Maybe she was just being a kid, dead or not. Maybe she was just playing with me. Maybe . . .

The flowers – who had left the flowers?

I swung around and began walking down the garden towards the gate. There were fresh flowers on her grave. Her parents were in New York with her grandparents. Were her other grandparents local? Did she have any other family living close by who would lay flowers on her grave? I somehow thought not. Jed hadn't mentioned any other family and I'm sure he would have, even if only in passing.

I opened the gate and strode into the wood, the dead leaves now a damp mess beneath my feet. I hurried through the trees, beginning to jog and then run, the compulsion to get to the grave and take a look at those flowers overwhelming me. Logic was telling me to slow down – what difference would a few more moments make? A little voice inside my head goaded me on, saying the opposite; that this was very important, maybe a clue, if not an answer to the whole mystery of Krystal's death.

I ran out of the trees and into the sunshine. Ahead of me I could see weather-beaten grey stone. I slowed to a trot as I searched for the collapsed part of the wall where I had entered the churchyard before, and then I was clambering over a heap of little more than rubble.

In the sunshine the cemetery looked a whole different place. I stopped just inside the boundary, scanning the rows of headstones. From memory, Krystal's grave was right over the other side of the cemetery, but last time I'd been disorientated by the mist and the disturbing thoughts flowing through my head. I started to weave my way through the tombstones.

Then I saw a tall, grey-coated figure in the distance, standing with its back to me, head bowed, and past it a glimpse of white marble – Krystal's grave?

I sped up, dodging past toppled headstones, trying to avoid treading on the graves of the dead.

The figure straightened and began to move towards the path.

'Wait!' I shouted.

The figure paused mid step and then set off again, hurrying to get away.

'Stop, please!'

If anything, he or she sped up.

I was running now, leaping over graves to try and catch up with the lone mourner, but then the figure disappeared around the side of the church.

'Damn.'

I carried on running until I reached the stone slab path leading around to the front of the church. I heard feet on stone, the creak of the gate, a car door slam, the revving of an engine and a roar as the car drove away with tyres screeching on tarmac.

I ran a few more steps, then ground to a stop. I was too late. I had missed him and as he clearly didn't want to talk with me, I doubted he'd be visiting again anytime soon. I turned and made my way back to Krystal's grave. Sure enough, there were fresh flowers lying just beneath the headstone.

I crouched down to take a closer look. This time they had left a small posy of pink and white carnations tied with a shiny silver ribbon. The sort of sprig of flowers a little girl would probably like. There was no card or anything else to identify who the mystery mourner had been. If it had been a member of the family, surely there would have been something – a message or endearment, perhaps?

A fat, fluffy bee, humming happily to itself, meandered its way past my ear to alight on a pink petal. I got to my feet and started back to the cottage. There was nothing else for me here.

When I reached the cottage and the half-open back door it occurred to me that, after all Jed's hard work to keep persons who meant me harm out, I had, with not a second's thought, run off, leaving the place vulnerable to anyone who happened by. Cursing myself for being an idiot, I began the process of walking from room to room checking for intruders with murderous intent.

I was too angry with myself to be scared. I marched through the house almost daring someone to be lying in wait. That was until I had checked my bedroom and walked back out into the hallway and my eyes were drawn upwards to the loft hatch.

My mouth went dry and suddenly it seemed unnaturally quiet. I could hear my heart thumping and feel the throb of its rapid beat at my temple.

I wasn't going to do it. It was one paranoiac step too far. I started towards the stairs, then stopped. Was it worth a sleepless night if I didn't check up there? With slumped shoulders I headed for the bathroom to get the pole and torch, all the while telling myself it was a waste of time and energy, but even so not believing it.

I reached up with the pole – and my mobile began to ring. *My first, my last . . .*

I dropped the length of wood and ran to the stairs, taking the steps two at a time. Despite my terrifying afternoon hiding on the cliff path and promising that I would carry my mobile with me at all times, I had left it on the kitchen table when I'd gone out this afternoon. I was definitely an idiot.

I jumped down the last couple of steps and flew along the hall. *My first, my last . . .* I grabbed the door frame and swung into the kitchen – to silence.

'No, damn you. No!'

I snatched my mobile up off the table and peered at the screen. No missed calls. No incoming calls for days. I flung the thing down, sending it spinning across the tabletop. I had heard it. I *had* heard it. I slumped down onto a chair and, elbows on table, flopped forward, head in hands.

I couldn't deny it any longer. I *was* losing it. There were no ghosts; no little girls in red cardigans, no barrel-chested psychopaths in grey, no dead fiancées calling me on the phone. I was having a breakdown.

I lifted my head and wiped my face with my hand and it came away wet. 'Oh, Kat. Why did you leave me?' and I began to sob.

* * *

200

I woke with a start, completely disorientated. Where the hell was I? I sat up, glancing around, and it was only the glow of the green fluorescent clock on the cooker that reminded me I was in the kitchen. I struggled to my feet and across the room to switch on the light. It was past nine and my eyes and head were throbbing, and my tongue filled my mouth like a flap of dried leather.

'God, I feel like shit,' I muttered, immediately followed by, 'I need a piss.'

I stumbled into the hallway and to the stairs, turning on lights as I went, at the same time it began to come back to me as to why I was in such a sorry state.

'Damn it,' and I felt my eyes begin to bubble up again. I rubbed the back of my hand across my face and started up the stairs. 'Hot fuck and damn it,' I said, but there was no heat behind my words; they sounded hollow, lost and defeated. I was even climbing the stairs like an old man, all hunched over.

I paused on the third step. 'You are so fucking pathetic,' I told myself, took a deep breath, straightened up, wiped my eyes and looked up to the landing above me.

I staggered, lurching backwards and almost fell before grabbing hold of the banister. The hatch to the loft was hanging open, the ladder was up, but the fucking hatch was open. How could that be? Unless . . .

I took a couple of deep breaths, trying to control the panic bubbling up inside me. I hadn't got as far as opening the hatch. The phone had interrupted me. I slowly walked up the stairs, eyes glued to the dark rectangle above me. Then it occurred to me that the need for caution was probably long past. I had been asleep at the kitchen table for hours. If whoever had opened the loft hatch had wanted to harm me, they would have done so. They certainly wouldn't have hung around all evening waiting for me to wake up.

The pole was lying on the carpet, but where was the torch? I glanced around the hallway. I had taken the torch from the cupboard in the bathroom, I remembered its weight in my hand. Then my mobile rang – or not. I certainly thought it had. I had dropped the pole and careered down the stairs to the kitchen, but what had I done with the torch? I didn't remember dropping it. I *wouldn't* have dropped it. I'd have been scared that I'd break it. Then again, I wasn't exactly thinking straight. When I heard the mobile's ringtone everything else went out of my head except my need to answer it. Answer it and what? Did I really expect Kat to be at the other end of it? Was she yet another phantom wanting to pass me a celestial message?

Then it occurred to me that maybe I'd taken the torch downstairs with me. Maybe it was sitting on the kitchen table. Well one thing was for sure – I was *not* going to go up that ladder to poke my head up into the loft space without a torch to give me a bit of light to look around. What would be the point?

I picked up the pole and lifted the loft hatch, slamming it into place with more force than was necessary, then stomped down the stairs again.

The torch wasn't on the table. Nor was it on any of the worktops, on the sink or on the floor next to the chair where I'd fallen asleep.

Where the fuck was it? I'd had it, I'd taken it from the bathroom cupboard. I'd had it in my left hand while the pole was in my right.

In an anxiety-fuelled frenzy I rushed around the kitchen opening every single cupboard and slamming it shut when the object of my obsession wasn't apparent. As I flung open the final cupboard and peered inside, seeing nothing but empty space I flopped down onto my backside in morose dejection. Where was it? Where could it be?

And once again I put my head in my hands and wept.

This time sleep didn't come to take away my misery, I just cried until I couldn't cry any more. Hardly manly, but that's how it was, and I wish I could say it made me feel better – it didn't. I felt alone, useless and scared.

When I eventually dragged myself up onto my feet, I was light-headed to the point I had to grab hold of a chair to keep myself upright. I was so dog-damned weary. I'd slept away half the evening and even so my eyes were so heavy I wasn't sure I would make it up the stairs before they drooped shut.

I staggered around the kitchen, one hand on the worktop or wall, and I barely had the wherewithal to switch off the light as I clung onto the door frame for support. Each step of the stairs could have been a mile up the Eiger, the way I was feeling.

When I reached the upstairs landing, the weight of my bladder reminded me I'd been on my way to the bathroom when I'd come across the open loft hatch. I could hardly be bothered, but if I didn't go now it wouldn't be long before I'd have to drag my sorry self out of bed unless I wanted to have a very messy accident.

I did what I had to do and forced myself to wash my face and clean my teeth, avoiding looking in the mirror – I didn't need to see my reflection to know I looked like shit – and shambled across the hallway to my room.

I didn't look up at the rectangular door in the ceiling as I passed beneath it. My head felt too heavy and, from the way I was feeling, should my nemesis come calling he would be doing me a favour when he shoved a knife into my heart or stove my head in as I slept. I was too bone-achingly weary to care.

I nudged open my bedroom door, too tired to lift my hand to push against it, and it slowly swung open. I shuffled inside, the bed filling my vision. Lying on my pillow was a single pink carnation. I sank down onto the bed, lay down and rolled over to face the flower.

'Krystal,' I heard myself mutter from a very long way away and my eyes fluttered shut.

CHAPTER FIFTEEN

Kat and I were sitting at the kitchen table. She was wearing the flowery yellow shirt she'd had on the day she died. It was soaking wet, clinging to her. Her short black hair was plastered to her head. A bottle of Sir Peter's Scotch was sitting on the table between us and she was running the tip of her forefinger around the rim of her glass while contemplating its contents.

'You're really not very good at any of this,' she said, looking at me.

A drop of water trickled down her nose, hung on its tip suspended there for a moment, before falling to splatter on the patch of skin between her breasts.

'Oh, come on, Jim. Think about it, why don't you?' She put the glass down and leant forward, placing her palms on the table either side of it. She was still wearing her engagement ring, which I knew wasn't right. She hadn't been wearing it when they found her, she'd thrown it at me an hour or so earlier. 'For God's sake, Jim, do you really want to die?'

'It'd be better than this.'

'Typical,' she said with a twist of her lavender-tinged lips, 'when the going gets tough . . .' She picked up the glass, glared at it and then her expression softened. 'At least you've had the balls to try and kick one habit.'

'It isn't a habit.'

'Hmm, it was becoming one.'

'Kat—'

She held up a hand stopping me. 'No time.'

'But—'

'No time,' she repeated. 'What you have to do is look at the clues you've been given. Remember what you've seen and been told.'

'Clues?'

'She's trying to tell you something and you must listen.'

'Why doesn't she speak to me? The reverend spoke to me, you're speaking to me, why doesn't she if she wants me to help her so much?'

Kat very slowly shook her head, droplets falling from the spikes of her hair to patter down on the floor around her. 'It's not her who needs helping,' she said, and her lips curled into that really sad half-smile she used to give me towards the end. 'It's too late for her,' and she got to her feet, 'but I'm sort of hoping it isn't too late for you.'

Then it was as though she was freezing, turning to ice or glass; she shimmered and glimmered and with a whoosh collapsed into a sea of water that washed across the kitchen floor, lapping against the walls and kitchen cupboards before disappearing in a hiss of steam that filled the room with clouds of mist.

And I was walking through the graveyard surrounded by swirling murk. Now and then I would catch a glimpse of red in the distance or hear a child's laughter, but however quickly I chased after her I could never get any closer.

'Krystal,' I called. 'Krystal – wait for me.'

She started to sing. '*Now I lay me down to sleep . . .*' and a huge grey figure loomed out of the ground in front of me, his enraged face filling my vision as his hands grabbed for me, his meaty fingers clutching at my throat, his thumbs pressing hard against my larynx.

I tore at his hands as he pushed me down, down, down into an open grave and as it all turned black I could see the blurred outline of a shadowy figure in red floating above us. '*Now I lay me down . . .*' and her voice faded away along with my vision.

I have never smoked in my life, but I'd have done anything for a cigarette to calm my tattered nerves. A stiff one would have been better, but I immediately pushed that thought away. Kat was right, it was a slippery road I wasn't ever taking again.

The clock said it was half past ten and I could only hope this wasn't the beginning of the same old pattern I'd gone through before, night after night of nightmares. I supposed I at least remembered this one – though I wasn't sure this was a good thing. I didn't want to remember Kat that way. A pale, cold corpse, still wet from the river they had pulled her from.

That day, just two weeks before our wedding, we had argued, she stormed out, two hours later I opened the front door to grim-faced police officers.

The coroner said it was suicide. Her mother and friends said I'd driven her to it and, to be honest, I'd believed them – until now. Or was it that I was just clinging onto the hope that Emma was right when she told me it was an accident? Right – *now* I wanted to believe it was possible to receive messages from the dead, but only when it suited me.

I got up to make myself a coffee. I'd have to risk it'd keep me awake half the night, though better that than more nightmares. As the kettle boiled, I stared at the steamed-up window, glad that it was preventing me seeing out into the garden. I gave a shiver as I remembered the figure I'd thought I'd seen loom up at me at Emma's, the same figure as in my dream. The man in grey.

Each time I'd seen his face, but I hadn't – not really. Not so I could describe it, anyway. It was somehow misshapen. No – smeared. It was like someone had painted his face then smudged it with their thumb. When I'd seen it through the window it had been distorted by the glass and maybe that's why in the dream it was unclear. All I could definitely say about his description was his face was twisted with rage.

And he was unshaven with a dark shadow of stubble upon his chin and upper lip. A bit like he'd been on an alcohol- or drug-fuelled bender. I recognised the look; a couple of times I'd seen it reflected back at me in the bathroom mirror.

I spooned some coffee into the mug, poured in the just-boiled water, then slopped in a drop of milk and wished it was a measure of something stronger. *Just for medicinal purposes. A small snifter won't do you any harm.*

I leant back against the sink and took a sip nearly burning my tongue. I cooled the coffee down with another drop of milk and sat down at the kitchen table.

So what now? Good question.

I reached out for the mug and my hand was shaking. I clenched my fingers into a fist a couple of times, then tried again. Better – my fingers were still trembling but not so much I was in danger of spilling my drink all down myself.

I leant back in the chair and took a sip from my mug. It occurred to me that in my dream I'd been sitting like this but nursing a tumbler of malt. What was it Kat had said? *What you have to do is look at the clues you've been given.*

Clues? What clues?

She's trying to tell you something and you must listen.

What? What is she trying to tell me? I thought about it for a few minutes. It was true that several times she or her dog had appeared when I'd been in danger. And the flowers – they were obviously . . . There had been a carnation on my bed. I jumped to my feet and headed for the hall. Was that an indication that I was right about the flowers and the person who had left them? Was she telling me I was on the right track?

I ran up the stairs. The hatch to the attic was still closed at least. I hesitated, looking up. Was the carnation on my bed her way of telling me that it was she who wanted me to go and look in the loft? But then why had my mobile rung to stop me? Maybe the carnation was telling me that my nemesis had been up there waiting. But then why not finish me off while I was sleeping?

This was getting me nowhere. I stalked into the bedroom. The carnation was still on the pillow next to where I had laid my head. I sat down on the bed and picked up the flower. 'What are you trying to tell me, Krystal?' I asked, rolling the stem around in my fingers as I studied the curled petals. 'What is it you want me to do?'

Of course, there was no answer, only silence. One thing was certainly becoming apparent, there was more than one force at work: Krystal and her dog, who so far had saved me in times of peril, and the man in grey, who whether alive or dead was trying to drive me to drink. I couldn't believe it was Krystal who had been responsible for the moving bottle of Scotch and glass.

Clues, Kat had said. The flowers at Krystal's grave were definitely a clue. If I could work out who had left them, I was pretty sure I would be well on the way to solving the whole mystery. Unfortunately, I'd blown it;

he or she would never risk visiting the churchyard again, at least not while I was still living in Slyford.

I frowned down at the flower in my hand. Why were they still leaving flowers? It was over two years ago since she'd died. Was it guilt? Whoever was at the graveside, although dressed in a long grey coat, wasn't 'the man'. The solitary mourner was tall and slim, I could see that much; 'the man' was big and bulky.

Then it hit me. It was a woman! I squeezed my eyes shut and tried to see the figure in my head and how they hurried from the grave and along the path. I'm pretty sure it was a woman. Now we were getting somewhere. I'd cut the potential candidates down by approximately half.

If you're right.

I know a woman's walk when I see one.

She was dressed like a man.

She was wearing a long grey coat; she could have been wearing anything underneath!

She was wearing trousers.

So? Some women wear hardly anything else. Jeans, slacks, trouser suits. In fact, I'd only ever seen Emma wearing trousers. And that made me pause for thought. Emma was tall and slim. Could it have been her at the churchyard? Could it be Emma who had been leaving flowers on Krystal's grave? She had obviously been fond of Krystal and her parents.

I went back downstairs, taking the carnation with me and avoiding the living room. I rummaged around in one of the kitchen cabinets until I found a fairly small glass and filled it with about an inch and a half of water as it seemed a shame to let the carnation wither and die before it had to. Then I wasn't sure what to do with it. Eventually I stuck it on the window sill, where it would at least get some light, and turned my back on it to sit down. I leant back in the chair to get back to thinking.

If it had been Emma at the church, she'd have stopped when I called out. She'd have come and spoken to me. Why wouldn't she?

Maybe she didn't want you to know.

I thought on it some more. No, it couldn't have been Emma. She *would* have spoken to me. Anyway, why would she drive to the church? She only lived about ten minutes away, tops.

Maybe she was on her way back from getting the flowers. There isn't a florist in the village.

I took a deep shuddery breath. If it had been Emma leaving the flowers – and it was a big if – why wouldn't she want me to know it unless she did have something to hide?

She didn't want to come into the cottage that morning, did she?

I frowned into my coffee cup. No, she didn't. At the time it had appeared almost like she'd been waiting for me outside the gate. I thought on it some more. A weird expression passed across her face when I'd invited her in.

I frowned into space. No, Emma was nothing to do with all this. Whoever tried to kill me had broken into her house straight after leaving the cottage. She was as much a victim as I.

But was she?

Someone broke into her house.

So she said.

Someone *had* broken into her house after leaving mine. She called Jed and he'd frightened them off.

Leaving an empty bottle of your whisky.

So?

My inner voice went silent and my mouth was suddenly very dry. Emma wouldn't. Why would she?

Unless she did have something to hide.

I gave a little shiver and I could feel goosebumps prickle my skin like someone had walked over my grave. Was it possible Emma had a key to the cottage? She'd been a friend of the Morgans. But why would she try to kill me? And what would have all the business with the whisky bottle have been about?

A drunken man with psychological problems breaks into an acquaintance's house, gets chased off, goes home, realises what he's done and in a fit of alcohol-fuelled remorse tries to gas himself, not realising it wouldn't work. He falls asleep or unconscious and when he comes to inadvertently blows himself up by switching on a light.

It all made a horrible kind of sense. But there was still the one big question – why?

I heated some milk in the microwave. I doubted it'd help me to sleep, there was too much stuff whizzing around inside my head, but I could do with a drink and milk was better than coffee. My gut was burning, and it didn't need any more caffeine. I was dyspeptic enough already.

If Emma was involved, was Jed part of this weird conspiracy too? He was a big hulking man. Was it him on the cliff top?

Then it occurred to me – the night of Emma's party he couldn't have been inside the house and outside the window at the same time. If anyone had really been there in the first place. I'd already more or less put that episode down to either my overactive imagination or another ghostly apparition like Krystal.

I just couldn't believe Emma or Jed were anything to do with what was going on with me. I'm pretty much sure Emma wouldn't hurt a fly. She was a kind, decent person. And Jed – for all his blather – was a kind and decent man.

No, I wouldn't believe it. One tall, slim woman putting flowers on a grave didn't make my friends murderers. There were probably lots of tall, slim women in Slyford, I just hadn't met any of them yet.

But I had, at Emma's party. There was Kathy what's-her-face; she was a tall, thin redhead with slightly buck teeth, and there was Darcy, I mustn't forget her. Come to think on it, most of the women there were slim if not tall, other than Miriam and another woman whose name escaped me, but I recalled her husband was a retired banker.

Little by little my anxiety levels began to drop. I'd been working myself up and seeing shadows where there were none. Instead of making mountains out of molehills, I should be trying to find out who *was* leaving the flowers, though I'd probably missed that chance.

I washed the mug and left it on the drainer, checked the back door and window were locked and, after taking one last glance around making sure everything was as it should be, switched off the light and then went through the whole rigmarole again and again throughout the whole house.

When I was finally convinced the cottage was locked up as tight as it could be, I used the bathroom, decided against taking a Bisodol for my burning stomach, and crossed the hallway to my bedroom, keeping my eyes down and averted from the trapdoor hatch above me. I was not going up there without a flashlight, and as the only one I'd had in the cottage had mysteriously done a vanishing act I wasn't about to be investigating up there anytime soon.

As I reached for the light switch just inside the bedroom door, I heard a child's giggle. I stopped, hand outstretched, and waited, listening hard. I was sure I'd heard a giggle, but it had been light and wispy, like it'd been tugged away by a gust of wind.

I clicked on the light and took a look around the room. It was as I'd left it. Covers rumpled, one pillow indented where I'd laid my head, a pink carnation lying on the other.

I started to pull my shirt up over my head and stopped, pulling it back down and jerking around to look at the bed. A pink carnation lay on the second pillow.

I wrapped my arms around myself. This was all getting too weird. Think, Jim, think. I'd definitely taken the flower downstairs. I'd put it in water, for fuck's sake. I turned to leave the room and stopped.

Little bitch playing with my head. Treating me like I'm fucking stupid. I'll show her. Little bitch.

The anger drained away, leaving me shivering. It was like before, it hadn't been me. It'd been like someone else had been inside my head. Even so . . .

I fumbled in my pocket to pull out my mobile phone. From now on I wasn't going to let them play with my head. Krystal or the mystery man. I took a couple of pictures of the carnation from slightly different angles and checked to see how they'd come out. Two pictures, both good, both showing a single pink flower lying on the pillow.

I stalked from the room and hurried downstairs. Clicked on the kitchen light and strode over to the sink. A small glass half-filled with water sat on the window sill – but there was no pink flower.

Little bitch.

I scrunched my eyes shut. I didn't want him inside my head.

I let out a shuddery breath and opened my eyes. There was still no flower. I lifted my phone and took a picture. Maybe I should have thought of this earlier when there actually was a flower in the bloody glass.

I shoved the phone in my pocket, grabbed the glass and strode out of the kitchen, switching the light off as I left and went back up the stairs to bed. I half-expected the loft hatch to be open again or the torch to have magically reappeared on the landing.

Neither had occurred. Nor had the carnation disappeared; it was still there on the pillow where I'd left it.

'I've had enough of this,' I muttered, picking up the flower and popping it into the glass of water and thumping it down on the bedside table. 'Krystal, if you want to tell me something just tell me, or at least make it obvious what you what me to know or do. I'm sick of playing games.'

I pulled off my clothes, throwing them in a heap on the floor. Not my usual way, but I was tired and fractious. The horrible irrational anger had gone, but I was left feeling irritable. I wasn't even scared any more. I just felt like I was the butt of some awful joke that everyone thought was funny but me.

I pulled back the duvet, dropped down on the bed and flopped back, wrapping myself up in a cocoon. I glanced at the bedside clock before pulling the cover up over my head. It was past midnight and I was too damn grumpy to sleep.

My last conscious thought was that I could smell the carnation even with my head under the covers.

* * *

I awoke to bright sunshine slotting under the curtains and the sound of birdsong, and when I rolled over to look at the bedside clock, the first thing I noticed was the glass containing a single pink carnation.

I supposed at least the damn thing hadn't disappeared again and I wondered whether the torch would turn up sometime today.

As it happened, I felt more cheerful than I had in days. Then I remembered the dreams. But that was just what they were, dreams. I'd worked myself up into a stew and it had given me nightmares, that was all. I wasn't about to let them bring me down. If I was having a breakdown it was of my own making. I had to pull myself together; I had to get on with my life. I couldn't bring Kat back and although I would never forget her, I couldn't make her the excuse for my life falling apart. That was all down to me.

I had to pick myself up, brush myself down and start all over again. Wasn't that a line from a song? I used the bathroom and cleaned my teeth with the line running through my head over and over again as I tried to remember the tune. By the time I bounced down the stairs I was whistling.

The whisky bottle was in the centre of the kitchen table along with two glasses, one in front of where I'd been sitting in my dream, the other where Kat had been. Mine was empty, hers had an inch in the bottom. I stopped in the doorway, staring at them as my good mood evaporated like a good malt will if left uncorked.

I closed my eyes and opened them again. It didn't do any good.

I pulled my phone out of my pocket and took a picture before stepping into the room and almost skidding over.

I looked down at the floor. The tiles were wet. They were wet. I rubbed my hand across my face. How could they be wet? I tried to think. I'd been in the kitchen since the dream. I'd had a cup of coffee. I'd been up and down a couple of times, once to put the carnation in water and once to collect the glass when the flower had somehow got back upstairs and onto my pillow.

I glanced at the window sill by the sink. No glass, no carnation – I didn't know whether to be relieved or not. I turned around and went out into the hall to the cupboard under the stairs. I was sure I'd seen a mop in there propped up in the corner. Sure enough there was, one of those with a sponge head and a handle-like contraption so you could squeeze it out into a bucket. There was one of those too – red, shiny and plastic with a white handle.

As I mopped the floor I wondered where all the water had come from. It hadn't been there last night, I was sure of it. In the end there wasn't that much, really. It came to barely an inch in the bottom of the bucket. I propped the mop up by the door outside in the garden to dry, then checked for leaks under the sink. I knew I wouldn't find one.

That just left the whisky and two glasses on the table.

I had not poured it – I knew I hadn't poured the inch of liquor that sat there beckoning to me.

Are you sure?

Positive.

Someone did.

But not me.

I went to pick up the glass and hesitated, my hand hovering above it. It wasn't even nine yet for God's sake, but – I could almost taste it.

No! In one fluid movement I picked it up, turned and tipped the inch of whisky down the sink. I'm not saying it didn't pain me – it was a waste of good booze – but it was better than the alternative.

I washed and polished the glass, picked up its twin from the table along with the whisky bottle and took them back to where they belonged. The cabinet was open with the key in the door.

I locked it and took the key across the room and dropped it into a small blue and white patterned dish on the mantelpiece. I was about to walk away but changed my mind. If it was the ghosts of the dead making my life a misery, they would find the key wherever I left it. If it was some unknown person who was still somehow getting into the cottage to mess with my head despite the change of locks, I should make it difficult for them. In fact, maybe I should make it difficult for me.

I did consider freezing the key in a block of ice and hiding it at the back of the freezer, but I didn't really want to have to explain that to Jed if one night he came back for a swift one. In the end I taped the key to the back of the small carriage clock on the mantelpiece and left it at that.

Now Jed had changed the locks, no one but I should be able to get in and out of the cottage. And Jed; he'd kept a key. Which had me starting to wonder all over again, were Jed and Emma both playing some weird sort of game with me?

No – they couldn't make me see dead children and priests. Anything that was going on was either all in my head or . . . or it was real.

CHAPTER SIXTEEN

On the spur of the moment I decided to forgo breakfast and coffee – I was drinking too much caffeine anyway – and take a drive over to Chalfont. I could always pick up something at the small cafe I'd visited with Jed. Basically, I just wanted to get away from the cottage. I wanted to mix with everyday, normal people. I wanted to get some semblance of a normal life.

I parked in the same small car park as before and stuck forty pence in the meter. A couple of hours would be more than enough and if I wasn't ready to go back, I could always drive on somewhere else.

I wandered up and down the high street window-shopping. The toyshop was still all kitted out for Halloween and some of the other businesses had put carved-out pumpkins, black paper bats and witches' hats in their windows getting ready for the celebration, although it was still over a month away.

I popped into a small general store and bought a newspaper. I hadn't seen or read any news since I'd been in Slyford St James, and with a jolt I realised I'd more or less cut myself off from the outside world.

As I went to cross the street to the small cafe, I saw two women I recognised and hastily stepped back onto the pavement. Darcy was striding along with Miriam by her side, almost having to trot to keep up with her.

Mixing with the living was one thing, but I had a feeling if I gave this pair any encouragement at all I might not be able to extricate myself from them. Jed had said as much.

I was tempted to dart into a shop doorway or turn my back to peer into a window, but the body language of both women piqued my interest and, although I took a couple of steps back from the kerb, I watched their passing and hoped neither would glance my way.

Darcy's lips were compressed into a thin, straight line and I could almost see the anger radiating off her. Miriam was chattering away as though oblivious to her sister's mood. Then all I could see was their backs. Darcy all stick-thin, straight and angular, even the set of her shoulders broadcast her disapproval, and Miriam all rounded, cushiony curves, giving the impression of good-natured contentment.

I couldn't help myself, I followed on along the opposite side of the road keeping a yard or so behind them, where they hopefully wouldn't see me should they look back. Then Darcy's head jerked around, and

I caught a side-on glimpse of her face. She wasn't just angry, she was furious. Her lips moved as she strode on. Miriam stopped mid step. I could see her reflection in a shop window. Maybe it was distorted by the glass, but her expression appeared cold and, for a second, she could have been a different woman to the one I'd met at Emma's party.

Her hand shot out, grabbing Darcy's arm, yanking her to a halt. 'You even think of going behind my back and I'll make you very sorry indeed,' Miriam spat loud enough to turn heads.

Darcy stared at her sister and she looked – scared. She abruptly turned away and kept on walking. Miriam glared after her and a moment later hurried along the pavement to catch her, and then the couple were hidden from view by other shoppers.

I was intrigued. What had that been all about? It appeared to be more than just a sisterly spat. It had looked serious.

I crossed the street to the cafe. It was time for my first coffee of the day and some breakfast. Once I'd settled down with my newspaper the Garvin sisters were all but forgotten.

I didn't want to go straight back to the cottage, instead I decided to drive around for a while. I managed to find a road that led down to the sea and wound around the coast for a few miles until it took me back up and along the cliff tops. It was certainly a beautiful part of the world and I really did wish I'd found my retreat from civilisation somewhere else other than Slyford St James.

High up on the cliffs I spotted a small lay-by, probably large enough for two or maybe three cars to park comfortably, and on impulse pulled in to admire the view.

The sky was clear with not one powder puff of cloud marring the blue. There was a breeze, but it did nothing to cool the sun warming my skin, instead it ruffled my hair and coated my lips with a salty glaze as I filled my lungs with air good enough to bottle.

The sea below was calm with not a white-tipped wave in sight. It sparkled and gleamed in the sunshine, and in a brief flight of fancy I thought if I could capture this moment and stay in this time and place for ever, I'd be a happy man.

For the second time in a day I wished I smoked as it would give me an excuse to linger a little longer. Then it occurred to me I didn't need an excuse, I could stay as long as I wanted. I wasn't a financial executive any more. I had nowhere to be and nothing to do. I was free.

A seagull cried out overhead and swooped down across the deep-blue expanse below me, and I shivered despite the sunshine remembering another day, another bird and a panicked race along the cliff path in fear of my life. My moment ruined, I climbed back into the car.

A few miles further on, the road swung away from the cliff and I came to a road sign directing me back to Slyford St James. I stopped at the junction and it crossed my mind if I carried on to the main road I could be back in London in four hours or so. It was so very tempting, but a white van pulling up behind me, and the realisation that I'd have to go back to the cottage if only to pick up my stuff, sent me back on the road to Slyford, although it was with a heavy heart.

At the next junction I turned left towards my temporary home and the urge to delay my return grew. I almost hoped that, for whatever reason, the road ahead would be closed and I'd have to go back the way I'd come, and then I could take the lane leading me back to the main road and London.

The white van took the turning to the right and, having no impatient driver behind me to make me hurry, I slowed down. I told myself it was to take in my surroundings, though in my heart I knew it was just to put off the inevitable.

If I'd been driving at my usual speed I'd probably never have seen the sign, or if I had I'd have ignored it, but to my right there was a narrow lane with a large gold engraved sign at its entrance directing traffic to Goldsmere House. There wasn't a National Trust sign or anything like that, it just looked interesting. To be truthful, at any other time I wouldn't have thought it interesting at all. Kat was the one for stately homes and grandiose gardens. If she ever did get me to walk around one with her, I spent most of my time moaning and grouching until we could leave to get down the pub. When I thought of how I'd behaved back then I realised what a prick I really was. How she'd put up with me for so long I'd never fathom. At the time I thought she was lucky to have me. What a tosser.

I drove past the turning, then thought what the hell and stuck the car into reverse and backed up until I could turn into the lane, and by the cringe it was narrow. For the first twenty yards or so I'd have had to reverse if I'd met someone coming the other way, then it widened out a bit and the high hedges on either side dipped down revealing acres of farmland.

Even so, it didn't have the feel of a driveway to a stately home. At the end of the lane I discovered why. It abruptly ended with a large turning circle of road surrounded by hedge on either side and a high stone wall with ornate but heavy steel gates to the front. The security cameras above the gates weren't lost on me. If this was a stately home, it wasn't one that opened to the public.

I swung the car around so I was side on to the gate, and wound down the window to peer at the brass plate screwed to the wall. 'Goldsmere House Care Home' it announced. Care home? If it was a care home it wasn't for old ladies in wheelchairs, that was for sure. Through the gate I could just make out another line of fencing. This time pointed V-shaped panels topped with razor wire. Nah, this wasn't some care home for the elderly, this was something else altogether.

I was tempted to get out of the car so I could take a better look down the drive to perhaps catch a glimpse of the building, but as I was about to unbuckle my seat belt I heard a weird whirring sound, and when I leant forward and looked up I could see one of the cameras turning to point down at me, its lens a glistening eye, cold, disapproving and menacing. I got the message. I closed my window, took off the handbrake and continued on my way.

When I reached the cottage, I sat outside in the car staring at the place. The thought of going inside and spending another afternoon on my own, followed by an evening and night of more of the same was too depressing for words. Even so, I couldn't sit in the car for the rest of the day.

I climbed out, slamming the door shut, and leant back against it peering at the empty windows of the cottage and the reflection of the sky and the few small clouds slowly crossing them.

All my previous gung-ho 'I'm gonna find out who's doing all this and solve the mystery' had dribbled away. What if there wasn't any mystery? What if I was just one seriously disturbed young man, who by a quirk of fate had met up with two eccentrics who instead of pulling me back to earth were feeding my delusions?

I locked the car, dropped the fob in my jacket pocket and pushed myself off the car, reaching for the gate. I took one step onto the path and thought *sod it*! I backed out, pulling the gate closed behind me. I was going to get a pie and a pint at the Sly. One pint wouldn't hurt me, but an afternoon with a bottle of Scotch beckoning just might.

I didn't pass a soul on the street and it crossed my mind that maybe in reality I was locked up in some place like Goldsmere House, surrounded by padded walls and wrapped in a straitjacket and everything else was just in my mind. Then I wondered why I thought Goldsmere House should be such a place, and the razor wire and pointed steel fences floated through my head.

The Sly was empty except for George and one old codger sitting on a barstool at the far end of the bar and Old Ginge, who was curled up on another.

'Afternoon, Jim,' George said, looking up from the glass he was polishing. 'The usual?'

'Please,' I said, getting up on the stool next to the sleeping cat. 'Can I get something to eat?'

George gestured with his head to a box filled with menus. 'Everything's on except for the mussels and duck.'

'Thanks,' I said, taking a menu from the pile.

George plonked the pint down next to me and I gave him my order, at the last minute forgoing the pie for scampi and chips.

I took a sip of my pint and I must admit it tasted really good.

'It won't be long,' George told me, returning from the kitchen.

'No rush.'

'So,' he said, 'are you keeping yourself busy?'

'Not really. I'm finding it a bit hard to settle.'

'Different pace of life to what you're used to, I expect.'

I shrugged. 'I guess,' I said, and then as an afterthought, 'I drove over to Chalfont this morning.'

'Oh aye.'

'Nice place.'

'It has a bit more going on over thar,' he admitted.

'George . . .' He looked up expectantly as I hesitated. 'Have you heard of a place called Goldsmere House?'

'On the top road?'

I took another sip of my drink and nodded.

'Hmm. Why d'you ask?'

'Oh, I just saw the sign as I passed and wondered what it was.'

'It's a sort of care home,' George said.

'Loony bin, more like,' the old boy down the end of the bar piped up. 'Loonies thar, the lot of them.'

George gave him a pained look. 'Now, Cedric, is that anyway to speak about them poor ald folk?'

'Don't you go all politically correct on me, George Duffield. The people that end up thar aren't right in the head and you damn well know it.' The old boy sunk the rest of his pint and dropped down from the stool. 'Criminally insane, I think is what they call them.' He pulled a leather purse out from his jacket pocket and slowly picked through the coins, counting them out one by one onto the copper bar top. 'Nutters the lot of them.'

George swept up the coins. 'See you later.'

'Yessum,' Cedric agreed and, giving me a curt nod, shambled out of the bar.

George dropped the coins into the cash register and shoved it closed. 'He's one of what we villagers call "local characters",' he said with a laugh.

'I guessed as much.'

'I gather there was a bit of an uproar here and in Chalfont when the Goldsmere first opened,' George told me. 'Cedric's probably old enough to remember it.'

'Why? The uproar, I mean.'

'Like Cedric said, the locals all thought they would be murdered in their beds by the "criminally insane" folk that'd be cared for there, but most of the residents are just old people with dementia and the like.'

'The security looks pretty intense for a care home.'

'You actually went up there, then?'

'Just being nosey, I suppose.'

'I think the security is mainly for show – just to keep the locals happy.'

'So you're not from around here?'

'Brixham, which isn't that far. Even so, I've been here ten years and the old'uns are only just beginning to accept me.'

'I haven't got much chance, then,' I said with a smile.

'You'll be all right,' George said with a chuckle. 'If Jed's taken a shine to you most of the rest of the village will too.'

'People around here think a lot of Jed?'

'He's a bit of an odd character, but yes, yes they do.'

'So he's a good friend as long as I don't let him "play with my head"?'

George gave me an apologetic smile. 'You know what he's like. All that mumbo-jumbo he comes out with when he's in his cups.'

'Yeah, I know what he's like.' I ran a finger down the side of my glass, tracing a line in the condensation clouding its surface. 'Does it get him into any trouble?'

George wrinkled his nose. 'Not often . . .' he paused as if thinking about it, 'but one time he had a real falling-out with one of the vicars from St Jude's.'

'I'd heard as much.'

'A nasty business.'

'Really?' He'd piqued my curiosity now. Emma had made it sound – how had she made it sound? Not as serious as George apparently thought.

He leant over the bar, moving closer as though not wanting to be overheard, although there wasn't a single other person in the room. 'Jed and Donald Pugh never really saw eye to eye, then it all came to a head one afternoon when we were holding a wake for ald Mrs Dutton.' George straightened up and his brow creased into lines as if trying to remember. 'We'd got over the initial weeping and wailing stage, not that there was much of that, she was very ald, in her nineties, and she'd had a good life. The sandwiches were almost gone, and everyone was getting merry, then suddenly from out of nowhere it all kicked off.' He shook his head almost as though he still couldn't believe what had happened.

'Kicked off?'

Without asking, George took my now-empty glass and poured me another. 'Take one for yourself,' I told him.

'Thanks,' and he poured himself a small Scotch.

'What happened?' I asked.

He took a slug of his drink. 'You know what? I'm still not exactly sure. It was all going really well. I think Jed'd had a few, though he was nowhere near blathered. Even the reverend had taken a couple,' George shrugged, 'and maybe that's what did it. Maybe it was the drink that gave the reverend that added bit of . . . I wouldn't say courage.' He thought on it for a bit. 'More like a "you know what, I'm going to tell it how I see it and be damned the consequences" feeling. Do you know what I mean?'

I took a chug of my beer and nodded. If I hadn't left Sir Peter's office that final day when I did, I'd probably have said a few things I really shouldn't have.

'It started over there by the door.' George gestured across the bar to the door leading to the lavatories. 'Whether one of them was on the way out and the other on the way in or whether the argument had started over the urinals, I'm not sure, but there was a shout and all the chatter went quiet.' He threw back the rest of his Scotch and rinsed the glass. 'I looked up wondering what was going on and saw the reverend and Jed both red-faced and almost nose to nose. Then the rev turned his back on Jed and began to push his way across the bar with Jed right behind him. He got as far as there,' George pointed to almost the slap-bang middle of the room, 'when Jed grabbed him by the shoulder and spun him around.'

'One scampi and chips.' I looked up to see a young woman appear behind the bar carrying a plate of what I assumed was my dinner in one hand and cutlery wrapped in a red paper napkin in the other.

'Here, luv,' George said, gesturing to me. 'Jim, this is my daughter, Lucy. Lucy, this is Jim, Slyford's newest resident.'

233

'Hi, Jim,' she said, putting the plate and cutlery in front of me. 'Any sauces? Vinegar?'

'Mayo, please.'

She smiled, flicking her long blonde hair behind one ear and moved off along the bar. I couldn't help but watch. She wasn't exactly pretty in the conventional sense, there was something more to her than that. Alluring – I'd call her alluring, at least that's the word that popped into my head. Tight blue jeans covered an equally small, tight derrière and her dark-blue T-shirt didn't do anything to hide her other curves.

'There you go, Jim,' she said, putting the jar of mayo down by my elbow. 'Anything else?'

'No, no thanks. This is great.'

'Enjoy,' she said and, giving me another brilliant smile, disappeared through a door that I assumed led to the kitchen.

'This looks good,' I told George.

He gave me a strange look and I hoped he hadn't noticed me eyeing up his daughter's attributes. I didn't want to fall out with my local's publican and ogling his daughter was probably a very good way of doing it.

'Scampi caught fresh this morning. My missus won't have any of the frozen packet stuff.'

I speared a piece of scampi and took a bite. 'Hmm. Tell her to never succumb to the dark side,' I told him, 'this is wonderful.' And I wasn't lying, it was the best scampi I'd had for a very long time.

I unscrewed the cap off the mayonnaise and spooned

a couple of large portions onto my plate. 'So,' I said, 'you were telling me about this falling-out between Jed and the vicar.'

'There's not much more to tell, really.'

'You said Jed grabbed the reverend and spun him around.'

'Yeah, he did that, then called him a sanctimonious old blatherskite.'

'Blimey, that doesn't sound very nice.'

'I think if it hadn't been for Pugh being a man of the cloth, Jed would've probably said something a lot worse – as it was, I think he was struggling to find an adjective,' George said with a chuckle.

'What did the rev say?'

'He said, "Call me what you will, but at least I'm not a charlatan and a con man playing on the emotions and grief of the bereaved." That's when Jed took a swing at him.'

'No?'

''Fraid so. Fortunately, as soon as I saw there was gonna be trouble, I'd got out from behind the bar and managed to get to Jed and grab his arm before he landed the punch. Otherwise he'd probably've been had up for assault.'

'Surely a vicar wouldn't press charges?'

'To be honest, I think Donald Pugh was disappointed I'd stopped Jed. In my opinion he was deliberately goading him, hoping he would snap.'

'Why?'

George shrugged. 'I have no idea, though he was playing with fire. Jed can look after himself.'

'Really?'

'Regular war hero,' he said, then leant towards me glancing around the bar as though not wanting to be heard. 'If rumours are to be believed, he and Reggie Mortimer were in military intelligence, but then you know village gossip.' He suddenly looked uncomfortable, as though realising he'd said something that maybe he shouldn't, and gestured to my plate. 'You'd better eat that before it goes cold.'

I looked down at my plate – that would definitely be a shame.

I savoured every mouthful. The scampi was wonderful, but George's missus had also done something extraordinary to the chips. They were chunky cut and she had basted them in something like a light, spicy batter before deep frying them. If I'd been intending on staying in Slyford for any length of time I think my waistline would soon start to suffer. The chips were to die for.

I made my pint last for as long as I could as the prospect of going back to the empty cottage still didn't fill me with a warm fuzzy feeling. I would have asked George more about Jed as his comment had intrigued me, but I had the impression from how he had immediately changed the subject that maybe he'd said more than he'd meant to and I'd be pushing it to ask any more. Eventually I drained the last drop, and with no further excuse to stay any longer, paid my tab and left George with only Old Ginge for company. Sadly, I hadn't caught another glimpse of Lucy, though it was probably just as well.

I'd enough problems without making George's daughter another. Still, I'd killed a couple of hours or so.

Back at the cottage nothing had changed. Though I'd had some more redirected post, probably mostly nothing of interest. I dumped my keys on the hallstand and hung my jacket on the post at the bottom of the stairs, then wandered through into the kitchen and dropped the post on the worktop and filled the kettle.

While I waited for the water to boil, I tore open the plastic envelope and flicked through my post. Two letters were from charities selling me raffle tickets, one was from a wealth management company and another was trying to sell me a wine club membership. I left them stacked in a pile by the sink to deal with later.

I made myself a coffee and stood sipping it as I stared out the window into the garden. The gate leading into the patch of woodland was ajar I noticed. Chances are I'd left it that way, I couldn't remember. It crossed my mind that I should go and close it. Instead I turned my back on the window, leaning against the sink as I finished my drink.

I chugged back the last mouthful and as I lowered the mug froze. In the middle of the table was a small tumbler containing the pink carnation. Groping behind me and not taking my eyes off the flower I put the mug on the draining board with a clatter. The last time I had seen the carnation and glass was upstairs on my bedside table. I rubbed my hand across my face. This was ridiculous. I shoved my hand in my pocket and pulled out my mobile and took a picture of the flower and glass upon the table. Then checked the pictures. It was a shame I hadn't taken a picture of the carnation in the glass by my alarm clock last night. Though what did the pictures prove? Nothing to anyone but me.

'Krystal, what's this all about? Are you trying to tell me something or are you just playing with my head?' Silence was the only reply. I felt my face grow hot. I was talking to myself now. No, even worse – I was talking to a child who had died over two years ago.

I supposed I should go and check upstairs to make sure it was the same glass and carnation. But I knew it would be.

I slumped down at the table and stared at the small pink flower. I could feel my face slipping into a morose scowl. I reached out and ran my fingertip across the soft crinkled petals. Who'd left the flowers at the grave? And was this one of them?

I pushed back the chair, the sound of its feet scraping the tiles breaking the silence with a shrill screech, and went to look out the window. The gate at the end of the garden was swinging slightly in the breeze.

'Fuck it, Krystal – do you want me to go back to the churchyard? Is there something I'm missing? Or are you telling me the flowers and the mystery woman who left them are important?' Then a thought struck me. 'It wasn't her who killed you, was it?'

Silence. There could be only silence. What was I expecting? Did I think she would talk to me? That would be too damn easy.

'Peter Davies spoke to me, even "the man" spoke to me, albeit in my head, why can't you speak to me, Krystal?'

Silence.

'Shit,' I said as I strode out into the hall, snatched my keys off the table, the ones with the dog whistle attached, grabbed my jacket and headed back into the kitchen and to the back door. This time I locked it when I left, and I closed the gate behind me and made sure the catch had taken.

I don't know what I was hoping for. I was pretty damn sure the mystery woman wouldn't be conveniently waiting by Krystal's grave for me to turn up. She hadn't wanted to speak to me before, so it was unlikely that she'd want to speak to me now. Still, I supposed it was better than sitting back at the cottage slowly going mad.

So much better to do it in a deserted cemetery.

I ignored my inner voice of reason. Or was it the voice of madness? A vision of me kneeling on the floor surrounded by four padded walls and wrapped up tight in a straitjacket flickered through my head.

I faltered mid stride. What the hell was I doing?

Does it matter?

I carried on towards the church. Maybe there was something else there Krystal wanted me to see.

I climbed into the churchyard over the same ruined wall as before and made my way through the headstones towards where Krystal was buried. This time, though, I paid more attention to the graves I was passing, after all I was in no hurry. On this side of the cemetery they were mainly very old stones, some so weather-worn and moss-covered that I could barely read the inscriptions, and there were a few that had totally collapsed in on themselves and lay in broken heaps.

Then there were a few dates I could read: 1785, 1803, 1918 and so forth, gradually getting newer as I grew closer to Krystal's stone. Then I reached the more contemporary gravestones carved out of black or white marble with gold or black lettering; 1963, 1969 and . . . As my eyes scanned the stones, I saw a splash of colour a few rows along and back from Krystal's resting place. More flowers.

I swung around and trudged through the knee-high grass between the graves to go and take a look. This was another well-tended plot. White gravel covered the grave with a matching white headstone inscribed in gold lettering. Marie Louise Baker born 1st May 1955 died 4th July 1983. I crouched down to take a look at the flowers. No little-girl pink for this lady, an arrangement of purple and blue, species unknown, at least to me. Kat would have known; she was the gardener out of the two of us.

They were beginning to wilt but were probably only a day or so old. Had they been left by the mystery woman too? Again, there was no card – wasn't that unusual? Didn't mourners usually leave a message of some kind for the ones they had loved and lost? I ran my finger down the blooms and onto the green stems until they reached silver ribbon. *Silver ribbon.*

I jumped up and strode between the stones until I reached Krystal's plot and crouched down beside it. The pink carnations were turning a little brown at the edges and beginning to wither without water, unlike their counterpart sat on my kitchen table, but it wasn't the blooms I was interested in. It was the ribbon – the *silver ribbon*.

Two small posies of flowers, both tied with silver ribbon and probably both left on the same day. What were the chances of two mourners visiting the cemetery and leaving flowers tied with identical ribbon and therefore from the same florist? It stood to reason that they were bought by the same person and at the same time.

A lot of conjecture on my part, I supposed. I stood up and looked around. But there were no other floral tributes, at least not recent ones. There were a couple of decaying bouquets that were probably weeks, maybe even months old as they were so brown and shrivelled, and a few plots had potted plants placed in front of the headstones, but most of these were dead or gone to seed. Apparently Slyford's dead were gone and mainly forgotten. But not Krystal or Marie Louise Baker and it made me wonder – who was she?

CHAPTER SEVENTEEN

The carnation and glass were still on the kitchen table when I returned to the cottage. I had half-expected them to have disappeared now I'd been to the cemetery. Or maybe that wasn't the message Krystal had been sending me, though I was hoping that Marie Louise Baker was another clue and I wasn't heading for a one-way ticket to Goldsmere House.

I went and got my laptop, setting it down on the kitchen table to power up. I doubted that a woman who had died in 1983 would show up anywhere, but I thought I'd give it a try. While I waited for the computer to come to life, I switched on the kettle, then slumped down at the table.

It was as I thought: no Marie Louise Baker came up on Google – well, not the one I was looking for, anyway.

On the off-chance I googled florists in the area. Obviously, nothing came up for Slyford St James, but low and behold the closest was in Chalfont. In fact, I remembered seeing it when Jed had taken me for the guided tour. I thought about it – yes, next to the pet shop on the opposite side of the road to the toyshop, and the image of Krystal's reflection next to mine floated through my head.

I pushed away the feeling of sadness that bubbled up inside my chest. Krystal was dead, she had been for two years now, and whatever I did it wouldn't bring her back.

But maybe it would lay her to rest.

Maybe it would. I could only but hope.

I stared at the screen of my laptop. So, now I'd confirmed that there was a florist in Chalfont, but exactly what good was it going to do me? If I was Angela Lansbury playing somebody or other Fletcher or that Inspector Barnaby from the fictional county whose death rate was probably ten times the national average, I would visit the shop and enquire if someone had recently bought two small bouquets tied with silver ribbon and if so who that person might be. As I was neither a police officer nor an interfering old busybody I couldn't really do either. I'd feel awkward and I doubt the shop assistant would tell me anyway – they would think I was odd.

Do you care?

That was a point – did I? They wouldn't know me from Adam, and they would hardly call the police for my asking the question. I could make an excuse, a valid reason for my asking.

I sipped on my coffee and pondered. Perhaps this was something I should talk over with Jed and Emma. Maybe Emma could go in and ask. I doubted it would sound so strange coming from a woman. Then I'd have to explain to them both what I'd been doing in the graveyard in the first place. Did I really want to share what even to me felt like moments of madness? Reflections of dead little girls being the least of it, I'm not sure what they'd make of roving carnations. That brought a smile to my lips; 'roving carnations' – said like that it definitely sounded weird, like perhaps the name of some 1960s pop group.

I was about to switch off my laptop and close the lid when I thought of something else to google just on the off-chance – Goldsmere House. I tapped in the name and pressed enter. It would at least tell me what they did there or the type of patients they took in. I was to be disappointed. It told me nothing – not a thing I didn't know, anyway. A map came up showing where it was and how to get there, but nothing about what the place was or what they did. Didn't those sorts of places advertise? Maybe not, maybe you got to know about institutions like Goldsmere House through referrals by your GP, and the place certainly didn't look cheap. Mental illness still had a stigma about it. It was something upper-class families of the 'unwell' kept under wraps, shame keeping them silent. *Great Uncle Charlie is residing at Goldsmere House* wasn't something discussed over afternoon tea.

Then it crossed my mind that 'there but for the grace of God go I'. A sobering thought, especially since the jury was still out on that one.

This time I did switch off the machine and close the lid. Maybe it wasn't such a good idea to involve Jed and Emma, though I guess I could ask them if they knew anything about Goldsmere House. I'd sleep on it.

The following morning I awoke to sunshine pouring in through the window and not a wisp of mist to be seen, which was a novelty. It was certainly turning into an Indian summer and I felt better than I had in days. There's nothing like bright-blue skies, birdsong and the warmth of the sun shining down on your face to boost the spirits.

In fact, for a moment, I even considered taking another walk along the cliff path; after all, it wasn't the place that was dangerous, just who I might meet there. Then I remembered the fear constricting my chest as I had raced up the steps from the beach and the pounding of my heart, so loud it'd made my head throb.

No, I'd give the cliff a miss. A walk through the village would suffice. It was a shame, though. Then I thought of Kat and how she would have loved it here. She would have spent hours walking along the cliff with a little dog like Benji bouncing along by her side. I really wished I'd let her have a dog.

And suddenly the sunshine and the Mediterranean sky had lost its appeal and my mood plummeted into what would have been morose depression if I let it.

'No,' I said, looking out of the kitchen window at the perfect day. 'No, I am not going to be that person,' and gave myself a mental shake. 'I am going out into the sunshine and I'm going to make the most of it.'

Before I had time to change my mind, I grabbed my keys from the table in the hall, shoved them into my pocket and went out the front door slamming it behind me. I was in two minds whether to get in the car and drive somewhere and got as far as opening the driver's door, but after a moment's hesitation I grabbed my sunglasses from the compartment under the dashboard and slammed the door shut. I slipped the glasses on, shoving their soft case in my back pocket, and started off up the lane towards the village.

I breathed in deeply as I strode along. The air smelt so fresh and full of the scent of greenery and warm earth that with each step and every breath my earlier cheer returned.

The sun warmed my shoulders and the back of my head. In the distance I could hear the sound of peacocks calling out and I remembered how content I'd felt sitting on Emma's terrace – or at least I had until it had all started to get so weird.

I pushed the negative thoughts away. Then I reached the cemetery. I averted my eyes and kept them fixed ahead until I passed the neglected graves and was in front of the church building. The dead *were not* going to lower my good mood this morning.

When I reached the lychgate I paused and glanced along the flagstone path towards the church. It had been impressive in its day and much bigger than I would have expected for such a small village, but then I had been surprised by the size of the cemetery. The stained-glass windows were still all intact, although streaked with grime and probably seagull shit. The leaded roof certainly had been splattered with its fair share.

As I continued on my way, I wondered what had become of all the old records and if the registry of births, deaths and marriages was still kept inside the church. I supposed it would be, unless someone from the diocese had come and taken them away.

When I reached the rectory I shivered, despite the warmth of the day; being even anywhere near the place gave me goosebumps. Even so, as I grew level with the front gate I felt my eyes drawn towards the building.

The front door was closed, thank God, and, if anything, the pathway to it was even more overgrown than I'd remembered, though truth be told I'd been trying very hard to push my two visits to the place out of my head for ever.

A small movement caught my attention and my eyes were drawn to the window of the study. The dingy, torn net curtain fluttered against the cracked panes for a moment, reminding me of a trapped moth. Then white fingers gripped the flimsy material, pulling it back, and a bespectacled pale face pressed up against the glass. The reverend smiled and waggled the fingers of his other hand in greeting.

My fist flew to my mouth as I fought to hold back the scream rising up in my throat, and his smile grew sad, then he raised a hand and beckoned to me.

I began to shake my head, but even as I gestured to him *no* my feet began to move towards the gate. I didn't want to go through that gate – but I did. I didn't want to walk down that path – but my feet weren't listening to my head. I didn't want to press my hand against the door and push it open – but it lifted of its own accord like I was a puppet and someone else was pulling the strings. My palm rested against the cracked and peeling paintwork, and the door swung open.

I didn't want to look up the stairs, scared of what I might see, but I did. Thankfully, there were just dusty, varnished steps and faded carpet; I don't think my heart could have stood seeing the previous horror. My feet carried on moving down the passageway, past the hallstand and to the study. Again, my hand lifted unbidden to press against the partly open door. It swung open with the creak of unoiled and infrequently used hinges.

If I could have forced my feet to have stopped moving, I would have. If I could have grasped the door frame to stop myself crossing its threshold, I would have done it, but it could have been me that was dead, my body animated by some ghastly black magic. I couldn't even close my eyes to blot out whatever abomination I was about to see.

I stepped inside the room – and everything went black.

It could only have been for a moment or two, just long enough for me to take a few steps across the room and around behind the desk, because when I came to that's where I was standing, my palms resting flat on its dark-green, embossed leather surface. It was probably just as well, as my legs felt shaky and I was breathing way too fast.

I reached behind me with one hand groping for the chair I knew should be there, and to my relief my fingers curled around its wooden arm and I sank down onto it before my legs gave way beneath me.

I scrunched my eyes shut and took a few seconds, forcing myself to take slow deep breaths. Had I passed out? If I had, surely I would have woken to find myself on the floor? It was stress. I'd blacked out due to stress.

I tentatively opened my eyes, scared of what I might see. Knowing he was dead, I wasn't sure I could have any sort of conversation with Peter Davies, not without either pissing myself or having a bout of hysterics. I was scared shitless.

Fortunately, for my underwear and self-esteem, when I made myself look around the room I was alone. The room was as I had left it the second time I'd paid a visit, more or less.

The only thing I could immediately see that had changed was that the black leather-bound Bible was now in the centre of the desk, directly in front of me, as though waiting for me to open it.

I took another deep breath, tried to relax and, I don't know what made me do it, I reached out and laid my palm on the Bible's cover.

And all the anxiety that had been threatening to overwhelm me drained away, leaving me feeling slightly light-headed, but in a nice way, like when you're just about to drift off to sleep.

I let myself sit there for a moment, nice and still and calm. Yes, I felt calm. I was no longer in danger of hyperventilating and my heart had slowed to a sure and steady thud. Then I realised I still had my hand resting on the Bible.

It felt cold and faintly damp to the touch. I was surprised the leather hadn't gone a little mouldy; in time I supposed it would and that would be a shame. It looked so old. I traced my fingers over the leather and opened the cover. I'm not sure what I was expecting, an inscription perhaps. But no, just a blank, yellowing page. I turned it over, expecting the title and perhaps date of publishing, but again another blank page. Then it was old, so maybe in the days when this was published this had been the way of things, perhaps allowing for pages of inscriptions if it had been bought as a family Bible.

I turned another page and it all became clear. This wasn't a Bible at all, I had just assumed from its appearance that it was. Inscribed on the page in copperplate print was the legend *Baptisms, Marriages and Burials in the Village of Slyford St James from 1780 to* – and that was it.

At last, something that might actually be useful, and I guess another clue provided by those who had gone before.

'Thank you, Reverend Davies,' I said out loud and hoped he heard me, though I'd prefer he didn't appear to accept my thanks. Seeing him at the window had been enough to practically make me go into meltdown.

I got to my feet. 'If you don't mind, I'll take this somewhere more comfortable,' I said, 'but I promise to bring it back.'

Again, I was relieved that he chose not to answer.

I picked the book up and stuck it under my arm. It was heavy, heavy and solid, a physical something of this world, not the next, and maybe that's why I'd found its touch so comforting. I half-expected the door to the study to slam in my face as I went to leave, but no, and neither did the front door. I closed the gate behind me and glanced back at the window as the curtain dropped down, veiling the shadow of a man standing behind it.

I raised my hand and waved. I think I saw the shadow wave back.

And my fear fell away.

I walked back to the cottage. I could hardly stroll around the village with the purloined, or should I say borrowed, registry beneath my arm.

I took the book straight to the kitchen and dumped it on the table and then went upstairs to get my laptop, spending a few minutes scrabbling around trying to find a notepad of some description and a pen or pencil so I could jot down any interesting information.

When I got back to the kitchen, I sat at the table arranging the bits and pieces I'd collected around me and, with a feeling of immense optimism that I might at last be getting somewhere, opened the book. Then it occurred to me that I really had no idea what I was looking for or where to start.

How about Marie Louise Baker born 1st May 1955 died 4th July 1983?

She was buried in the cemetery, so even if her baptism wasn't registered her burial would be, I'd have thought. I opened the book roughly in the middle and still had to flick through a considerable number of pages before I reached the twentieth century. I kept turning the yellowing sheets until I reached May 1955. If Marie Louise Baker had been born in Slyford St James she would probably appear here somewhere during the month of May.

I ran my finger down each page peering at the handwritten scrawl. The vicar of the time had obviously trained in medicine, his handwriting was damn near illegible. Even so, I found her. Baptism 15th May 1955 of Marie Louise, daughter of Ronald Baker, Royal Air Force, and his wife, Delia Baker, born 1st May 1955.

So, it looked like poor Marie had never married. I flicked through the pages until I found July 1983. Again, I ran my finger down the page. This reverend had flowery yet legible handwriting, so when I found myself slipping into August – there had been several weddings and births this month and two funerals, but neither of them Marie's – I was a little perplexed. I ran through the month again, but nothing, so I carried on into August – and there she was, 20th August 1983, well over a month after her death.

I frowned down at the page – wasn't that a bit unusual?

It had taken almost as long before Kat's funeral.

But that was because there had to be an inquest. Then the penny dropped: Marie must have died in unusual circumstances.

I sat staring at the page. So, what happened to you, Marie? What is your connection to Krystal and why does someone still leave you both flowers?

Then a horrible thought occurred to me – had Marie also been murdered? Had she been murdered by *the man*? If she had, it was over thirty years ago, so he must be at least fifty by now – or he'd started his murderous career very early.

I made myself a sandwich while I thought on the Marie/Krystal connection for a bit. Then I tried Google, but news that was over thirty years old, from a small village in the middle of nowhere, was hardly likely to have made it onto the worldwide web. Eventually I ended up staring at the entry in the register, tapping the end of the pencil against my bottom lip and wondering where to go from here.

I knocked back the last of my coffee and grimaced. It was cold and when I looked back at the clock I could see why; it was now coming up to three.

I mulled on all that I'd learnt, which wasn't much and a lot less than I'd hoped, and I realised it was no good. I needed Jed and Emma's help. Had I been clutching at straws, I wouldn't even have considered it, but there was a reason Krystal kept leading me to the cemetery and Peter Davies had beckoned me into the rectory. There was a connection between Krystal and Marie – I was sure of it.

I switched off my laptop, got to my feet, stretched, rotated my shoulders and decided to give Jed a ring. He might be able to throw some light on the mystery of Marie, even though she'd been dead over thirty years. Jed had told me he'd been born in Slyford, and I wasn't sure how old he was now, but if there'd been some kind of scandal, he might have been old enough to remember it or the gossip afterwards.

He answered on the fourth ring and our conversation was short though not particularly sweet.

'Hi, it's Jim.'

'What's up?'

'Can I see you? There's something you might be able to help me with.'

'I'm guessing you're not talking about cutting the grass or fitting some more locks.'

'Nah, the other stuff.'

I heard him sigh. 'I'm at Emms'.' I heard muffled voices, then, 'Emms says to come over now and you can join us for afternoon tea. We'll be round the back.'

'Thanks. I'll come right over.'

He gave a grunt. 'You do that,' and the line went dead. It occurred to me that he didn't really sound very happy about it, which made me pause for thought. I hoped I hadn't interrupted anything.

I shoved the register under my arm, grabbed my keys

like her should be able to rest in peace.'
,' I told him.
on grew grim. 'I know,' he said, 'and I
time we listened to what she has to say.'

from the hall table and as an afterthought took my jacket off the banister and slung it over my shoulder. It was warm out now, but it could be another thing by the time I left Emma's.

Emma was pouring tea as I climbed the steps to the patio. She smiled in my direction and gestured with her head that I should take the empty seat. Jed nodded hello and his expression was welcoming enough, so I guessed his earlier brusqueness might be down to just not liking talking on the phone.

'Goodness,' Emma said, seeing the book under my arm. 'What have you got there?'

I put it on the spare seat beside me as I hung my jacket over the back of the chair and sat down. 'It's a long story.'

'We've time,' Jed said.

So I told them. I told them everything. I hadn't meant to. I didn't want them to think I was going crazy, but once I'd started it all sort of started to tumble out.

Once or twice I saw them exchange glances, but they didn't interrupt, which must have taken some doing. Had I been listening to my tirade I think I wouldn't have been able to help myself.

Mysterious figures in the cemetery, roving carnations, silver ribbon, long-dead priests, even I thought I sounded bonkers, especially when I explained how I thought Krystal was trying to give me clues.

Did I mention her reflection in Emma's or the shop's windows? No, I kept those occasions to myself. They were a couple of pieces of strangeness too far.

'So you think this person, this woman, left the flowers on both graves?' Emma asked when I finally stuttered into silence.

I took a sip of my now stone-cold tea and grimaced. 'I think so. I saw the fresh flowers on Krystal's grave the first time I went to the cemetery and hadn't given it too much thought other than to who might have left them. Then I wondered why Krystal would have led me there in the first place if not to see the flowers and perhaps meet Peter Davies.'

Jed and Emma exchanged another look.

'I know it sounds mad, but I had this urge to go back to the churchyard and when I did, I saw the woman and the fresh flowers.'

'Then a carnation from the bouquet appeared on your pillow?' Emma asked and the gentleness of her voice wasn't lost on me.

'I know it sounds crazy, but yes.'

'And it moved?'

'It didn't exactly move – more like relocated. And that's when I decided she must be trying to tell me something. So I went back and found the other bouquet tied with the same ribbon.'

'So from this you're surmising the mystery woman left both bouquets?' Jed said.

'It would be logical, I suppose. Not many of the other graves are so well-cared for or receive regular flowers,' and I know I sounded a little terse.

If Jed noticed he didn't show it.

'And you say thi[...]

I folded my arms [...]

'It could be she [...] somewhere?' Emma [...] people went travellin[...]

'She was hardly a [...]

'In those days yo[...] Some went travelling [...] or Morocco and beca[...] them in some places li[...]

'Hmm,' Jed growled [...] was it disbelief? It could [...]

'More tea?'

I shook my head, s[...] I was bordering on b[...] from him to give Em[...]

'Jed?' He glanced [...] cup. 'Tea?'

He gave her a di[...] into space.

'Jed – what is [...] asked him.

His shoulders s[...] face her his express[...] would, but maybe [...] promise to myself [...]

She leant forw[...] 'What promise?'

'When Krystal [...]

back. A little[...]

'But she's[...]

His expr[...]

think mayb[...]

CHAPTER EIGHTEEN

We finished our tea in silence, then Emma led the way inside and through to her sitting room. It was here where I'd first heard Krystal speak, albeit via a tape recorder. The same one Emma now placed on the coffee table as we sat. Jed took an armchair, Emma and I perched on the sofa. I'd expected us to have gathered around a table in the semi-dark and to link hands. That's what they always do in films, but then this wasn't some melodrama or ghost story – or was it? I was beginning to feel like I'd somehow been sucked into some low budget, made-for-television movie destined to be shown either late at night or on bleak, winter weekday afternoons.

Jed settled in his seat, leaning back against the floral upholstery. I shifted on the couch trying to get comfortable. I had a feeling we could be in for a long afternoon. Jed's eyes flickered shut almost as though he'd dozed off and

Emma leant forward slightly, hands gripped together on her lap. She was far from relaxed, she was almost vibrating with tension, which fuelled my own.

I tried to calm myself and fight back the anxiety gnawing at my gut. This was ridiculous. Sunlight was pouring in through the window, bathing us all in its glow and making the room as far removed from the fictional darkened parlours where these sort of activities were carried out as it could possibly be. There was no need for me to be afraid. This is what I told myself, but a deep primal fear of the unknown was causing my heart to pound and a steel corset to wrap itself around my chest, making it hard to take in anything more than the shallowest of breaths.

Seconds stretched into minutes and I began to wonder whether Jed really *had* fallen asleep. I glanced at Emma and she was staring at him with an intensity that made me shiver. This was getting all too extreme for me. I was about to get up and say I had to go. As much as I wanted to solve the mystery, I wasn't sure this was the way to do it. There was something about this that was setting off all sorts of alarm bells in my head. There was a wrongness to this. My anxiety was turning to dread. Something terrible was about to happen, I could feel it.

I opened my mouth to speak, but it was as though I'd been struck dumb as I couldn't form the words, I couldn't speak. I tried to get to my feet, but I couldn't stand, I couldn't move. It was as though all my joints had suddenly locked solid.

I heard Emma suck in breath, and she reached out to turn on the tape machine.

'Do you really want to be inside my head?' Jed said, but it wasn't Jed really. His lips moved but the words that came out weren't his, nor was the voice. It dripped with malevolence and sly glee. 'If you want to see inside my head, then come on. Come on in, if you dare.' Jed's eyes snapped open and he was looking directly at me. But it wasn't him. Just as the words weren't his nor were the eyes burning into mine, sucking me in, dragging me inside his head and into the asylum that was his mind.

Through white, blurred corridors echoing with screams and manic laughter we raced, his mind clinging onto mine. At the end of the corridor a door loomed ahead and we were heading straight for it at speed then, at the last moment, it swung open and I saw a window and to one side of it a bed and on the bed lay a man. I could see his eyes moving in erratic spasms beneath closed lids and white drool running from the corner of his smiling mouth as I was propelled towards him.

I tried to hold back. I tried to wrench away from him, and he began to laugh as I was sucked through flesh and bone and brain, and then all I could see were blurred images of his memories as I flew through one and into another. Children playing, a chained dog barking and snarling, a baby crying, a procession of people dressed in black. And behind all this a cacophony of wind and wailing voices and music – yes, there was music, but the discordant notes were whipped away by the wind.

The images in his head flew past me, or more accurately I flew through them, so fast I could hardly register one before another was crowding in on me. I was glad it was so fast. I was glad I couldn't see more clearly as some of the half-viewed technicoloured pictures he showed me hinted at a vileness I didn't think I could bear to have floating around inside my head.

Then we started to slow. These images he really wanted me to see, he wanted me to know of what he'd been capable, of what he'd done. A girl's tear-stained face, her eyes wide and terrified, a silver band of duct tape sealing her mouth, bright-red beads of blood running down porcelain skin. A woman at the top of a staircase, her lips pinched, her cheeks flushed with anger. Small hands shoving her in the back, a tumbling body somersaulting down carpeted stairs to finally come to rest, eyes open and neck twisted at an unnatural angle.

Stop, I wanted it to stop.

A chubby-faced young woman, vaguely familiar, kneeling on all fours, skirt hitched up around her waist, knickers pooled at her knees. *The man*, I somehow knew it was him, pumping, pumping, pumping. I could hear him laughing in my head as I fought to break free of him.

Then children in a schoolyard. White shirts and socks, red cardigans and grey skirts and shorts. The school at Chalfont. I think I glimpsed Krystal amongst them. Then the front of the cottage, my cottage. The face of a woman smiling pleasantly. Krystal and Benji hopping from rock to rock on the beach. Krystal and

Benji running, their backs disappearing into the mist.

Come back, you little bitch. Think you can make a fool of me.

No! I struggled against his will. I knew where this was going, and I didn't want to see any more. I didn't want to see Krystal's crumpled body at the top of the stairs. I didn't want to see what he'd done to Benji.

But he did. He wanted me to see his finest moments. Benji barking, snarling, showing teeth, bouncing back and forth, trying to protect his young owner. A hand around the little dog's throat. His body hitting the wall and sliding to the floor. Then, thankfully, momentary darkness before more images crowded around me as I was sucked into his vortex of madness. A white face in the dark. Peter Davies, backing away, his face full of fear.

Sanctimonious God-botherer.

The cliff path. I was in his head as the man ran along the cliff path. There was someone ahead of him waiting. His euphoria changed to confusion and . . . We were falling, falling, falling . . . *Bitch!*

Then silence and pitch-black dark for a few seconds before it began to get light and my hearing began to return, bringing with it the sound of ragged breathing, hiccupping sobs and the weight of an arm around my shoulders and a hand holding tightly onto mine.

'Jim? Jim! Can you hear me?' A voice coming from so far away. 'Jim?'

I opened my eyes. Jed was crouched down beside me, and Emma's hand was in mine.

'What happened?' I managed to say, but my voice came out as more of a gasp.

'I have no idea,' Jed said, 'I thought you were having a fit.'

'Make yourself useful and get Jim some tea.'

'The last thing he wants is tea, woman,' Jed grumbled, and the next thing I knew a tumbler was being pressed into my hand.

I looked down at the glass and had to rest it on my knee as my hand was trembling so badly I was in danger of slopping the amber liquid that half-filled it.

Emma gave my other hand a squeeze and let it go as she unwrapped her arm from around me. 'Do you want to talk about it?'

I took a sip of my drink and then another, and it wasn't until I felt the warm trail the liquid left down my throat and into my chest that I realised how very cold I was.

'In a mo . . . m . . . moment,' I said, and God help me my teeth were actually chattering.

'Well, I will say one thing,' Jed said, flopping back down into the armchair, 'you are sure full of surprises.'

I put my drink down and looked around for my jacket, belatedly remembering I'd left it outside.

'Can I get you something?' Emma asked.

I shook my head. I didn't want to send her running all over the place for me.

'You're shivering,' she said.

'Cold.'

She and Jed exchanged one of their looks and he got

to his feet. 'I think Jim left his jacket on the patio,' Emma told him and with a nod he was gone.

'What happened?' I asked again. 'Jed was meant to be contacting Krystal.'

'It's not an exact science,' she said with a tight smile. 'A psychic doesn't necessarily contact the person they are trying to reach. If there's another spirit waiting . . .' She trailed off as Jed came back into the room holding my jacket.

'Here,' he said, handing it to me.

To my embarrassment I had trouble standing up and, in the end, just shrugged my way into it while still sitting.

'Did you get anything useful?' I said, nodding towards the tape machine.

'Not really,' Emma replied, reaching out for the machine and clicking a button, I assume to wind it back. 'Jed said a few words.'

'Then he was gone,' Jed said with a shudder, 'and I was damn glad of it too. He was . . .' He shuddered again. 'He made me feel horrible inside. Dirty and slimy.'

I knew what he meant. I felt like I'd been dragged through a sewer and it had left filthy tidemarks throughout my whole body, but nowhere near as bad as inside my head. It was so bad I could almost taste it. I drained my glass, but I had a feeling it would take more than half a glass of good malt to wash this nastiness away. I was hoping it would eventually fade to nothing as I didn't think I could go on living feeling like I did at this moment. I felt soiled. And, as for the images floating around inside my head, I wanted them washed away, and it was something I didn't think a long, hot shower was ever going to achieve.

'Are you sure you're ready for this?' Emma asked, her finger poised over the play button of the recorder.

I wasn't, I really wasn't, but I wanted to get it over with. Then maybe I could get this dreadful feeling out of my system. 'Yes,' I lied, and she turned on the tape.

A few seconds quiet, then, 'Do you really want to be inside my head?' a voice said, and hearing it again it sounded sly. Sly and malevolent. 'Come on. Come on if you dare.'

I heard a gasp and a sharp intake of breath. 'Oh, bugger that.' Jed's voice.

'What happened?' Emma.

'Something, someone really nasty—'

'Ahh. Ahh.'

'Jim? Jim?'

'No, don't touch him, Emms.'

Then just me groaning and sounding like I was trying to speak.

Come back, you little bitch. Think you can make a fool of me. The man's voice, me speaking but his voice.

'Dear God.' Emma.

More groaning. *Sanctimonious God-botherer.*

'What do you think—?' Emma

'Shush.' Jed.

Bitch!

'Ahh . . . Ahh . . .'

'It's over,' Jed said, and then there was a click as I assume Emma had turned off the recorder and then nothing but the hiss of a blank tape until she clicked the off button.

'Who is he? Who is this man?' Emma asked.

I slowly shook my head. 'I have to think,' I said to nobody in particular.

'What did you see?' Emma asked.

'I'm not sure. There was so much, it was like he was taking me for a trip through his memories. Almost like he was showing off.'

Jed gave a little shake of his shoulders. 'He was only in my head for barely a minute and that was long enough. The man was loathsome.'

'Is,' I said. '*Is* loathsome.'

'I still can't believe he's alive.' Jed's bushy eyebrows bunched into a frown.

'Well, I do. Though, if I'm right, he might as well be dead.'

'Explain,' Jed said.

'Can I have some paper and a pen?' I asked Emma. 'I want to write a few things down before I forget.'

She got up and hurried out of the room.

'Then I want to forget them for good.'

Jed didn't say a word, but I could see from his expression that he understood. He said the man was loathsome and he was right. This unknown man was also something far worse. He was evil and it was his inherent evilness that kept his spirit active while I was pretty sure he was lying in a vegetative state in a hospital somewhere.

When Emma returned with the paper, I scribbled down all I could remember of the images I had seen from the first moment I'd been dragged into his nightmare world until we had fallen off the cliff, which I think we had. And as I wrote, as I made myself remember, a few terrible truths began to become very apparent. Krystal hadn't been the first and she certainly wasn't the last.

When they realised that they wouldn't be getting anything out of me until I'd finished my note-making, Emma led Jed out of the room, and I heard them whispering as they went off somewhere together.

I had just finished and was reading through what I had written down, making sure I hadn't missed anything and trying to make sense of it all, when Jed returned with a glass of red wine in each hand. He put one on the table in front of me and settled back down into the armchair.

'Emms is making us some dinner,' he said.

'That's very kind of her.'

'She's a kind woman.'

I dropped the notepad onto the coffee table, rubbed my eyes and stretched. Funnily enough, I felt better for having written all the bad stuff down.

'Finished?' Jed asked, gesturing at my notes.

'Hmm, as much as I can remember,' I told him. 'It was so fast and a lot of the images I saw were blurred into each other.' I hesitated. Was it fair to burden him, and I supposed Emma, if he chose to tell her, with what I thought I now knew? Would it be fair not to?

'What?' he asked.

I picked up my glass of wine, then put it down untouched. 'The man, I . . .' I changed my mind and reached for the glass again. I took a sip, not really knowing how I was going to put into words the suspicions I had.

'Go on, lad, spit it out.'

'Krystal wasn't the first,' I practically whispered.

He leant forward in his seat, stared at me for a moment, then let out a ragged sigh. 'He was only in my head for a very short time, but it doesn't surprise me.' He got to his feet. 'Come on, I think Emms should hear what you have to say.'

'Are you sure? I mean, does she need to hear this?'

He gave a snort of humourless laughter. 'Don't even think of keeping anything from her. It would be more than either of our lives would be worth,' and with that he picked up the notepad and pen, handed them to me and led me out along the corridor and to the kitchen.

Emma was doing something interesting with chopped tomatoes and the scent of frying garlic and onions set my taste buds tingling. I was suddenly a lot hungrier than I'd thought I'd be; a few minutes earlier I'd felt sick to my stomach.

'I have one rule,' she said with a smile as soon as we walked into the room, 'we only talk about pleasant subjects until after dinner. I don't want to end up putting most of this in the bin.'

'If that's your spaghetti Bolognese you're making, nothing could possibly put me off finishing it and asking for seconds,' Jed said.

Emma brushed a strand of hair behind her ear and smiled at him. 'I've made some garlic bread.'

Jed grinned. 'My favourite.'

'I hope you like garlic,' Emma said to me, 'otherwise I'm afraid Jed and I won't be very nice to know for the rest of the evening.'

'One of my favourites too,' I told her.

The spaghetti was wonderful. I don't know what she'd done to the Bolognese sauce, but it was the best I'd ever tasted. It had once been my signature dish – not any more. Mine would taste for ever bland in comparison.

We talked, at least they did. Mainly about people they knew. The village committee, local characters, George from the pub, and my ears pricked up when they mentioned his daughter.

'You've heard Lucy's back?' Jed said.

'It's a shame,' Emma said. 'Lucy's such a nice young girl.'

'George is as pleased as punch.'

'He would be,' Emma said with a sniff. 'No one would be good enough for his daughter.'

'Well, he was right about her fella.'

'Have you met Lucy yet?' Emma asked.

'Yesterday, I popped in the pub for some lunch.'

'She's a lovely girl.'

'She seemed very nice,' I said and for some unfathomable reason I felt my cheeks starting to warm.

'She moved to London for a while, but it didn't work out,' Emma said, 'so she's back.'

'Boyfriend trouble?' I asked, keeping my head down as I wrapped the last few strands of spaghetti around my fork.

'Hmm, he made the mistake of trying to treat her like a doormat,' Emma said.

Jed chuckled as he licked garlic butter from his fingers. 'The way George tells it, I think it was probably the biggest mistake of the fella's life. She was out the door like a shot.'

'She's not nursing a broken heart, which is the main thing,' Emma said.

'Nah,' Jed said. 'She's more angry than upset.'

'Good, I don't like to think of a nice young woman like her grieving over some ne'er-do-well.' Emma stood up and started to clear the dishes. 'Lemon meringue pie, anyone?'

'You're spoiling us, Emms.'

'I'll take that as a yes, then,' she said with a laugh.

'If you thought the spaghetti was good, Jim, you wait until you try Emms' lemon meringue.'

I was feeling full to burst, but when she put the pie on the table my mouth began to water. I could actually smell the lemon as she cut through the spiky crust and scooped the first slice onto a plate.

Then there was silence except for the clink of cutlery against dishes and sighs of contentment.

'Am I too old for you to adopt me?' I asked as I

dropped my fork onto the scraped-clean dish and flopped back in my seat feeling pleasantly sated. Emma laughed as she stood to collect the dishes. 'Here, let me,' I said, getting up to join her.

'You sit down,' she said. 'The most strenuous thing I'm about to do is load the dishwasher.'

I sank back down onto my seat as Emma bustled about the kitchen. I noticed when she leant across the table to collect the cream jug she rested her hand on Jed's shoulder and gave it a little squeeze. Things were obviously moving on between the two of them and it made me happier than I would have imagined.

Dishwasher loaded and glasses replenished, Emma led us back to the living room where we would 'be more comfortable'.

I was halfway to the kitchen door before I remembered the notepad and retrieved it from beneath my chair where I'd put it while we ate. When we spread ourselves back around the coffee table, I noticed that my friends' smiles had faded away.

I got straight to the point. 'I think "the man",' as we all called him now, 'had killed before Krystal and, from what I saw, Peter Davies's death wasn't suicide.'

Emma's hand went to her throat as if imagining the rope around her own neck. 'You think he killed Peter?'

I lay my hand on the notepad resting on my knee and nodded. 'Yes.'

Jed rubbed his beard, staring at me through narrowed eyes. Though he might have been looking in my direction, he wasn't seeing me, he was mulling over what I'd said.

Emma was watching him. She had told me he had found the reverend's body and was no doubt wondering how he would react to this news.

'Do you know,' Jed finally said, 'I always had a funny sort of feeling about his death. I tried to tell myself it was the shock of finding him the way I did, as the police didn't appear all that interested, but it always struck me as strange.'

'How do you mean, Jed?' Emma asked.

'Hanging yourself from the banisters – I don't know. It was too awkward somehow. The rope would have to be short enough that you were left hanging, but long enough that you could launch yourself off the top step. If you were in the frame of mind you wanted to kill yourself, it was too much like hard work when you could fling yourself off the cliff or take an overdose of something or other.'

Emma frowned at him as she thought about it. 'Maybe he didn't have anything to overdose on.'

'If he took the time to buy the rope and then measure the amount he'd need and the height from where he would have to jump, I'm sure, given the time he must have spent planning it, he would have thought of a better way.'

'It could have been a spur-of-the-moment thing.'

'The rope was new, the police said that much. *And* he didn't leave a note.'

'Are you sure it wasn't suicide?' Emma asked me.

I flicked through the pages of the notepad until I got

273

to the place where I'd scrawled *Sanctimonious God-botherer*. 'I saw Peter Davies. He was backing away from me – him. He was backing away from him and he was scared. More than scared. He looked to me like a man who was frightened for his life.'

'But you said the images were blurred into each other they were so fast,' Emma said.

'He seemed to linger on the ones he enjoyed the most,' I said, and Emma's excellent dinner suddenly felt like it was weighing very heavy in my gut and I felt a little queasy. Maybe it was the light in the room, but I had the feeling Jed and Emma were both feeling the same.

'What makes you think he's killed before Krystal?' Jed asked after a while.

I looked back at the notebook on my lap and laid it on the coffee table. 'It's in my notes, but,' I had to swallow twice before I could continue, 'from the images I saw, from the things he showed me, I think he started on animals and then progressed to children. His first was a . . .' I looked up and saw Emma's stricken face and lapsed into silence. She didn't need to hear some of what I'd seen. I was sure it was going to haunt me and didn't want it doing the same to her.

Jed obviously thought the same as he looked from her to me and back again. 'Maybe we should leave all this until tomorrow.'

Emma wrapped her arms around herself as if she was now cold. 'How would that make this any better? We need to find him and stop him. Now.'

'The thing is,' I said, 'although I think he's still alive he might as well not be.'

'You said that before,' Jed said.

I nodded. 'He's in some kind of coma.'

'He can't be,' Jed said.

'I saw him. He was lying in a bed with all sorts of wires and tubes coming out of him.'

'I hate to piddle on your bonfire, Jim, but if that's the case, who the hell tried to kill you and broke into The Grange? Not to mention scared the shit out of you on the cliff path?'

I reached out for my glass of wine and took a swig. 'I don't know,' I admitted, avoiding Emma's eyes by staring into the bottom of my glass.

'Wait a minute,' Emma said, looking from Jed to me, 'what are you both not saying?'

Jed leant back in his seat crossing his arms and fixed me with a penetrating stare, no doubt leaving me to break the bad news.

'Here's the thing,' I said. 'If I've understood everything I saw correctly, there's not just one killer – there's two.'

CHAPTER NINETEEN

Jed and I walked home to the sound of the dawn chorus, and despite being up all damn night he insisted on taking a look around the cottage with me before leaving.

'And who's going to make sure no one's lying in wait for you when you get home?' I'd asked him, and he'd given me a look that had made me shiver, and not for the first time it crossed my mind that Jed hadn't always been the village handyman. Sometime before I left Slyford, if I ever built up the nerve, I'd have to ask him.

I was so wound up I didn't think I'd be able to sleep and, as the only drink I had left in the cottage was coffee or alcohol, I made do with a glass of water instead of being complicit to my own sleep deprivation. As it happened *this is a waste of time: I'm never going to drift off* was my last thought as I fidgeted myself down under my duvet and instantly fell asleep.

It was coming up to noon when I eventually woke from a surprisingly dreamless slumber and the stain I'd thought had been indelibly marked on my psyche from my frenzied journey through 'the man's' gallery of insanity had faded to a mere smudge.

The notepad was downstairs on the kitchen table where I'd left it when Jed and I had stumbled in earlier that morning. I knew I should read through its pages and try and glean as much as I could from my scrawled notes, but having slept so well and the images of the night before having almost faded away, I didn't want to deliberately put myself back inside 'the man's' head. I didn't want his wet dreams to become my nightmares.

I ate my lunch staring out through the kitchen window at the beautiful day outside, pointedly ignoring the notebook, although it was as if I could hear it calling to me. It started as a whisper and with each passing minute its grumbling grew and grew until, by the time I'd washed my plate and left it to drain in the dish rack, it was practically screaming *I let you have your restful night, now READ ME!*

I still chose to ignore it. I mean, what was I thinking? It was a notebook, for Christ's sake. I stalked out of the kitchen into the hall, grabbed my keys off the table and, not bothering with a jacket, went outside, slamming the front door behind me.

I would go for a drive to clear my head. Great idea. I set off with no thought as to where I was going, I didn't really care. At this point anywhere but the cottage was a good place to be.

I drove around aimlessly, first heading inland into the countryside, along winding lanes bordered by green rolling fields inhabited by white fluffy sheep and some that were a curious rusty red. At first, I thought their fleeces had been stained by the red clay soil, but when I saw others of a similar colour with the same puffball coats in other fields, I realised they must be of a specific breed.

After about an hour I found myself driving back towards the coast and along a road from which I could get an occasional glimpse of the sea as it dipped and climbed and curled its way back towards Slyford.

My good spirits had returned, and I resolved to put the notebook away in a drawer somewhere – out of sight and out of mind. Writing it all down had unwittingly helped to cleanse my soul. I remembered enough of the relevant stuff for it to be helpful – I didn't need reminders of 'the man's' atrocities. They were helpful to no one, least alone me.

An image flicked into my head. A baby . . . I slammed my foot on the brake. I sat there for a moment sucking in air. I glanced in the rear-view mirror and thanked God the road behind me was clear. I switched on the radio, turned it up loud and, as soon as my shattered nerves would let me, continued driving.

I sang along with the radio. I supposed it was my version of sticking my fingers in my ears and whistling so

I didn't have to hear, or in my case see, what I didn't want to. It appeared to work.

It wasn't long before I was driving along a road I thought I recognised. I was definitely on my way back to Slyford. I reached a crossroads – yes, I did remember this – and drove straight across. The road narrowed and high green hedgerows rose up flanking me on either side, then a turning and a sign for Goldsmere House.

I found myself swinging the car into the lane and I had no idea why. Shit! From memory there was nowhere to turn around until I reached the care home and the end of the lane. There were a couple of passing points, but even then the lane was far too narrow to manage a five-point let alone a three-point turn.

When I reached the turning circle I swung the car around, my intention being to keep on driving, but as I drew parallel with the heavy, ornate steel gates my right foot hit the brake and I jerked to a stop.

'What the—?'

I put the car into neutral and sat there staring at the steering wheel for a few seconds. What the hell was wrong with me? A strange mechanical noise and the sound of tyres on gravel made me glance to the left across the passenger seat. The gate was opening as a car approached from along the drive.

'Hell,' I muttered and edged the car around so I was out of the way of the oncoming vehicle. It made sense to let it go first. I had nowhere else to be and hadn't the faintest idea where I was going anyway.

I glanced out the window expecting a gesture of thanks from the driver for moving out of their way as the car drifted by almost as though it was in slow motion, although from the sound of the engine I was sure it had in fact sped up.

There was no gesture. I suspected from her grim expression she was so wrapped up in her own little world that she hadn't noticed me. It was probably as well. I suspected Goldsmere House was the last place Darcy Garvin would have wanted to be seen, but it did beg the question – who on earth was she visiting?

I turned the radio down a tad for the rest of the journey, my mind occupied by the Garvin sisters and why one of them would be spending a late September afternoon at what the old guy – Cedric – had called a 'loony bin'. Not politically correct, but, judging by the security, it did make me wonder.

I glanced at the clock on the dashboard. It was after three, but I was pretty sure the Sly served food all day and I was getting hungry. A little voice in my head whispered that it was more likely gossip I was hungry for and it was probably right, though, from what Jed and Emma had said about the Garvin sisters, I doubted George knew very much about them as they had probably never set foot in his establishment.

I dropped the car off at the cottage, knowing I would have at least one pint and a drink-driving conviction was definitely one problem I could well do without. Not that

I'd ever seen a policeman of any description patrolling or even driving through our little village.

If I'd hoped to have gleaned any information from any of the Sly's patrons I was out of luck. It was empty apart from Old Ginge curled up on a stool and George sitting behind the bar and reading the newspaper. He looked up as I walked in and was pouring me a pint before I reached him.

'Any chance of something to eat?'

'Anything you want except for the mussels and dressed crab.'

I took a quick look at one of the menus lying on the bar. 'Cod and chips would be good.'

'You won't be disappointed,' he said with a grin. 'Do you want peas or salad with that?' He leant across the bar and whispered, 'My girl makes a mean honey and mustard salad dressing.'

I took the hint. 'Salad, thanks.'

'Good choice,' he said over his shoulder as he went out back.

I made myself comfortable on the bar stool next to the cat and took a mouthful of beer. It looked as though George was doing the crossword – badly. Several answers had been crossed out or inked over and there was a whole list of words in the margin that had been slashed through. I never understood the appeal; I was more of a Sudoku man.

'So, what have you been doing with yourself?' George asked, taking his place back at the bar.

'Not much. Slept late, went for a drive, came here.'

'Late night?'

'Early morning,' I told him.

'Not drinking with Jed?'

I nodded. 'And Emma.'

'Nice lady.'

'Yeah, she is.'

'I'm surprised she's never remarried, but then from what I hear, Reggie Mortimer was a hard act to follow.'

'Really?'

'Hmm, he'd been gone about five years before I came to Slyford, but to this day everyone speaks highly of him.'

'You said he and Jed were military intelligence.'

George shrugged. 'That's what the rumourmongers say.' He paused for a moment, then moved a little closer to me. 'I don't know about Reggie, but here's the thing – I wouldn't at all be surprised if it was true of Jed. He's very tight-lipped about what he got up to while he was in the army.'

'A lot of soldiers who've seen action are,' I said. 'My grandfather, for one. It wasn't until he was dying that he ever spoke about what had happened to him during the war.'

George thought about it and nodded. 'Yeah, I guess you're right. The real war heroes never do.' He picked up his pen with a sigh.

I took another mouthful of beer and nodded towards the newspaper. 'Stuck?'

He grimaced. 'I don't know why I bother.' He picked

up his pen and poked it at a clue. 'Do you know what this even means? Leave after faulty rivet becomes source of imbalance?'

To me it sounded like utter nonsense.

'Vertigo,' Lucy said, squeezing past him to put my meal on the bar.

'Really?' He frowned down at the paper.

'Dad, you're reading the cryptic clues. You know you can never work them out. It's these ones you want,' she told him, pointing at a column on the other side of the crossword grid.

He scowled at the paper and then flapped it shut, folded it and shoved it along the bar away from him. 'Bloody thing.'

'Hi, Jim,' Lucy said to me as she put napkin-wrapped cutlery next to my plate. 'Can I get you anything to go with that? Tartar sauce, vinegar, mayo?'

'Mayo, please.'

'A man after my own heart,' she said and disappeared around the back to return a few moments later with a small earthenware pot piled high with the white, creamy condiment. 'Enjoy.'

'Thanks. I'm sure I will.' And I did. George was right about the salad dressing. It made what I would usually consider rabbit food actually surprisingly edible. Not as good as the batter-basted chips, but good nevertheless. At this rate I was going to have to start doing a whole lot more walking as, between Emma's cooking and the pub, I was going to start piling on the pounds.

'Another pint?' George asked.

'Better not,' I said, albeit reluctantly; this was another bad habit I shouldn't be getting into. *Better than drinking alone*, my inner voice told me, but I ignored it. It was probably better that I didn't drink at all.

I heard a phone ring from out back, muttered conversation and Lucy popped her head through the door. 'It's the brewery.'

George gave a grunt. 'Look after Jim, will yer,' he said and lumbered off, leaving his daughter smiling after him.

'He's not always such an old grump,' she said.

'He's always been friendly enough to me.'

'So he should. Mind you, as this is the only pub in the village, he can get away with being an old curmudgeon.'

'Does it ever get busy?'

'Weekends mostly, but we do all right. There's usually at least one customer in at any one time throughout the day and there's the regular evening crowd.'

'You know Jed?'

She laughed. 'Everyone knows Jed. Dad said he'd taken you under his wing.'

'He looks after the cottage where I'm staying.'

Her smile slipped a bit. 'The Morgans' old place.'

'Yeah.'

'It was a real shame about them. Nice people.'

'I heard.'

She gave a little shiver. 'I still can't believe it.'

'What?'

'Their little girl. She was such a sweetheart.'

'You knew them?'

'A bit. I used to see them around, you know.'

'How about the Garvin sisters?'

She wrinkled her nose.

'You don't like them?'

'There's something off about them,' she said, then blinked as though she was surprised she'd said it out loud.

'What do you mean?'

'I don't really know. It's just – Darcy's a bit prim, but she's all right. What you see is what you get, but Miriam' – she gave a little shiver – 'there's something about her that makes me feel downright uncomfortable. Like all her motherly bluster is a veneer and beneath it is something really . . .' She gave a small laugh. 'Sorry, I'm talking utter rubbish. Forget I ever said anything,' and went to move away.

'No, don't go,' I said.

She hesitated, then gave me a smile that made my heart give a little flip. 'All right – just a minute until Dad finishes on the phone. I can't have you getting lonely out here all on your own.'

'No,' I agreed, 'that would never do.'

She sat on her father's stool. 'So, Jim Hawkes, how long do you intend to stay in Slyford?'

'Not sure. I've rented the cottage until mid October, but they said I could stay for longer if I wanted. The Morgans apparently would prefer longer-term lets.'

'I guess they're hoping someone will fall in love with the place and make them an offer.'

'Jed said as much. He doubted they'd ever come back.'

'Would you want to if you were them?'

'No. Too many memories that's why . . .' and realising what I was about to say I stopped.

'That's why . . . ?'

Then I thought, what did it matter? She'd no doubt find out eventually anyway, either from me or from someone else once I'd gone. 'I lost someone about two years ago and it's the memories that make it so hard. That's why I had to get away. It was getting to me.'

'I'm sorry,' she said. 'How terrible for you.'

I forced myself to smile. 'How about you? Do you work here full-time?'

'Hell, no! Dad, Mum and me together twenty-four seven would be a right recipe for disaster. We'd end up killing each other,' she said with a laugh. 'I'm just here for a break.'

'You don't live in Slyford?'

'Not at the moment,' she said as George appeared beside her. 'But never say never,' and she gave me a wink before disappearing through the door out back.

I paid George and left the pub in a bit of a stupor. What had the wink meant? Did she like me? I thought maybe she did and I'm pretty sure if I could have seen my own face it would have a stupid smile plastered right across it. Then the image of Kat, dripping wet and sitting at the kitchen table, flashed into my head and I immediately felt guilty.

It's been two years, Jim – you have to move on.

Can I, Kat? Can I really?

You have to.

Yeah, I guess I did. That had been my whole problem and why I'd chucked in my job and left the city.

When I reached the rectory, I kept my eyes fixed straight ahead. I couldn't be doing with any more of that weirdness, though at some time, as much as I didn't want to, I'd have to come back to return the registry that I'd left at Emma's. At the end of the lane leading to the cottage I slowed down. The churchyard and rectory were no stranger than the very place I lived.

As I approached the front gate I glanced at my car, and it was oh so tempting to just get into it and drive away. But I couldn't. I'd let Kat down and I wasn't going to do the same to Krystal. Maybe that was why I was here. Maybe this was my chance for absolution.

Absolution? I paused as I put the key in the lock. That was a peculiar word to describe it. Next I'd be thinking along the lines that what was happening to me now was my penance. The idea made me shiver and not for the first time I wondered what the hell was going on inside my head.

I threw my keys on the hall table and went straight up the stairs to the bathroom. As I washed my hands, I caught a glimpse of myself in the mirror and it was like looking at a me from some alternative universe. It was me, I knew it was, but I looked so . . . different.

My hair needed cutting. It was well down over my collar and had become shaggy and wild. Despite my thinking I'd be soon in need of going on a diet, my face appeared less soft and rounded and I had a tan. If I'd been wearing a thick woolly jumper, I could have mistaken myself for a local fisherman.

I stared at my reflection for a few seconds and actually, even though it wasn't my usual clean-cut, city-slicker look, I liked what I saw. And it crossed my mind that Kat would have probably liked the new me too.

I went into the bedroom, sitting down on the bed to take off my shoes and socks and slip on my deck shoes. Maybe not so much a fisherman as a beach bum. The idea wasn't so bad and made me chuckle, my spirits lifting.

I bounced down the stairs to the kitchen. I'd make myself a coffee and go and sit outside in the garden to make the most of the sunshine while we still had some. We were almost into October, before long it would be winter and, as I walked into the kitchen, I wondered whether, when it did come, I would still be here in Slyford.

Nah, why would I be? I'd be back in the city. I'd be . . . I reached for the kettle and froze. No, no, no, no, no, no, no! This couldn't be happening. I was tempted to close my eyes and feel my way out of the kitchen like I'd been struck blind, but I knew I wouldn't, couldn't. I slowly turned around.

The carnation was still in the glass on the table, but it was sitting on the right-hand page of the open notebook. The notebook I had abandoned on the table last night and not opened since.

It had called to you and you ignored it – ignoring it now?

I guessed not. Though I wanted to.

I put the kettle on and set about making a coffee, delaying the inevitable, I suppose. I opened the back door and put my coffee mug outside on the doorstep, and then with a heavy heart went back to the kitchen table to collect the book. If I was to read it, I was going to do it outside in the sunshine, maybe then it wouldn't seem so bad, maybe then I wouldn't feel so cold.

It was open at the last page of my notes. I took the glass containing the carnation off the page and sat it down back in the middle of the table. A pen was lying in the spine of the notebook. Not Emma's pen, I'd left it behind at her place, the pen I used for making a list of things I needed to buy. It had black ink; Emma's had been blue. The last words I'd written were: *Someone pushed 'the man' off the cliff. Someone had tried to kill the killer.* The word 'someone' had been underlined each time it had been used in black ink. Not just once but with several angry slashes so hard it had scored through the paper.

I took the notebook and pen and went outside, sinking down onto the back step next to my mug of coffee. I took a swig and returned my attention to the notebook. *Someone had tried to kill the killer.* And someone was making damn sure I knew it.

In all, I had written six and a half pages of notes when I flicked through and counted them. As I turned the pages

I looked out for more black ink upon the pages. I wasn't sure if I was disappointed or not when I found none.

I closed my eyes and massaged the bridge of my nose. In the distance I could hear the call of a peacock and wondered where it lived.

When I opened my eyes, a sudden movement and a flash of red at the bottom of the garden made my heart jump, but when I really looked it was just a robin hopping along the top of the fence.

I slowly exhaled and returned my attention to the notebook. *Someone had tried to kill the killer.*

He had been running along the cliff path. I thought on it a bit. I hadn't recognised the stretch of path, but then I'd only walked it once, on my return I'd been running for my life. I did know he was running in the opposite direction to Slyford. I closed my eyes again and tried to remember how it had felt. How *he* had felt. He wasn't panicked. He was running but it wasn't to get away it was to get somewhere. It was to get to someone. He was jubilant and he wanted to share his jubilation. There was a figure waiting, waiting close to the point not far from where I'd seen him when I'd been down in the bay.

He slowed as he reached the point, his jubilation turning to confusion and then anger. *Bitch!* And then he was falling and as he fell, she turned and walked away. A tall, slim figure dressed in grey.

When I opened my eyes, I could feel my heart pounding in my chest and my mouth felt very dry. She'd tried to kill him but hadn't succeeded. He was alive – just.

Oh my God. Was it the same woman I'd seen at the cemetery? Was that why she left flowers for Krystal? Was it because she knew what 'the man' had done?

I took a swig of my coffee, but it most definitely wasn't hitting the spot. Tough. I wasn't about to start drinking whisky so early in the afternoon. I turned to the first page of the notebook and began to read.

CHAPTER TWENTY

By the time I'd finished a chill had crept into the air and the bottom of the garden was cloaked in shadows. I was cold, but not just my skin. It felt like the chill had sunk deep into my bones and my heart had frozen into a lump of ice.

I knew I shouldn't have read the notes. I knew I'd been granted a reprieve when my subconscious had let the terrible images fade away. It was my mind's way of coping. Making what was indescribably awful bearable. Now I'd made myself remember, it'd be there for good.

You know what they say – if you can't stand the heat . . .

I rubbed a hand across my face and it came away wet. I shouldn't have read the fucking thing. Why had I? What purpose did it serve? I should never have even written it down. I climbed to my feet and staggered inside. I should never have written it down.

It made you feel better.

But not now. Not now I'd read it. Oh my God, Kat – he killed a baby. He killed a tiny baby.

And you can't do a thing about it.

He killed Krystal. I know he did.

And you can't do anything about that either.

I threw the notebook down onto the table almost causing the carnation to topple from its glass. A second empty tumbler sat next to it and beside it was a bottle of whisky. Not the good stuff. That was long gone, the empty bottle used as incriminating evidence against me had 'the man's' plan worked.

I sat down at the table. But 'the man' couldn't have been responsible, could he? He was lying comatose in a hospital bed. So who had tried to kill me, and was it the same person who had tried to kill him?

I'd been so sure it was 'the man'. I'd seen his hulking bulk up above me on the cliff top. True – he too had been wearing a long, grey coat, but it wasn't the same person I'd seen hurrying from the cemetery and possibly the would-be assassin I'd seen in his memories.

Did this mean there were not one or even two killers – there were three?

'The man' I was now sure had killed Peter Davies as well as Krystal and, if the mad rampage through his memories was anything to go by, several more poor souls, including a tiny infant. A second person, who I was pretty sure was a woman – *Bitch* – had tried to kill him. So, who was it who had turned on the gas in the cottage and lit the candle? Who was it who had left the empty whisky bottle at Emma's? Who was it I'd seen on the cliff top?

But did you? You have been seeing things.

No – there's a difference between seeing things and having things mysteriously move around the house.

Shall we make a list?

I looked down at the whisky bottle, now in my left hand while my right twisted at its cap. I dropped it on the table as if burnt and it was only the notebook that stopped it rolling off the other side to smash on the floor.

You can't really believe you saw a dead child running through the cemetery? You can't really believe you saw her reflection in a window?

I . . .

As for the dead priest – even your pair of bonkers friends have trouble with that one.

'I spoke to him,' I said to the empty room. 'I spoke to him.'

Did you? Did you really?

All right – who exactly did light the gas and leave the empty bottle at Emma's? Who left the carnation? Who's been moving the fucking bottle of whisky?

Who do 'you' think? Poor, poor Jim. All alone and slowly losing it. Guilt does that to a man. Guilt and self-loathing.

Stop it!

And you should feel guilty, you should loathe yourself.

'I said stop it!'

You might as well have thrown that poor young woman into the river yourself.

'No,' I said, but it came out more as a gasp because the voice was right. It was so fucking right. And I hunched forward over the table, covered my face with my hands and began to sob.

Why not have a drink, Jim? It'll make you feel so much better.

I wiped my face with my shirtsleeve, still snivelling. The bottle was upright on the table and the tumbler was half full of golden liquid.

Just one. You know you want it.

I reached for the glass, fingers outstretched and—my mobile began to ring.

My first, my last, my . . .

I staggered to my feet, groping in my back pocket, but it wasn't there. I was sure I'd had it. No – it was coming from out in the hall. I blundered across the kitchen, knocking the table as I went. The ringtone was playing in the hallway. My jacket. My jacket was hanging on the post at the bottom of the stairs.

I rummaged in the pockets in a frenzied panic. I had to answer it. I had to answer it before she rang off. If I could just hear her voice one more time. If I could just hear her say she forgave me.

I had the phone in my hand. I looked down at the image on the display. Her face leapt up at me. I swiped my finger across the screen and put the phone to my ear. 'Kat!'

Nothing.

'Kat? Can you hear me? Kat?'

There was something there. I could hear something other than silence.

'Kat, please. Please!'

Then it did go dead.

'Kat. Oh, Kat,' and I sank down onto my knees. 'Oh, Kat.' I wiped away the tears that began to well up. 'Enough. Enough,' I mumbled to myself. I was not going to be that man. That's what *he* wanted. *He* wanted me to break down and fall apart. *He* wanted me to think I was going mad. Is that what had happened to him?

I climbed to my feet, shoved the phone in my back pocket and returned to the kitchen. The open notebook and half a glass of whisky were where I'd left them. The other glass was on its side, water all over the table. A casualty of when I'd knocked it as I careered out of the room, I supposed. I picked up the glasses, dropping them both in the sink and grabbed a handful of kitchen towel to mop up the water.

I wiped the table and then knelt down to soak up anything that may have dripped down onto the floor. What was left of the carnation was scattered beneath the table. It looked as though someone had crushed the head within their fist and then wrenched the petals from the stem, throwing them down in impotent rage.

It brought a grim smile to my face. 'Not getting all your own way, then,' I muttered to myself as I swept the petals up into the paper towel.

I had half-clambered to my feet when I noticed a small sliver of white poking out from beneath one of the table legs. I bunched the towel around the petals, dropping it on the table and crouched back down.

It looked like a white business card had somehow got caught under the foot of the table leg. Probably one of Jed's, I thought to myself.

I reached out and flicked up the edge with my nail, taking the corner between my thumb and forefinger and giving it a tug. The table moved slightly but the card didn't budge. It was well trapped. I scrambled a little closer and took hold of the table leg with one hand, lifting it slightly while pulling the card free with the other.

'Doesn't say much for my housekeeping,' I said, getting to my feet and glancing down at the card.

It was blank on one side and when I flipped it over in a plain black font it read: *David Baker – Handyman – No Job Too Small*.

Not Jed's card, after all. Where on earth had this come from? I closed my eyes as black despair rose up inside me. Not another mystery. Not another ghostly happening. My eyelids snapped opened. No – I remembered. The card wasn't some supernatural joke being played on me. It wasn't me playing tricks on myself during some fugue of mental illness. I'd been searching for Jed's card and when I took it from the pinboard I'd dislodged this one. I'd seen it flutter to the floor but was distracted by Jed's knock on the door and then had forgotten all about it.

I looked back down at the card. The name was vaguely familiar. David Baker, both fairly common names. Hadn't I worked with a David Baker?

Why would the Morgans have had another handyman's card? They trusted Jed enough that they left him with keys to the cottage and in charge of maintenance while they were away.

I dropped the card on the table. Maybe this David Baker was trying to drum up trade and had popped it through the Morgans' letter box. I supposed it didn't hurt to have a standby in case of an emergency.

I picked up the kitchen towel I'd wrapped around the mangled carnation and dropped it in the bin. Pity – I'd liked the pretty pink flower. It reminded me of Krystal.

The two glasses were in the sink where I'd left them, one still half full of whisky.

It'd be a shame to waste it.

I picked it up and with a flick of the wrist poured it away. I still had half a bottle and I could always buy more. I washed the glasses, dried them and, picking up the bottle from off the table, carried them through to the living room and locked them back in the cabinet where they belonged.

I was going to hide the key again, but then thought *why bother?* I doubted it would make the slightest difference.

I returned to the kitchen – the further I was away from that bottle of whisky the better.

Perhaps you should've emptied the whole bottle down the sink.

Perhaps I should have.

I sat back down at the kitchen table. The notebook was lying where I'd left it, the pen by its side.

'Who are you?' I muttered to myself, tapping the notebook with my forefinger. 'Whoever you are, you are sure one sick fuck.'

Takes one to know one.

'Least I've never killed anyone.'

Are you sure?

I flipped the notebook shut and got to my feet, pushing the chair back hard enough that the legs screeched against the floor tiles. I strode towards the door and then, as an afterthought, turned back and picked up the business card and shoved it in my back pocket.

You can run, but you can't—

I slammed the kitchen door hard enough that the wall shook, pulled on my jacket and, picking up my keys, strode out the front door, again slamming it probably harder than I should have. Halfway along the lane I suddenly realised I had no idea where I was going or what I was going to do when I got there. But I couldn't go back. I couldn't sit there alone for one moment longer. I knew for a certainty if the loneliness didn't drive me mad, the voices in my head most certainly would.

Or was it too late? Back in the city I'd had fits of depression and bad dreams, but I'd never heard voices or seen dead people. My doctor had been so positive that I wasn't having a breakdown, but could she have been wrong?

'What's wrong, Jim? You look like you've lost a fiver and found a quid.'

I flinched and the smile slipped from Lucy's face to be replaced by concern.

'Are you all right?' she asked, laying a hand on my sleeve.

'I'm fine,' I said, forcing my lips to curl into a smile, but I think it must have looked more like a grimace as she didn't appear convinced.

'Yeah, right.'

'No, really,' I said, pulling myself together. What must the woman think of me?

'You sure?'

'Just deep in thought.'

'Sorry I made you jump.'

'That's OK. Maybe it's just as well, I'd probably have got run over by a bus or something.'

'Fat chance around here. There're only two a day.'

'So I've heard, though I've never actually seen one.'

'Were you going to the pub?'

'No,' I said, not wanting her to think I'd no life at all. 'Just taking a stroll.'

'Mind if I join you?'

'No, not at all. I was wondering where to go, actually.'

'Come on, I'll show you my favourite walk.'

And as she linked her arm through mine and turned me around, I just knew where she was taking me, and sure enough, she led me along past my lane towards Emma's house and the cliff path.

'It's almost dark,' I said, hoping to put her off.

She rummaged in her pocket and held up a torch. 'I used to be a Girl Guide.'

'Really?'

She looked at me, pulling a face and then began to laugh. 'Nooo!'

And soon I was laughing too and, despite our destination, feeling one hundred times better than I had only fifteen or twenty minutes before.

It was actually too dark to go very far and we turned back after only ten minutes, but she told me where it led to and how I could get down to Fisherman's Cove or another small bay a bit further along, and if I was really feeling energetic, I could walk all the way to Chalfont. It was all stuff I already knew, but I enjoyed listening to her.

'If you like, we could walk to one of the bays tomorrow. The weather's meant to be fine,' she said, and I heard myself saying yes, I'd like that very much.

'I'll knock for you about ten, or is that too early?'

'That's good for me.'

'Well, I suppose I'd better get back. I told Dad I'd help him finish up.'

'I'll walk with you,' I said.

'No need.'

'I'd like to.'

I saw her teeth glint in the dark as she smiled. 'Good.'

I saw her to the pub and watched her go inside but didn't go in myself. I wasn't sure what the score would be with

George and decided it was probably best to leave it that way, or at least until Lucy and I'd had our day out together.

I was up and dressed by eight-thirty after a surprisingly good night's sleep. I couldn't help thinking these mood swings from the lowest low to a happy high weren't a good sign, but happy was definitely better than sad so I'd make the most of it while I could. Besides, I didn't want Lucy to think I was bad company.

The notebook was still on the kitchen table where I'd left it and it did cross my mind that I wouldn't much care if it disappeared like my original set of house keys. Unfortunately, lately things were more likely to appear from nowhere than for ever vanish.

I munched on a slice of toast and washed it down with a mug of coffee, not knowing whether we would stop anywhere for something to eat or even where she was intending to take me. I guessed if we walked all the way to Chalfont, we could get a bite of something there.

At ten on the dot there was a knock on the front door and just seeing her standing there as I pulled it open made my welcoming smile twitch up a notch or two.

'Come in a sec while I grab my sweatshirt,' I said, seeing the cardigan she had tied around her waist, and gestured for her to come inside.

'Hopefully we shouldn't need them, but the weather around here can take a sudden turn for the worse.'

When I came down from the bedroom, she was standing in the doorway to the kitchen. 'It's a nice little cottage,' she said, 'and you've a lovely garden.'

I gave a non-committal 'hmm' as I opened the front door and gestured for her to go first, noticing she had a blue rucksack on her back.

'Do you want me to take that?'

'Huh?'

'Your bag?'

She grinned at me. 'You can if you like. It's not too heavy,' she said, shrugging it off of her shoulders and passing it to me. 'I'll carry it on the way back when it's lighter.'

'What's in it, anyway?' I asked as she helped me put my arms through the straps and heave it up onto my back. Despite what she said, it was heavy enough, though once I'd got it sitting comfortably it didn't feel particularly weighty at all.

'Provisions,' she said.

'Provisions?'

She stuck her arm through mine and steered me towards the gate. 'You'll see.' And off we went.

The morning couldn't have been more perfect. The usual ever-present mist had burnt away before we had even reached the cliff path, and the sun shone down from a deep-blue sky warming the back of my head. Even the air smelt good, warm and scented with fresh vegetation and grass with a hint of dry earth.

If I'd been worried about whether we'd have anything to talk about I needn't have bothered. We could have been old friends who just hadn't seen each other for a while. We compared notes on London and the places we'd both been to. I obviously knew the city better than she did, but she had a pretty impressive knowledge and there were a few places we both knew fairly well.

She didn't mention her ex and I didn't enquire, and similarly I didn't say anything about Kat, for one thing I didn't want Lucy's sympathy. Anyway, during what I supposed was our first date was hardly the time, though I'm not sure there ever would be.

There were places when we had to walk single file, but mostly when we reached the narrower stretches of path Lucy just snuggled closer to my side and held onto my arm tighter.

'Where are we heading?' I asked after a while.

'I thought we could go down to Saint's Bay and have a picnic. It's a bit of a steep climb on the way back but it's worth it.'

'It can't be as steep as the steps down to Fisherman's Cove,' I said, and for a moment in my head I was running up those steps once again in fear of my life.

'So you have been this way before.'

'Once.'

'And last night you just let me prattle on like an idiot.'

'I liked listening to you prattle on,' I told her with a smile, and she began to laugh.

'My grandma would say you have a silver tongue, Jim Hawkes.'

'I *did* work in the city.'

'Hmm, that would explain it. What were you?' She stopped mid stride and let go of my arm, turning to look me up and down. 'You don't much look like a city slicker.'

'I'm not any more.'

She squinted at my face. 'I bet with a haircut and an expensive suit you'd look the part, though.'

'I guess I did once,' I admitted.

'Finance, I bet.'

'Yep.'

'Investment banker?'

I shook my head as she slipped her arm back through mine and we started back off along the path. 'Banker is about right, though.'

She turned her head so she could look at my face. 'You said that as though you despised what you were.'

I kept my eyes straight ahead. This I did not want to talk about. If I despised myself, what would she think of me?

'Let's just say it was making me into a person I suddenly realised I didn't want to be.'

She was quiet for a few moments, then said so softly I wouldn't have heard her if we hadn't been walking so close together, 'I can relate to that.'

I glanced her way and her expression was grim. This was not a good way to start a first date.

A gull cried out above and a cricket chirruped from within the long swathes of grass stretching out to either side of us, and a smile returned to her lips. 'I love it here,' she said. 'It makes me realise why I came back. If I never see London again, I'll be happy.'

'Really? Don't you miss it?'

'Do you?' she asked, looking at me again.

I frowned at her for a moment, then felt a smile tugging at my lips. 'At this precise moment – no, not at all.'

She began to laugh, and it was infectious. For the first time in over two years – maybe even longer – I was having pure, uncomplicated fun and I was happy, really happy.

We carried on past the turning that led down the long flight of steps to Fisherman's Cove towards the point where I'd first seen 'the man' on that fateful afternoon, and I had to suppress a shudder. I forced the apprehension that threatened to darken my mood away; I was buggered if *he* was going to ruin my day. Anyway, if he was a figment of my overwrought imagination, as the voice inside my head would have me believe, why should I let him?

The path followed the cliff as it curved around and to the point that stuck out in a high jagged tip overlooking the sea. I couldn't help it but as we began to get closer, I kept looking for the place *she* had been waiting for *him*; the place where *she* had tried to push *him* to his death. We must have passed it, I was sure it was somewhere just before the incline to the point, but if we did, I missed it.

When we reached the tip of the point the path had been widened by hundreds, or maybe even thousands, of walkers' feet as each one had pressed a little closer to the edge to get a better view. There was now a tubular, metal safety rail supported by similar posts driven into the rock to hold back the masses. It was largely unnecessary; if someone were to slip and fall the worst that would happen was they'd get entangled in the brambles and other vegetation covering the rock face before it dropped away into the sea. 'The man' hadn't fallen from this place, of that I was sure, and for some reason it made me relax a little. I was not going to think of him any more – not today, at least.

We stood there for a while, the wind blowing our hair about our faces and turning our cheeks pink, as we looked out across a sparkling sea that appeared as though it could go on and on for ever. Our shoulders were touching and if her arm hadn't been through mine, I would have been tempted to drape mine around the back of her neck – nothing too heavy, just rest it there and gauge the reaction. It was probably just as well I couldn't, maybe it was too soon, I didn't want to make things awkward between us and potentially end our date before it'd even begun.

'I love it here,' Lucy said.

'I can see why.'

She smiled up at me. 'Come on,' she said, taking my hand and drawing me after her.

When Lucy had said the climb down to Saint's Bay was steep she hadn't been joking, and for the most part there weren't any steps to help us on our way, just a well-trod, zigzagging gully trodden into the rock between the vegetation. Here we did have to walk in single file. I let her lead the way and was glad I'd opted to wear trainers. Lucy almost skipped down the path like a mountain goat, whereas I took it slow and steady. For one thing I didn't want to reach the bottom puffing and wheezing like an old man – this wouldn't impress her at all. And I was finding I wanted to do that more and more with each passing moment.

The path ended with a flight of steps carved into the cliff like at Fisherman's Cove; even so, they were steep and weathered so smooth that in the wet they'd probably become lethal.

It was worth the climb. The bay was small, sandy and secluded with a small island about twenty metres from the shore.

'When the tide's out we can wade to it,' Lucy told me.

Again, she took my hand and led me across the sand and over some rocks close to the cliff face, past some pretty impressive rock pools. Behind them and to one side was a small cave completely hidden from the beach.

'I used to come here as a child,' she told me. 'It was my secret place.'

She helped me off with the backpack and began to unload its contents. A bottle of white wine and two cans of beer went straight into a nearby rock pool to keep cold and the rest she stowed in the shaded entrance to the cave.

'Want to explore?'

I nodded my agreement and then we were off over the rocks like two excited kids, stopping at every pool to check it for marine life. It was a good place. Small blennies and shrimps hid in clumps of weed and hermit crabs scuttled across the sandy pool bottoms alarmed by our figures looming over them and blocking out the light.

Sheltered from the wind it felt warm in the sun, warmer than one would expect on a late September day. We cooled down by taking off our trainers and padding along the shoreline with the sea lapping around our ankles and the wet sand scrunching between our toes. We laughed, we laughed a lot, actually, and for the first time since I'd arrived at Slyford St James it occurred to me that if most days were like this one, then yes – yes, maybe I could make this isolated place my home.

Lunch was good. Lucy had brought chicken, salad and a bottle of her delicious, home-made dressing to slop over it. She had laid a blanket out on the sand for us to sit on and while I had a beer, she sipped the white wine as she told me about her childhood in Devon and I told her about mine in the suburbs of London.

'Do you think you might stay?' she asked.

'If you'd asked me yesterday, I would have said no. Today,' I shrugged and smiled at her, 'today I'm not so sure.'

'There're worse places to live.'

'You'd not go back to London?'

She gave a small laugh and ran her finger around the rim of her glass her eyes on its contents. 'I don't think so. I never got used to the hustle and bustle. I never got used to the constant hum of the city. I don't suppose you'd even notice it, but to me there was never quiet. Never silence.'

I thought about it and I supposed she was right. At night, when I walked to the pub or back from Emma's with Jed, apart from the sound of our own voices and our footsteps echoing along the street there was hardly a sound other than maybe the occasional call of an animal crying out across the countryside. During the day it wasn't much different. Apart from the odd car passing through the village every sound was natural: birds singing, peacocks calling, insects buzzing. She was right, now I thought on it, in the city it was never silent – not really.

After we'd finished eating Lucy flopped back on the blanket and I laid down resting on my elbow so I could watch her face as she was speaking.

She closed her eyes. 'Hmm, this is nice.'

If she'd been wearing anything on her lips it was gone now, which was probably just as well, they already looked too kissable by far. Her nose twitched and she raised a hand to flick away an imaginary fly.

I don't know when I'd become such a coward. In London I'd snogged the face off many a girl I'd met only a few minutes earlier when on the dance floor of some club. I suppose the difference was I'd never intended or wanted to see them again; with Lucy it was different.

Then I thought of Kat and it was like a cloud had drifted across the sun.

You have to move on, Jim. Don't make me an excuse for fucking up the rest of your life.

'Why so serious?' Lucy had opened one eye and was shading it with the back of her hand as she looked at me.

I made myself relax. I was not going to fuck *this* up. 'I was just wondering if it was worth risking a slapped face if I reached over and kissed you.'

She closed her eye and rested her hands across her stomach. 'You'll never know unless you try,' her expression inscrutable, 'but be warned – I know t'ai chi.'

I was in a quandary. I'd planted the idea in her head, but she hadn't exactly given me the thumbs up.

Her eye opened again. 'What's the matter, Jim? Scared I'm going to turn you into a pile of chopped liver?' Then her lips began to quiver, and she started to laugh. 'Come here, why don't you?' and she reached up, hooked a hand around the back of my neck and pulled me down to her.

The kiss was soft and sweet, and I could feel all the sense I was born with deserting me. I wasn't ready for a relationship. I wasn't in the right place inside myself to start a new relationship. I didn't even know if I'd still be in Slyford St James this time next week. All this went through my head and mattered for probably a nanosecond, then I was kissing her back and it was like our lips were meant for each other.

Soft kisses became a little bit more as I wrapped my arms around her and we snuggled up close, but as much as I wanted her, and I wanted her a lot, somewhere at the back of my mind I had this strange little feeling like I was being . . . tested. There was nothing in her kiss or in the way she pressed against me to suggest this; it was just, I don't know, maybe intuition.

So, I stroked her hair, nuzzled her neck and resisted everything but non-threatening foreplay as if we were fifteen-year-old virgins. When eventually I lay flat on my back and she snuggled up against my chest I was pretty sure it'd been the right move. That didn't stop me from being rock hard, but in a funny way even that was good, like a promise of good times to come.

We lay there for a bit, me stroking her hair and Lucy resting her hand on my chest right above my heart as though checking I had one and it was hers for the taking.

'Want another beer?' she asked.

I kissed the top of her head. 'I'll have a drop of wine if there's still some going.'

She gave me a hug, then pushed herself onto her knees and lifted the bottle so I could see it was over two-thirds full. 'Plenty,' she said and got another glass out of her rucksack.

I sat up to join her and shuffled back so I was leaning against a rock. She passed me a glass and I took a sip. 'Still cold,' I said.

'Hmm. Lovely.'

'Yes, you are.'

She grinned at me and moved closer, so she was sitting next to me, our shoulders brushing. 'So are you, actually,' she said, 'for a Londoner, that is,' and there was something wistful in her voice that made me turn my head to look at her, really look at her.

'Something you want to share?' I asked, knowing there damn well was something, but not sure what.

Maybe the ex, maybe something or someone else, but my money was on the ex.

She gave a little sigh. 'Not really, not here, not now.' When she looked at me her smile was overbright. 'I don't want to spoil our day.'

'Hey, whatever you say, unless it's "I never want to see you again", won't spoil it for me.'

She turned onto her knees and, putting her glass down beside her, took my head in her hands and gently kissed my lips. 'You're a good man.'

It was my turn for a smile to fade. 'No – no, I'm not, but I'd like to be.'

She stared into my eyes as though searching for my soul. 'I think you're probably better than you know. Anyway, I think I'd like to find out.'

'Good,' I said. 'I'd like that too.'

We packed up our things pretty soon after that. We finished off the wine as it would be one less thing to carry, and despite her arguing, I carried the rucksack. With the food and wine gone it was pretty light with only our empties, cutlery and the blanket to carry away with us.

We took the climb up from the bay slowly, not just because it was steep, but I think neither of us really wanted our day to end. When we reached the top, her hand slipped into mine and we started the slow walk home, and it was slow. After a while I slipped my arm around her shoulders and now and then we would stop to look out over the sea and have another kiss. It was weird, though. It was almost as though we both felt like it was the last time we'd be together before a long, enforced separation, and what made me think that I'll never know.

Maybe we were just scared it was too young and fragile to last, or maybe it was something to do with us both having our own demons rampaging around in our heads. I knew I had mine and now I'd a suspicion I wasn't the only one.

All too soon we were stepping off the path and into the lane leading us home. I really didn't want this day to end and I didn't want to say goodbye. The memory of the bitter-sweet feeling I'd felt earlier making me scared that when we parted it would be for good.

When we reached the end of my lane we stopped. I wasn't sure whether to invite her back or whether this would appear a bit forward, like I was after something and she'd have a pretty good idea what.

'I'll walk you back,' I said.

'You can – later. Do you mind if I use your loo?'

'No, not at all.'

'If I go back now, Dad will only have me washing glasses and stacking dishes,' she said as we started off towards the cottage, and I must admit there was a spring to my step that hadn't been there before. This was until I heard the mower going from what could only be my back garden.

'I don't believe this,' I muttered as we reached the gate, and Lucy started to laugh. I glanced her way. 'Do you still want to come in?'

'When a girl's gotta go a girl's gotta go, and anyway,

Jed might be many things, but he's not a gossip. My reputation will remain intact.'

I didn't want to disillusion her – to my way of thinking Jed gossiped as much as the next person.

I opened the front door and directed Lucy upstairs, then walked through to the kitchen to unlock the back door and go out into the garden. Jed had his back to me and looked as though he was finishing up. He pushed the mower back and forth two or three more times then killed the engine and pulled a large white hanky from his back pocket and wiped it across his brow.

'It's not Thursday, is it?' I asked, and he swung around, his face creasing into what looked to me like a relieved smile.

'Friday, actually. I missed yesterday and was going to leave it until next week, but Emms was worried, you see, and when you weren't here when I arrived, I thought I might as well . . .' and he gestured around the garden.

'Worried?' I asked, latching onto what he had said about Emma.

'She thought we'd have heard from you after the other night and when it was coming up to two days and not a word,' he gave a shrug, 'she started to think the worst.'

'The worst?'

'Like maybe you'd – I don't know, gone back to London, drunk yourself into a stupor, had an accident,' he lowered his voice, 'been murdered.'

I started to feel really bad. Of course they'd been worried. 'I'm sorry I just—'

Before I could say any more, Jed's attention shifted to over my shoulder and his face lit up into a beaming smile. 'Hello, Lucy, my love.'

'Hi, Jed. Keeping busy, I see.'

'No rest for the wicked.'

'Shall I put the kettle on?' Lucy asked, touching my arm.

'Thanks,' I replied with a smile and had to force myself to drag my eyes away from her backside as she sauntered back into the cottage as though it was the most natural place in the world for her to be.

When I turned back to Jed, he raised an eyebrow and grinned. 'I can see why we haven't seen hide nor hair of you today.'

'I'm sorry you were worried.'

He flapped a hand at me. 'Emma will be pleased you've been enjoying yourself for once.'

'You'll come in and have a coffee when you've finished up?'

'If you're sure?'

'Of course,' I said and went back inside to see what Lucy was doing.

She was standing in the kitchen, leaning with her back against the kitchen sink waiting for the kettle to boil, but my eyes were immediately drawn to the open notebook lying on the table. Had it been open when I'd walked through the kitchen earlier? I didn't think so. I glanced Lucy's way and she smiled in a way that made most of the brains I was born with disappear down south. It wasn't the look of a woman who'd been reading something they really shouldn't have.

I flipped the notebook shut and moved to stand in front of her, pushing it firmly from my mind. It was a day for good thoughts not those nightmares are made of. They would no doubt come when she'd left for the night.

She reached up and slipped her hands around my neck and I moved in for the kiss. 'I could get used to this,' I whispered against her cheek.

'Hmm, so could I.'

'When you're not at the pub, where do you live?' I asked.

'I'm staying with a friend in Exeter, but it's only temporary, until I find a place of my own.'

'When are you going back?'

'Trying to get rid of me already?' she said, but her eyes were twinkling.

I didn't get the chance to reply as there was a rap on the door and I jumped away from her like a startled cat.

'Come in,' I said, hurrying to the door.

I heard Lucy chuckle, but when I glanced around she was busying herself with making the coffee.

I pulled the door open. 'Come in,' I said again.

'Are you certain?' Jed whispered to me.

'You'd better,' Lucy called, 'I've poured you a coffee.'

Jed took his usual seat at the table and I joined him while Lucy lounged against the sink. His eyes went straight to the notebook and then to mine and I could tell he was dying to say something, but he very sensibly kept it to himself. Whatever it was I'm sure it wasn't something Lucy should hear.

'Have you had a good day?' he asked.

'I took Jim to Saint's Bay.'

'Nice spot.'

'I enjoyed it,' I said.

'Next time we'll have to walk to Chalfont,' she said.

'I'd like that.'

'I'm working tomorrow,' she said. 'Letting Mum take a day off for once, but maybe the next day if the weather holds – if you're up for it?'

'Sounds good to me.'

Jed took a swig of his coffee and put his mug down next to the notebook, giving me a pointed look. 'Then I'll come around tomorrow, if that's OK? Just to finish tidying up the garden.'

'Fine by me.' And it was. There were a couple of things I wanted to ask him, one being did he know who it was Darcy Garvin might be visiting at Goldsmere House. I wasn't sure whether it was important or not, but I'd been drawn to the place for a reason.

Lucy asked Jed about what he'd been up to, I think probably to stop him feeling awkward, and we chatted about this and that until he downed the last of his coffee and got to his feet.

'I'll be off now,' he said, 'and I'll see you tomorrow – about nine?'

'That's good for me,' I said, seeing him out the back door.

He hesitated just outside, and I took the hint and walked with him around to the front.

'I'm really sorry you and Emma were worried,' I said as we rounded the side of the cottage and out of Lucy's earshot.

'You're all right, that's the main thing.'

'I do need to speak to you.'

'You can do that tomorrow. I think you have better things to be doing with your time at the moment,' and he slapped me on the back as we reached the front gate. 'It'll do you good to mix with someone of your own age instead of us two old fogies.'

'I'll see you tomorrow.'

'That you will, lad, that you will,' and with a farewell flip of the hand he started off down the lane and didn't look back.

I watched him until he turned the corner and then wandered back around the side of the cottage and into the kitchen. Lucy had washed the mugs and was sitting at the table in the spot Jed had so recently left. The notebook was unopened and where I'd left it.

I bet the nosey bint's been sticky-beaking.

And I had to fight back a sudden surge of anger. Not now, not now.

Butter wouldn't melt; little prick tease.

Stop it.

'Are you all right?' Lucy asked, turning in the chair to look at me.

I took a deep breath and forced myself to smile. 'Sorry, miles away.'

She rose from the chair to walk around and stand

in front of me, reaching up to run her fingers down my cheek. I wrapped my hand around hers and moved it to my lips, kissing her knuckles.

'I can stay for a while longer,' she said and her voice had a slightly husky sound to it that was enough to let me know Lucy might be a lot of things, but I doubted very much a prick tease was one of them, and I think *the man* knew too as his voice grew silent.

CHAPTER TWENTY-ONE

I walked Lucy back to the pub just after closing time. The lights were on, so I assumed George and his wife were still clearing up.

'Do you think I should come in and say hi?' I asked.

She grinned at me. 'Better not.'

'You think your parents will mind – you know, you seeing me?'

'No, not that it's any of their business, but I'll get the third degree out of the way first.'

'Oh?'

'Nothing to worry about. If we start seeing each other regularly, then we can do the whole meeting the parents thing.'

'I hope we will.'

She smiled up at me. 'So do I,' then she gave me a kiss that had me wishing I could drag her back to the cottage, whispered 'goodbye' and disappeared inside.

I could hear voices before I'd even had a chance to turn away. I hesitated a moment, waiting for gruff anger, then heard feminine laughter followed by a masculine chuckle. Lucy could probably wrap George around her little finger like most daughters could their fathers.

The walk back to the cottage was a lonely one, though I couldn't believe how happy I was. Floating-on-air happy was about the gist of it. Once inside I locked up and then set about washing the glasses and dishes from the makeshift picnic supper we'd had in bed. I'd had no white wine, but Lucy said the red went better with the cheese and crackers, which was about all I had that didn't need cooking – and who had the time for that? We certainly didn't.

I went around checking all the windows and the outside doors, even though I'd checked them all before I went out that morning and quickly again before walking Lucy home. I wondered whether I was getting a bit OCD. Then I supposed someone having tried to kill me would excuse me if I was. I quickly pushed the thought from my mind. Tonight, I was going to be happy. I'd had a good day and an even better evening, and I was damn well going to have a good night.

And, strangely enough, I did.

Jed was early, arriving just as I was pouring the boiling water into my mug. I was beginning to think he could smell a mug of java or a glass of the hard stuff from a mile away.

'Want one?'

'Wouldn't say no,' he said, sinking down at the table.

I handed him a mug and then slouched down into the seat opposite, the notebook on the table between us seemingly filling the space.

I stretched out my hand, laying it on the book and sliding it towards me. I flipped the cover open, leafing through the pages until I reached the last sheet of my scrawled writing. Then I pushed it back across the table to Jed.

He looked down at the page, then his eyes lifted to meet mine.

'What does it mean?'

'I think he's trying to let me know that someone tried to murder him, though why *he* should think I'd care I haven't a clue. He was – is – a monster as far as I'm concerned.'

'You couldn't have . . .' he trailed off, rubbing his chin and grimacing. 'Sorry, stupid question.'

'Not really. I've been asking myself the same thing.' Or at least the voices in my head had been inferring it, but I wasn't about to tell Jed that. He might be open-minded when it came to the supernatural, but I doubted that open-minded.

'Can I read it?' he asked.

'Do you want to?'

'Not really, but I think maybe I should.'

I gestured for him to go ahead. With a sigh he pulled a glasses case out of his top pocket, and perching a pair of those half-lens spectacles on the end of his nose, began to read, his forefinger tracing his progress.

I finished my coffee and washed up our mugs, then generally pottered about leaving him to it. Judging by the speed of Jed's finger crossing the page it was going to take him some time. After ten minutes or so I went outside into the garden just for something to do as being in the kitchen watching him read was beginning to make me feel claustrophobic and antsy.

I was sitting on the doorstep when the door opened and he joined me outside. With a grunt he lowered himself down to sit beside me. I glanced his way; his expression was grim, his eyes narrowed and fixed at some point at the end of the garden. His usually ruddy complexion had taken on a sallow look.

Twice he opened his mouth to say something and twice his lips pressed back together in a thin line. I'd always thought Jed was probably about fifty, maybe fifty-five, but this morning he looked like if he wasn't already collecting his pension it could be sometime very soon.

The third time he opened his mouth he managed to speak. 'You saw all that, did yer?'

'In glorious Technicolor.'

He let out a long deep breath and shivered. 'There've been a couple of times that I've considered my gift to be something I wouldn't wish upon my worst enemy, but,' he paused and shuddered, 'what you've written in that notebook, what you say you saw—'

'Did see, Jed, I did see it,' I told him, my voice little more than a whisper.

He nodded and I could see his jaw muscles working like he was grinding his teeth or trying very hard to speak but nothing was coming. 'What you saw was like looking into the depths of hell.'

'I know.'

'How can you live with it?' he asked, at last turning to look at me.

'Yesterday I would have told you I wasn't sure I could.'

'And today?'

'Today I have hope.'

'Lucy?'

I looked away. 'I know it's early days and nothing might come of it, but I'm moving on. I've a reason to go on that has nothing to do with dead children and murdered priests.'

'But will he let you go?'

I laughed. 'No. No, he wants something from me. I'm sure of it.'

'And Krystal?'

'To me, she's the important one.'

Jed took a deep breath and then clambered to his feet and held out his hand to pull me up after him. 'It's too early for a drop of the hard stuff so if you don't mind, I'll have another mug of coffee.'

'Tell you what – how about we go for a drive over to Chalfont and I'll buy you a coffee and a muffin?'

He gave me a strange look. 'What's over at Chalfont?'

'I'm not sure, but humour me.'

He clapped me on the shoulder. 'All right, I hadn't much planned for today anyhow.'

I made straight for Goldsmere House. As we turned down the lane Jed shifted in his seat and frowned through the windscreen. To his credit he didn't say a word until I pulled up outside the main gate.

'If you're thinking of having me committed, I'm pretty sure you'll find you need at least two doctors' signatures on the papers,' he said, peering down the drive.

'So, it is an asylum?'

Jed turned in his seat to look at me. 'So some of the locals would say, but as far as I know it's a private care home for patients who can't be looked after in run-of-the-mill old people's homes.'

'How do you mean?'

'Old people with dementia and the like. Not all care homes will take them. Dementia can be a terrible thing, makes some poor souls violent and others just can't look after themselves in even the most basic way, if you get my meaning.'

I leant forward so I could get a look through the gates and up the drive to the building. Judging by the security Goldsmere House had in place, I suspected it didn't have anything to do with old people with incontinence problems. It also looked too high-tech just to be a show to pay lip service to the locals and their concerns.

'It's private, you say?'

Jed nodded and rubbed his beard. 'I've heard it's mighty expensive, and by the looks of it I think I've probably heard right.'

I looked towards the cameras on the top of the gates and sure enough they were pointing down at the car. I took off the handbrake and shifted into gear. If I wasn't careful, I was going to make someone in there start wondering about me and I'd have trouble coming up with any sort of logical answer as to why I kept turning up outside their gates.

'Why the interest?' Jed asked as we pulled back onto the main road.

'I wasn't really sure until the other day when I found myself turning into the lane for no apparent reason and pulling up outside the gate.'

'Do you think this is where *he* is? In your notebook you say there was a man in a hospital bed.'

'Possibly, but here's the thing. When I was here last time a car was leaving, so I pulled to one side to let it pass, and you'll never guess who was at the wheel.'

Jed frowned at me. 'Someone we both know?'

I nodded.

'Not Emms?'

'Why would Emma be visiting the place?'

Jed let out a relieved sigh and began to laugh. 'No reason, but you were beginning to make me wonder.'

'No, who else do we both know?'

Jed's brow creased in concentration. 'No idea.'

'Darcy Garvin.'

Jed's eyebrows shot up into his shaggy fringe. 'Darcy Garvin? No. Are you sure?'

'Absolutely,' I said.

'Well I never,' Jed said and sank back down into his seat. He didn't say another word until we reached Chalfont.

I parked in the same small car park behind the shops and after I stuck some change in the meter, we went straight to the small cafe Jed liked so much.

Once we'd placed our order and Lil had disappeared behind the counter to make our coffee, I started back where we left off.

'So, can you think of why Darcy would be at Goldsmere House?'

Jed shook his head. 'No, not at all.'

'Elderly parents?'

'No, as far as I'm aware they were brought up by their grandmother. Their parents died when they were little more than toddlers, from what I've heard.'

'And there were only the two of them?'

'Aye. Them and the old girl.'

'So they've always lived in Slyford St James?'

'As far as I know,' he said, but there was an edge to his voice.

At that moment Lil appeared with our order and she and Jed exchanged pleasantries while she laid the table and presented us with our order.

When she was gone, I watched him stir his drink. I was missing something, I was sure of it. 'I thought you'd always lived in Slyford?'

He didn't look up from his cup. 'Slyford born and bred.'

'But you haven't always lived there.'

He glanced up at me, dropped the spoon on the side of his saucer and leant back in his chair, fixing me with an inscrutable stare.

'No, I went away to boarding school when I was twelve.'

'Really?' Now he had surprised me.

'Yep.'

'So the Garvin girls would have only been kids when you left?'

'Possibly. I didn't know them then. I knew their grandmother, everyone did, she thought she was lady of the manor and we were all her serfs.' He began to laugh. 'She had an old roller and a chauffeur who was a hundred and ten if he was a day. He used to ferry her around the place while she sat in the back with her nose in the air like she could smell the great unwashed walking the streets around her.' He paused rubbing his head. 'Come to think of it, she used to live at The Grange. It was sold on not long after she died, probably to pay death duties, I shouldn't wonder.'

'So, you came back when you finished school?'

'For a while, but not really to stay until about twenty years ago when my ma died. She left me the house, so I've been here ever since.'

'So you came back about the same time as Emma and her husband moved here.'

'A bit before.'

I thought about it for a moment. 'Emma told me . . .'

What had Emma told me? Then I remembered. 'Emma told me you used to look after the garden at The Grange, and when she and her husband moved in you carried on looking after it for them.'

'That's right.' He started peeling the corrugated wrapper away from his chocolate muffin and paying it a lot more attention than it warranted.

'But you were friends with Reggie and Emma before.'

Jed placed the muffin back on its plate and gave me a very long, hard look. 'Not everything is some great mystery, you know.'

'Then why make it seem like it is?'

He breathed out a long and ragged breath as though releasing some pent-up emotion. Anger perhaps? Or something else? 'I met Reggie when I was in the army. We were friends, and when he married Emma, she became my friend too. Reggie's health began to deteriorate, and they wanted to move away from the city. They came to Slyford to stay for a while and when I heard The Grange was going up for sale, I told them. They bought it, I continued to keep it tidy, and there you have it.'

But that's not all the story.

I let it lie. It was, when all was said and done, none of my bloody business, but that didn't stop me from wondering.

'So, going back to Darcy – why do you think she was up at Goldsmere House?'

Jed returned to picking at the wrapping around his muffin. 'No idea, but I could ask around a bit. There's a few old boys at the pub who have never left Slyford for more than a couple of weeks at a time, except for perhaps during the war, and they'll flap their chops for the price of a pint.'

'Cedric?'

'Aye, he's one,' Jed said with a laugh, his humour returning now we were on a safe topic. 'You've met him, then?'

'He's the one who told me Goldsmere was a "loony bin".'

'Not one for political correctness is our Cedric, but if anyone knows anything interesting about the Garvin girls it'll probably be him.'

'I saw them in the street just outside here a few days ago,' I said, suddenly remembering. 'I think they were having a row. Darcy looked furious and Miriam was practically having to trot along to keep up.'

'I'm not surprised. They may be sisters, but they're like chalk and cheese. About the only thing they have in common is their interest in spiritualism,' Jed said, breaking a piece of his muffin and popping it into his mouth. His face lit up as he chewed on it. 'Heaven.'

I broke a lump off mine and for a minute or so both Jed and I munched away happily in silence, washing the chocolate sponge down with swigs of coffee.

'They argue like cat and dog.'

'Pardon?'

'Darcy and Miriam.'

'Siblings can be like that.'

'Hmm. That was good, thanks,' he said, screwing up

the empty paper wrapper and dropping it on his plate.

I caught Lil's eye and she hurried over with the bill. 'See you both again soon, I hope,' she said, beaming after seeing the over-the-top tip I'd left her.

'Next week, if not before,' Jed told her. 'Emma's got a hairdressing appointment, so I expect I'll bring her over.'

We said our goodbyes and took a leisurely walk back to the car. It was quiet out on the street. A car was idling outside the paper shop just up the road and an overwrought mother was trying to calm a screaming infant as it struggled in her arms while her other child tugged at her skirt shouting 'Mummy, mummy' as he pointed at something in the toyshop window. I noticed a poster had joined the Halloween display advertising fireworks as the next of the year's main events, reminding me winter would soon be on its way despite the warm weather we were having.

'Do you want to come back to Emma's?' Jed asked as we drove out of the car park. 'I know she'd like to see you.'

'If we won't be intruding?'

'It's a nice day. We'll drag her out to the pub. If anyone can get old Cedric talking it's Emms. She's more subtle than I am, so it won't be so obvious that we're digging.'

It was a good idea. I hardly wanted either of the Garvin sisters to find out I was enquiring about them. Particularly if one of them knew 'the man' and had tried to do away with him. As far-fetched as it might seem, it could have been Darcy I'd seen pushing him off the cliff, and it could have been Darcy I'd seen at the cemetery. Then again it could have been someone else altogether and her visit to Goldsmere House could have been to see an elderly family friend or neighbour.

Perhaps Jed was right – not everything was a mystery. In this particular case, though, I wasn't so sure. I felt like I'd been drawn to the place, and if I had it'd been for a reason.

We dropped the car off at the cottage before walking around to Emma's, seeing as there was a possibility we'd be going on to the pub. We found her sitting out on her terrace reading the newspaper and nursing a cup of tea. On seeing me she got up and gave me a huge hug.

'I'm so glad you're all right,' she said. 'I was worried.'

I felt my cheeks heat up enough to glow. 'I'm sorry,' I told her. 'I should have at least called you or Jed.'

'No matter. No matter,' she said, patting my arm and gesturing that I should sit. 'Tea?'

'No thanks,' I replied.

'Jed?'

'Me neither, thanks. We've just got back from Chalfont and a couple of Lil's muffins.'

'So,' Emma said, turning her attention back to me. 'Jed tells me you've been stepping out with Lucy Duffield.'

And if my cheeks hadn't been red before they certainly were on fire now.

'Emma! Give the lad a break.'

'Jim doesn't mind, do you, Jim?'

'You're embarrassing him.'

'You're not embarrassed, are you?'

'Um . . .'

'Emms, I could boil a kettle on his face.'

'She's a lovely girl,' Emma said, unperturbed.

'Yes,' I said, 'she is.'

'Maybe you'll think twice about leaving?'

'Maybe.'

'Emma,' Jed interrupted and shot me an apologetic look, 'you know the Garvin girls pretty well.'

She gave him a quizzical look. 'As well as one can do, I suppose. They're a strange pair. Miriam prattles on, but not about anything much that really matters.'

'I seem to recall they were brought up by their grandmother.'

Emma frowned as she thought about it. 'I'd not heard that one.' She frowned some more. 'Do you know something? Now I think on it, I don't really know much about them at all.'

'What do you mean?' I asked.

'It's as I said. Miriam does most of the talking.'

'She can talk for England that one,' Jed mumbled.

Emma shushed him with the flap of her hand. 'But it's about nothing personal.'

Jed stroked his beard, staring at her for a moment. 'Do you know what? You're right. When I think about it, I know nothing much about them either, and anything I do I reckon is hearsay.'

'Where did you hear about their parents dying and them living with their grandmother?' I asked.

'It wasn't from them, I'm pretty sure,' he said. 'My ma probably told me. I knew they lived with the old girl as I'd sometimes see them in the back of the car with her, when I came home from school for the holidays.'

'Why so interested?' Emma asked.

'Jim here saw Darcy coming out of that care home on the way to Chalfont.'

'Goldsmere?'

'The same.'

Emma turned her attention back to me. 'You think she might be visiting this man you keep seeing in your head?'

I shrugged. 'It's a possibility.'

Emma wrapped her arms around herself and shivered.

'Are you cold?' Jed asked.

She shook her head. 'No, not cold.' She gave him a tight smile. 'Afraid . . . I feel afraid.'

CHAPTER TWENTY-TWO

Jed said Cedric usually arrived at the Sly just after twelve and stayed there nursing a pint to almost two. The only time he missed his lunchtime pint was when his daughter came over once a week to do his washing and cleaning and drop off a load of dinners she had precooked for his freezer.

'He may be an old curmudgeon,' Jed said, 'but he loves his daughter.'

Sure enough, when we walked in, he was the sole patron and sitting at the end of the bar. George was poring over his newspaper, pencil in hand. I wasn't sure what his reaction to me would be after my day out with his daughter, but his smile was welcoming enough, though it was probably more for Emma's benefit than mine or Jed's.

'Two pints and a VAT,' Jed said, 'and put one in the pipe for Cedric and yourself while you're at it.'

'You won the pools or something?' Cedric asked.

'Nah, just thought I might raise a smile on your miserable, old face.'

Cedric grinned at him showing missing teeth. 'Well, you got your wish. Thanking you.'

'And how are you, Cedric?' Emma asked.

'Pretty well, all considered.'

'Becki been around this week yet?'

'Tomorrow. This week she's coming tomorrow as she's got a thing at little Maisie's school the day after.'

While Emma chatted to Cedric, George poured and served our drinks, then went out back. When he returned he was followed by Lucy.

She gave me a slow, warm smile that had my heart doing cartwheels and then leant across the bar to give me an unexpected peck on the cheek. I heard Jed chuckle from beside me, but I didn't care.

'Just thought I'd pop out to say hello,' she said. 'You still on for tomorrow?'

'Looking forward to it.'

'Good,' she said.

'Can I buy you a drink?' I asked.

She glanced at her father. 'Go on, take a few minutes – we're hardly busy,' he told her.

She grinned at me. 'Then yes, please, a white wine would be good.'

'Put it on my tab,' Jed said and raised a hand to stop me before I could argue. 'This one's on me.'

'Thanks, Jed.'

'You two young folk sit down, we'll be with you in

a bit,' Jed said, passing Emma her drink and joining her and Cedric. Crafty old goat, he was giving me and Lucy some space and at the same time keeping her out of the way while he and Emma tried to get some information about the Garvin girls from the old man.

We sat down at Jed's usual table, leaving his seat in the corner free.

'I wasn't expecting to see you so soon,' Lucy said.

'I think Emma and Jed are trying their hands at matchmaking.'

'A bit late for that,' she said, her eyes sparkling.

I took hold of her hand. 'Yeah, just a bit.'

'They'd make a nice couple themselves.'

'I think so.'

'Maybe we should try a bit of the same with them.'

'No need,' I told her. 'They'll get there in the end.'

'If they haven't already.' She took a sip of her drink. 'I hope the weather holds for tomorrow.'

'They're saying this could go on right into October.'

'It'd be nice.'

'Your dad was OK about you seeing me, then?'

'Surprisingly enough, yes, he was.'

I raised an eyebrow at that. 'Surprisingly?'

'I don't think I've ever had a boyfriend who he's liked, but when I said I was going out with you for the day he didn't bat an eyelid.'

'Maybe he doesn't expect it will last,' I said, looking down at the fingers curled around mine and giving them a squeeze.

She squeezed back. 'I think it's more like he's expecting it will.'

I mulled on that for a bit while Lucy sipped her wine. At one time such a comment from a new girlfriend would have seen me running for the hills, instead I could feel my lips curling into a stupid smile.

'Are you all going to stay for lunch?' Lucy asked, glancing towards where Jed and Emma were still chatting to Cedric.

'I probably shouldn't, but your mother's chips are to die for.'

'Ah, her secret recipe.'

'Do you know it?'

She tapped the side of her nose with her forefinger. 'It's a secret passed down from mother to daughter.'

'In which case I'm going to have to buy a deep-fat fryer.'

She grinned at me. 'I'd better get back to work if I'm going to be cooking up a load of Mum's chips.' She knocked back the rest of her drink, gave me a quick peck on the lips and got to her feet. 'I'll see you before you go.'

I returned her smile, then watched her walk away until she disappeared out into the kitchen.

'Well, it was lovely speaking to you, Cedric. Give Becki my regards,' I heard Emma say, and she and Jed made their way over to the table as the old boy paid up his tab.

'We're going to eat,' Jed said as he sank down onto the chair opposite. 'You want something?'

'At a risk to my waistline, I think I will.'

'Della's chips?' Jed asked with a chuckle.

'Oh yes.'

'They are exceptionally good,' Emma said, handing me a menu. 'Every time I eat here I promise myself I'll have salad, but I always succumb.'

George appeared from behind the bar to take our orders. As soon as he'd gone out back and we were alone, Jed and Emma moved their chairs in closer, leaning over the table.

'Learn anything interesting?' I asked, and realised I was whispering.

'We did, though Cedric's probably left us with more questions than answers,' Emma said, 'but it reached the stage that if I'd asked him any more he would have begun to wonder why we were so interested.'

'So, what did you find out?'

'To start with, the Garvin girls were indeed brought up by their grandmother. Apparently, their mother died when they were both very young. Miriam wasn't much more than a toddler.'

'I was right about Darcy being the eldest,' Jed said.

'I was sure Miriam said something about looking after the baby,' Emma said with a puzzled frown, her brow knotted as though she was trying to remember.

'Cedric said there was some sort of scandal back in the early seventies concerning their father, Phillip Garvin. He couldn't remember what it was all about, but he did recall that there was a woman involved and old Ma Garvin got sonny Jim out of the way pretty damn fast.'

'This was after their mother died?'

'So Cedric said.'

'But why would the girls' father getting into a new relationship cause a problem?'

Emma gave a sigh. 'The young woman was probably considered unsuitable. Apparently, the Garvins were old money and those sorts of people have expectations of their children and the social standing of their potential spouses. With me and Reggie it was the same. It didn't go down at all well with his family when he married me.'

'Really?' I asked, surprised.

'Again, they were old money, but Reggie didn't care.'

'I should bloody well think not,' Jed said, and Emma patted his hand.

'Reggie stood up to his family, apparently Phillip Garvin didn't,' Emma said.

We sat in silence for a few moments. Then a thought occurred to me. 'Do you think this woman was pregnant?' I asked.

'Pregnant?' Jed said in surprise.

I shot him a look. 'Why else would his mother get him out of the way so quick?'

Emma leant back in her seat. 'It makes sense. Not so many young women were on the pill in those days and certainly not in rural areas like here,' Emma said.

'I wonder what happened to her,' I said.

'She can't have stayed around here, otherwise everyone would have known about it,' Jed said.

'They probably paid her off,' Emma said, and with that Lucy and George came over with our meals, ending our deliberations.

We didn't resume our conversation until we were walking home. I'd said a quick goodbye to Lucy, and she promised to be knocking on my door at ten the following morning, which made me happier than I'd have thought possible. Consequently, I was practically walking on air when we left the pub. Jed and Emma soon brought me back to earth with a bump.

'What happened to Phillip Garvin, do you think?' Emma asked.

'Ah,' Jed said, and there was something about his tone that made both Emma and I look his way. 'Now there is a story.'

'Jed?'

'He never came back to Slyford St James.'

'What? He deserted his children?' Emma was outraged.

'Not really, though I suppose he did in a way. By all accounts he was a weak man.'

'Sounds it – ditching his girlfriend and running away on his mother's say-so,' Emma said.

'Well, after hearing what Cedric had to say, a few things are beginning to make sense,' Jed said. 'I was only about nine or ten when this was all happening so none of it meant much to me, but I do remember Phillip's funeral.'

'He died?' I asked, glancing his way.

Jed gave a bob of the head. 'It was very sudden, rumour had it that it was suicide, but the family said a hunting

342

accident. Anyway, the village practically closed down for the morning. I still remember the coach being pulled by four black horses. They were the blackest creatures I'd ever seen.' We stopped at the corner of my lane. 'I said that to my ma, and you know what she said?'

Emma and I both dutifully shook our heads as he looked at us in turn. 'She said they were nowhere near as black as Ma Garvin's heart.'

'What did she mean by that?' Emma asked.

Jed stroked his beard in thought. 'I have no idea,' he said. 'When I tried to draw Ma on it further, she refused to say any more and clipped me round the ear for being a nuisance. To be honest, I'd pretty much forgotten about it until today.'

'I wonder what drove him to suicide?' Emma asked.

'If it was suicide, Emms – it was only a rumour. You know what it's like around here.'

'I suppose,' she said with a sigh.

'Well, I'll be seeing you,' I told them.

'What are you doing tomorrow?' Emma asked.

'He has a date with the lovely Lucy,' Jed said before I could answer, and it felt like my cheeks had turned the colour of cherries.

Emma's face lit up. 'You make a lovely couple.'

'Easy on, Emms, it's only their second date.'

'I reckon she could be the one,' Emma said.

'You'll scare the poor lad off.'

'If he's stupid enough to let Lucy slip through his fingers without at least making a play for her, then she

343

deserves better. You men can't see what's right in front of your noses,' Emma said, and she wasn't smiling. Then she gave me a brisk kiss on the cheek and was marching off towards The Grange with Jed staring after her with a nonplussed expression upon his face.

'What's got into her?' he muttered.

I couldn't help myself and started to laugh. 'I think you'd better try and catch up with her to find out.'

He pulled at the end of his beard. 'Women! I don't think I'll ever understand 'em.'

'I don't think you're meant to,' I told him.

He gave a grunt in farewell and strode off along the lane after Emma. I was still chuckling when I let myself into the cottage. I had a feeling Emma was perhaps getting fed up with waiting for Jed to make the first move.

The notebook was in the middle of the kitchen table where I'd left it. I ignored it. I didn't need to read it again and, in fact, it would probably be best if I destroyed it. They were the demented ramblings of a seriously sick mind and I really didn't want anyone reading them and thinking they were mine. They'd lock me up and throw away the key.

It was a sobering thought and the two pints I'd sunk at the pub had suddenly become as alcoholic as water. I picked up the notebook, opened it and, gripping hold of the first four pages, ripped them out from the spine. I threw the book onto the table and, taking the sheets of paper in both hands, tore them in two, then scrunched them into a ball and threw them in the bin.

'Good riddance,' I whispered to myself and slumped down at the kitchen table.

I probably sat there for less than thirty seconds before I was on my feet again and delving into the bin to retrieve my scrawled notes. Tearing them in two just wasn't good enough. If something inexplicable happened to Emma, Jed or me between now and when I emptied the bin and the rubbish had been collected, I knew exactly what would happen. Inspector Barnaby's clone would get his sidekick to go through my rubbish, they would find the notes and job done – I was the psycho who had committed whatever foul play they were investigating.

Then I wondered what the fuck I was thinking.

They tried to kill you and frame you once – who's to say they won't try again?

I let out a shuddery breath. I knew I was letting my paranoia get the better of me, but the notes had to go. Jed had read them; he knew what they said. He knew what we were dealing with. No one else needed to know.

I threw the crumpled paper in the sink, tore another page from the notebook and turned on the hob, holding the edge of the sheet into the flame until it blackened and flared. Then, cupping my hand around the flame, I took the couple of steps to the sink and held it to the pages until they too caught alight. I added some scrunched-up kitchen roll to the fire and kept it burning until every last scrap was burnt to blackened fragments, then turned on the tap and washed them away.

Even that wasn't enough. I rinsed the stainless steel bowl around with bleach to get rid of the residue and gave it a good clean, then poured more bleach down the plughole and ran the hot tap until the water steamed.

'Let's see you put that all back together again,' I said, and immediately wished I hadn't as it was almost as though I was setting my nemesis a challenge. Then I realised how mad that sounded, even to me.

I poured some more bleach down the sink, stomped out of the kitchen and into the living room and spent the afternoon channel-hopping.

By eight o'clock I was sorely tempted to make for the pub, not for a drink – well, maybe for a drink, but mainly to see Lucy. When I was with her all the bad stuff disappeared. With her I felt good about myself. The thing was I didn't want her to think me too keen. I'd learnt from experience there is a fine line between making a girl feel like you were more than a little interested in a good way as opposed to that you were practically stalking her.

So at eight-thirty I ate baked beans out of the saucepan, had one can of lager while watching a ridiculously awful talent show and was in bed by ten.

Bad move – I tossed and turned and just couldn't nod off. At eleven-thirty I switched on the bedside light. It was no good, I was never going to fall asleep. I swung my legs out of the bed, pulled on a pair of jeans and stepped into my deck shoes to pad downstairs in search of something to read. There were plenty of books in the living room. I'd given them a cursory look when I'd first arrived, but not much more, though I was sure that there must be at least one novel or biography that would capture my interest.

I was to be disappointed. My first impression when I'd arrived was the right one, most of the books had been provided by the estate agent to make the place look more homely. There were books on gardening, there were books on the countryside, there were books on Devon and the surrounding area, there were books on Devonshire fauna and flora – but not one of interest to me.

I flopped down on the settee and let my eyes drift around the rest of the room. Then I noticed a few more books lying on their sides in a pile in a small corner cabinet. I got up to take a closer look. I was desperate now. If one of them was about anything other than plants and the Devonshire countryside, I'd give it a go.

I crouched down in front of the cabinet to take a look. There were three in all, two slim, hard-backed volumes and one paperback that looked like it could be a novel. I reached in to grab all three and rocked back on my heels to balance the pile on my knee.

They had been Krystal's books, I was pretty sure. The novel was one of the Narnia series. I'd read it as a boy. The two others were illustrated storybooks and well thumbed. Probably her favourites from when she had first learnt to read. I was proven right when I opened the cover of the first storybook. She had written her name in stilted blue crayon capitals at the top of the first page.

My legs began to cramp, so I eased myself to my feet and sat back down on the settee, the three books on my lap, and started to slowly turn the pages.

'Oh, Krystal,' I murmured, 'who was it that hurt you and Benji?' and I wondered whether I would ever find out and whether I'd be sorry if I did.

CHAPTER TWENTY-THREE

I awoke to a persistent buzzing sound and the realisation that sunshine was pouring in through the window and I was curled up on the sofa in the living room.

'What the f—?'

Then I heard the rattle of the letter box and a voice calling my name. Lucy! I scrambled off the sofa and hurried out into the hallway, thanking God that when I'd come downstairs the previous night I'd pulled on a pair of jeans and hadn't come down in my underpants, or even worse – naked.

'Coming,' I called, and when I wrenched open the door after having to faff about with the bolts at the top and bottom of the door together with the chain Lucy took one look at me and burst out laughing.

'Late night?' she asked.

I gestured that she come in and moved to one side.

'Oh, you know, it was one of those when I just couldn't settle so I thought I'd try and find a book to read and ended up falling asleep on the sofa.'

'Hmm, I'll make some coffee, shall I?'

'You're an angel,' I told her, giving her a peck on the cheek and backing towards the stairs. 'I'll be down in a jiff.'

'Take your time,' she said. 'I'll not be going anywhere.'

I probably set a record for showering and cleaning my teeth. I'd been so looking forward to seeing her again and she was probably now thinking I was a prize jerk. Having heard that she'd just finished a relationship with another idiot, it wasn't exactly the impression I was aiming for.

When I finally made it downstairs, she was sitting at the kitchen table sipping coffee and a second mug was on the table waiting for me.

She looked up with a smile that warmed my cockles and slowly rose up from her seat to wrap her arms around my neck and give me a welcoming kiss, which let me know that I hadn't blotted my copybook – yet.

'Shall I make you toast?' she asked.

'No thanks,' I said, hugging her to me. 'I didn't eat until late, I was still full up from lunchtime and those chips.'

I reluctantly let her go so we could both sit down to drink our coffee. Had we been a bit further on in our relationship I might have just carried her upstairs. I was hoping if I played my cards right, we might finish our day the way we had before and, if so, I wasn't about to complain.

This time her knapsack was pretty light, containing only two bottles of water, a couple of packets of crisps and dry-roasted cashews.

'We'll get something to eat in Chalfont,' she said.

'Will anywhere be open? It's Sunday.'

'There're two pubs and a couple of tea rooms, so never fear – you won't starve,' she said with a chuckle.

'A bit of abstinence will probably do me good,' I told her.

She gave me a very slow and sexy smile. 'That, I very much doubt,' she said, and I know she wasn't talking about food.

This time I did wrap my arm around her shoulders as we walked along and never had anything felt so natural. We talked a bit, laughed a lot, and it was like we'd known each other for years.

It was a perfect morning. If there had been a mist it had burnt off long since leaving a bright-blue sky with only one or two puffballs of white chasing each other across the horizon. The sun was hot on the back of my head and I was grateful for my longer than usual hair protecting my neck from getting burnt.

The fine weather had the yachting brigade out in full force and from the cliff top we could see a steady stream of boats making their way along the coast and further out to sea. Closer to the shore there were a couple of lads on jet skis darting back and forth and it crossed my mind that, if I should stay on in Slyford, having a boat or some watercraft might not be such a bad idea. Lazy days spent with Lucy out at sea, swimming and fishing. Then making love below deck and being rocked to sleep by the gentle rhythm of the waves. That would be an idyllic way to spend my self-imposed retirement from the City. It was something to think on.

Then I realised I was actually planning a future for myself that had both Lucy and Slyford in it.

'What?' Lucy said, studying my face.

'Sorry?'

'Your expression – you were obviously thinking of something good.'

'Just thinking.'

'About what?' she asked and punched me on the arm.

'About you and me on a boat, actually.'

Her expression became slightly puzzled. 'On a boat? Doing what?'

'What do you think?'

Then she gave me that full-on sexy smile she was so good at, which had all the senses I was born with travelling down south. 'Have you got sea legs?'

'You don't need them when you're lying down,' I replied, and I figured it must have been a good answer as she stopped walking to pull me into a long, deep kiss that had me thinking that maybe we should skip lunch and head on back home.

'Hmm,' she said when she finally pulled away, 'at this rate we'll never get to Chalfont.'

'Maybe we should . . .' and I gestured with my head back the way we had come.

She pressed her fingers to my lips. 'Huh-uh, mister. I promised you a trip to Chalfont and a trip to Chalfont you shall have. Anyway, didn't you say something about abstaining?'

And so, it went on. She teased me, I teased her back and by the time we reached the end of the path and stepped out onto the lane leading down to Chalfont I was more than a little in love.

Lucy told me that the best pub was at the far end of the village and suggested we walk down one side of the road and return on the other so I could investigate the village shops. I didn't have the heart to tell her I'd already visited Chalfont a couple of times with Jed and once on my own. We stopped at the window to the toyshop. I would have walked on, but Lucy pulled on my arm, drawing me to a standstill.

'I loved this shop as a kid.'

'I thought your parents didn't get the pub until about ten years ago.'

She pulled a face, her expression a little sheepish. 'I was almost thirteen when we came to Slyford St James and really too old for looking in toyshops, but this one always had such wonderful displays. I mean, look at it.'

She was right, it was a great display and I thought of Krystal's reflection next to mine. Krystal had been only six when she died, and she would have looked in this shop window with the wondrous eyes of a child.

'Do you want kids?' Lucy asked, and it was such an unexpected question for a moment I was dumbfounded.

'I . . . I . . .' Then instead of making a complete twat of myself I stopped and thought about it for a bit. 'A few months ago, I would have said no – definitely not. Now I'm not so sure,' and Krystal's sweet little face floated through my head.

'Why do you think that is?' she asked, and I squeezed her hand.

'I was selfish. A typical self-centred, career-obsessed male.'

'Was it losing your partner that made the difference?'

'No,' I said, shaking my head and suddenly feeling really small and ashamed; for two years it hadn't made any difference at all. 'It was coming here.'

I think she realised she had touched on a nerve, as she went very quiet as we continued our way along the street, and I was beginning to think I must have blown it big time. *Fuck it, fuck it, fuck it* was running through my head and I had no idea of how to unfuck it.

She squeezed my hand. 'I think most people are, at some time, not the person they'd wish to be,' she said very quietly.

I stopped to look down at her bowed head. 'Lucy?'

When she looked up her eyes were overbright. 'At least you're trying to turn your life around. Some people never do,' and I was pretty sure she was talking about her ex.

'Want to talk about it?'

Her smile was more of a grimace. 'I never want to talk about it again and I certainly don't want to spoil our day.'

I stroked the hair away from her brow. 'What's past is past,' I told her.

Her smile returned, maybe not so bright, but it was at least a smile. 'When we get to the pub, I'm going to make a toast to new beginnings.'

The pub was more for locals than tourists. It was small and quaint with a very limited menu. Oak beams darkened by age had me ducking my head, and the white paintwork still had a patina of nicotine despite the smoking ban. I had the feeling this was the type of place that probably had late-night lock-ins for locals, when all the rules and regulations went out the window.

'Hello, Lucy, my love.' The buxom, young barmaid lifted a hand and waved as we pushed our way past a group of old boys to get to the bar. 'How are you keeping, my darling?' she asked, leaning across the bar to give Lucy a hug and air kiss. Her eyes darted to me and back to Lucy. 'And who might this be?'

'I'm good, thanks, and this is Jim,' she said, gesturing to me. 'Jim – Rose.'

We swapped the usual 'nice to meet you' and Rose asked, 'What can I get you?'

I ordered a lager for me and a white wine for Lucy in between the two girls making small talk. There were too many customers for them to chat for long, and as soon as we'd been served Lucy led the way to an empty table in the corner.

'It gets busy in here.'

'Mainly locals.'

'I guessed as much. You come here often?'

'Nah,' she said. 'Rose and I went to school together and our parents being publicans gave us something in common, so we used to hang out a bit.'

'Nice place.'

'The choice of food's pretty basic, but it's good.'

We both opted for a ploughman's and I went and put the order in.

'You local?' Rose asked as she scribbled down what we wanted. 'I've not seen you before.'

'I'm renting a cottage in Slyford St James.'

'Nice place.'

'I like it.'

'Some of the locals are a bit weird, don't you think?' I just looked at her. 'You know, there's that fellow that talks to dead people. Then there're those batty sisters.' She gave a shiver. 'Them two really give me the creeps.'

'You mean the Garvins?'

'Hmm, that'll be thirteen-ninety.'

I gave her the money and tried to think how I could get her to elaborate without being too obvious. 'Why do they give you the creeps?'

'I suppose that's a bit unkind. It's not so much them as their whack-job cousin.'

'Cousin?'

'*Rose*,' a voice boomed.

She glanced over her shoulder at the portly man squeezing past her. 'Well, he is, Dad.'

'The poor chap is as good as dead, so show a bit more respect.'

Rose rolled her eyes as she handed me my change and moved in close to whisper, 'Total whack-job.'

I headed back to the table with my head spinning. So, it was their cousin who was in Goldsmere House. Some things started to make a good deal of sense.

All through lunch I had to make a conscious effort to concentrate on what Lucy was saying to me as all sorts of things were whirring around in my head. A couple of times she had to repeat what she had said, but it was getting loud in the bar, and pretty much packed to capacity. Had we arrived twenty minutes or so later there would have been standing room only.

On the way back I forced the Garvin sisters out of my mind. I was not going to mess things up with Lucy. No way.

If she noticed I was a bit quiet she didn't say anything, but then she was too, and I hoped it wasn't anything to do with our previous conversation outside the toyshop. I had put my arm around her shoulders and she hadn't pulled away, so I took that as a good sign. When we reached the point, we stopped to look out to sea at all the sailing boats that were scattered across the horizon.

When I glanced down at her she was smiling at me. 'What?'

'Penny for them?'

357

'I was just thinking this is perfect – you, me, here, the weather.' I wasn't exactly lying, all those things were true – what I was really thinking was I hope I haven't blown it with her because it *was* perfect – or as perfect as it could ever be.

She reached up to hook her hand around the back of my neck and stood on tiptoes to kiss me. It was then that I knew I hadn't blown it yet and if I did so in the future, I was a fucking idiot. She was the one. Kat's face skittered through my head and I knew I should feel guilty. Damn it, I did feel guilty, but I had to move on. I might have behaved badly, I mightn't have treated Kat as well as I should, but I didn't make her kill herself. It was a choice she'd made – if it was true – and in my heart I'd never really believed it. Kat was too strong. She would never have taken her own life. That's what I hoped, that's what I wanted to believe.

When we reached the end of the cliff path and walked out into the lane we stopped to kiss again, and I hoped this meant she'd be coming back with me. I slipped my arm around her waist and she leant her head against my chest as we carried on walking, and when we reached the end of the lane she didn't stop or turn towards the village centre and the pub, she automatically turned towards the cottage. I kissed the top of her head and she snuggled up against me.

We'd almost reached the turning into my lane when from behind us I heard the sound of an engine. The road was narrow, so we broke apart and stepped to one side to allow the car to pass. Lucy took hold of my hand as we waited, and I smiled down at her before looking towards the passing car. Two pairs of eyes appeared to bore into mine and I could feel the smile slip from my face.

Darcy Garvin's expression was of haughty disapproval, which was mirrored by her sister's, though as soon as she saw me looking their way Miriam smiled and waggled her fingers at us. Then they were gone, and Lucy was putting her arm back around my waist, blissfully unaware of the feeling of foreboding sinking into my heart.

CHAPTER TWENTY-FOUR

As I opened the front door to the cottage, I tried to push the Garvin sisters out of my head, at least temporarily. I would phone Jed tomorrow morning to discuss what I'd learnt, there was no immediate rush. I had new locks on the doors to the front, back and bedroom. Anyway, they'd have to be mad to try anything so soon.

Once again, I had to stop myself and wonder what the hell I was thinking. They were two middle-aged women, for goodness' sake, though the evidence did appear to be stacking up against them. There had to be a logical explanation, I told myself, there just had to.

Yeah – like you're totally losing it!

There was that too.

'Ground control to Major Jim,' I heard Lucy say, and I realised she was halfway up the stairs and I'd ground to a halt on the first step.

'Sorry, just wondering whether I should bring the wine and cheese up now,' I improvised.

'Hmm, wine would be nice, we can get the cheese later.'

'I've only red, I'm afraid.'

'Red's good.'

'You go on. I'll be up in a minute.'

I hurried into the living room to grab a couple of wine goblets and a bottle of red from the drinks cabinet, then hot-footed it up the stairs. Lucy hadn't got very far, she was standing just inside the bedroom doorway.

'Wine all sorted,' and then I saw what had halted her progress into the room. On the wall above the bed scrawled in crimson paint or maybe lipstick was one word. *CUNT*.

'What the fuck?' I said.

'Who? Who would?' Lucy's voice was shaking.

'How, is more the question. I've had new locks fitted,' then belatedly realised that was something I should have probably kept to myself.

'You've had trouble before?'

'A bit,' I admitted, thinking quickly. 'Probably kids.'

'Have you told the police?'

'No point, nothing was taken.'

'But that,' she pointed at the wall, 'that looks personal. Like someone's having a pop.'

She was probably right, but unless I could find a forced window there was only one explanation – or two, if I didn't discount that I could be going mad and doing these things in some sort of fugue state. Whoever or whatever kept moving the whisky bottle and glass had written the message on the wall.

'I'd better go and get a cloth and some cleaner,' I said, putting the red wine and glasses down on the bedside table.

'Aren't you going to call the police?'

'Do you really think they'd be interested?' I said, walking to the door, then as an afterthought I took my mobile out of my pocket and took a picture. 'Just in case.'

I stomped down the stairs. This wasn't at all the end to our perfect day that I'd planned. I couldn't imagine Lucy'd feel particularly amorous now, and definitely not in that room.

I rummaged under the sink and found a couple of new dishcloths and some strong cleaning spray. If it was lipstick I was in with a chance; if it was red paint I was buggered. When I stood up and turned around Lucy was behind me.

She held out her hand. 'Here, let me do it while you have a look around and figure out how they got in.'

'Thanks,' I said, handing her the spray and cloths. 'If it's paint give us a shout and I'll see if I can find some white spirit.'

I followed her out of the kitchen and watched her walk upstairs, thinking that she really did have a nice backside. She must have felt my eyes upon her, as when she reached the top, she half-turned her head and said, 'You'll go blind,' which made me laugh despite everything.

I started in the living room. I was really only doing

this for Lucy's sake as, since almost being murdered in my bed, my paranoia had me checking windows and doors every time I left the house or went to bed. I'd checked them last night and I'd checked them this morning before we left – but I hadn't. I'd been in a hurry because I'd overslept.

Still, I had checked them the night before and the night before that. So they would be locked. Definitely.

Being an old cottage, most of the windows had sash cords. The Morgans or their predecessors had obviously been pretty security conscious as each window had been fitted with a fairly basic but efficient security device, which effectively screwed the window shut. This obviously could be unscrewed if you wanted the window open. I'd never unscrewed any of the devices. Since the incident with the gas, I'd checked they were screwed up tight, but never had I unscrewed them. In fact, as far as I knew, they were all seized up. Even so, I checked them.

Then I went along the corridor to the dining room. I only ever went in there to check the windows as I always ate at the kitchen table. There were two windows, both with sash cords, both screwed shut. I tried to tighten the screw on each window and neither would move even a fraction.

It was exactly as I thought. No one could get into this house unless they had a key.

I was about to walk away, but as I turned from the window I caught a glimpse of red outside in the garden. I spun around, laying my hand against the window and moving in close to peer outside, but there was no one there. I let out a shaky sigh. God help me, I wasn't sure whether I had wanted to see a small figure waving at me from the lawn or not. I think deep down inside I did.

I lifted my hand from the windowpane and it gave a little judder. I'd have thought no more of it – they were old windows, they weren't a tight fit – but something made me stop. I leant in close to try and tighten the screw a little more and the bottom windowpane moved, but the top one to which it was meant to be screwed did not.

I peered at the screw, then grabbed it between my thumb and forefinger and gave it a tug. It moved and once again the top pane didn't. My stomach gave a little flip. I took a deep breath, reached for the catch in the middle of the window and pushed it to open. It moved with hardly any resistance at all. I pressed my hands against the frame and pushed upwards. The window slid open with barely a sound. Someone had cut through the security screw and now I knew how someone had been getting inside the cottage. All it would take was a thin blade or strip of metal pushed between the window frames and slid along to push open the catch.

Lucy was cleaning the last of the scrawl off the wall when I returned to the bedroom. 'You haven't got some other girlfriend somewhere who has a grudge?' she asked. It *had* been lipstick and it'd left a stain on the paintwork, but it was better than what had been there before. 'Mind you, she must be some old dragon to wear a colour like this.'

'I thought red was popular.'

'With supermodels and old ladies. Mere mortals like me would look stupid. Or worse – tarty.'

'Never in a million years,' I said, though with all that was whizzing around in my head I was surprised I was capable of coherent conversation, let alone flirting. It was suddenly like there was two of me, one stumbling around in total confusion while the other was cool, calm and collected, saying the right things, going through the motions.

Lucy sprayed a bit more cleaner onto a fresh cloth and attacked the pink smear that now coloured the wall.

'I don't think it's all going to come out,' she said, kneeling back on the bed to peer up at her handiwork.

'I'll repaint it.'

'Find out how they got in?'

'Not a clue,' I said, the lie tumbling from my lips with frightening ease.

Jim, you have to stop lying to people you love.

It was true – I did, but I couldn't tell her the truth. How could I? It would lead to me having to explain a whole load of things that I could barely comprehend myself. Seeing dead children being the least of it.

'That's a bit of a worry.' She glanced over her shoulder to look at me. 'They must have got in somehow.' She scrambled off the bed. 'Come on, let's take another look around.'

I was about to try and dissuade her, but the calm calculating side of me stepped in. *If she finds the window lock that's been tampered with, in her mind she'd have solved the mystery; if she doesn't, what does it matter?*

I took the ruined dishcloths and cleaner in one hand and she grabbed hold of my other and led me from the bedroom and down the stairs. We started in the kitchen, and while I threw the cloths away and stowed the cleaner under the sink, she checked each window and the door.

'You sure do lock up tight, don't you?' she commented upon seeing that the back door was not only locked but bolted at top and bottom.

'Comes from living in London,' I said.

'Hmm.'

She stalked off into the hall and into the lounge. She checked each window thoroughly and I noticed that not only did she check the screw locks, she also tried rattling the windows in their frames.

'I can't see that they could have got in through any of these,' she said as she slid past me and back out into the hall and made for the dining room.

She went through the same rigmarole and upon reaching the last window she noticed that there was something wrong within a nanosecond and had the window open.

'Little sods,' she said. 'They've cut through the lock.'

'How on earth did you notice that? I had no idea.'

Jim! I know, another lie.

'Well, at least you can screw it shut for the time being.'

'I'll get Jed to take a look at it tomorrow,' I said.

'I don't suppose they'll come back tonight,' she said, 'if it is kids.'

'Who else could it be?'

She closed the window and took a step back from it, her brow creased into a worried frown. 'I don't know. You tell me.'

I obviously wasn't as convincing a liar as I thought. 'I'll see if I can find a drill and a screwdriver.'

She followed me out into the hall, where I poked around in the cupboard under the stairs. I was sure I'd seen a rusty, old biscuit tin in there containing various bits and pieces, including a few tools.

'Ah, here we go,' I said, seeing the tin wedged into the corner at the back. I took it into the kitchen and placed it on the table to prise off the lid.

'Anything useful?' Lucy asked.

'I have a drill, at least,' I said, holding up a hand-operated contraption that had probably been invented at the time of the ark.

Lucy screwed up her nose. 'I could always pop home and borrow something off my dad.'

'Where's your sense of adventure?' I laughed and lifted it up, furiously turning the handle.

'It'll take you hours.'

'Have you something better to do?'

Her lips curled into that very sexy smile of hers. 'Now you mention it . . .'

'I'll be quick.'

'I hope not.'

'With the screwing.'

'That's what I'm afraid of.'

'Of the window,' I said with a chuckle.

In the end it took about twenty minutes and I had it screwed so tight they'd never be able to push anything between the two frames to cut it through. I'd go around all the other windows in the morning when I was alone. I didn't want Lucy to know I was worried.

Surprisingly enough, Lucy wasn't at all put off by what had been scrawled across my bedroom wall. Now that it had dried the resultant mark wasn't so obvious. It would still need repainting to cover the rose-coloured smear, but I didn't have time to worry about that as Lucy was giving me more pressing things to occupy my mind.

Later, when we were sitting up in bed drinking red wine and eating cheese and crackers, Lucy's eyes wandered back up to the stain on the wall.

'Do you really think it was kids?'

'Who else? Nobody much knows me here and I can't imagine I've pissed anyone off so badly in only two weeks that they'd want to break in and write obscenities on my bedroom wall.'

'I s'pose not,' she said, popping a piece of cheese into her mouth.

'I mean, to do something like that you'd have to be more than a little crazy, wouldn't you have thought?'

Lucy shivered. 'Is that meant to make me feel better?'

'I was only joking,' I said, lying through my teeth as, yes, to do something like that, you would have to be crazy and it was as scary as hell.

At about eleven she climbed out of bed to get dressed and go home.

'Can't you stay?' I asked.

'Mum and Dad are fairly broad-minded, you have to be running a pub, but where his little girl is concerned, Dad can be a bit . . .' She paused for a moment thinking about it. 'Let's just say – overprotective.'

'I can't say I blame him,' I said, climbing out of bed and pulling on my jeans.

'You don't have to get up.'

'I'm not letting you walk home alone.'

'What about you, walking back all alone?'

'That's different.'

'I've not had anyone breaking into my house and writing obscenities on the wall.'

'Kids,' I told her, 'just kids.'

'But still . . .'

'No arguments. If your dad found out that I'd let his *little girl* walk home alone, I doubt he'd be well impressed.'

'Hmm, I guess that's true enough,' she said, hooking her hands around my neck and giving me a kiss.

'I thought you were going home.' I laughed.

When we reached the pub there were still lights on in the bar. 'Dad waiting up, I expect,' she told me. 'Most regulars are gone by ten on a Sunday night.'

'Shall I come in?'

'Nah. Maybe tomorrow night. That's if you're free tomorrow evening?'

'I'll have to check my hectic schedule.' She thumped me on the arm.

'Dad's given me tomorrow night off.'

'OK, I'll take you out somewhere for dinner.'

She grinned at me. 'How about I come and cook for you? Then we won't waste half the evening driving around South Devon.'

'Are you sure? It's a bit of a busman's holiday.'

'Totally. See you about six?'

'Looking forward to it,' I said, and she melted against me. When she pulled away, I felt like she'd taken a little piece of me with her.

I watched her go inside, waited until I heard voices, then started back to the place that, despite everything, was beginning to feel like home.

CHAPTER TWENTY-FIVE

I spent the morning going around all the windows putting in a second screw. It took a while with the old hand-turned drill and manual screwdriver, but I found it therapeutic. *I* was doing something to protect myself. *I* was taking some kind of control. Once I'd completed this task, I walked around the outside of the cottage, checking each window. Visibly nothing had changed, but when I tried forcing a thin-bladed knife up between the window frames it was nigh on impossible.

Satisfied with my morning's work, I set about giving the kitchen a bit of a clean. If Lucy was taking the trouble to cook for me, I could at least make a bit of an effort to clean and tidy the place.

I did have another go at the bedroom wall, but nothing was going to shift the remainder of the lipstick stain, so it looked as though I'd either have to repaint or lose my deposit.

By eleven-thirty I'd put off the inevitable as long as I possibly could. With a heavy heart I rang Jed. I didn't have a choice; pretending that nothing was wrong, when very clearly something seriously was, wasn't going to help anyone, least of all me. I was the one with the problem – no one else.

His phone rang six times, then went to voicemail. I would have phoned Emma, but I didn't have her number. I decided to give it twenty minutes. After procrastinating all morning, I was now feeling anxious and desperate to speak to them. After ten minutes I tried again. Six rings and again to voicemail.

'Fuck it, Jed, where are you?'

Ten minutes later six rings and to voicemail. Something was wrong. I was absolutely sure of it.

I didn't know Jed's address, but I did know where Emma lived.

I grabbed my keys off the hall table and strode out of the house. By the time I reached the end of the lane I was running.

I stopped outside Emma's gates. They were wide open and the feeling of foreboding I'd had from the moment my first call to Jed had gone to voicemail almost overwhelmed me. Something terrible had happened.

As I walked up the drive, I heard the peacock cry from the back of the house. Usually its call made me feel at peace, this time it sounded plaintive, desolate even. By the time I reached the front door my heart had worked its way up into my throat, and I was so afraid I could hardly stop my hand from shaking as I reached for the doorbell.

I pressed the button and could hear the strident ring of the bell echoing around the house as though it was an empty tomb, and the thought made me shiver.

'Come on, come on.' I rang the bell again, stabbing at the button once, twice, then a third time.

Then, through the bevelled glass panel down the centre of the door, I saw a figure approaching.

'Thank God,' I muttered to myself, the tension relaxing a bit.

The door began to open, and I forced my lips into a smile, which instantly fell away when I saw the expression of the young woman who had opened it.

Her blue eyes were red-rimmed and bloodshot, her nose a shiny pink. She started to speak, but before she could utter more than a couple of words her tears overflowed, and she raised her hand to her face to dab at it with a scrunched-up tissue.

'What's happened?' I asked. 'Where's Emma?'

'Mrs Mortimer . . .' She stopped to gulp back tears. 'Mrs Mortimer,' she gallantly tried again, but her voice broke. She took a deep breath. 'Mrs Mortimer's had an accident. They've taken her to Torquay Hospital.'

'Do you know where Jed is?'

'There. He's gone there.' It made sense of why he'd not been answering his phone; you often had to turn off your mobile in most hospitals.

'Thank you,' I said and turned to leave.

'Mr Hawkes,' she said, and I looked back. 'Are you going there? To the hospital, I mean?'

I nodded. 'Jed might need – you know.'

'Tell him we're all praying for her.'

I nodded again as I had no words. This was more than a small household accident. This was serious.

I ran back to the cottage and jumped straight into my car. I wasn't sure what I was going to do when I got to the hospital, but I had to go.

As I drove, all sorts of scenarios were running through my head as to what had happened to Emma. I should have asked her maid, but I hadn't had the wherewithal. I'd been too shocked. Now my imagination was working overtime. The girl had said an accident – but what the fuck did that mean? From her tear-stained face, I didn't need to be psychic to know it was more than a cut finger or grazed knee.

I followed the signs and did an illegal right turn at the traffic lights leading up into the entrance to the hospital and realised I couldn't actually remember any of the rest of the journey; it had passed in a complete blur. I managed to find a car park with a few empty spaces and enough change to feed into the meter. Then I went in search of the accident and emergency department. Fortunately, there was a board with a diagram of the hospital and where all the departments were, in relation to where I was parked. Even so, it was a maze.

When I eventually found the waiting room it was almost full with people. Some, I assumed, waiting for loved ones while others clutched crudely bandaged arms or injured hands wrapped in towels to their chests. There were a couple of young women with grizzling children huddled on their laps, and several old folk in wheelchairs parked at the end of rows. Jed was nowhere to be seen.

I made my way to the reception desk in a daze. Had Jed left already? I hadn't seen his car in the car park, but then the place was littered with them. Anyway, he could have gone in the ambulance with Emma. It would probably take the bravest of paramedics to convince him otherwise.

Shit. I'd been poncing about screwing up windows and cleaning the kitchen all morning when I should have been here. I should have been here.

One receptionist was on the phone while the other was in earnest conversation with a man I assumed was a doctor from his white coat and stethoscope slung around his neck. I must have looked distraught as the lady on the phone looked up at me and with a sympathetic smile held up one finger and mouthed, 'One moment.'

The moment appeared to go on for ever. I glanced down at my wrist, but I no longer wore a watch. I pulled my mobile from my back pocket – twelve fifty-six. I put it away and stood there fidgeting until the receptionist put down the phone.

'Can I help you?'

'Mrs Emma Mortimer. She was brought in earlier, she's had some kind of accident.'

'Are you family?'

'No, I'm . . . I'm her partner's nephew. I think he's probably with her. Jed Cummins is his name.'

'One moment,' she repeated and started looking at her computer screen. 'All right Mr . . . ?'

'Hawkes, Jim Hawkes.'

'Right, Mr Hawkes, if you take the lift over there to level two and turn right, you'll find seating at the end of the corridor. You can wait there.'

I nodded my thanks and made straight for the lift.

I've never been particularly fond of hospitals. The last time I'd been in one was when . . . My throat closed up. There was no point thinking about then, this was now, and I prayed to God that this visit was going to have a better outcome.

Jed was sitting in the corner, arms resting on thighs, head in hands. I hesitated and for a moment considered returning to the lift. He might not want me here: he might think I'm intruding; he might even blame me.

He must have felt my eyes upon him as he looked up and stared at me with bloodshot eyes. I took a step towards him and he stood. I couldn't read his expression. I carried on walking and he started towards me. We both stopped when there was about a yard between us.

I had to swallow a couple of times before I could bring myself to speak. 'How is she?'

His brow bunched and his cheeks kind of twitched like he too was having trouble finding his voice, or was it that he was trying to keep it together?

Then he took that one last step and pulled me into a bear hug that was tight enough my ribcage screamed for mercy. I didn't care, I was too frightened to care. My big strong friend was clearly a mess and my fear for Emma shot through the roof.

'Jed,' I said when he abruptly let me go, finally remembering himself. 'What happened? Is Emma OK?'

He pinched at the bridge of his nose, surreptitiously wiping his eyes. Then his hand ran down his face to finally rub at his beard.

'I don't know. They've taken her for scans. She's got head injuries, you see.' He jerked his head towards the seats and we both went back along the corridor to sit down.

'What happened?'

His shoulders slumped. 'I don't know. I arrived at Emms' the same time as the girls this morning. We found her at the bottom of the stairs.' His eyes filled up and he pulled a huge white hanky from his pocket. 'She was so cold. So very cold. At first, we thought . . . I thought she was – you know.'

'Had she been there all night, do you think?'

Jed gave a bob of the head. 'That's why they're so worried. If she's been unconscious all night . . .' He didn't have to say any more – I got the picture.

We sat there in silence for a bit. What was there to say? Well, probably a lot, but not much of it mattered at the moment.

'Jed?' He looked up at me. 'What do you think happened? I mean, was it an accident?'

His eyes widened and he stared at me. 'What do you mean?'

'Do you think she fell?'

Jed carried on staring at me, but he wasn't really, his mind was far away and from the tightening of the lines around his eyes I guessed it wasn't in a very good place.

'Has something else happened?' he asked at last. 'Something I'm not aware of?'

So I told him. I told him about the chance comments made by Rose and her father, seeing the Garvin girls and their expressions as they passed me and Lucy on the road, the foul word scrawled in over-red lipstick on my bedroom wall, and the sabotaged window lock leaving the cottage open to someone so they could come and go as they pleased.

'We need to get those windows locked up tight,' Jed said. 'I'll come over later, when I know . . . you know?'

I put my hand on his arm. 'All taken care of. I did it this morning before I tried ringing you.' I ran a hand through my hair. 'Wish I'd tried phoning you first now.'

'Jim, there was nothing you could have done. There was nothing either of us could have done.'

I guessed he was right, but it didn't stop me from feeling shitty about it all.

'I've never liked those two old hags,' Jed said out of the blue.

'It's all conjecture,' I told him, like I had told myself a hundred times or more. 'I mean, why would either of them try to kill me? Or Emma, for that matter? There's no good reason for it.'

He shook his head. 'None of it makes sense. But you've been seeing these things for a reason. The dead have been giving you clues for a reason.'

'Well, I wish they'd give me more than clues. I'm not

Miss Fucking Marple,' I said, which did raise a glimmer of a smile from Jed.

I went and got some coffee for the pair of us, more for something to do than anything else. I also picked up a couple of sandwiches. I suspected they'd end up in a bin somewhere, but they were there if either of us wanted them.

When I returned, Jed was talking to a doctor. They were both standing, which I took as possibly a good sign. Didn't they usually ask you to sit when they were about to give you bad news?

I heard Jed ask, 'Can I see her?' I didn't hear what the doctor said, but as Jed started along the corridor beside him, I assumed the answer was yes.

Jed gave me a shaky smile as we passed. 'I'll be back in a few minutes,' he told me and then was gone.

I sank down onto the seat I'd occupied before and, putting the sandwiches and Jed's coffee on the floor between our chairs, began to sip mine. The coffee was hot and wet, the best that could be said of it. So, I sat and waited and, having nothing better to do, began to mull on the chain of events from my arrival in Slyford St James until this morning.

Jed was gone more like twenty minutes, but when he returned the smile on his face as he approached me eased away some of the tension.

'Well?' I asked, standing.

'She's sleeping now. They're going to keep her in overnight and do a few more tests when she wakes up, but the doctors are pretty confident that the worst she has is a concussion.'

'Thank God.'

'I've always said she was a tough old boot,' his voice cracked, and he had to look away.

'Did she regain consciousness?'

Jed nodded. I guessed still finding it difficult to speak.

'Did she say what'd happened?'

'No. She was still a little confused. She couldn't remember anything after getting ready for bed.'

'Is that normal?' I asked in alarm. 'Memory loss, I mean?'

'Apparently,' he said. 'Come on, let's get out of here. I'll come back this evening.'

'When's visiting hours?'

'Six-thirty they told me.'

It was only when we'd reached the ground floor that I remembered the sandwiches I'd bought. I kept on going. The sooner we were out of there the better.

It was as I thought. Jed had gone with Emma in the ambulance, so I drove him back to the village and, on the way, we returned to the subject of the Garvin girls.

'So, if I've got this right, Darcy and Miriam have a cousin and it's him that's in Goldsmere.'

'That was the gist of what Lucy's friend and her father said.'

'I've never heard of them having a cousin.'

'But as you and Emma said, neither of you really know them *that* well,' I said as I slowed down to let an old boy with a Zimmer frame cross the road.

'Did they tell you anything else? Like his name?'

I frowned at the windscreen, trying to recall exactly what

they had said. Then I remembered Rose had mentioned Jed, not by name, but it was him she was talking about all right. That made me smile, but I thought it best not to mention it. I doubted, somehow, he'd be thrilled as being known as 'that fellow that talks to dead people'.

'She called Darcy and Miriam the "batty sisters" and said they gave her the creeps, though when I asked her why, she did go on to say it wasn't so much them as their cousin.'

'Did she say why?'

'Not really,' I told him, 'only that he was "a total whack-job" and that's when her father butted in telling her to show more respect as "the poor chap was as good as dead".'

'I wonder what she meant by "total whack-job"?'

'I didn't get a chance to ask.'

I drove on while Jed sat silently, I assumed mulling on what I'd told him. 'Oh shit!' Jed said, though it was more like an exhalation of breath. 'They were there. Don't you remember? They were there – they heard you, they saw you. You changed, Jim, maybe only a bit, but you changed. Neither Emma or I recognised him, but Darcy and Miriam would have, if he was their cousin.'

I glanced across at him and he was rubbing at his beard, his eyebrows knotted together as he stared straight ahead.

'Take me back to Emms',' he said. 'I want to listen to that tape again.'

CHAPTER TWENTY-SIX

We drove the rest of the way in silence. I'd always thought the Garvin girls to be a bit odd, but surely neither of them was a potential murderer?

But you saw one of them push the man off the cliff.

I saw someone push the man off the cliff. It could have been anyone, he didn't show me a face, though it was definitely a woman – he called her a bitch.

I drove the car up Emma's drive and parked right out front. The same girl as before answered the door and let us in without question.

'Can I get you anything to take in to Mrs Mortimer?' she asked.

'Maybe some wash things, hairbrush, you know that sort of thing.'

'I'll go and pack her overnight bag,' she said and left us to it.

The tape machine was on the sideboard in the lounge. Jed fiddled about with it a bit, running the tape back and then forward until we got to the section recorded the night of Emma's party. I really didn't want to hear it again, but Jed appeared to think it was important.

'. . . *hide. He found me. Had to run. Make him stop. Make him go away.*'

'*Oh my God.*'

Jed stopped the tape for a moment. 'That was Darcy,' he said, 'and Miriam telling her to be quiet.' He clicked the tape back on.

'*He's coming. He's coming.*'

'*Do you think that's it?*'

'*I don't think so; look at him,*' Emma's voice and then several gasps.

'*Oh, dear Lord,*' Darcy again.

Then the man's voice. '*Where are you? Little brat. Think I'm stupid, do you? When I find you I'll show you who's stupid. I'll show you. When I find you I'm going to make you sorry. I'm going to make you very sorry indeed. Little bitch.*'

'*You have to make him stop,*' another voice, Peter Davies. '*He's going to hurt more children. You have to find him and make him stop.*'

'*Oh my God, oh my God,*' the woman's voice I'd heard when I came to my senses, then another low, barely distinguishable voice snapping at her to shut up.

Jed clicked off the tape.

'At the time I thought their reaction was odd,' Jed said,

383

stroking his beard. 'I mean, they were always begging me to hold seances.'

'It fucking scared me,' I said, gesturing with my head to the tape machine. 'I still can't believe all that stuff came out of my mouth.'

Jed ignored me. 'I'd've thought they would've been delighted, but they both looked scared – and now I know why. They recognised him. Miriam wasn't telling Darcy to shut up so she could hear, she was telling her to shut up before she gave something away she really shouldn't.'

'Okaaay,' I said, 'so they recognised the man as being their cousin and it scared them, I get that, but later they were asking Emma whether I held seances.'

'And Emma told them no. Don't you see? They were checking to find out whether you were likely to give the game away while holding another seance or having a psychic turn.'

'But nobody but them recognised him.'

'But if there was to be a next time someone else might. Just because neither Emma nor I have met their cousin it doesn't mean no one else has. It's a small community.'

'But you've lived here all your life.'

Jed gave a small and bitter laugh. 'I was sent away to school and then went straight into the army. Apart from a few holidays, I never came back until about twenty years ago.'

And that made me wonder, but his expression brooked no questions. He'd once told me that not everything was a mystery – maybe not, but I could tell when a person was keeping secrets. But then it was Jed's secret when all was said and done, and if he wanted to keep it to himself it was up to him.

'So, how do we find out more about this cousin? He's the key to all this.'

'How can a man who's half-dead be so dangerous?' Jed said, though from the way he said it he knew it was true.

This mystery man was dangerous – dangerous, nasty and malevolent. I'd felt it. He'd been inside my head and I'd been inside his, and a very dark and deeply unpleasant place it had been.

The maid, who Jed called Tilly, returned with an overnight bag for him to take into Emma.

'I've put in enough bits and bobs to last her a couple of days, just in case,' she said with a smile, though her eyes still looked red and puffy.

'I should be bringing her home tomorrow,' Jed told her.

'Let's hope so,' Tilly said and was about to leave, then hesitated. 'By the way, Miss Garvin rang just before lunch. She was very upset when she heard what'd happened to Mrs Mortimer.'

'What did she want?' Jed asked.

'She didn't say. When I told her Mrs Mortimer was in hospital, it sort of knocked the wind out of her sails.'

'Which Miss Garvin was it, Tilly?' I asked.

'Miss Darcy, I think. That's why I was a bit surprised. She always seems a bit of a cold fish to me. If it'd been Miss Miriam, I could've understood it. She gushes for England that one,' she gave a sniff, 'not that it means a thing. Miss Darcy may be cold, but Miss Miriam,' her shoulders wriggled as if shivering, 'she loves others' misfortunes, she do.'

Jed and I exchanged a glance. 'What do you mean?' he asked.

She gave a sniff. 'Remember when the Morgans' little girl died?' Jed nodded. 'Well, obviously they weren't at the following committee meeting, never came again, but as you'd expect, everyone was talking about it. There was Miss Miriam saying how sad it was and dabbing at her eyes, but afterwards I saw her.'

'Saw her what, Tilly?' Jed asked.

'When she thought no one was looking, for all her tears, I saw her smiling.'

'Could be you were mistaken,' I said.

'No, Mr Hawkes, I know what I saw. That woman is just plain nasty. Now, if there's nothing else I'd better get on.'

After she'd gone Jed and I exchanged another glance, and Jed blew out through pursed lips. 'I'm beginning to get a completely different picture of the Garvin sisters to the one I'd had before,' Jed said. 'I'd always thought them harmless old biddies.'

'We don't know that they're not.'

'Hmm, now say that like you believe it.'

'It's a big jump from being possibly a bit malicious to being a potential murderer.'

Jed rubbed at his beard. 'I think maybe we should take a trip over to Chalfont.'

'Why?' I asked.

'Because that's where you got to hear about the Garvins' "whack-job" cousin. And where better to get gossip than the village pub?'

'Now?' I asked.

'Now,' Jed said, glancing at his watch. 'We'll just have enough time to get over there for a quick bite and for me to get back for a wash and brush up before going to see Emma.'

I parked in the pub car park. Being a Monday afternoon, it was almost empty and inside the bar was quieter still. Rose was sitting behind the bar reading a magazine, and when she looked up and saw me her lips curled into a smile, which made me think that Lucy should perhaps be a little more careful about who she chose as friends.

'Hi, Jim,' she said, 'I wasn't expecting to see you so soon.'

'Just passing,' I said.

'What can I get you?'

Jed reluctantly went for a half of ale while I made do with a pint of soda water with a splash of lime. We also ordered a couple of sandwiches.

'Yesterday you mentioned the Garvin girls' cousin,' I said, jumping in with both feet, 'and your father gave the impression he wasn't too good. Jed here wondered which one it was. He hadn't heard that he'd taken ill.'

Rose looked up from Jed's half-pint she was pouring. 'As far as I know there's only the one and that thar's that David.' She gave a shiver. 'Didn't like him, but wouldn't wish what happened to him on my worst enemy.'

'What did happen?' Jed asked.

Rose put Jed's glass down on the bar and started pouring me a lime and soda. 'Tragic accident, they all say, but damn weird to my way of thinking.' She took a quick look over her shoulder, no doubt to make sure her father wasn't listening, and moved in closer. 'You must have heard about it,' she said to Jed. 'Happened a while back. He fell from the cliff path just a bit past the point. You'd have to be a fool to manage to fall from thar.'

'So, what do you think happened?'

'I reckon he jumped,' she said, 'jumped before someone found out what he'd been up to.'

'And what *had* he been up to?' I asked.

She glanced around again. 'He was always hanging around outside the little kids' school. I heard he'd even tried to get a job there once, but ald Mrs Peterson wasn't having none of it. She knew a wrong'un soon as look at 'em.' She plonked my drink down in front of me and took my money. 'I think a few people were getting suspicious,' she said, handing me my change. 'Maybe even someone had it out with him, said they were going to report him.' She gave a derisive sniff. 'Anyway, when they found him, he was still alive, but only just. Idiot – if you're going to do that sort of thing at least make sure you do it proper. Now he's up there at Goldsmere House with about as much going on in his head as a cabbage, so I've heard. Good riddance too.'

Sadly, I was pretty sure Rose's confidence was misplaced. If he'd been a danger before, as far as I was concerned, he was now doubly so – but how? How could a man in a coma be playing havoc with my life? And why? I'd never met the man.

But you have – inside your head. He knows you know what kind of monster he is. He knows you're going to expose him for what he's done, and he can't allow that.

Jed asked that I drop him off at Emma's, saying he'd forgotten something and, by the time I swung into her drive, we had talked ourselves round and round in circles.

'It's all in my head – it must be,' I said, pulling up outside the front door.

'Someone trying to kill you, and creeping around outside Emma's bedroom wasn't inside your head.'

'Maybe it was. Maybe I walked in my sleep.'

'You believe that?'

'I really don't know what to believe any more.'

'He got inside my head too,' Jed said, his voice almost a sigh. 'I remember how it felt; I remember how it made me feel. It was like my head was full of poison. The man was pure evil.'

I didn't disagree. I'd felt the same.

'Give my love to Emma,' I told him. 'If they don't let her come home tomorrow, I'll pop over to the hospital to see her in the evening.'

'I'll see you tomorrow,' he said as he climbed out of the car. 'And Jim,' he bent down to look back at me, 'be careful.'

'I'll do my best,' I said, trying to smile, but I'm not sure I succeeded.

He gave a grunt and slammed the door shut. I watched him until he reached Emma's front door.

It was almost five-thirty when I walked up the path to the cottage and not a moment too soon. During the drive back from Chalfont the sky had darkened to grey, and black storm clouds had begun to chase across the heavens. As I turned into the lane the first plump drops of rain splattered against the windscreen.

I went straight upstairs, undressed and threw myself into the shower. All the talk about the Garvins' cousin and how he'd invaded my head had left me feeling dirty. Sadly, the shower wouldn't be able to wash away the filth lingering inside my psyche.

By the time I'd showered and changed the rain was drumming against the windows and I heard the first rumble of thunder in the distance. It was almost six o'clock and Lucy was going to get soaked. I tried ringing her mobile, but it went straight to voicemail and it occurred to me I was getting a lot of that these days. I thought about phoning the pub to tell her I'd come and get her but realised I didn't have the number. And anyway, she was probably halfway across the village and already soaking wet.

I grabbed my keys off the hall table and made a run for it. In the few seconds it took me to run down the path and jump into the car my shirt was plastered to my back. At this rate we'd both need a change of clothing by the time we got back. The thought that we could always get naked while our clothes dried out brought back the smile to my face.

I made it across the village without seeing her and was pulling up outside the pub when my mobile went *ping*. I pulled it out of my back pocket and smiled. I had a text from Lucy. I clicked on the message and my smile disappeared.

If you ever want to see your whore again you will do exactly as you're told. Understand?

I stared at the screen. What was happening? What was Lucy playing at?

The phone pinged again, and another message popped up.

I said, do you understand?

Then I did understand, I understood only too well. He had Lucy. The motherfucker had Lucy, but how on earth could that be?

Yes, I replied, *I understand.*

Good. Wait for instructions. No police or game over for your filthy little slut. Understand?

Yes, I typed, though I had to do it twice as my fingers had apparently stopped functioning.

I swung the car around and drove back to the cottage, all the time wondering what the hell I was going to do.

CHAPTER TWENTY-SEVEN

By seven there had been no further messages and I was going not so quietly mad. I paced around the cottage, my stomach in knots and my heart pounding, mobile in hand, hardly able to take my eyes off the screen while I waited for another message.

Then it rang and I practically dropped it in my hyped-up state of anxiety. The screen said Jed was calling.

'Not now, not now,' I said to myself, but swiped the screen to answer the call anyway.

'Jim,' he said without any niceties, 'we have a problem. Emms is awake and I'm afraid we're going to have to involve the police, there's no other way.'

'No!' I practically shouted. 'No, you can't.'

'Jim? We have to. Someone tried to kill Emma. Someone pushed her down the stairs.'

'He has Lucy,' I said, and I could feel my eyes bubbling

up. 'He has Lucy and he says I'll never see her again if I don't do as he says and that includes not calling the police.'

'Who has her?'

'How the fuck should I know?'

I heard Jed suck in breath. 'Well – how did he make contact?'

'With her mobile. He texted me on her mobile.'

'Oh bugger!' and I heard someone say something to him and there was a muttered conversation. 'Where are you now?'

'At the cottage.'

'Wait for me there. I'll be straight over.'

'What if he sends me another message?'

'Let me know,' and with that he hung up.

Time seemed to go into slow motion, every minute taking an age. I should be doing something. I should be trying to find Lucy. Where the fuck could he have taken her? But *he* couldn't have taken her anywhere – *he* was in a high-security care home. Unless he wasn't as ill as they thought, unless it wasn't as secure as they thought – but that was mad, wasn't it? I'd seen him in there connected to a whole load of wires and tubes.

You didn't really see anything. You only saw what he wanted you to see.

'Come on, Jed, come on.' But Jed was miles away and all I could do was sit and wait, unless I did call the police. Whenever these situations occurred on the telly, I usually shouted at the screen for the hero or heroine not to be such an idiot and of course they should go to the police. They were the experts and how the hell would the villain know anyway? Now I was in the self-same position it didn't feel so easy. Terrible things could be happening to Lucy while I waited for Jed or another message, but even worse things could happen to her if I didn't do as I was told.

A zigzag of lightning lit up the sky and after a count of about five seconds there came a crash of thunder that was loud enough to make me jump. The rain was now lashing against the kitchen window and the inclement weather conditions would hinder Jed's journey back from Torquay.

There was another ping from my mobile.

Sitting comfortably? Your bitch is.

And there was a close-up of Lucy tied to a chair, head slumped forward, her hair a tangled mess, hiding her face.

Or maybe not.

'What the fuck do you want?' I shouted at the phone lying on my palm, then jabbed my finger on the letters at the bottom of the screen.

What do you want? I typed.

This time there wasn't any instant response. I waited and waited for what felt like eternity but was probably only a few minutes. This was driving me insane.

What the hell do you want? I typed again.

Nothing.

I looked at the picture of Lucy again. At least I had something to show the police if it came to it. Maybe that was the answer, maybe this was what I should do – go to the police.

Where was the nearest police station? I had no idea – it

could be anywhere. Knowing my luck, probably Torquay and I'd pass Jed on the way there.

Then there was a *thump, thump, thump* on the door, sending my heart right up into my mouth.

I dropped my mobile onto the table and grabbed the largest knife I could find. What I thought I was going to do with it I had no idea. I wasn't exactly thinking straight. All sorts of visions passed through my head, and by the time I reached the door I was expecting to open it to find no one there, but instead a package on the doorstep containing something terrible, like one of Lucy's fingers – or worse. One of the final scenes from the film *Seven* floated into my mind, the distraught Brad Pitt peering down into a box containing his wife's severed head.

I flung the door open. If 'the man' was there waiting for me with an axe, chainsaw or some other lethal weapon I didn't care, it had to be better than this.

Jed stepped straight inside, rain running down his ruddy cheeks and dripping off the end of his nose. He certainly wasn't dressed for wet weather this evening.

His eyes went to the knife I was brandishing in my right hand, though he didn't pass any comment. 'Have you heard anything more?' he asked.

'Yeah,' I said, leading him into the kitchen. I picked up my phone and handed it to him. 'I asked him what he wanted, but I've had no reply.'

Jed studied the picture of Lucy and I saw that same mean expression I'd seen before creep back onto his face.

'I don't know what to do,' I said, dragging my hand

through my hair as the awful sick feeling of despair bubbled up inside of me. 'What should I do?'

Jed glanced at me, then back to the image on the screen. 'Come on,' he said, handing me the phone.

I followed him out into the hallway. 'Where're we going?'

'To have a long conversation with the Garvin sisters about their cousin David.'

'Do you think they'll help us?'

'They'd bloody better,' he mumbled as he threw open the front door.

I just about had the wherewithal to pull on my jacket and grab my keys, but I was dressed about as well as Jed for the conditions and we were both dripping wet by the time I slammed the door to his Jaguar and settled back into the seat.

Jed started the engine and fiddled with the heater in an effort to clear the mist clouding the windscreen. After a few seconds he gave up and pulled out a cloth from the glove box, swiping it across the glass to leave a trail of tiny, shining droplets in its wake. With a grunt he put the car into gear and slowly reversed down the lane until he could turn around, which was no mean feat as I doubted he could see a thing out the back.

The road through the village was deserted and the few street lights barely cut their way through the murk. The storm had darkened the skies and it could have been midnight instead of mid evening.

Lights glowed from the windows of the Sly as we

drove past, and I felt awful knowing George and his wife were in there serving customers with hardly a care in the world, while their daughter was in the hands of some unidentified, crazed psychopath.

'Do you think this David had a partner in crime?' I said, thinking out loud.

Jed didn't take his eyes off the road ahead. 'Did you see anyone else in his head?'

'Only his victims and the woman who tried to kill him.'

'I don't know, Jim, there's something really odd about all of this.'

'Odd? The whole fucking thing is odd,' I said, getting angry. 'This is a small country village, where the most exciting thing that should be happening is someone's pet cat going missing. That's why I came here and ever since I've arrived my life has turned to shit.'

'Your life was already shit,' Jed said with a snort, '*that's* why you came here.'

I couldn't argue. 'Well, it got a whole lot shittier.'

'And if I told you it was going to get worse before it got better, I'd probably be right,' Jed said. 'I think whoever is doing this is trying to force the pace. He wants you gone and by hurting Emma he thought you'd be on your own tonight. He obviously didn't realise how tough she can be.' He paused for a moment as he brought the car to a halt. 'Or how angry I can get.' He turned the engine off and killed the lights. 'Come on – let's do this thing.'

'What are we going to say?' I asked. 'We can hardly tell them we think their comatose cousin is somehow

397

threatening Lucy's life, has attacked Emma and has tried to kill me.'

The inside light clicked on as he opened the driver's door and I caught a glimpse of his grim expression. If I was Darcy or Miriam upon seeing that look, I'd tell him anything he damn well wanted to know.

Jed strode around the car and up the path towards the house, seemingly oblivious to the rain lashing down upon us. The building was in darkness apart from a crack of light I could just make out through the glass panel in the front door, probably coming from an ajar door to the kitchen or a living room.

Jed wasn't in the mood for niceties. He thumped on the door four times, left it barely a second and thumped again.

I grabbed his arm before he could do it again. 'We want them to invite us in, not call the police,' I warned him.

He let out a shuddery breath and gave a bob of his head.

Light bloomed in the hallway as a door opened. 'Who's there?' a tentative voice called.

'Jed.'

'Jed?'

'Is that you, Darcy? I need to speak to you.'

The hall light came on and the shadow of a slight figure moved slowly towards the door. I'm not sure whether some sort of sixth sense kicked in, or whether it was just my powers of observation, but my anxiety levels jumped up another notch and at this rate I had the feeling I might end up having a heart attack before the end of the evening.

'Something's wrong,' I whispered out of the corner of my mouth.

I heard the drawing of bolts and, with the clink of a chain, the door opened a crack and Darcy peered out of the gloomy passageway.

'Jed?'

'Can we come in? We need to speak to you and Miriam.'

I could only see one side of her face through the crack in the door and the one eye flicked my way. Her head and shoulders slumped and with a weary sigh she pushed the door closed.

Jed raised his fist to thump on the door again, but I stopped him as I heard the rattle of the chain. Darcy opened the door and stepped to one side, gesturing for us both to come in. She led us down the corridor and into a small sitting room. One lamp in the corner by a large, lumpy armchair gave the room some muted light. A glass of some golden liquid rested on a small table beside it. Darcy obviously didn't believe in half measures as the glass was almost three-quarters full.

She sank down onto the chair and gestured that we should also sit.

'Maybe we should do this in the kitchen,' I said, 'we're both pretty wet.'

'No matter. The furniture will dry,' she said, and her voice sounded lost, like all hope had deserted her.

'Where's Miriam?' Jed asked. 'I'd rather not have to do this twice.'

'She's not here,' Darcy said, reaching for the glass and taking a slug. Tellingly she didn't offer us a drink.

Jed and I exchanged a glance. 'Where is she on a night like this? It's filthy out there.'

Darcy looked up at us with haunted eyes and although half her face was in shadow, I could see there was something wrong with it. Her left eye wasn't much more than a slit, her eyelid a sliver of liver.

'Jesus, Darcy, what happened to you?' I asked, leaning forward in my seat.

She lifted her left hand towards her face not quite touching her skin with her fingertips, before clenching her hand into a fist and letting it drop back into her lap.

She took another swig of her drink. 'What do you want?'

'Someone pushed Emma down the stairs last night and now they have Lucy,' Jed said, getting straight to the point. 'I don't know how or why but we think it all has something to do with your cousin David.'

Darcy gave a start at his name and her hand was shaking as she placed the tumbler down onto the table.

'Is Emma all right?' she asked.

'Yes, thanks to her hard head, but Lucy isn't.' He glanced my way and gestured towards Darcy. 'Show her,' he said.

I stood to pull my mobile out of my back pocket and clicked on the message showing the picture of Lucy and held it out to Darcy. She stared at it in my hand as though it was something alien to her.

'Take it,' Jed snapped, and Darcy flinched.

She slowly reached out her hand and clasped her fingers around it. When she looked down at the screen her lips pressed together into a thin, bloodless line. This time her expression was not one of disapproval, it was more like she was trying to hold in a scream or howl of agony.

When she looked up her eyes were brimming with tears. 'David isn't our cousin,' she said at last. 'He's our brother.'

'Brother?' Jed said.

And something I'd heard before went click in my head. 'The rumour about Darcy's father and a liaison with some girl,' I said. 'That's why he was sent away. He'd got her pregnant.'

Darcy grimaced and reached for her glass. 'Marie Baker,' she said. 'She was our nanny for a while. Then she just left out of the blue. It wasn't until years later we realised that the little boy being brought up by our aunt in Chalfont was actually our brother.'

'David Baker,' I said as another bit of information floated up out of my subconscious.

'What?' Darcy said. 'No, David Carlisle, he's known as David Carlisle.'

'There was a business card tucked in the corkboard back at the cottage – David Baker, handyman.'

'Oh my God,' Darcy said. 'Oh my God.'

'Darcy?'

Her one good eye was huge and full of despair. 'I didn't want to believe it was true,' she whispered, 'but deep down . . .' She let out a shuddery sigh and slumped further into her seat.

'It's you who visits Krystal Morgan's and Marie Louise Baker's graves?' I said.

She gave a small bob of the head and looked back down at the picture of Lucy before dropping my phone into her lap. 'She's at The Grange. There's a larder off the kitchen.'

'The Grange?' Jed and I both asked at the same time.

'It was our family home until grandmother died. It was sold to pay the death duties, that's when we were sent to live with our aunt in Chalfont. That's when David . . .' Her voice cracked.

'Who is it that has Lucy?' Jed asked. 'We know David's in Goldsmere House.'

Darcy gave a bitter laugh and reached for her glass, grasping it between both hands as she knocked back what was left. 'You know nothing,' she spat.

'Then why don't you tell us?'

'We haven't time for this,' I told him. 'We have to find Lucy.'

'Who is it that has her?' Jed repeated.

'Right from the start I knew something was wrong with him,' Darcy said, ignoring the question. 'He looked like an angel, but even as a child his heart was as black as any demon's.'

'Jed, we need to go,' I told him.

'Who has Lucy?' Jed repeated again.

Darcy slammed her empty glass down on the table making us both jump. 'Who do you think?' she said. 'Who's not here?'

'Miriam?' Jed said.

'Miriam – David. I'm not sure where one ends and the other begins any more. Some days I don't even know which one I'm talking to.'

My mobile pinged. Darcy picked it up out of her lap and glanced at the screen. 'I think you might want to see this,' she said and handed it back to me.

Meet me at the point. Come alone.

'Is she crazy? It's blowing a gale out there,' Jed said, looking over my shoulder.

'No, she's not crazy,' Darcy said, 'it's worse than that. He consumed her. David gradually, insidiously worked his way into her head until all she could think about or care about was him. After his . . . his accident, I thought she was getting better. I thought at last she was free of him.' She looked at me. 'But, oh so slowly, she gradually began to change. David would keep coming through in things she said and did. Then *you* came to Slyford and she got worse.'

'Me?'

She gave a bitter laugh. 'Yes, you. You and your little performance at Emma's. I told her to leave you be. I told her you wouldn't realise the significance.' She shrugged. 'Miriam probably would have listened, but David . . .' She grimaced. 'Since that night she . . . he's been obsessed with you.'

My mobile pinged again.

I said meet me at the point!

'I should reply,' I said.

'Tell her yes,' Jed said. 'I'll go to The Grange and see if I can find Lucy.'

'What if Miriam takes Lucy with her?' I asked. 'She can't leave any loose ends and Lucy would definitely be a loose end.'

'We should call the police,' Jed said.

'No!' Darcy said. 'No. It's bad enough David being in that terrible place, but Miriam as well – then he would have won.'

'What on earth are you talking about, woman?' Jed asked.

I grabbed Jed by the arm. 'Come on,' I told him. 'We'll go to The Grange on the way to the point. I'll text back when we're on the move.'

For a moment he was as immoveable as a statue as he glared down at Darcy, but then with a grunt he let me pull him towards the door.

Back in the car I began to text as Jed drove. I kept it short and sweet.

All right, was all I wrote.

CHAPTER TWENTY-EIGHT

The ground floor of The Grange was lit up like a Christmas tree and the front door was ajar. Jed paused on the doorstep and, gesturing for me to stand to one side and behind him, slowly pushed the door open. I'm not sure what he was expecting, but he was being very careful, that was for sure, and there was something in his posture that brought home to me that this man really had once been a soldier.

Once inside he moved from room to room, each time pausing on the threshold, each time taking it slow as he opened the door. As we entered the kitchen it finally occurred to me that he was checking for booby traps.

'Jed, Miriam's a middle-aged woman not Al-Qaeda,' I whispered.

'You saw what was inside his head – you saw what he's capable of,' he hissed back, and that had me biting back any further criticism. He was right. I knew exactly what David Baker, or should I say David Carlisle, was capable of: murder and torture and more.

As soon as we walked into the kitchen, even if it hadn't been for the open front door, we would have known that Darcy hadn't lied. One of the kitchen chairs lay on its side. It was as Darcy said, there was a larder at the back of the kitchen. Another kitchen chair, slashed duct tape hanging from its arms, was crammed into one corner. A roll of the stuff lay on a shelf along with a very sharp carving knife, its gleaming blade dulled in places by smears of blood.

'Oh my God,' I groaned. 'Oh my God – Lucy.'

Jed crouched down by the chair. 'Keep calm,' he told me. 'There's not enough blood for it to be life-threatening. I think he or she was just trying to frighten her – and maybe you, if you came here.'

'Well they've succeeded,' I muttered as my eyes roamed the cramped room looking for more evidence they'd been here. But Jed was right, there was no more blood and there would have been. There'd been plenty in my frenzied journey through David Carlisle's psyche.

'She must have taken Lucy with her.'

'You really think Miriam is behind all this?'

'Who else?'

My mobile pinged again before I could think of a reply.

Where the fuck are you?

I'm on my way, I texted back.

If you dont hurry there wont be nothing worth coming for.

'What the fuck does that mean?' I said, showing Jed the text.

'He – she – it is trying to panic you.'

'How can you be so calm?'

Jed just grunted. 'We need wet-weather gear if we're going to the point.'

'You're coming with me?'

'You don't think I'd let you go on your own?'

'The text said I had to.'

'Fuck the text! If you go on your own, I'd bet nineteen to the dozen that you won't be coming back – and Lucy neither.'

'But—'

'But what? Miriam is at best deranged or at worst she's been taken over by someone so incredibly evil they don't care what they do. Either way you need help.' He strode through the kitchen and out into the hall, and after one more glance at the bloodied knife I followed him.

Jed went straight along the hallway to a small lobby at the back of the house, taking off his jacket as he went. I followed on behind, now not so sure what I should do. What Jed said made sense, but if he came with me it could make a bad situation a whole lot worse.

'Maybe we should call the police,' I said.

Jed reached up to take down one of the long, waxcd raincoats hanging off a line of hooks on the wall. 'And how would a load of plod marching along that narrow cliff path make this any better? You involve them now and you'll leave them no way out. Never corner a rabid dog, lad.' My expression was no doubt distraught as his softened. 'Don't worry, lad, I do have a bit of experience in this sort of thing.'

'You said you were a soldier.'

He laughed. 'Military Intelligence, that's how I met Reggie.' He handed me the coat. 'This used to be his. Emma uses it now but it's large enough to fit you.'

Jed took down another and pulled it on. He then passed me a pair of wellies. They were a size too big, and I assumed also Reggie's, but better that than slipping and sliding around in the pouring rain.

When we'd both changed we looked like a couple of North Sea fishermen, but at least we wouldn't be getting any more soaked than we already were.

Outside the weather hadn't changed any. Flashes of silver zigzagged the sky, lighting up the drive, followed by booms of thunder that were getting louder, closer. We hurried out along the lane to the path to Fisherman's Cove.

'I can't see a thing,' I said.

'Here,' Jed said, and a beam of light appeared as if by magic. 'You take it and lead the way.'

'She'll see us coming,' I said, but still took the offered torch. It was one of those big buggers you see the American police force use on TV, and I must admit I felt a little better having the weight of it in my hand, if for no other reason than it'd make a good weapon.

'Probably best to hold it down low and pointing at the path. It might stop her from doing something stupid.'

'She already is doing something pretty fucking stupid.

408

How on earth does she think this is all going to end?' I shouted back at him, in an effort to be heard over the tempest going on all around us.

If he replied I didn't hear him. I wasn't even sure if he'd heard me. But now I'd asked the question it'd set me pondering on the answer. If Miriam was truly somehow possessed by her illegitimate brother, because this was what Darcy would have us believe, did he or she really care? Miriam could possibly have no idea of what she was doing, or if she did was so in David's thrall that she would do whatever it took to keep him happy. The vision of the chubby-faced young woman on her knees flashed through my head – had that been Miriam? Had David been abusing her when he was little more than a child? This didn't get any better. One thing was for certain, David would try to protect himself, meaning he wouldn't want anything to happen to Miriam, the person giving him a physical body.

Then I wondered what the fuck I was thinking. We were talking about possession, for fuck's sake.

He's been inside your head and you've been inside his – you've seen it is possible.

It can't be.

You've been seeing ghosts for the past two weeks – you didn't think that was possible either.

I still don't.

What then? You'd prefer to believe you were mad? Grow up, Jim – this isn't all about you. Think of someone else for once in your life. Think of that young woman,

409

who could possibly die tonight, think of Krystal and what happened to her.

It's Miriam who's mad. She must be. I was arguing with myself now – desperate to make some sense of it all. She only thinks she's possessed by David – that's the logical answer. It was, but in my heart, I knew it wasn't the correct one.

A hand touched me on the shoulder, and I whirled around. Jed moved in close and cupped a hand to his mouth, bringing it close to my ear.

'Best I hang back a bit,' he told me. I went to hand him the torch. 'You hold on to it,' he shouted, 'if worse comes to worst you can always use it as a club,' and with that cheery bit of advice I carried on walking and within moments realised why it was here that Jed had chosen to start to keep back. I had reached the most exposed stretch of path.

Although there was some way to go before I reached my destination, the path curved around the cove below and even through the pouring rain I could see the shadow of the point jutting out into the sea like a huge black beast. Another bright flash illuminated the headland, followed almost immediately by an almighty crash. I strained my eyes to peer across the bay in those few brief moments, but if Miriam and Lucy were there, I couldn't see them.

I trudged on through the dark. I kept the torch pointed down at the path, so I could see a few steps ahead, but it was barely making an impression. How Miriam had managed to coerce Lucy into going with her I had no idea,

410

and the image of the bloodied knife skittered through my mind and I felt sick to my stomach.

By my reckoning, I'd almost reached where the path dipped and a second branched off down to Fisherman's Cove when I heard a sharp, high-pitched yap from ahead of me. I stopped dead, peering into the black, not daring to lift the torch. Then I heard it again, closer now. I raised the torch a tad so it was angled onto the track about a yard in front of me. Another yap, and just on the edge of the beam I saw something move. I raised it a little higher and to the left.

Krystal was crouched down, her little dog squirming within her arms. Her eyes were wide and fearful as she looked at me. I sank down to her eye level and she lifted her forefinger first to her lips and then to point along the path and to the right.

Benji continued to struggle until he managed to manoeuvre himself around, so he was facing to where she had pointed. He yapped again and then snarled, showing teeth. Krystal petted his head with the hand she'd used to point.

They were warning me of something or, should I say, someone? No, something was probably right, my own argument that Miriam was deranged I now recognised as merely a wishful fantasy. She was possessed by something, that something being the entity that once had been David Carlisle.

'Is it him, Krystal? Is it really him?' I whispered, though no one could hear me over the howling wind.

Her bottom lip began to tremble, and she nodded.

I climbed to my feet and glanced back over my shoulder. I could just make out the bulky silhouette of Jed a few yards back down the path. Keeping the torch pointing straight down I hurried back to where he stood.

'Trouble ahead,' I said into his ear.

'Where?'

'I think he may be lurking at the top of the track down to Fisherman's Cove.'

I didn't need to see his face to know that his eyebrows had probably bunched together into his caterpillar frown. 'How?'

'Krystal told me,' I said and walked back to where Krystal had been waiting.

She was still there, but my flashlight found her now standing in the middle of the path as it first illuminated her black shoes then white socks. I didn't dare raise the torch any higher, but then, somehow, I could see her, as though she was glowing with some inner light. It wasn't bright, just enough to see her there. She pointed again along the path and to the right. I switched off the torch and hefted it in my right hand, holding it just above the lamp to use the handle like a club.

To my relief I could still see her. She crouched down to let Benji scramble to the ground, then the pair of them trotted off along the path and, to my disappointment, slowly faded away. It didn't matter, she had told me what I needed to know. I kept my eyes to the right, searching the shrubbery for a bulky shape. The path began to slope downwards, we were approaching the track down to the cove.

I gripped the torch and raised it slightly getting ready for any attack. I could feel my heart pounding in my ears and a trickle of sweat run down my spine. I saw the black mass of undergrowth begin to thin and then a gap. I lifted the flashlight to shoulder height and there was a roar, more like a howl, and something barrelled into me.

The ferocity of the attack bowled me off my feet and into the bushes to my left. A figure loomed above me. A flash across the sky illuminated the bulk towering over me in stark relief. I couldn't make out any features within the hooded raincoat, but I did see a glimmer of metal as an arm rose and came swinging down towards me.

Surrounded by the shrubbery I couldn't roll away, I was trapped. I flung up the arm holding the torch, swiping it across my body. I felt the clash of metal against metal as I knocked the blade aside hard enough to make my fingers tingle.

There was another roar and, as I struggled to get off my back like some overturned beetle, I saw the arm rise again. I grabbed hold of the torch at both ends and threw it up in front of me hoping to deflect the second blow, but it never came. The figure was whipped away.

A yell was followed by a shriek and when I managed to pull myself onto one knee, I could see two figures wrestling on the path a few feet away.

In the dark it was impossible to see who was who. Just two shadows separating then merging into one, locked in mortal combat. I clambered to my feet and got ready to hit out with the torch, but hit out at who? If anything, the rain had got worse and was falling like a curtain between me and them.

A flash across the bay half-blinded me, and a second later a boom loud enough to make my ears ring made the ground tremble beneath me, then a yell and a figure bounding away leaving the other in a crumpled heap. I switched on the torch and dropped down beside Jed. He was lying on his side clutching his shoulder, and it might have been the torchlight, but his usually ruddy complexion was a sickly white.

'I'm fine, I'm fine,' he said, although he was anything but. I could see blood seeping through his fingers and his breath was coming in gasps.

'Jed, you need help.'

'It's my bloody shoulder – I won't die, Lucy might. Get after Miriam – get after her!'

I didn't want to leave him, but he was right. I had to get to Miriam before she got to Lucy. I ran.

CHAPTER TWENTY-NINE

I ran with the torch shining ahead. There was no point hiding my progress now, she knew I'd be after her and she knew she had to get to Lucy before I caught her. If Lucy was still alive. I couldn't think that she wasn't. I couldn't let myself believe she could possibly be dead. I'd let Kat down. I couldn't let another woman I loved die because of me.

Running in wellington boots isn't easy at the best of times, but when they're a size too big, the weather conditions are apocalyptic and you're negotiating a slippery narrow track it is nigh on impossible, but still I somehow ran. I had to.

Above the pounding of the rain, the howling of the wind and the crashing of the waves below me I heard Benji bark. He'd never let me down before, so I switched off the torch and slowed to a trot, my eyes straining to see the path ahead – and a memory flickered up out of my subconscious.

'The man', David, thought he was so clever, but I had seen – he had let me see. David running along the path, jubilant. Wanting to tell Miriam what he'd done. Wanting to let her know what a clever little psychopath he was, but instead finding the other sister waiting for him. Waiting at the one place on the path where an abrupt and unexpected push would send him tumbling to the rocks below.

And even though I could hardly see a thing I knew the spot wasn't more than a few yards from here and Miriam – David – would be waiting. I slowed right down, peering through rain that was falling like stair rods.

There was another yap, so close that the terrier must be right by my side. I stood stock-still, the rain stinging my skin as it pounded my face. I pulled the hood back, so I at least had some peripheral vision. Another yap a few feet ahead and to my right. I slowly let my eyes scan the edge of the path.

Come on, you bastard, come on. A voice growled in my head.

Was he trying to goad me? Or did he not realise I could hear him, feel him, sense him?

Come on, you fucking bastard. Just a few more steps.

Could he see me? I couldn't see him. I stood my ground.

Bastard . . . and my head was suddenly awash with the nightmare ravings of the man I now knew to be David Carlisle. It was like a sluice had been opened as the sick fantasies of what he wanted to do to me spewed out in a vitriolic stream. I gritted my teeth to hold back my gasps as each atrocity punched into my psyche. Then, in amongst the sewer that was his mind, I saw glimpses of Lucy.

Lucy leaving the Sly dressed in knee-length wax jacket with flat cap covered by a hood. Lucy on the ground, eyes closed, a dark patch bruising her temple. Lucy bound to one of Emma's kitchen chairs with duct tape across her mouth, eyes wide and scared, trying to scream against the tape as the kitchen blade hovered inches from her face.

I felt like I'd been punched in the stomach. Oh God, Lucy.

And it was as if the Almighty had heard me as there was a flash of lightning that I'm sure hit the cliff, the resultant boom rocking me on my feet, but in that one moment I saw him – her – it – standing just three feet away from me and, in that split second, I knew what Darcy had told us was true. I could see it was Miriam, but although it was her face staring out from beneath her hood, it wasn't really. It wasn't just the snarling lips or the manic eyes, there was something masculine there: a hardening of her soft cheeks, a tautening and darkening of her jaw and upper lip.

Then the light was gone, and she was coming at me, arm raised, knife in hand. I lashed out with the torch and was rewarded with a solid thump hitting her right shoulder, but it wasn't enough to take her down. I didn't give her time to recover. I swung the torch again, and this time it smashed into the side of her head. She gave a yelp, and abruptly turned and began to run away.

I hesitated for a moment – was it a trick? Would she abruptly turn on me with that damned knife before I had a chance to stop? The vision of Lucy staring in terror at the kitchen knife we'd found smeared with blood flashed into my head and it was enough to spur me on. She must have hidden Lucy somewhere and I had to follow. I had to be right behind the thing that had been Miriam when it got there.

We were almost at the point and at last the rain eased, the flashes of lightning were fewer and the following booms of thunder fading into the distance. Black storm clouds still chased across the sky, but they were moving on, and occasionally the moon peeked out, bathing the landscape in its pale light, if only for a moment or two.

Now and then I caught sight of a figure charging along the track ahead of me. For a big woman Miriam was certainly fast on her feet as she was getting further and further ahead of me, and if she got to Lucy before I could catch her . . . My fear for Lucy was the impetus I needed to push myself even harder and the next time I caught sight of Miriam I was catching her.

The moon came out as the path ahead dipped and for a few yards the point was out of sight and then, when I ran up the next incline and rounded a bend, I was on the last upward stretch and had a clear view of Miriam ahead of me. Her age must have been beginning to tell as she was slowing, but then so was I. My heart was pounding, my legs were tiring and my calves were burning, but I had to catch her, I just had to.

I was about ten yards behind her when she reached the top. I forced myself to speed up, even though I knew I could be running into a trap. I had no choice. Then the path evened out and I was running towards the viewing point and there was Miriam.

She threw back her hood and reached down, knife in her other hand. I stopped as she pulled a figure off the ground.

What you going to do now, you little fucker?

She didn't say the words, but I heard them as clear as day. Miriam pulled Lucy against her and pressed that lethally sharp knife to her throat.

Lucy's face was pale beneath streaks of what could have been mud or blood in the moonlight. I could see tape stretched across her mouth and wrapped around her ankles, her hands were hidden from view behind her back – I assumed they were taped too. She was between me and a demented psychopath and there wasn't a thing I could do to save her.

There was no way I could see this ending well. This being that was David had made it clear he was going to murder Lucy in front of me. It would be either me dead or him, and he was confident it would be me. He'd killed before and enjoyed it. He didn't believe I had it in me. He believed I was weak – and he was probably right.

'So, Jim – what are you going to do now?' Miriam's lips moved, but the voice was deeper and rough-sounding. She laughed and pressed the point of the knife into the crease in Lucy's neck just below the jaw. Lucy winced and a teardrop of blood, black in the moonlight, slowly ran

419

down her neck mingling with the rain and staining the collar of her T-shirt.

'Why are you doing this?' I said.

'*Why are you doing this?*' she sneered. 'Why do you think?'

I shook my head.

'Because I can,' and she pressed the blade into Lucy's cheekbone.

'Don't!'

'*Don't!*' she mimicked. 'Don't what, Jim? Don't cut your whore of a girlfriend's face to ribbons? Don't cut out her eyes and force them down her throat? Don't throw her off the cliff? *Don't hurt her?*' She moved the knife until it was resting just below Lucy's eye. 'No chance. I want to see you suffer. I want to see you snivelling like a little kid. I want to hear you begging for her life and then, when I've finished with her, I want to hear you begging for your own.'

The rain had subsided to not much more than a drizzle so we didn't need to shout to make ourselves heard, and the moon was turning the landscape silver, so I could see Miriam and Lucy clearly. This, unfortunately, meant David could enjoy himself. Not much fun in playing with Lucy and me if we couldn't hear or see what was going on.

'On your knees,' Miriam spat at me. 'Get down on your knees and beg.'

I did as she said; I didn't have a choice. I got down on my knees, a muddy slurry instantly soaking through my jeans and chilling my bones.

'See him now, you little slut? See your big man down on his knees to me.'

Lucy's eyes fluttered shut for a moment and, when they opened, she looked me straight in the eyes and although I'm sure she was scared there was a steely resolve in her expression.

'I can't hear you,' Miriam said, pointing the knife at me. 'I told you I want to hear you beg.'

Lucy was still staring at me, and she gave an almost imperceptible shake of the head and then her legs appeared to give way beneath her.

'What are you doing, you little bitch?' Miriam was having trouble keeping Lucy upright. She had hold of her arm, but Lucy was slipping down to the ground.

'She's passed out,' I shouted at Miriam, although I could see Lucy's eyes were wide open and knowing if either of us were to have a chance of making it out of this alive I would have to take probably the only opportunity I would get. I jumped to my feet and threw myself across the few yards between us.

Our tormentor was wrong-footed. She was off balance as she tried to drag Lucy to her feet and taken completely by surprise as I ran at her screaming my lungs out. Lucy slipped from Miriam's grip and, seeing me coming, curled up into a ball, making herself as small as possible, rolling to the right.

Miriam stumbled backwards a couple of steps, but almost immediately regained her composure and lifted the knife getting ready to strike, but too late. At the last moment I turned sideways on and barged into her with my shoulder; to my way of thinking I was more likely to survive a stab to the back than one to the gut.

If she did land a blow, I didn't feel it. I hit her hard, sending her staggering backwards and into the tubular guard rail with a grunt of pain. I stayed pressed against her and grabbed for her throat, aware my shoulders and back were exposed.

I caught a whiff of lavender perfume reminding me that this was a middle-aged woman I was attacking, and it proved a costly distraction. She sensed my momentary hesitation and smacked her forehead into mine, making me see stars and knocking me back, leaving enough room to free the hand holding the lethal blade. She lashed out. I heard a muffled scream from behind me and just in time leant back as the knife skimmed across the front of my coat.

Miriam let out a roar of frustration and came right at me again. At some point I'd dropped the torch and had nothing to defend myself with as she rushed me, arm raised and knife flashing in the moonlight. I was back-pedalling as fast as I could, not daring to take my eyes off the figure descending upon me in an apoplectic frenzy. Her lips pulled back in feral fury, spittle coating her lips.

I lifted up an arm to protect my face, skidded on a loose stone, tried to right myself and then my feet flew out from beneath me and I hit the ground, smacking the back of my head. My vision turned red then black, and if it hadn't been for Lucy I might just have given into the darkness. I saw a shadow amongst all the black and I rolled to the left hearing the ring of metal against stone and the force of a presence on the ground next to me. I kept rolling and then struggled to stand. Miriam was also clambering to her feet.

She turned on me with a snarl. 'Don't think you're going to get away from me, little man.'

I couldn't argue. I couldn't draw enough breath to speak.

'But first I'm going to deal with your little bitch.'

She abruptly swung around and stalked towards Lucy, who was struggling to get off her knees. Miriam raised the blade above her head, and I heard her laugh. Male laughter. Deep, resounding, masculine laughter.

'You're not going to be so pretty when I've finished with you. No more prick teasing for you. No decent man will ever look at you again.'

Knife or no knife I had to stop David; it might be Miriam's body, but it was him pulling her strings. I launched myself at her back and once again barged into her with my shoulder. She went down with me lying on top of her, her right hand stretched out, fingers scrabbling, to reach the knife that had slipped from her grasp.

I crawled up her body, keeping her pressed down in the mud as I desperately tried to get to the knife before she did. She wriggled and strained beneath me. This time, any thought of the person I was fighting being an older woman was driven from my mind. I pressed my knee into her back and slammed her face down into the dirt, and still she tried to throw me off as her fingers bit into the earth, inching that little bit closer to the handle of the knife.

I kept my hand on the back of her head, grinding Miriam's face into the mud and rock as I reached out with my other hand. Whether she could somehow see I was going to get to it before she did, I'll never know, but she abruptly bucked beneath me, throwing me upwards as she made one last lunge for the knife. Her fingers curled around the handle. I heard her cry of triumph and then she was pushing down with both hands, levering herself up while I tried to cling onto her.

Frantic beyond reason, I clenched my fist and hammered it into the side of her temple – once, twice and a third time. I could have been hitting a brick wall for all the good I was doing. Miriam was an overweight, fifty-something spinster and yet her body was taking everything I could throw at it. David must be giving her this additional strength.

Miriam was twisting around beneath me and if she managed to get onto her back, I would be at the mercy of the lethal weapon she had in her grip. I pummelled at her head, but it was no use. Then with one massive heave she turned over and in desperation I rolled away from her, the knife narrowly missing my right cheek.

For such a bulky woman she was quick on her feet. I'd only just managed to position myself between her and Lucy when she was coming at me, knife extended.

Her face was a bloody mess, but even so she was grinning at me with scarlet-stained teeth. She turned her head and spat. I think I'd broken her nose. I backed away until I was next to Lucy and, not taking my eyes off the

424

advancing woman, helped her to her feet, then pushed her behind me.

'Ah, isn't that sweet?' David said. If Miriam was still in there she was completely dominated by her sibling, there wasn't a shred of her standing there. The body, maybe, but the way she spoke, the way she stood, even the way she held her head – this was David. 'Time to say goodbye.'

I glanced back at Lucy. She was pressed up against the guard rail. I supposed to help keep her standing. The expression in her eyes said it all, she knew we were done for.

'No,' I said. 'No!'

'No what, little man? No, I'm not going to kill you? No, I'm not going to—'

Now I lay me down to sleep.

David stopped, his mouth dropping open as he looked about him and a glimmer of Miriam appeared. 'What?'

I pray the Lord my soul to keep and a dog barked.

Miriam was looking back and forth, and even spun around to look behind her, unfortunately David wasn't stupid enough to let her turn her back on us for long.

'How are you doing that?' David said, glaring at me.

'Doing what?' I asked.

And if I die before I wake.

'You know! You fucking well know!'

I shook my head.

I pray the Lord and the air quivered as slowly a small figure began to materialise between us.

I don't know if Lucy could see her, but the thing that had once been Miriam certainly could. She began to back away, and as she did there was a bark and a small terrier bounded forward to bounce up and down, barking and snarling a few feet away from her.

'Get away from me!' Miriam shouted, and I'm sure it was Miriam, as her eyes darted from Krystal to Benji.

My soul to take.

'You can't hurt me. You're dead. Dead,' David snarled.

Benji wasn't much acting like a dead dog, and I was pretty sure he'd more on his mind than savaging Miriam's ankles. Going for the throat was more likely.

Now I lay me . . .

'Shut up. Shut up,' Miriam cried and lifted her hands to cover her ears. David was made of stronger stuff. Miriam's face hardened and her hands dropped away.

'You can't hurt me.'

What's the matter, David? A voice said, and standing next to Krystal was another figure I recognised. Peter Davies. He and Krystal took a step towards Miriam, who almost fell in her haste to back away from them.

'Get away from me.'

It's time to atone.

And other figures began to appear, first as shadowy silhouettes, but gradually growing in substance until, although still apparitions, they were recognisable as having once been human.

I moved to stand beside Lucy, and she looked up at me with terrified eyes. I glanced back at Miriam and, while her mind was clearly on other things, I pulled the duct tape from Lucy's mouth as gently as I could.

I was still carefully easing it off when she started to speak, unable to contain herself any longer. 'Can you see them?' she asked. 'Can you see Krystal and Benji?'

'Yes, how about the others?'

'What others?'

When I looked back 'the others' had joined Krystal and the reverend and were slowly descending upon Miriam. Her head was jerking from side to side, her face a mask of fear.

'The dead can't hurt me!' she shouted, but Peter Davies knew who was talking.

Maybe we can, maybe we can't, but the living most certainly can.

A sly expression crossed Miriam's face and David was back and in control. 'What? Him?' he sneered pointing at me, and the spirits began to laugh. He froze for a moment and his mouth dropped open into an 'O'. 'No,' David roared. 'No! Darcy, you bitch!' and if any tiny part of Miriam had been there before, she was gone now as her face contorted into a masculine mask of rage. 'You're not going to win, you sanctimonious bastard,' he snarled at the reverend. 'If I go, I'm going to take them with me,' and ignoring the apparitions between us he raised the knife to head height, the lethal blade glinting viciously in the moonlight, and hurled himself straight towards Lucy and me. The phantoms dispersed like smoke as he ploughed through them, leaving a trail of mist in his wake.

I had no weapon with which to defend myself, but I didn't hesitate, I threw myself forward. I heard Lucy cry my name as the creature that once had been Miriam Garvin and I collided, my shoulder hitting him in the chest. He staggered back a few steps, but I hadn't even winded him. He gave a cry of triumph and I leapt back as he took a swipe at my unguarded belly.

The raincoat billowed around me engulfing the blade, but barely for a moment as it sliced through the thick waterproof material as though it was a slab of cream cheese. I was in no doubt if it connected with me, I was a dead man. It would cut through flesh with just as much ease.

He began to laugh. 'Prepare to die, Jim Hawkes.' And he strode towards me, the knife once more held at head height. 'But don't worry. I'll leave enough life in you that you can watch me take your slut to pieces before I end your miserable existence.'

I glanced about me. I had nowhere to go. Lucy had dragged herself along the railing behind me so she was out of the way, but other than running for it, which wasn't an option, I had no choice other than to try and fight him off.

Lucy must have known what I was thinking. 'Run, Jim, save yourself!'

'No,' I said, straightening up and raising my fists. 'I'll not leave you.'

David laughed again.

The clock's ticking, David. I heard Reverend Davies say.

'But not fast enough to save this piece of shit,' and with another stride he was upon me.

His arm drew back, he began to grin, and the blade surged towards me. I ducked to his left away from the knife and thumped him as hard as I could with my right fist, hoping to connect with his kidneys. As my wet-weather gear had saved me from his knife, his cushioned the blow, making it as ineffective as the punch of a child.

As I moved to pass him, he swung around following me, leaving my back wide open to that vicious blade. Lucy screamed as I spun around to face him. The knife rushed towards me and I felt it caress the sleeve of my coat as I jerked away. I didn't have time to thank my good fortune as he kept on coming, a relentless force. He might only be in a vehicle of flesh and blood, but there was no doubt in my mind that I was locked in mortal combat with a supernatural entity. Even his face appeared demonic as the light from the moon danced across his features before being briefly obscured by clouds time and time again.

Then he gave a yell and rushed at me, flipping the blade from one hand to another as I raised my arm to block it. I was back-pedalling again, desperately trying to get out of the way of that blade, too slow, too slow. I saw the knife coming, arcing down towards me and there wasn't a thing I could do to stop it. I heard Lucy cry out again and as the blade scythed towards me, I trod on something hard. I skidded, fought to regain my balance, he lunged at me and I stumbled and fell.

My back hit the ground, jarring my body and knocking the breath out of me, but there was no time to think about pain, no time to think about anything other than the creature trying to kill me. I scrabbled, trying to get to my feet, but I was too late. He loomed over me, knife pointed at my unprotected chest and his expression triumphant. I was about to die.

Tick-tock, David! Tick-tock! I heard the reverend whisper.

David snarled. 'Too late for Jimbo here.' He drew his arm back. 'Much too late.'

He stepped forward so his legs were astride me and dropped to his knees, pinning me down.

'I did so want to make your last moments memorable,' he said, 'but apparently my stupid fucking sister is about to bugger it all up. Nevertheless, I can still make it bloody and painful.' He lowered the knife, so the tip of the blade hovered about an inch from my right eye. 'Maybe I shouldn't kill you. Maybe I should just cut you so badly that you'll spend the rest of your life wishing you were dead. Doubt your pretty young slut will want you then.'

He lowered the knife a tad more. I flinched, turning my head to one side. With his free hand he grabbed hold of my chin and twisted my head around so I was looking at him.

'Kind of fitting that my face will be the last thing you ever see,' he said, laughing.

'No,' I said and grabbed hold of his wrist. Had he balls I would have tried to punch him in them, but as he hadn't, I used the other hand to strengthen my hold on the arm with the knife at the end of it and at the same time I began to struggle.

By God, he was strong. I couldn't hold him back. The knife thudded down just missing my right ear. He wrenched his arm upwards pulling me with it, but I wasn't about to let go. With his free hand he punched at my face. It grazed my chin, but it was his left hand and there was no real power behind it.

His lips twisted into a grimace and he tried again. This time he scuffed the side of my head, but my arms were beginning to weaken. He was pushing down and I was trying to push his arm upwards. I was fighting a losing battle and had seconds before it would be game over. He knew it too. He began to laugh.

Then I heard Benji barking and Krystal began to sing. *Now I lay me . . .*

His lips twisted into a grimace.

And if I die before I wake . . .

The muscles in my arms were trembling as the knife filled my vision.

I pray the Lord . . .

Then Peter Davies said, *my soul to take.*

David's laughter died on his lips. 'Darcy, you fucking bitch,' he snarled and a myriad of emotions flashed across his face. Contempt, anger and finally a sly smile, which lasted only a second before he drew in a shuddery breath and the expression changed to confusion. Miriam – I was sure it was Miriam – looked down on me and then to the knife in her hand.

'What?' she cried, and the hand dropped to her side with a gasp.

'David?' she whispered. 'David?'

A tear slipped down her cheek. 'David!' she cried. 'Nooooooo!' and it was a wail from the heart, pathetic and full of despair. 'Nooooo!' She staggered to her feet. 'No. No, it can't be.' She stepped away from me. 'Darcy! Darcy – no! What have you done? What *have* you done?' and she threw back her head and let out an anguished howl, the howl of heartbreak and a woman bereft. A howl that I imagined would echo in my memory for all time. Her cry had barely faded away before she began to run. She ran towards Chalfont, coat flapping behind her, with Benji bounding along snapping at her heels.

On legs like rubber I clambered to my feet. 'What just happened?' I said.

If Krystal and Peter Davies knew they didn't say, though they both had sunny smiles as they slowly faded away, leaving Lucy and me alone in the pale moonlight.

CHAPTER THIRTY

I found the torch. It was what I had trodden on and had almost been my undoing.

'I don't understand what just happened,' Lucy said, as I slowly unpicked the tape binding her. I couldn't find Miriam's knife and guessed she must have taken it with her.

'It's a long story.'

'We've got a long walk home.'

'There's no time,' I told her. 'We've got to hurry. Miriam stabbed Jed.'

But when we reached the spot where I thought I'd left him, Jed was gone, so I told her – everything. I thought she deserved it, although I wasn't sure how much she'd believe. She listened, not interrupting, and when I'd finished she passed no comment and instead told me how she'd been knocked over the head as she'd left the Sly to come to the cottage and when she'd come to she'd been in Emma's larder.

'I should take you to hospital. You could be concussed.'

'When we find Jed, you can take us both.'

The lights were still on at The Grange when we walked up the drive, and I wondered if Jed would have gone there to ring for help as we'd seen no sign of him at all on the way back. Tellingly, his car was gone.

'Maybe he drove himself to the hospital,' Lucy suggested.

'Maybe,' I said, 'but knowing him, I doubt it. Do you know where he lives?'

'The other end of the village, just past the Sly.'

'Do you feel up to taking me there?'

'Come on,' she said, holding me by the hand, and I wondered at the strength of this woman. She had been assaulted, held hostage and terrorised, yet she was holding it together when most people would have been a total mess.

We went back to the cottage and picked up my car to drive to Jed's, and when Lucy told me to pull up outside a grand-looking house at the other end of the village, I thought she must be mistaken.

'This is where Jed lives?'

'His family home,' Lucy told me, and once again it occurred to me that there was an awful lot I didn't know about Jed. The man was an enigma and I said as much to Lucy.

'I know,' she said. 'There are lots of rumours, but that's villages for you.'

'His family must have been well off,' I said, looking up at the building.

'Rich, ruthless and heartless, so I've been told.'

I frowned at her. 'What do you mean?'

She pulled a face. 'You know what Jed's like, how he gets messages from the dead?'

I nodded. 'He's never hidden the fact.'

'Well, story has it that as soon as his mother realised he was *different*,' Lucy grimaced, 'she tried to beat it out of him. When that didn't work, she had him sent him away to boarding school.'

'That's terrible.'

'It gets worse. When he came home for holidays, she virtually shunned him. Apparently, she considered him an abomination against God and didn't mind telling him so. When Jed grew up, not wanting to return to a home where he knew he wasn't wanted, he joined the army straight from school. It was only when his mother died that he came back for good.'

'Poor bugger,' I said.

'It's sad. He's such a nice bloke.'

She was right, he was, and I was worried about him. The house was in darkness and when I knocked on the door there was no reply. I tried the bell. Its strident ringing echoed throughout the corridors making the house sound empty and hollow as though abandoned and filling me with disquiet.

'No answer,' I said getting back into the car. 'I hope he's all right.'

'He probably did drive himself to hospital,' Lucy said, hugging me to her. 'If not for himself, to be with Emma.'

'Well, that's where I'm taking you.'

'Huh-uh. I'm fine.'

'You were knocked out, not to mention terrorised by a lunatic.'

'I just want to go home,' she said.

'OK, but I'd better come in with you. If your dad sees you like this . . .'

She put her fingers across my lips. 'I meant your home,' she said.

So that's where we went.

I did try phoning Jed while Lucy was in the shower, but I went straight to voicemail, so I left a message asking him to phone me as soon as he could. My gut instinct was to phone the police. Miriam, or even worse David, was still out there somewhere, and while one of them was none of us were safe, but I needed to speak to Jed first. If we called in the police, we had to all be telling the same story, and that couldn't include possession and ghostly children.

I was checking the windows and doors when my phone went ping. Jed had sent me a message.

At hospital. All well. No police until we speak. See you tomorrow a.m.

I felt weak with relief. Jed was OK and I guessed he was of the same opinion as me, we needed to get our story straight if we were to involve the police. I shambled towards the shower, hoping it would wake me up a bit. We were all safe, but we weren't anywhere near out of the woods. I wouldn't be happy until I knew where Miriam was.

By the time I'd finished in the shower, Lucy was fast asleep. I was bone-tired, but I didn't dare join her. I locked and bolted the bedroom door and dragged the chair from under the window to next to the bed. Then, armed with the largest knife I could find in the kitchen, I sat down to wait for morning. It wasn't long before my eyes began to droop, as any fear I might have gave way to exhaustion and, as my eyes finally fluttered shut, I thought I heard a child's laughter. Maybe it was my imagination, but nevertheless, for some reason I found it comforting.

I woke up to an empty bed and the patter of rain against the window. Our Indian summer appeared to have come to an end.

I wondered if Lucy had crept off home, but when I crossed the hallway to use the bathroom, I caught a waft of frying bacon floating up the stairs and decided things were definitely looking a lot better than they had the night before. I'd been sure that in the clear light of day she'd probably not want another thing to do with me.

I found Lucy downstairs in the kitchen cooking bacon and eggs, wearing one of my T-shirts and not much else. 'I was going to bring you breakfast in bed,' she said upon seeing me.

'How're you feeling?'

'Good, actually. I've a bit of a bump on my temple, but that's about it.' I lifted her chin to look at where Miriam had pierced her skin with the knife. 'I think it felt and looked worse than it was.'

'Won't your mum and dad be worried where you are?' I asked.

'They know where I am.'

'Really?'

She giggled. 'I phoned them, silly.'

'Won't they mind? I mean, you being here.'

'I am a grown-up in case you hadn't noticed,' she said, putting her arms around my neck and then proceeded to give me a hint of how grown-up she could be. Before I could take it any further, she batted my hands away. 'First, we have breakfast.'

'What about after?'

Her lips curled into a sexy smile. 'Maybe, if you eat all your bacon.'

It all felt so normal, us sitting there together eating bacon and eggs, drinking tea and making small talk, but the spectres of David and Miriam were there even if both Lucy and I were trying to ignore them. When every bit of bacon was eaten and the last drips of egg yolk were wiped from our plates we lapsed into silence. It was almost as though we suddenly realised that what had happened the previous night wasn't a dream and although we had escaped, more or less unscathed, it was by no means over. We might not have wanted to get the authorities involved, but something did have to be done.

I slipped my mobile from my pocket to check for messages while Lucy was putting the plates in the sink.

'Anything more from Jed?' she asked when she saw the phone in my hand.

I shook my head. 'He did say he—' and I was interrupted by a *bang, bang, bang* on the back door.

'Jim?' I heard a familiar voice call.

When I unbolted the door, Jed was standing outside with Emma by his side.

'Thank God,' we both said at once and then began to laugh.

'Come in, come in,' I said, moving aside.

'I'll just put some clothes on,' I heard Lucy say from behind me and glanced around to see her disappearing out into the hall.

'Tea – coffee?' I asked, gesturing for them to sit and make themselves comfortable.

'Are you and Lucy all right?' Emma asked. 'We've been worried.'

'No more than we have about Jed,' I said. 'How's your arm, by the way?'

'Good, thanks. Bit stiff, but good.'

'You can't believe how relieved I was when I got your message. When we couldn't find you, we didn't know what to think,' I told Jed over my shoulder as I poured the tea. 'So, what are we going to tell the police?' Jed and Emma exchanged a look. I handed them both their drinks with a frown. 'What's happened?' I asked, as I

439

was pretty much sure that something significant had.

'David's dead,' Jed said.

'What? How?' I was aware of Lucy slipping back into the room and joining us at the kitchen table, but my eyes were on Jed. 'I mean, how can he be?'

'Darcy found me as I was trying to get back to Emma's. She patched me up and I think seeing what David had made Miriam do she realised enough was enough. I drove her up to Goldsmere and she gave permission for them to turn off the life support.'

'Can they just do that?' Lucy asked.

'Apparently. Darcy and Miriam had him moved into private care because the doctors at the hospital wanted to let him slip away more than a year ago. Over the past few months the doctors at Goldsmere have been saying the same, but Miriam wouldn't hear of it and I guess now we know why.'

'So, they just did it last night?'

Jed nodded. 'Darcy had already put the wheels in motion, that's why she'd been up at Goldsmere the day you saw her. The hospital was only waiting for her final say-so and last night she wasn't about to be refused. To be honest, she was desperate. When she saw what Miriam had done to me, she was terrified of what she might do to you and Lucy. She hoped if he was dead, he'd no longer have a hold over Miriam.'

'Where's Miriam?' I asked.

Jed and Emma exchanged another look and I could tell by their expressions that this wasn't going to be good news. 'Don't tell me – she's gone to the police and I'm going to be done for assault.'

'She's dead,' Jed said, his voice not much more than a whisper.

'She can't be,' Lucy said, looking from me to Jed and Emma then back again.

'They found her this morning. She'd jumped from the cliff above Saint's Bay.'

'Oh, shit.'

'We think she couldn't bear to go on without David, he'd been with her so long,' Emma said. 'Darcy told Jed that Miriam and David had been very close long before his accident.'

I looked down into my tea. I doubted Darcy realised how close – or then again, maybe she did.

'Poor Darcy,' Lucy said.

'To be honest, I think it was almost a relief for her,' Jed said. 'She told Jim and me that ever since David's "accident" Miriam has been becoming increasingly unstable.'

'Do you truly believe Miriam was possessed by David?' Lucy asked, giving me an apologetic look.

Jed stared into his coffee cup for a few seconds and when he looked up, he suddenly looked very old. 'Yes,' he said. 'Yes, I truly do.'

When I saw Jed and Emma out, I watched them walk up the path and I noticed Jed put his arm around her waist, which made me smile. He deserved to be happy, they both did.

'So,' Lucy said when I returned to the kitchen, 'do you think it's all over?'

'I hope so,' I said.

'I'm sorry if it appeared I didn't believe you, it's just that it was all so weird. I mean, seeing dead people.'

'You saw Krystal and Benji,' I said.

'And the reverend.' She shook her head as though she couldn't believe it herself. 'At first I thought I was hallucinating, but when I realised you could see them as well . . .' She shrugged. 'I didn't really know what to think.' She gave me a crooked smile and got up to throw her arms around my neck. 'But I do know it's something I'd prefer to forget.'

'You and me both,' and with that I took her by the hand and led her back upstairs to the bedroom.

CHAPTER THIRTY-ONE

I stood staring at myself in the bathroom mirror for some time. I was actually looking pretty good considering the battering I'd had from Miriam. She'd been one strong old bird. It was a shame about her.

But all that was over and done with and I'd already decided that today was going to be the first day of the rest of my life. I might even put an offer in for the cottage. I'd think on it.

I smiled at my reflection. I could get used to this shaggy-haired beach boy look. I switched off the light and padded back to the bedroom.

Soft grey morning light was beginning to creep into the room and the birds were announcing the dawn with their melodic chorus. Lucy lay on her side, her lips slightly parted. She was such a pretty, young thing.

I stood there just drinking in the birdsong, the musky

smell of sex and Lucy's sweet expression, and the rise and fall of her breasts.

Yes, life was definitely looking up and she and I were going to have so much fun.

Little bitch.

ACKNOWLEDGEMENTS

First off, I would like to thank Sebastien de Castell for his generosity in introducing me to his agent, the lovely Heather Adams. Heather also deserves a big thank you for her time and patience and for taking such good care of me and my writing career. I would also like to take this opportunity to thank my editor, Kelly Smith, and all the folk at Allison & Busby for their faith in me and *The Evil Within*.

As with most things, family is very important and my significant other is the best, particularly when it comes to patience. Once I'm in mid flow absolutely nothing gets done except for my writing, so a huge thank you, Howard, for your understanding and support.

Finally, I must mention my mum and dad, Ruby and Jack, and my brother Michael. Sadly, they had all passed on before I became published, but they were always supportive in everything I ever did and would be so very pleased and proud of my new-found career.

S. M. HARDY grew up in south London and worked in banking for many years. She has now given up the day job to allegedly spend more time with her husband; he, however, has noticed that an awful lot more writing appears to be going on. She currently lives in Devon. *The Evil Within* is her first paranormal mystery novel.

smhardy.co.uk   @SueTingey